Maria Lewis

THE GRAVEYARD SHIFT

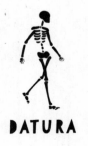

DATURA

DATURA BOOKS
An imprint of Watkins Media Ltd

Unit 11, Shepperton House
89 Shepperton Road
London N1 3DF
UK

daturabooks.com
twitter.com/daturabooks
Long Time Listener, First Time Killer

A Datura Books paperback original, 2023
Copyright © Maria Lewis, 2023

Cover by Sarah O'Flaherty
Edited by Gemma Creffield
Set in Meridien

ISBN 978 1 91552 306 8
Ebook ISBN 978 1 91552 309 9

Printed and bound in the United Kingdom by TJ Books Ltd.

9 8 7 6 5 4 3 2 1

For Kodie Bedford, the Blak Final Girl

CHAPTER 1

Mera Brant couldn't get the blood off her skin. She was scrubbing and scrubbing, but the substance had dried and stuck to her flesh. She flinched as it yanked against the hairs on her arm.

She turned the shower on, watching as the mix of cocoa powder, food dye, water and powdered sugar began to drip slowly from her body. The water at her toes turned red, fake blood spiraling into the drain like a scene from *Psycho* as she cranked the hot tap.

Stepping out fifteen minutes later, she looked longingly at the fluffy, thick white towels folded in a neat pile nearby. She was tempted, but Mera knew her roommate Jiro would lose his mind if she ruined one with red-brown stains. He was staying at his boyfriend's place overnight, so if she used one and had it cleaned before he got back after work tomorrow evening...

Forget it, she thought. *Not worth the drama.*

She reached for the black, tattered towel that belonged to her instead and wrapped it around her body with a sigh. As she walked through the house, Mera savored the fact Jiro wasn't there to tell her the music was "too loud" or "too weird." No roomie though, no problem. She had her phone synched to the Bluetooth speakers and cranked the volume as she nodded along to the beat. She grabbed a plastic bag from the kitchen and continued the path to her bedroom. The wooden floorboards creaked under her feet, the noise coming to a stop only when she did.

A pile of bloody – and sticky – clothes sat in the corner of her bedroom. She used the plastic bag like a glove as she picked them up, maneuvering the items until they were inside and tying a neat knot. She didn't know why she had expected to salvage the blouse and jeans she'd worn that evening, but it was clear they were *beyond* repair.

"No, you have not time travelled back to the sixties and yes, that was Bobby 'Boris' Pickett's Halloween classic 'Monster Mash' from 1962," the voice on the radio chirped once the song faded away. "Before that we had 'Alone in the Graveyard' by Gravediggaz and French sisters the Orties with 'Plus Putes que toutes les Putes' from the feminist cannibal movie *Raw*, which put me off meat for a month FYI. My name is Tinsel Munroe and you're listening to a very special, very spooky edition of *The Graveyard Shift* right here on 102.8 HitsFM."

Mera unrolled the poster she'd won that evening at a back-to-back screening of the first five movies in the *Halloween* franchise. She had been hoping to bump into the guy she'd been chatting to on the uUp app; this was part of the reason she'd gone so hard on her costume. But he'd been a no-show. She had all but a second to feel disappointed before her phone buzzed on the bed.

Guess who got held up at work, a uUp message read, followed by a sad face emoji. Her pulse quickened as she realised it was from *him*. She slipped into an oversized shirt, grabbing the bag of clothes and house keys, as she walked towards the backdoor.

I'm guessing you, she typed in response, before switching on her phone's torch light and stepping outside.

The October evening was weirdly chilly for Melbourne as Mera negotiated her way through the blackness of the small backyard that sat at the rear of the terrace house. *It's November now,* she thought, mentally correcting herself as she realised it was already 12.30am. She took it one metre at a time, careful not to collide with the outdoor boiler and bruise herself, like she had done countless times while making this same trip. The phone only illuminated what was directly in front of her and she came to a stop once the different coloured wheelie bins swam into view.

Hurling her ruined clothes inside and slamming down the lid, she turned back towards the house and froze. Something dark flashed past her line of sight and towards the house.

She blinked, urging herself to see the route more clearly with the gentle glow from the kitchen illuminating a small portion of the backyard. The outlines of various objects – the boiler, two bikes, gym equipment – were just visible. She couldn't see anything that didn't belong or had just moved, but that didn't stop her heartbeat pounding in her chest. She crept forward, eyes scanning for the next flash of motion.

Logically she knew it was most likely the neighbour's cat, Wilko, but Mera was thinking about Michael Meyers and how she'd just spent the past few hours watching him murder babysitters. Clothes hung suspended from the washing line, swaying ever-so-slightly in the breeze as she felt goosebumps prickle up over her skin.

Her phone buzzed in her hand, causing her to leap about a foot in the air. Glancing at the screen, she let out a shaky breath as she read the latest message.

I'll definitely be there tomorrow night, it said. *Even if the final films are inferior to the first.*

She smiled, the text doing something to relieve the tension. She typed her response as she walked back inside, closing and locking the door behind her. A song she didn't recognise was playing and she swiped her phone screen until the 102.8 HitsFM app appeared. Cover art for MC Hammer's 'Addams Groove' sat under the "now playing" tab. She laughed, the gesture easing the discomfort she'd felt just moments earlier. *The Graveyard Shift* might have truly fallen off the deep end with this selection.

She grabbed a bottle of water from the fridge, taking a sip as she began washing the plastic containers she'd used in a hasty attempt to make fake blood. Mera crinkled her nose at the grossness of it all as she scrubbed the caked substance loose. Her phone pinged again just as she was finishing up and she dried her hands, eager to read the message.

Are you hearing MC Hammer right now? he asked, clearly knowing she'd be listening to the show.

Tragically, yes, Mera answered. She paused for a beat, carefully positioning herself in the best light as she took a selfie and pulled a disgusted face to send back to him.

I can't believe Jiro is letting you listen to this nonsense publicly.

She smiled and typed, *He's not, I have the house and terrible nineties theme songs allll to myself.*

Are you sure?

Mera frowned at his response, watching as he sent her selfie back to her but with the background zoomed in. The light from her bedroom down the hall had cast a shape on the wall. The shape looked like a person.

Her eyes widened and she spun around. There was nothing there now. She tried to settle the panic in her chest, telling herself it was a myriad of things: Halloween, being home alone, the horror movie binge session she'd just participated in, even the music. Yet Mera couldn't shake the feeling as she stood there, perfectly still, straining to hear anything unusual.

Something wasn't right.

Turning down the radio volume slightly, she grabbed one of her hockey sticks from the closet as she crept towards her room. Clenching the handle tightly, she peered through the doorway. The space was undisturbed, everything left exactly the way it had been. Mera let out a long, shaky exhale. Stepping inside, she closed the bedroom door behind her and rested against the wooden frame with relief. Loosening her grip, the hockey stick dropped to the ground as Mera began typing a reply.

Hahaha you're hilarious. I'm also mad at myself for not immediately assuming you did that in Photoshop.

Running her hands through her hair, Mera bounced on to her bed and positioned the cushions for maximum comfort. She impatiently watched the moving dots on her screen that meant he was writing a reply, her thumb poised over the keyboard to respond quickly.

"It turns out I can and will touch this, as that was MC Hammer with 'Addams Groove' from the 1991 film *The Addams Family*," the announcer's voice said through the speakers.

"And since I profoundly miss the days of rap theme songs that tie into movies, before that we had 'Deepest Bluest' from LL Cool J. Now, the first person to call through and tell me what film that's very obviously from will get two tickets to the premiere of–"

Mera jerked upright, not even needing to hear the rest of the sentence before she was hitting the number for 102.8 HitFM's call line. It was saved in her phone under "favourites" specifically for occasions like this. In the past she had gotten lucky, as not that many people listened to *The Graveyard Shift* compared to the station's other shows, and she'd managed to snag a few Blu-rays. Tonight, she was much more hopeful as she heard the tone ringing down the line.

Come on, come on, come on, she thought, hopping up off her bed.

"Happy Halloween! This is Tinsel Munroe and welcome to *The Graveyard Shift*. Caller, who am I speaking to?"

"Hello!" she squeaked with excitement, unable to help herself. "I'm Mera! Mera Brant."

"You wouldn't happen to be the same Mera who called in a few months ago for the Jordan Peele triple bill prize pack, would you?"

"Yes, that's me!" She smiled, stoked the host remembered.

"Well, look out fellow listeners cos not only did Mera get through first on the call line, but this girl also knows her shit."

She laughed, feeling herself blush at the compliment despite the fact no one could see her.

"Okay, so, Mera, I have high expectations here. For two tickets to the premiere of Joe Meyer's new flick, what movie was LL Cool J's track 'Deepest Bluest' released to promote?"

Her mouth was open to reply when she hesitated, hearing a creak behind her. Frowning, Mera lifted the phone away from her ear to double check she had definitely heard the sound.

"Mera, hello? Are you there?"

"Um… yeah," she replied, uncertain. "I'm here."

"Do you need me to repeat the question?"

"No, no, I know it," she answered, eyes darting over everything around her. She was sure she had heard something.

"Bonus points for dragging out the tension there, kiddo."

"It's *Deep Blue Sea* from 1999," Mera said.

"Damn, you're coming through with the release year and everything! Knew you wouldn't let us spooky sisters down."

Half a smile was playing on her lips as she went to respond, but she stopped completely. A cheap IKEA rack that hung most of her clothing was swaying slightly, the hem of a dress rocking backwards and forwards with movement. She could hear the announcer's voice down the line, talking incessantly as she ran through the details of the prize, but Mera had ceased to fully hear them. Her eyes were instead fixated on the thick set of boots she could see among her collection of shoes. They didn't belong to her and worse still, she was fairly sure they were attached to a person. They started to move.

"Someone's in my room," she said, practically barking down the line in panic.

"Uh, what?"

"SOMEONE'S IN MY ROOM!" she shouted, as the clothing rack was thrown forward and a dark figure lurched out from behind it.

"That's very–"

"THEY'RE TRYING TO ATTACK ME, HELP!"

The dark figure blocked the only entry and exit of the room. There was barely any space for Mera to flee as she jumped up on to her bed in panic. Somehow, she held on to the phone, screaming into it as she kicked out at her attacker. The figure ducked the blows and grabbed for her legs at the same time.

Quickly growing tired with the skirmish, the assailant swiped forward with a silver flash that Mera didn't register until pain seared across her leg. She dropped down to the mattress with a scream, clutching at her calf muscle as blood bloomed from an enormous slice running down her limb diagonally. Her own panicked cries were mirrored back at her through the speakers. Mera thrashed and punched at the figure as they bore down on her with the blade.

Her attacker had the height advantage, and her attempts to fight them off were in vain. The knife sunk through her flesh and into the soft material of the mattress underneath, again and again and again. Mera's eyes locked on the blood-splattered screen of her phone in her outstretched hand as it slowly slipped from her grasp, landing with a clatter on the floor.

A groan escaped her lips, but the sound was lost as the killer stepped away from her body and turned up the volume on the speakers.

Mera's last moments were silenced under the pulse of a new track, her lips mumbling final words that were never heard under the rising swell of a saxophone.

CHAPTER 2

The teen was gawking at Tinsel Munroe like she was a freak. To be fair, that was entirely her intention. The boy had been unable to stop looking since she hopped on the tram. Tinsel did her best to hide a smirk as she flicked her eyes away from him, catching her reflection in the darkened glass.

A skeleton was looking back at her, a permanent scowl painted on her face with the outline of bones and teeth in white, juxtaposed against an inky black. She had spent a solid hour in front of the mirror, blending and shading and contouring to make sure her make-up was just right. *Thank God for TikTok tutorials*, she thought, blinking with slight agitation due to the unnatural grey contacts she was wearing. Closing her eyes, she let the movements of the tram rock her into a drowsy comfort as she clung to the railing where she stood.

"Next stop: Federation Square," a polite voice said through the speakers.

Bracing her feet as the locomotive shuddered to a halt, she threw two shoulder bags over one arm and an enormous pumpkin under the other. The teen wasn't the only one who tossed her a strange look as she navigated her way through the chaos of people pushing to get off and on one of Melbourne's busiest tram stops. But that was fine, she expected the looks, anticipated them even.

It was All Hallow's Eve and Tinsel considered it a personal

failure if her chosen costume didn't raise a few eyebrows. She passed four women dressed in matching *The Nun* costumes who shouted "Hi!" at her excitedly, plus a couple outfitted as Chucky and Tiffany, who nodded at her in solidarity.

Besides that, there really weren't as many folks dressed up as she would have liked. She put it down to the fact this Halloween had fallen on a Wednesday night. Friday night Halloweens were always the best, as the parties dragged out through the weekend. Mid-week Halloweens, like this one, were always a bummer.

It was a shame, really. If there was anywhere in the city you were likely to bump into costumed adults it was here, wedged between one of the world's most visited film museums, the outdoor hub of Federation Square, and the bustling Flinders Street Station. Pausing once she made it across the other side of Swanston Street in the usual pedestrian scramble, Tinsel sighed. Looking up at the huge, domed roof of the train station, her gaze focused on one of the many enormous clocks that ticked closer and closer to her airtime.

It didn't matter that it was past 10pm, this part of Melbourne city was always awake. As it creeped closer to summer, even more so as people flocked to Fed Square to watch the free movie screenings and sporting events that were broadcast on the massive outdoor screens. There had even been an all-ages showing of *Paranorman* that evening to tie in with spooky season. But those crowds were long gone as she cut through the large, paved atrium and darted around outdoor beanbags that would have been packed with families just a few hours earlier.

Tinsel was headed towards the most unusual looking building in Fed Square – the massive structure looked like several dimensions had folded in on each other as different geometric shapes collided. The bulk of the space was occupied by the Australian Centre for Moving Image (ACMI), a place Tinsel could easily waste hours of her life in, browsing exhibitions about the dawn of cinema or catching a James Whale retrospective in one of the theatres.

A much smaller portion of the building, however, was her destination. The radio station 102.8 HitsFM rented a multi-floored office there in one of the city's most sought after locations.

Tinsel was used to the idea of her night beginning just as everyone else's was ending, and she waved at the security guard through the glass. He frowned, not moving for a few seconds before something like recognition crossed his face. Hopping out from behind his desk, he hit a button and the doors swooshed open.

"What, you too good to swipe yourself in now?" he smirked, crossing his arms.

"Malu, my man! We both know you have nothing to do for at least eighty-five per cent of your shift. Is swiping a girl in so much trouble?"

"If she's bringing a giant pumpkin into the building, yeah."

"It turns into a carriage later."

"*And* you're a bloody big skeleton," he laughed, looking her up and down. "You come from a party or something?"

"It's Halloween. Of course I went to a party first."

"Awrite, tell me: who's throwing a party that slaps on a Wednesday night?"

Tinsel hesitated, knowing he had her there.

"Okay *fine*, it was a movie marathon. But there was booze and everyone was dressed in costume, so it was basically a party."

"Not by any reasonable person's standards."

"I know," she admitted. "It killed me a little bit inside. But hey, if you keep being snarky I won't give you the Trick or Treat baggie I made you."

Malu's eyes lit up, huge muscles flexing as he made a sweeping gesture with his arms.

"By all means, come in."

Tinsel laughed, depositing the purple and orange-striped bag at his desk. "You're so easy to please."

"What's in here?" he asked, ruffling through it. "Oh, a Pinky bar!"

"I made an Aotearoa-themed one just for you," she winked. "Can you open the barriers for me too?"

He did as she asked, and Tinsel called out a thank you as she shuffled sideways towards the elevator that would take her up to the third floor. Using her elbow, she hit the button and waited patiently for it to arrive. During the day, this place would be populated with people coming and going. The radio station was just the tip of the iceberg, with most of the bodies in the building belonging to those in the sales and marketing departments. That's what had kept HitsFM afloat when other networks had slowly folded over the past ten years. Yet during her shift, Tinsel and Malu were usually the only two people in the building: at least until the early morning producers and news readers came in.

"You better play some LL Cool J tonight," the security guard called to her as the elevator doors pinged open.

"It's the Halloween show, what song of his could possibly work for that brief?"

"*Deepest, bluest, my hat is like a shark's fin*," Malu rapped at her, then rolled his eyes at the blank expression on her face. "From *Deep Blue Sea*. That's a horror movie!"

"It's a survivalist action movie."

"It counts!"

"Barely," she huffed, stepping inside the elevator.

"You better play that song. You know I'll be listening!"

"Yeah yeah," Tinsel chimed, as the doors slid shut. He would be tuning in, but not out of choice: whatever was live on-air was played throughout the station building. Malu had to listen to her nightly show, *The Graveyard Shift*, whether he wanted to or not. Every few hours when he did his foot patrol of the studio, he'd share his opinion on whatever she'd played so far. Tinsel always anticipated his immediate feedback.

Stepping out of the elevator, she wrangled with her own pass to let herself into the studio. The show before hers was wrapping up so the host, Luiza, wouldn't be free to get the door for her the way Malu had. Rushing to her desk, she set down her things and quickly logged into her desktop.

"'Deepest Bluest,'" Tinsel whispered to herself, typing the song title into a search engine as quickly as she could. "Huh, what do you know…"

She doubted it would be in the station's internal song database, which only held the current top forty hits and a few thousand classics. Anything else had to be sourced by the hosts themselves, so she downloaded the song from iTunes. *You owe me one dollar and forty-nine cents, big man*, she thought.

Dashing to the bathroom and heating up a microwave meal on the way back, she grabbed what she needed and hovered outside the studio. Above the door was a big light, illuminated in warning red to indicate that whoever was inside was presently live on the air. Tinsel could barely hear anything from the other side; the walls were so carefully soundproofed that everything was muffled.

When the light switched to green, she twisted the door handle and made her way inside. Sliding a pair of headphones off her head, Luiza looked up at the disturbance and burst out laughing.

"Ha, you fucking mad woman! I knew you'd dress up."

Tinsel beamed at her, doing a gratuitous spin so Luiza could digest the full effect of the outfit.

"Here," she said, handing Luiza her own bag of Halloween treats. She snatched it up greedily, inspecting the contents for a second before eyeing what else Tinsel was carrying inside her Mary Poppins bag of goodies.

"Oooooh, what about the rest of that stuff?"

"That's for the studio. Figured I'd decorate the place for my show tonight and everyone else's for the rest of the week."

"Holy shit, you properly carved a pumpkin and everything. Where did you even get that?"

"I have a connect."

"Did you make pumpkin pie too?"

"No, Christ, who do you think I am? Martha Stewart?"

Luiza laughed. "Nah, you would have come in a prison jumpsuit."

Tinsel rolled her eyes and began laying out the decorations she had brought with her, including rubber bats, ghost lights, a tasselled garland in orange, black, purple and green, cardboard skeletons and a few packets of synthetic cobwebs. There were some ornamental spiders and fake limbs in there as well and she happily occupied her final chunk of freedom by carefully arranging everything to her liking. Tossing the leftover Blu-Tac back in her bag, she flopped down on the studio couch with a contented sigh and began picking at her dinner with a fork. She was quiet as the warning light flicked from green to red overhead again. Luiza readjusted the headphones on her ears as she back-announced the last few songs.

"Yeah that has gotta be one of my favourite tracks off the new Hurray For The Riff Raff album, and before that we had an older gem, 'Pa'lante' from her 2017 release, *The Navigator*."

Tinsel watched as Luiza's hands moved over the control deck, fading out the final seconds of the song as she began speaking over the top of it.

"We're nearly out of time here on *The Apéritif*, your Monday to Friday show that stimulates the musical palette. My name is Luiza Curser and up next, we have my girl Tinsel Munroe with *The Graveyard Shift* and listeners, I gotta tell ya, she loves Halloween so much that she has rocked up in a full-on costume and even decorated the 102.8 HitsFM studio. I'm legit so impressed, pics are gonna go up on our social channels within the next few, so make sure you're following #TheGraveyardShift and it's not too late to send through your ultimate spooky jams. But first, here's a message from our sponsors."

Clicking so the right scheduled ads would play, Luiza's eyes stayed occupied on her screen as she kept talking to Tinsel.

"Alright, I've just got the lead out to go after these songs and then it's all yours, baby girl."

"You're a dreamboat, thanks," Tinsel told her, swallowing the last unsatisfactory bite of microwaved pasta and tuna. Getting to her feet, she ditched the meal in the bin and grabbed a Vanilla Coke from the mini-fridge that sat in the studio. The whole space was decked out to provide as much comfort as possible, with not one but three couches assembled on the other side of the massive bench that contained most of the important hardware. There were stools on one side, with headphone jacks and microphone stations at the ready for any visiting guest. On the other – the side Tinsel was intimately familiar with – sat two computer screens, which she began opening up to the appropriate windows she needed. There was a third, slightly different in size from the others, which had HitFM's internal Content Management System (CMS) running at all times. It showed a list of what was currently being played, ads that had to be broadcast, a schedule of what songs the presenter had positioned next and a countdown timer to the following show.

Tinsel and Luiza performed an awkward dance as each woman switched between the screens, the former getting ready for her show and the latter preparing to log off for the evening.

"You came in later than expected," Luiza muttered, scrolling through social media and choosing a few final messages to retweet.

"It's entirely Halloween themed tonight, obviously, so I came in earlier on Monday and Tuesday to have the whole thing prepped."

"Ha, I should have known, you big nerd. I've gotta stay back tonight so I can come in late on Friday."

"Bring your laptop in here," Tinsel offered. "I could use the company."

"Yeah, I don't know how you do it every weeknight with those hours? It would kill me."

Tinsel shrugged. She really didn't have much choice in the matter. She had worked her ass off to get a gig at 102.8 HitsFM, toiling in community radio for years while doing a Bachelor's Degree in Communications at the same time. It was the same entry route for a lot of people at the station. Tinsel knew that to improve her chances at becoming a presenter, she needed to be able to produce as well. She'd gotten lucky at first, only serving as an assistant producer on the afternoon *Drive Show* before a spot opened on the evening slot, jokingly called 'the graveyard shift' due to the hours: 11pm to 6am, Monday to Friday. It wasn't ideal, but it was her foot in the door and that's all she needed.

"Damn," Luiza whispered, looking over Tinsel's shoulder at the track list. "You've got Dead Man's Bones, The Cure, Graveyard Train... you're going deep on this."

"This is my third Halloween show, you gotta offer more than 'Thriller'."

"Whatever you say. You want me to get some pics for social? This song has two minutes to go."

"Yes please," she grinned, tossing Luiza her phone. "Make me look svelte."

"You're a skeleton," her friend answered, drily.

Tinsel switched it up with a few different poses, grateful that she and Luiza had been colleagues long enough now that the woman knew all her good angles. Double checking the time, she quickly sent out a few images across *The Graveyard Shift's* Twitter, Instagram and Facebook page as she watched the minutes tick closer. Tinsel had already uploaded a TikTok video earlier in the night, plugging the show from the site of the movie marathon she had hosted.

Right on 10.58pm, she and Luiza switched spots as Tinsel

took control of the decks. With Luiza leaving to stretch her legs and take a much needed bathroom break, Tinsel was left with the studio all to herself. This was what she was used to: the office quiet on the floor around her, the other studios that looked into hers dark and empty, her reflection just visible on the glass across the opposite side of the space.

She could see the lights of the city outside the only outdoor-facing window, reminding Tinsel there was a world out there and that most of the people in it were asleep right now. Her adrenaline kicked up just a little as the digits changed to 10.59 pm and she took a final sip of her soda. As the closing chords of the song played out, she dropped the volume and hovered her finger over the button that would take her live. With a steadying breath, Tinsel pushed it.

"Happy Halloween creeps and psycho killers – qu'est-ce que c'est? My name is Tinsel Munroe and welcome to this very special, very spooky edition of *The Graveyard Shift*."

As she spoke, she moved the cursor of her mouse to a sound effect she had cued and ready to go the second she finished her sentence. It was one of dozens she had downloaded specifically for that evening's show. Tinsel paused as thunder and a creepy laugh punctuated her words.

"Luiza didn't lie, the studio tonight looks like a scene from a Wes Craven movie and if you want to see it for yourself, why not check us out on social media…"

She rattled off the appropriate plugs for *The Graveyard Shift*'s internet presence, knowing these lines so well after three years of doing the show that she sometimes spoke them in her sleep, according to her boyfriend. Already she could see a few people using #TheGraveyardShift to wish her Happy Halloween. She kept speaking as she absentmindedly retweeted them.

"I have so many graveyard bops, undead bangers and horror jams for you this evening and into the morning, you are not gonna want to go anywhere this October 31st. Plus! I've got a chat coming up with Joe Meyer, who's third film *Band Candy* just played at the 'Toronto After Dark' film festival. I know a lot of you are really excited about it and there'll also be an opportunity to win tickets to the Australian premiere. I'll be opening up the phone lines, so strap yourselves in. First up, we've gotta start with a classic, yeah, you know what it is... who ya gonna call?"

She waited until the beginning of the *Ghostbusters* theme played through her headphones, which was the same feed her audience would be hearing, and with a nod she switched off the live button. The audio in the studio cut out every time the light was red and when it was green, the show played softly through the speakers as a back-up mechanism so she could hear what was going on. It wasn't until she was halfway through the second song of the night that Luiza returned, eyes wide and a huge smile plastered on her face as she bopped her head to the beat of 'A Nightmare on My Street.'

"First Ray Parker Jr, now DJ Jazzy Jeff and 'The Fresh Prince of Bel-Air!'" she exclaimed. "Kid, I did not think you had it in you! So, it's not gonna be kitsch jams all night?"

"Those are coming," Tinsel laughed. "I'm just warming up. But first, 'I'd Rather Be Burned As A Witch.'"

Luiza fist pumped with genuine joy as Eartha Kitt purred through the speakers. Tinsel was unable to help the shimmy of her shoulders as she danced along to the track behind the decks. It was easy to fall into her usual rhythm, setting up a list of three to four songs and two ads before she would need to pop back and provide some living, breathing human commentary.

With her entire body stretched out along the length of a couch, laptop positioned on her stomach, Luiza added her insights on the song selection every few minutes. Tinsel was surprised to find she was a 'This Is Halloween' fan – "Danny Elfman still fucks" – but made a gagging sound when 'Pet Cemetery' from the Ramones came on.

"No, you have not time travelled back to the sixties and yes, that was Bobby 'Boris' Pickett's Halloween classic 'Monster

Mash' from 1962," Tinsel said, back-announcing the song. "Before that, we had 'Alone in the Graveyard' by Gravediggaz and French sisters the Orties with 'Plus Putes que toutes les Putes' from the feminist cannibal movie *Raw*, which put me off meat for a month FYI. My name is Tinsel Munroe and you're listening to a very special, very spooky edition of *The Graveyard Shift* right here on 102.8 HitsFM."

She paused again, hitting the cue for a dramatic wolf howl that rung out.

"Before the break I asked what's your favourite werewolf movie, and things are about to get a little hairy here at Hits as I go to the phone lines."

There was a landline next to the controls, mainly used for internal communications as everyone had their phones on silent in the studio and things were often missed. But during her show, Tinsel would open up the lines to try and engage the listeners, and she had cultivated a loyal and active audience that way. As the past series of tracks had played out, three callers rang through and after a brief interaction with her, she had placed them on hold where they would hear the show for a few minutes before she picked up again.

"Hello there, caller, you're on *The Graveyard Shift*. What is your name and what is your favourite werewolf movie?"

"Oh my God, hi, happy Halloween!" the bubbly voice squeaked down the line.

"Happy Halloween to you too!" Tinsel laughed. "What's your name?"

"Um, I'm Auli'i and, like, *What We Do in The Shadows* is my favourite. Does that count?"

"You're damn right it counts, werewolves not swearwolves! Thanks for listening Auli'i."

Unclicking the girl's line – number one – she switched to the next caller.

"Hi, you're on with Tinsel, what's your favourite werewolf movie?"

The crackle of a party could be heard in the background as the caller shouted over the ruckus.

"*The Wolf*!" the guy yelled.

"*The Wolf?*" She thought she misheard. "With Jack Nicholson?"

Luiza sat up on the couch, shaking her head across the studio in disgust.

"Yeah, yeah, from the nineties!"

"Sir, you are terribly mistaken, that is barely a movie. But happy Halloween anyway!"

"Yeeeeeeeew!" His voice was met with an echo of other revellers as she switched to the third and final caller.

"You're on 102.8 HitsFM, favourite werewolf movie – go!"

"Oh, I have two! Can I say two?"

"You can say two, I'm feeling generous."

"Cool, uh, my name is Andy and *An American Werewolf in London* is the first and *The Howling* is the second."

"Andy, thanks so much and thanks to everyone who called in with their interesting choices – *The Wolf* guy, I'm talking to you specifically."

Her caller laughed down the other end and she faded him out, eventually ending her call as she scheduled the next track.

"On that note, Andy, let's listen to an oldie but a goldie with 'Werewolves of London' by Warren Zevon then coming up afterwards, 'Mama Werewolf' by Brandi Carlile and 'Wolf Like Me' by TV On the Radio."

Setting the headphones down and stepping away from the mic, Tinsel pulled several darts free from the target board that hung on the studio wall next to a huge, illuminated version of the 102.8 HitsFM logo.

"What's *your* favourite werewolf movie?" Luiza asked, watching as Tinsel took her time aiming.

"I'll give you a pair. The OG – *Wolf Man* with the boys, Bela and Lon. Then *When Animals Dream*. You?"

Luiza shrugged. "I liked that Marvel one, *Werewolf by Night*."

"It rips," Tinsel confirmed.

"I still think you're crazy for taking calls."

"I like it," Tinsel replied, throwing the first dart. "It builds a relationship with the listeners. And it keeps me company when you're not here."

"It's just so much extra work – oh, bull's eye!"

"See, but, if I didn't take calls, all I'd be doing in between announcements is this shit."

"You'd probably make more money as a professional darts player."

"And I'd get to hang out in pubs."

Malu popped by soon after, waving at her from the other side of the studio glass as she was live on air, mouthing the words 'Where's LL?'

Tinsel grinned, flipping him the bird, before he strolled off to the rest of his rounds. She had gotten so caught up in her job she didn't realise Luiza had been quiet for a while. Glancing from behind her screens, she saw the woman fast asleep on the couch. Smirking, Tinsel snuck over and placed her friend's laptop on the ground instead of the precarious angle it had been resting at. There were a few blankets stored inside the hollow of one of the footstools, so she grabbed one and threw it over her before ducking back behind the mic with just seconds to spare.

"It turns out I can and will touch this, as that was MC Hammer and 'Addams Groove' from the 1991 film *The Addams Family*," she said, back from the break. "And since I profoundly miss the days of rap theme songs that tie into movies, before that we had 'Deepest Bluest' from LL Cool J. Now the first person to call through and tell me what film that's very obviously from will get two tickets to the premiere of Joe Meyer's new movie *Band Candy*, which is happening in Melbourne next week on Thursday, November 9. We've got an interview coming with Joe in just a few minutes so call through on 1800 HITS FM –

that's 1800 448 736 – if you have the right answer and want those tickets. But first, a word from our sponsors."

Luiza stirred just as the first ad began to play, groaning as she sat upright. Cracking her neck, she used one of the remotes to turn on the flat screen television that was mounted into the wall. The thing was permanently on mute, but some presenters liked to have a visual going on in the background.

"How long was I out?" she moaned.

"Truthfully, I'm not sure," Tinsel admitted. "I think you went down somewhere before 'Demons' by What So Not."

"Gah! The one song I actually like. I should get out of here, wife's gonna be spewing and I'm not gonna get anything else done to–"

Tinsel held up her hand to shush Luiza, with five seconds to go before she was back live on air. Her colleague nodded to let her know she understood, and Tinsel counted down the remaining time on her fingers as the light switched over from green to red.

"Happy Halloween, this is Tinsel Munroe and welcome to *The Graveyard Shift*," she chirped, picking up the first call that had buzzed through on the landline. "Caller, who am I speaking to?"

"Hello!" a voice replied. "My name is Mera Brant."

Tinsel was smiling as she continued the conversation and retweeted a group shot from a Halloween house party where the caption said they were playing the show. At least somebody was.

Luiza got to her feet quietly, folded up the blanket and packed up her things.

"Okay so, Mera, I have high expectations here. For two tickets to the premiere of Joe Meyer's new flick, what movie was LL Cool J's 'Deepest Bluest' released to promote?"

Tinsel's attention was half divided between the social media and the show, so it took her a little longer to react to the silence on the other end.

"Mera, hello, are you there?"

"Um yeah, I'm here."

"Did you need me to repeat the question."

"No, no, I know it."

There was another awkward pause, and Tinsel shot Luiza an annoyed look. "Bonus points for dragging out the tension there, kiddo."

"It's *Deep Blue Sea* from 1999."

"Damn, you're coming through with the release year and everything! I knew you wouldn't let us spooky sisters down. Okay, for a bonus round can you tell me what line from 'Deepest Bluest' is actually from classic LL Cool J banger 'I'm Bad' which was released waaaaay back in 1987 off his second al–"

"Someone's in my room."

"Uh, what?"

"SOMEONE'S IN MY ROOM!"

Tinsel flinched at the sudden increase in volume sharp in her ear as the woman screamed. An amused smile played on her lips, somewhat appreciating the skit.

"That's very–"

"THEY'RE TRYING TO ATTACK ME, HELP!"

She pulled one headphone away from her ear, unable to properly make out any other words as the caller continued to shout. She could make out a series of grunts down the line and Tinsel looked across at Luiza, who was frozen as she also listened to the scene play out.

After taking a beat, she rolled her eyes at Tinsel. The caller's line went dead, with the dial tone now the only thing she – and her listeners – could hear.

"Well, there's always bound to be one prank call every Halloween show," Tinsel sighed. "At least no one has attempted their best Ghostface voice but hey, the night is young and that was *not* an open invitation."

She scheduled the next song, increased the volume and brought it in early.

"So I guess I've still got passes to the *Band Candy* premiere! Heck, since Mera graciously already answered the question these will just go to the next caller who rings through. In the meantime, here's 'Let's Have a Satanic Orgy' by Twin Temple followed by 'The Mummy' from Benji Hughes to wrap up."

The phone rang almost immediately and thankfully she was able to offload the tickets. Tinsel managed to get the guy's email address and contact details to send through to the film publicists without further incident. Hanging up, she took a moment to give Luiza a quick farewell hug.

"You know that's not gonna be the only weird call you get tonight," her friend warned, embracing her. "Remember that guy who used to ring in while he was jerking off?"

"I've worked really hard to forget it, so thanks for resurrecting that horrible memory."

"I'm just saying…"

"Get outta here, catch Zs for me."

Tinsel whacked her on the butt playfully before dashing back to promo the Joe Meyer interview with audio from the *Band Candy* trailer. She tried to keep the energy up as the hours ticked by, but 3am was always the toughest: that was usually when the stragglers began to tune out and head to bed as well. Social media quieted down and even the chatty emails from Malu came to a stop. The only benefit was that it meant she had enough time to take a break – she programmed six tracks in a row so she could slip to the bathroom and wash off her skeleton makeup. Straight up soap and water wasn't going to cut it, but Tinsel had brought her toughest foaming cleanser from home and with less scrubbing than you would expect, her own face was looking back at her in the mirror.

"Guh," she said, using a make-up wipe to get whatever was left clinging to her skin. Slipping into clothing that would get her less attention than a Halloween costume on the walk home, she quickly brushed her hair straight so that her fringe and bobbed haircut were perfectly aligned. When she returned to the studio,

Tinsel felt a slight morsel of relief as she looked at the clock and realised how much closer it was to her shift being over.

Pulling a stool behind the decks, she put on the headphones as the *Stranger Things* theme played out.

"Welcome back from the Upside Down," she purred into the mic. "Friends don't lie, my name is Tinsel Munroe, and we are inching ever closer to the end of my time with you on *The Graveyard Shift* tonight. But don't worry, I've saved some good stuff until the end including *The X-Files* techno remix – you're welcome – and the late, great MF Doom's 'Hey!' Right now though, this is 'Halloweenie III: Seven Days' by Ashnikko."

Grabbing a container from the mini-fridge that housed chopped fruit and yogurt she had prepared earlier, Tinsel began eating in small bites as she touched up her appearance. Most other people in the city probably didn't care about how they looked at 5am in the morning, but most other people didn't also have a job where their bosses had to see them at such an ungodly hour. Tinted moisturiser, a touch of concealer, highlighter that doubled as eye shadow, mascara and a line of liquid eyeliner on her top lid had her looking – and feeling – a little bit more like herself.

Usually Tinsel had her make-up done when she started her shift, with a liberal application of setting spray to keep everything in check until the morning, when she could roll out of the studio fresher than the people rolling in. It was a little thing, but it gave her a feeling of pride and professionalism. While *The Graveyard Shift* was a stepping-stone for her, one that she'd hoped to have been out of within two years, things hadn't exactly worked out that way.

All it meant was Tinsel had to work a little bit harder, a little bit longer, and she was sure her efforts would eventually land her a daytime slot or even early evening. Her third year at 102.8 HitsFM was nearly up, with everyone's contracts either renewed or terminated over the December break, and she couldn't afford to sleep on her goals.

One of the lights in the studio across the hall blinked on. Tinsel straightened up as she watched the breakfast show newsreader Killara Clayshore moving through the space. She was always the first to arrive, settling in front of her station with a cup of coffee as she scrambled to catch up on the overnight news and put the first morning bulletin together.

The executive producer, Tim Franklin, would arrive next, working from the studio Tinsel was situated in as he began setting up the screens for *Breakfast with Ryan and Shea*, which was the station's real money maker. Each host had a six-figure salary, both of them celebrities outside of the station thanks to side careers as stand-up comedians and occasional television hosts. Tinsel tried not to think about the fact that she could barely afford to split her rent with her boyfriend, telling herself repeatedly that everyone had to start somewhere.

"If it isn't Doctor Christmas Jones," a voice said, the studio door opening as Tim revealed himself behind it.

"If it isn't the man with the worst, most outdated Bond references."

"Hey, your parents named you Tinsel. I'm therefore allowed to make jokes about it. And whoa, the studio – this looks amazing! Ah, happy Halloween to me?"

"And to all a good fright," Tinsel beamed, smiling sweetly as she held up her hand to warn him she was about to go live. Tim was a veteran of the industry, having worked in radio for over thirty years and had long since lost the nervous twitch a newbie had when operating in a live mic environment.

"'Last Living Souls' by Gorillaz was what you just heard, followed by 'Mo Murda' from Bone Thugs-N-Harmony off the *Fear Street: Part One – 1994* soundtrack and then something a little bit jaunty given the hour: 'Spookie Coochie' by Doechii."

Tinsel quickly bridged the gap into the advertisements, before shuffling to the side so Tim could begin logging in next to her.

"God that coffee smells good," she muttered, not looking up as she began closing the windows of all the tabs she had open on screen.

"My offer still stands," Tim replied. "If you want me to grab you one on my way in, I'll do it."

"Nah, I need to be absolutely munted when I walk through the door so I can go straight to sleep. Coffee is counterintuitive."

"Any issues overnight? No system freeze?"

"Please, like that's a problem. I can just go into the server room and reboot it myself."

"Atta girl. But seriously–"

"Nada. It was a really fun show, I think you would have liked it. All Halloween themed and–"

"I saw some of the preliminary numbers, it did well."

"*The Graveyard Shift* was even the number two trending topic in Australia last night," she whispered, giving him a nudge with her elbow. "Behind 'Halloween' of course."

"Of course."

Tinsel didn't add that it was largely because there wasn't much in terms of competing trends in the evening, when most of the daily news cycle had died down. She wanted to impress Tim: he was a star-maker, and she knew she'd need his endorsement if she was to work her way up at the station.

"Alright, things are all good to go on my end," he said, turning to her expectantly. "You got one more in you?"

"That I do," Tinsel answered, listening as the last line of an advertisement played out in her headphones.

"Ghouls and goblins, I'm afraid that is all we have time for on what has been the Halloween edition of *The Graveyard Shift*. My name is Tinsel Munroe, but rest assured I'm about to put a stake in the heart of this show with five excellent tunes: 'Witchyman' by Cain Culto, 'Dracula's Wedding' by OutKast and Kelis, the haunting 'Supiria' theme by Goblin, 'Teenage Witch' by Suzi Wu and my personal favourite, 'Demon Rock' by Letters to Cleo. I'll catch you all later this evening."

It felt good to liberate herself from the cords of the control deck, spinning away from the panel and computers as Tim gleefully took over. Shrugging into her satin bomber jacket, she opened her mouth to tell the executive producer she would catch him later when the door to the studio burst open.

"Yeah, but that's what I'm saying! Belichick can't be your solution to every problem you have as a team – EP Tim, what up!" interrupted Ryan.

"This Patriots shit gets old, and you know it. Morning Tinsel, love what you've done with the place," said Shea, following him in.

"Ryan," she waved, by way of greeting. "Shea."

"You do all this yourself? Overnight?" Ryan asked, as he crouched down to examine the pumpkin she had carved.

Shea moved slowly around the room, taking it all in. "I could have sworn we had an Occupational Health and Safety policy about carving pumpkins in the studio."

"We do!" Tim barked, not looking up from behind the computer screens at his two breakfast hosts. "The policy is no idiots are allowed to wield knives in the building, which excludes you two. Tinsel, however, is not an idiot."

"My God," Shea sniffed, putting a hand to heart. "Calling me 'not an idiot' might be the nicest thing you've ever said to me, Timmy."

"Don't call me Timmy." He pointed his fingers squarely at the hosts, clicking to get their attention. "You two, will you get in front of the bloody mics and settle in? We're live in three."

Shea took a sip from the enormous mug he was holding, slowly sauntering to the position Tim had indicated.

"Actually," Ryan began. "The news bulletin takes a whole four minutes, so technically we're not live until four past six."

"Basically we're early," Shea quipped.

Ryan nodded. "Beyond punctual."

This was a morning ritual: the boys arriving with minutes to spare and Tim attempting to berate them, while secretly being glad they had showed up at all. Grabbing her bag, Tinsel went to make her exit while they were in the throngs of their daily bickering when Ryan's outstretched arm grabbed and stopped her.

"Where you going so fast?" he asked, a smile plastered on his face as his eyes looked her up and down. "You disappearing out of here before we've even had a chance to admire the latest ensemble?"

"Ensemble?" Shea scoffed. "You sound ridiculous."

"You *look* ridiculous. What's with your bleached tips 'n' shit?"

"It's from the sun, I told you!"

"Yeah, yeah. Anyway, Tinsel: what are these, pedal pushers? You know I love this whole mod, rockabilly thing you have going on. Very sexy."

She resisted the urge to yank her arm free and visibly shudder, largely because she was used to it at this point. Tinsel sensed Tim's eyes on them, watching the scene play out as he usually did every morning when Ryan tried flirting with her in various forms. He was married, of course, with two kids. It was never the single men shooting their shot, but always the boyfriends and husbands unloading their clip in the DMs of her life. The breakfast host also had a terrible reputation in the industry for hitting on anything with a pulse. Due to the timing and proximity, Tinsel was usually the first person to cop it at the start of every day.

"Bro," Shea said, not looking at his colleague. "You prep those questions for the Bruno Mars interview? He's in at eight."

"Huh?" Ryan grunted, letting go of her arm, clearly distracted. She shot Shea a grateful look, mouthing the words "thank you." He nodded slightly in response.

Tinsel took the opportunity to get out of the studio as quickly as she could. She didn't make it much further than the doorway though, nearly walking headfirst into their station manager, Rushelle Li.

"Oh, sorry," Tinsel murmured, stumbling backwards. "I didn't see you."

It was unusual for Rushelle to be there at such an early hour. Even more unusual was the fact the station's big boss was dressed in a pair of sneakers and jeans. Tinsel frowned, thinking that she had never seen her in anything but a coordinated pantsuit and heels.

"Tinsel, good, I was hoping you'd still be here," she said.

Blinking, Tinsel realised that was probably the longest sentence the woman had ever spoken to her.

"Oh, I was just heading out," Tinsel answered, noting the two figures standing behind Rushelle. "Is there something you need me for?"

"Yes, these men are homicide detectives. They'd like to talk to you for a moment."

"Really? What's this about?" she asked, trying to keep the panic out of her voice as her mind immediately raced to thoughts of her sister or parents in a horrible accident. She cast a look over her shoulder and through the thin slit of glass in the studio wall; she could see Tim staring back at her with concern.

"This is better done in private," the older of the two men said. "I'm afraid there has been a murder."

CHAPTER 3

Tinsel was doing her best to remain calm on the outside, but inside she was a nervous ball of jitters. Rushelle placed a steaming cup of tea in front of her, and took the seat next to Tinsel as they stared at the detectives across from them. They were sitting in one of 102.8 HitFM's boardrooms surrounded with glass walls, meaning they were visible to anyone in the main part of the office even if they couldn't be heard. Thankfully people were still rolling in, Tinsel noted, but there had been enough around to see her being walked into the room by Rushelle and two cops.

Of course, they couldn't be mistaken for anything *but* cops. With their guns strapped to their hips and stiff posture, it didn't matter that one of them was hot while the other was trying to project a surrogate dad vibe. They screamed "police" with their every movement, and as a young, brown woman living in the world, Tinsel wasn't too fond of the police. She took a slow sip of her tea in order to calm her anxiety.

"What can I help you with?" she asked, having felt only slight relief when she learned they weren't there to see her about a loved one. They'd assured Tinsel of that out in the hall, but Rushelle had remained by her side anyway and insisted she needed to sit in on the meeting for "legal reasons."

"Is that necessary?" Rushelle asked, as the younger detective slid a small, digital voice recorder on to the table.

"It is, I'm afraid. This is just a line of enquiry at the moment, but having our conversation on file will help us down the line."

"It's fine," Tinsel told them both. "Really, I want to help any way I can... As soon as I know what this is about."

"I'm Detective James and this is Detective Senior Sergeant Diraani," he said, smiling at her in a way that was friendly but also highlighted the laugh lines around his eyes.

The older cop took over, flipping open a small notepad as he consulted what was written there. "Last night, or this morning, rather, shortly after midnight the neighbours of a Mera Brant called police to report a disturbance at her property. Officers at the scene discovered Miss Brant deceased. Due to the nature of her injuries, we're treating the matter as a homicide."

The name flagged something in Tinsel's mind, but she couldn't immediately recall what it was as she concentrated on the information detectives were telling her.

"Her mobile device was discovered near the body, the last call being registered to this station we believe shortly before her time of death. The number is 1800–"

"–448 36," Tinsel finished, earning an interested stare from the officer.

"That's our call line," Rushelle said. "When we run competitions or have people dial into the show, that's the number they call. It's 1800 HIT FM."

"Miss Brant dialled this number and was on the line for several minutes," Detective Senior Sergeant Diraani frowned. "We were told here by your station manager that you're the only one who works the overnight shift, is that right?"

"*The Graveyard Shift*," Tinsel corrected. "That's what my show is called. I work from eleven through to the breakfast show at six. It's supposed to be the dead zone."

"Do you remember speaking to anyone last night?" Detective James asked. "Were there any–"

"I know her," she whispered, shock spreading through Tinsel's limbs as she realised why the victim's name was familiar.

Detective James leaned forward in his chair. "You know Miss Brant?"

"I mean, not *know* her know her," Tinsel clarified. "But she called into the show last night. She's called in a few times."

"Was there anything unusual about the call?" the older detective questioned.

The silence was heavy as Tinsel attempted to take another sip of her tea, her hand shaking enough that it was noticeable to the other people in the room.

"Tinsel..." Rushelle started, straightening up in her chair.

"I thought it was a prank," she whispered, eyes wide as she looked at the two detectives. "It was our Halloween show, you know? There's always at least one or two people calling in pretending to be Hannibal Lecter or something."

"When was this?" Detective Senior Sergeant Diraani was scribbling notes.

"Uh, I'd have to check the logs but around twelve thirty maybe? A little bit after?"

"And you were alone in the studio?"

"No, I mean, usually I am but Luiza Curser was there as well. She stayed late after her shift. She heard the call too."

"Luiza hosts *The Apéritif*," Rushelle supplied. "It's the mid-evening show from six until eleven after *Drive* finishes."

"Wait," Detective James said, putting up his hand. "What do you mean 'heard the call?'"

"It was live," Tinsel explained. "I opened up the lines and a woman called Mera Brant rang through to try and win tickets to a movie premiere."

"Walk me through exactly what was said."

"It was a question about a rap song, she answered and then... I don't know, I thought she had dropped off the line. She went quiet, I prompted her, and she spoke up and..."

Tinsel's throat felt thick as she swallowed, realising for the first time just what she might have heard. Rushelle's hand touched her wrist gently, a gesture of sympathy. Her eyes felt like they were filling to the brim and she blinked rapidly, trying to keep it together.

"She said... she thought someone was in her room," Tinsel answered, her voice shaking. "It was just a comment at first and then she screamed it. She was shouting and I could hear something. I didn't know what it was – *oh God*! I could have done something." She slapped a hand to her mouth, struggling with the notion. "Couldn't I?" she asked. "I just thought it was a joke."

"All the shows have had them," Rushelle said, speaking rapidly. "People who call in, make creepy comments or weird sounds. Tinsel gets a lot of them because of her show's timeslot and the fact that she's..."

The station manager trailed off, meeting Tinsel's gaze before looking away.

"Any young, attractive woman on-air gets those calls," Rushelle muttered quietly. "It's just part of the job, unfortunately."

Tinsel felt the gaze of Detective James burning through her and she looked back at him, the penetrating stare intense.

"Have you had any of those calls lately?" the older detective asked.

"No," Tinsel answered, still looking at his colleague. "Not since there was a guy who used to call up and wank off. After about the third time, I realised it was the same person and I passed the number on to one of my bosses who passed it on to the police."

"We have records of that, if you would like to see them," Rushelle supplied.

Detective Senior Sergeant Diraani sighed, putting down his notepad with frustration.

"I'll need copies, definitely, but what I'm more concerned

about is that it sounds like this murder was recorded live on-air. Is it stored in some way, so that people can listen it to it after the fact?"

Tinsel nodded. "It's up on the website now. Soon as I finish the show, I clip it and post it so people can listen if they missed it. It's the same with every show here, they stay up for at least a month."

"What happens after a month?"

"The archive is wiped and the episodes are lost."

"Server storage fees are too high to host them any more than four weeks," Rushelle explained. "But some of the presenters keep select episodes on their own hard drives."

"We're going to need a copy of the recording from last night's show," Diraani told her. "As well as a log of all the calls you received during the broadcast."

"Tinsel, you can get those for the officers, can't you?" her boss asked.

"Of course," she replied, feeling somewhat numb.

"And last night's episode will need to be pulled from the website as quickly as possible. The media will have a field day if they get hold of it."

The older detective got to his feet, the other officer following, signalling the end of the informal interview.

"What about the listeners?" Tinsel asked. "People heard the show, thousands of them, all around Australia. Worldwide too, through the stream. As soon as the victim's name gets out–"

"We're hoping to keep a lid on this for as long as possible," Diraani said. "Obviously this exchange needs to stay between us, as well as any other details discussed with management."

"Of course," Rushelle nodded, seemingly obedient.

Tinsel was sceptical. A story like this would inevitably get out. A murder broadcast live on-air during a Halloween-themed radio show? It was too horrible to stay under wraps.

"Excuse me," Tinsel said, rushing from the room and

towards a staff kitchenette next door. She barely made it in time, her stomach wrenching as she vomited into the silver sink. Breathless, she stayed leaning over the edge for several moments before turning on the tap and washing her sick away. She reached for a paper towel, but touched an outstretched hand instead, making her jump.

"Here." Detective James was standing beside her. Tinsel took the paper towel from him and wiped her mouth with a trembling hand. Cold and clammy, she took a moment before straightening up and leaning against the sink. He stayed next to her, both of their backs resting against the counter as they looked out at the 102.8 HitsFM office.

"Thank you," she croaked, finally.

He nodded, crossing his arms over his chest as they watched Rushelle walk the other detective to her office. Tinsel recognised one of the station's lawyers waiting there, hair in disarray. They'd obviously come straight from bed.

"You couldn't have done anything."

"Huh?"

"What you said in there," the detective continued. "You couldn't have done anything. Even if you'd known it was real and not some joke, by the time you hung up, called the police and we got over there, it still would have been too late."

She let that sit with her for a moment, still too overwhelmed by everything to process it properly. It was a small grace he had given her, but it was a kindness.

"How did she die?" Tinsel asked.

"We're still waiting on the autopsy results."

"If you were to guess?"

"I don't guess, I have to know."

"Uh."

An awkward silence fell between them, lasting only a few beats before he huffed and spoke up.

"It was a sharp implement. Probably a knife of some description, with a serrated edge, ranging seven to nine inches in length. Cause of death could have been damage to an internal organ, blood loss, any number of things from a weapon like that."

"She was stabbed to death?"

He nodded, Tinsel feeling like she might throw up again. Instead, she turned around and started running water from the tap, the sound and movement of it soothing her. Splashing water on her face, Tinsel took a steadying breath.

"Come on," she said, leading him through the pathway of mostly empty desks. "I'm this way."

She pulled out Luiza's chair for him to sit in as she logged back into her computer and began pulling up the files the police needed. Grabbing a USB from the tray in her top drawer, she quickly deleted what was on it and dragged the archived *The Graveyard Shift* episode on to it. A progress bar popped up on her screen, showing her what percentage had been transferred over numeral-by-annoying-numeral.

"It's a big file," she said, by way of explanation.

Detective James nodded, seemingly uninterested at her attempt to fill the silence as he tapped the head of a Boris Karloff Frankenstein bobblehead she had sitting on her desk.

"You have a lot of these," he said, examining the rest of her figurines.

"They're Universal movie monsters." One look at the blank expression on his face told her he didn't get it. "Classic horror movie monsters, like The Mummy? Wolf Man? Gill-Man? Dracula?"

"I saw the Tom Cruise *Mummy* movie."

"I'm terribly sorry for your loss."

He smiled, clearly fascinated by her desk display, which was like a mini-shrine to all the things she loved.

"It's funny, this doesn't look that different to her room."

Tinsel stiffened just as she was reaching for the USB. "The victim's?"

"Yeah."

"Huh. That makes sense, I guess. After all, she listened to the show."

"What do you mean?"

"Well, it is technically 'the graveyard shift' – that's what everyone in radio calls those hours – but I actively named it *The Graveyard Shift* to reflect the kind of show it is."

"A horror radio show?"

"Not many people listen during the hours of eleven to six compared to the other shows, so when I took over from the last guy I pretty much had free reign to do what I wanted. Genre is my love."

Tinsel handed him the USB.

"Last night's show is on there. I added the log of all the numbers that called through and messages received on the text line."

"Text line?"

"People know the number, it's on all our official social media pages. They occasionally send a message through – usually a song request or something like that. If we have a guest, it might be a question they want you to ask them in the interview. People tend to tweet the show using a hashtag as well, so I downloaded the archive for that too and other social updates."

"This is all on here?"

"It is."

"Thanks," he said, looking at the device with newfound respect. Tinsel nearly left it at that, but she wanted to know. She was desperate to.

"The murder weapon, the person who did this, neither of them were there?"

Detective James glanced at her. "At the crime scene? No, just the deceased."

"Do you have any suspects?"

"I can't discuss that kind of thing but… we're gonna get the guy, I promise."

"What makes you think it's a guy?"

"Experience," he shrugged. "Statistics. Also the... *physicality* of the scene."

His colleague walked out of Rushelle's office with the station boss and lawyer in tow. They made a beeline for Tinsel's desk, curious glances following them from the skeleton staff in attendance.

Tinsel tried not to think about the newsreaders and the info they would try to get out of her. She quickly got to her feet when the others joined them.

"I've got the contact details for yourself and Luiza Curser here," Diraani said. "We're going to be in touch with both of you, hopefully get you down to the station this evening or tomorrow for some follow up questions and an official statement if that's OK."

"Sure," Tinsel nodded. "Do I need a lawyer or–"

"We're going to send Stu here with you," Rushelle noted, gesturing to the dishevelled lawyer. "With both of you. And if there's anything else the officers need, Stu will be their point of call."

"Thank you for your time, Miss Munroe, Mrs. Li." Diraani shook both of their hands in a somewhat formal gesture. Detective James gave them all stiff nods. Tinsel watched the expanse of his back as he moved through the hallway to the exit. As they were about to step out of the door, he hesitated and looked back at her for a moment, offering a small smile.

"Look, I don't want to be that person," the lawyer muttered. "But do all detectives look like that?"

"Stu," Rushelle scolded. "Someone has died!"

"And someone is *living*. He's cute, no? Oh look, he left his card on your desk, Tinsel. Do we think he's straight or can I swipe this?"

She dragged her eyes away from the now empty doorway, meeting the gaze of Stu who had a playful smirk resting on his face. Tinsel realised what he was doing with his attempt to cheer her up and lighten the heavy mood. She had only met him once, briefly, at an office Christmas party, but she appreciated his gesture nonetheless.

"I might need that," she said, taking the business card from him as he attempted to fan himself with it.

"Besides," Rushelle sighed, leaning against Tinsel's desk. "You're married. Leave the hot cops to the eligible bachelors."

"You're married too, ma'am."

"I wasn't talking about me." Rushelle undid her ponytail, shaking her hair loose before tying it back up again.

"Should I... go home?" Tinsel asked, unsure what they were supposed to do next.

"Yes," Rushelle said. "Try and get some rest while you can and take your mind off this. Before you go though, I'd like to debrief properly in my office. Stu, if you wouldn't mind grabbing Tim for me as well? He'll kick off, but tell him it's important and that I demanded it."

"He's going to shoot the messenger," the lawyer answered in a sing-song tone.

It wasn't even 7am yet and Tinsel already felt bone tired as she followed her boss towards her office.

In direct contradiction to her fatigue, Tinsel hit the pavement. She needed it for the same reason she always needed it: to clear her head. And today, her head was not just in need of clearing, it needed an exorcism. The thoughts that were spinning in there were downright demonic and the voices she was trying to keep at bay were scaring the shit out of her.

A woman was murdered. A woman was murdered while talking *to her* live on-air. And she had heard the whole thing.

Tinsel felt her throat clench up like she was going to be sick again and she tried to ignore the sensation. Instead, she concentrated on her breaths. She focussed on the sound of her footsteps as she plodded along the footpath. She was intimately acquainted with every line, every crack, every pebble on this five-kilometre trek that she walked every day, twice a day.

She had never been a big exercise girlie, but Tinsel had found motion always helped her think. Since the journey from her office to home was almost a straight line, it was very much a no-brainer. She made it her routine, usually skipping the tram unless the weather dipped into what she called Melbourne hardcore: hail, torrential flooding, random fog.

Tinsel's route was along a main road. Since hers was a city in the true sense, she felt pretty safe weaving among the throng of human traffic heading into boutique bars and lining up for restaurants at night. On her way home, it was the hustle and bustle of early morning exercisers making penance in lycra, dog walkers and coffee-addicts. Yet feeling safe and being safe were two different things, which was why she had a switchblade disguised as a cute, pink key *just* in case. When you pressed the heart detail, the blade popped free.

She felt ridiculous clutching on to it now – the office calamity meant she had left much later than she usually would have. Her timing collided with school drop off: the bikes that whizzed by her were not the road racing kind, but instead touted wooden buckets loaded with kids. Toddlers with backpacks that dwarfed their tiny frames waddled past like determined tortoises, exhausted parents trailing behind. They looked how Tinsel felt and she was relieved when her destination loomed in the distance.

At first glance, it appeared like a mini version of New York's flatiron building. The Fitzroy Pinnacle straddled the space between two streets, the pub stretching backwards in an odd triangular shape and reaching upwards just the same. It had a generous second storey flat and then a third, which contained the remnants of a bell tower.

Back when she was still at uni, and still slogging on community radio, she had worked behind the bar at The Pinny, as it was more commonly known. Even now she picked up the occasional shift there, but only when there was a staffing emergency. Mostly she just hung out on the back stoop at the staff entrance with her mates Gee and Ray, smoking ciggies and gossiping on their break. It was her connections there that had scored Tinsel the deal of a lifetime: fantastic proximity to alcohol, live music and cheap rent.

Few people wanted to live above a pub and the owner Jorro had been constantly looking for ways to occupy the generous quarters upstairs. Tinsel had come to the rescue, asking if he'd consider renting it to her and her boyfriend, Zack. When the pub was at its loudest Monday to Friday, she was at work. And on the weekends, she was usually down amongst the fray. It was the ideal scenario, even if it did always take a few goes jiggling her key in the lock of the staff entrance before she was able to get the door open.

Closing the door behind her with the sole of her foot, Tinsel inched around the kegs of beer waiting to be brought into the bar for that evening's shift. Her footsteps sounded as heavy as they felt. She thudded up the wooden staircase to her flat, holding on to the handrailing for dear life as she moved in a zombie-like trance towards the smell of eggs.

Zack was waiting for her in the kitchen, and it was testament to her emotional and physical exhaustion that she didn't read his mood right away. It wasn't until she'd looped her bag on a hook next to the doorframe and kicked off her shoes that she realised he was pissed.

She paused, eyes drinking in the tattoos that started at his feet and worked their way right up to under his ear like an inky turtleneck. It was a hazard of the job; he worked as a tattoo artist for a studio just around the corner. Her name was on his skin somewhere, which probably would have been a red flag to most. Yet this was Zack: he also had the name of Polly, his first dog, inked inside a love heart on his wrist.

Tinsel wondered if maybe he had already heard what happened and was annoyed that she didn't call him first. She dismissed that thought almost immediately though, realising there was no way he could have known. And judging from his dark expression, she wasn't about to tell him.

"I tried calling," he said, by way of hello.

"Oh-kay," she replied cautiously, trying to get a feel for the eggshells she was walking on. "I've been a bit busy."

"That's the thing with you, isn't it? You're always busy."

She opened her mouth to snap a response, but froze when her eyes settled on the two plates in front of Zack. They had once been warm; delicious chili scrambled eggs were stacked on top of a thick slice of rye, with chunks of goat cheese sprinkled on top. Her favourite. Tinsel closed her eyes, a pang of regret and guilt coursing through her.

"Too busy for me," he continued. "Too busy to–"

"I'm sorry," she snapped, the words coming out harsher than she meant them. "I forgot, Zack."

"Bullshit. You never forget anything. You can name every dumb B-movie ever made without blinking, but can't remember when you're meant to meet your boyfriend – who you live with – for breakfast?"

"There was just a lot going on this morning!" she protested, the rebuttal sounding lame even to her ears.

"Yeah, well," Zack said, picking up both plates. "I've got a lot on this morning too. And I still skipped the gym to make you breakfast." To punctuate the point, his foot hit the lever on the bin and the lid popped up. He dumped both meals – plates, cutlery and all – in the trash.

Bit dramatic, Tinsel thought, biting her lip to stop herself verbalising the comment. It would only add to his annoyance.

"I'm trying, Tin," Zack huffed. "I'm really trying but fuck, you don't make it easy."

With that, he stormed past her. Tinsel was unable to speak or move, and just stood there in the kitchen, staring at the bin, feeling like shit. She listened to Zack moving through the apartment, the familiar jangle of his keys followed by his footsteps thudding down the stairs and the ultimate slam of the door.

Things had been tense between them lately. The on again/off again excitement that energised their first few years together had long worn off. The pro of the hot make-up sex was no longer worth the con of the drama that remained.

Their beef over the past few months was distance, which seemed like a weird thing to say about someone you lived with. But *The Graveyard Shift*'s hours meant they were like ships passing in the night, never getting to see each other enough according to Zack. Tinsel hated when her job became a sticking point. He worked out of a popular local joint, Wallace and Marshall Tattoos, but technically he was a freelance artist who rented a space there and could make his own schedule. Tinsel had never had that luxury and as far as she was concerned, if Zack could follow his passion and she had no problems with it, she expected the same to be true for her.

Tinsel had said these very things to Zack, and he had folded after their last big fight. Breakfast that morning was supposed to be an olive branch. They had agreed he was going to get up early and make food so they could eat together before work each day. She, in turn, was going to take less hosting and emcee gigs that bled into their weekends and time off-air. Except she had forgotten. Sure, sure, extenuating circumstance and all that but... she still felt bad somehow.

There was little else to do but fish the crockery Zack had tossed out of the bin. The frying pan with the remnants of the eggs was still on the stove, along with the mixing bowls and the half-cut loaf of bread that scattered crumbs all over the kitchen counter. So, she rolled up her literal sleeves, filled the sink with warm water and soap, and started scrubbing. Her relationship was a mess that she seemingly couldn't clean up, but this she could.

When she was done, Tinsel stood in the empty space nibbling on a piece of bread absentmindedly. She was usually asleep by this time of day. Instead, she was the kind of exhausted that left her alert and grimy. A twenty-minute shower didn't help and neither did the fresh pair of satin pajamas she slid into. With the bedroom door shut and the blinds pulled, she plunged herself into darkness.

But 10am rolled around and then 11, with Tinsel wide awake and flat on her back in bed as she stared at the ceiling. She couldn't stop thinking about Mera Brant, replaying the call over and over in her mind. Sitting up, she kicked away the covers and started rummaging through one of the compartments in her bag. Her breathing stilled as she held a USB in her hands, containing all the same files she had given to Detective James.

She wasn't sure why she had done it at first, it just seemed important that she had the information too. Tinsel tapped her fingernail against the plastic casing, fighting the urge to open up the file and listen to Mera's voice. *It won't help*, she thought. *It will only make it worse.*

With an agitated grunt, she got to her feet and began throwing on the same clothes she'd stripped off a short time ago. Running a comb through her hair, she grabbed her backpack and a pen from the mug that contained about twenty of them sitting on her bedside table. She scrawled a note for Zack telling him she'd gone to her sister's, knowing he wouldn't see it until he got home late that night but, in the moment, really not caring about the blue this was likely to cause as well.

A short train ride later with cat-eye sunglasses covering the significant bags under her peepers, Tinsel craved one thing and one thing only: the manic energy of her sister's presence.

CHAPTER 4

"Jesus Christ, you're pale as hell," Pandora said, by way of greeting. A smiling baby on her hip, she followed up with: "You need a tan."

"I'm ethnic," Tinsel growled in response, stepping over a toy truck and into the house. "I don't need a tan."

"Crabby, aren't we?" her sister teased, as she did her best to restrain her three-year-old son he made a sprint towards the open door. "Uh-uh, not a chance, Mad Max."

Tinsel automatically plucked the giggling baby from her sister and spun her around in the air before settling her in the cradle of her arms in one smooth motion. That left Pandora to handle her eldest, Max, whom she dragged by the collar of his shirt back into the house.

"I swear, I'm gonna duct tape you to a chair, mate," she told him.

"Mate," he replied, doing a close to perfect impression of his mother. "Mate mate mate mate matematematemat—"

"Oh my God," Pandora growled, throwing the blond boy over her shoulder as he laughed and squirmed. "Get your tubes tied, sis, I'm telling you. It's not too late."

"What's tubes?" Max asked.

"Your Auntie Tintin's tubes. I'm trying to save her."

Tinsel smiled through her cooing to Airlie as she took her over towards the couch. She could hear her sister wrangling

45

Max back into the playpen area she had built, designed for the specific purpose of keeping him in one place for a prolonged period of time. He had skipped a key step in his developmental growth, going straight from crawling to sprinting and never looking back. Pandora swore that seventy-five per cent of her day was trying to keep track of him. That wasn't an issue for her daughter, with the almost-one year-old barely mustering more than a steady waddle on her chubby legs when she felt like it.

"What's more extreme than ADHD?" Pandora asked, flopping on to the couch with a sigh. "ADH-DD?"

"What would you know about double Ds?" Tinsel replied, sticking out her tongue as Airlie stared at her, eyes and mouth wide. "Your mum has itty bitty titties. Yeah, itty bitty, that's what she has."

"At least I can walk down stairs without being in physical pain. You wanna make us a cup of tea? I'll take Airlie."

"You will not," Tinsel said, feigning outrage. "She's my sweet, fat baby."

"Who hopefully never learns anything from her brother, the boy destined to be a getaway driver and live a life of crime. 'The action is the juice!'"

Tinsel got to her feet, propping Airlie on one side of her body as she strolled into the kitchen, moving around with ease. She knew this place as well as she did her own home, which wasn't surprising given she spent so much of her time there.

"What are you doing here anyway?" Pandora called from the lounge, rolling on to her side to open her laptop on the coffee table. "It's rare you emerge before 3pm on a good day. Aren't you gonna be buggered for your shift?"

"I have the night off," Tinsel answered, the teacup clinking as she stirred two teaspoons of sugar into her sister's mug. "And tomorrow night."

"What? Since when?"

She took her time to reply, making two trips back to the

couch with each mug before grabbing a container of several sliced strawberries from the fridge for Airlie: they were her favourite. Popping the kid on her play mat on the floor, she handed her the Tupperware before settling back with her own cup. All she needed was one sip, digesting it slowly, before she began relaying the night and morning's events to an increasingly shocked Pandora. She took her second sip only when she had completely finished the story, her sister sitting upright and blinking at her in shock.

"So, they – Rushelle and the station – thought it was probably best if I took the rest of the week off. Luiza too. They have a duty of care or something like that. One of the producers is clipping together a 'best of' show for the both of us."

"And then... what? You go back on Monday, like nothing happened?"

She shrugged. "I guess so."

"They're completely bonkers if they think that's going to do anything. I guarantee you, the only thing that will be different on Monday is *everyone* will know the story."

"Pandora..." she cautioned, worried for the first time as her older sibling began furiously typing on her laptop.

"Mera Brant – oh! I found her socials, but nothing else. That means the media doesn't have a name yet. Do you think–"

"No," Tinsel said, cutting her off before she had a chance to finish.

Pandora bit her lip, shoulders deflating for a moment. Tinsel watched the internal battle going on in her sister's head as she went back and forth about how far to push it.

"I could break the story."

"And I could break ya neck."

"*Tinsel.*"

"Tintin!" Airlie babbled, punctuating the sentence with the kids' nickname for her.

"This is not something for your true crime blog, okay? This is something that's actually happening *right now*."

"All true crime is happening *right now*," Pandora harrumphed.

"Will you check your ambition for five minutes, please?"

"You're one to talk."

They fell into a silent truce, neither willing to sacrifice ground as they sat there with their arms folded, mirror images of each other.

Pandora had studied law at university and was currently working on a Master of Criminology at the University of Melbourne a few days a week while caring for Max and Airlie. She had married her high school boyfriend, Brian Smith, when she was in her twenties and had started popping out kids a few years later.

Compared to Tinsel's dating history, her twenty-nine-year-old sister had a disgustingly stable relationship with a really decent guy. She'd never been actively single – not since she and Brian got together when they were fourteen – and Pandora had never seemed to question this decision the way Tinsel second-guessed every choice she made.

"When you've found The One, why keep looking?" was Pandora's mantra.

Brian worked in tech, running the global operations for a sports broadcaster, and earned a salary that kept them both afloat. When Pandora was in class, he worked from home and looked after the kids simultaneously. Sometimes Tinsel was called to help out, but more often than not, she volunteered her services: Max and Airlie were the loves of her life.

Pandora's third child, however, was a true crime blog. She had started it back when she was a first-year law student. It had always been a passion project and she had built up an impressive audience of mostly international readers over the years. The site earned money in ad placements and with the tenth anniversary of *Pandora's Box* approaching, her older sister was trying to convince Tinsel to launch a tie-in podcast with her. Tinsel said she'd produce it and handle the technical side of things, but outside of that, she wasn't sure she had anything to offer. That was Pandora's area of expertise, not hers.

"Fine," her sister said, interrupting her train of thought. "I won't write anything about it if you don't want me to."

"I could get in trouble from the police, Pandora. They might still be trying to notify her next of kin. They might not want the public to know the things they told me if it means they could catch this guy."

"You still got the detective's card?"

"The old one or the hot one?"

"The hot one, obviously."

She plucked it from her wallet and handed it to her sister. Pandora examined the tiny rectangle of card like it held some secret only she could see. She switched her attention to her computer in an instant and tapped away.

"*Detective Vic James*. Is this him?" her sister asked, sliding the laptop across to Tinsel.

"Damn, yeah. You found him quick."

"Puh-lease. Huh, he's smart. His Facebook page is completely locked."

"The only thing you can see is that profile pic," Tinsel murmured, attempting to navigate further.

"He's really cute," Pandora continued. "Got that tall, dark and handsome thing going on. I wonder if that's why he was so chatty: he's got a thing for you."

"After half an hour of watching me stutter and cry in a boardroom? Oh yeah, what a meet-cute."

"When do you have to go back into the station?"

"I don't know. It's supposed to be sometime today or tomorrow, but they said they'll call me."

"What did Zack say?"

Tinsel let the question hang in the air for a beat before casting her sister a nervous glance.

"I haven't told him yet."

"Tinsel!"

"Tintin!" Airlie exclaimed passionately.

"I know," she said to both of them. "I was going to tell him this morning and then we got into a stupid fight and... I thought I'd wait until tonight when he's finished work and we have time to talk about it properly."

Pandora took a pointed sip of her tea, saying everything with the way she was not saying anything.

"Not every couple are you and Brian," Tinsel whined, giving her sister a playful whack on the arm. "It's not healthy to tell each other everything."

"You're right, a fifteen-year relationship isn't healthy at all."

"Shut up."

"Five years married."

"Oh my God, okay, I get it. I said I'll talk to him. He's just not... you."

Pandora arched an eyebrow, sitting down her teacup as she pulled Tinsel in for a hug.

"Am I the first person you've spoken to about this outside the office?"

"Yeah."

"Not mum or dad?"

"No, you know how they are. Dad will start trying to therapize me and mum will–"

"I get it," Pandora said, rubbing Tinsel's back affectionately. "Okay, when you go into the police station next, you do not speak to them until the lawyer from the station is present."

"Stu?"

"Yeah, whatever his name is. You got his number?"

"Uh huh. Collected his card too. And he's got mine. Wait, can't you represent me?"

"You don't need representation, you're not a suspect. But this is a murder investigation, so the presence of a lawyer is non-negotiable."

"Fine, so can it be you?"

"Hell no! I can't represent you if I want to write about it."

"Pandora!"

"Everything I hear in there will be useless, I'll be unable to publish it."

Tinsel wiggled free of her grip, deeply annoyed. "You promised you wouldn't write about it."

"Firstly, I didn't promise. Secondly, I agreed that I won't write about it... until someone else publishes the name. I won't break the story, but I also won't *not* write about it either."

"You're unbelievable," Tinsel huffed, getting to her feet and snatching up Airlie. The baby had strawberries smeared around her mouth like she was a bloodthirsty zombie. "Your mother is unbelievable, I hope you know."

"What are you doing with her? That's my one normal child, leave her be."

"She needs her nappy changed, I can smell it."

Tinsel hung the toddler in front of Pandora, pushing her butt as close to her sister's nose as she could.

"Ergh, get that thing away from me. Okay, okay, point made."

Tinsel carried Airlie to the change table, Pandora trailing after her as she verbally worked through her process.

"I'm going to write the story now," she started, "but I won't publish it until it's live somewhere else first. That way you won't get in trouble."

"I will if you put in details that no one else has, things only I could know."

"There are dozens of people who work at 102.8 HitsFM. That place is leakier than Airlie's nappy. Thanks for that, by the way."

"You're welcome," Tinsel responded, wiping between the kid's many fat rolls.

"So as long as I don't publish anything that someone at the station couldn't have leaked me, I think you're safe. Legally too, cos I'd never reveal my sources."

"How kind."

"Besides, we have different last names, we look completely different, no one from a glance is even gonna know we're related."

Pandora had a point; her naturally red hair and face dotted in ginger freckles seemingly proving the argument as Tinsel cast a sideways glance. Brian sometimes jokingly called her Princess Merida and it was a fair description. Tinsel's appearance was as close to opposite as you could get. Her skin was dark and so were her features, with black, glossy hair, deep brown eyes, thick black eyelashes and eyebrows all indicative of her Indian heritage.

That's about all she knew of her background, Pandora too, as both the girls had been adopted by academics Eugene Roe and Abigail Munnet when they were babies. Their parents were both professors at the University of Sydney, their father in psychology and their mother in radical feminist theory. That's why – even though they were married – Abigail had refused to take Eugene's name in order to "buck the patriarchal legacy of cattle branding women during the institution of matrimony." Their mother had told Pandora that she "respected each woman's choice" when she got married to Brian and decided to take his surname – Smith – but Tinsel had long suspected the grey-haired rebel was quietly disappointed by it.

To be fair, it was probably the only thing her older sister had done in her entire existence that had disappointed their mother. Eugene and Abigail had joined their surnames to create Munroe, making sure Tinsel and Pandora would grow up and go through school feeling united. Now she was the only one left with it, Pandora having shrugged it off like an old cardigan as she started her own family. Looking down at Airlie, who was attempting to blow raspberries at her, Tinsel didn't feel like it was such a bad thing in the moment.

Rebuttoning the babe's jumpsuit, she handed her to Pandora as she thought about her sister's proposal.

"Alright, you can write the piece and have it ready to go," she conceded. "Especially if they still haven't caught the guy. Who knows, the post may help."

"Definitely!" Pandora beamed. "I'll even let you look through the first draft. Say, you don't happen to have the USB with the audio on it with you, do you?"

Tinsel hesitated before answering. "The kids cannot hear it."

"Ha, of course not!" she laughed. "What kind of loose unit parent do you think I am? I'll set them up in the lounge with *Kangaroo Beach*, we can listen on headphones. That is, if you want to listen again?"

Tinsel felt her chest clench at the thought of it, but she also knew that it was inevitable. She was going to listen to it again, whether it was now or at 2am in the morning when she was so plagued by the memory she couldn't sleep. She'd much rather take the plunge in the comfort of her sister's house with a chubby babe in arm's reach if she needed something to cuddle. With a stiff nod, she agreed.

"Great," Pandora beamed. "I'll get the emergency vino."

With her headphones in and her favourite playlist on blast, it was a weird sensation as Tinsel sat on the train travelling home instead of to work like she usually would at that hour. She always took her allocated six weeks vacation per year from the first of December, not returning to the station until it was ratings season again in January like most of her colleagues. That meant a long time between breaks and Tinsel was so used to her routine, it was strange when she was forced out of it.

Watching suburbs whir by outside the window, sun properly setting on the horizon, she was grateful that Pandora and Brian lived on a train line close to her. Reservoir was an easier place to get to on public transport than it was by car, and she wasn't sure if her nerves were fit for driving on Melbourne roads at the moment. As she started to recognise the swelling, green scenery that lined the tracks, she got to her feet with the anticipation as her stop at Clifton Hill station was just a few minutes away.

Tinsel was going to the tattoo shop first, even though she knew Zack worked late on Thursday nights and wouldn't be finished for a few more hours. Her sister's scolding had been right for the most part: she needed to tell him, and she needed to tell him now.

Passing the colourful, hand drawn art of the pedestrian underpass and joining the tide of bodies that took the stairs up out of the station, she didn't have far to go. She jumped on a tram for a few stops then hopped off at Nicholson Street. She slowed to pat an overweight bulldog tied to a street sign out the front of a convenience store, the gesture doubling as a way to avoid the charity mugger complimenting people on their hair, outfit, smile, in order to get them to sign up to their cause.

Wallace And Marshall Tattoos was weirdly wedged between an accountant's office and Madame Fazell's Psychic Readings. It was always busy, with milk crates positioned out the front of the store, usually occupied by people drinking coffees they'd bought from a nearby cafe or having a sneaky beer. She didn't recognise any of the faces there tonight, but she nodded at them anyway just to be polite as she stepped inside.

Cypress Hill was blaring from the speakers positioned all around the two-storey building, meaning there was no escaping the whims of whoever was in charge of the music that day. It was a democracy, so each of the five artists in residence had a turn at controlling the playlist. The other two days of the week went to their receptionist, Nancy, and the apprentice, Fredrico.

"Hey, Tinsel," Nancy chirped, her thin, inky eyebrows rising with surprise. "I didn't expect you in tonight, don't you usually have the show?"

"Usually. But I've got the night off. You reckon I can grab him for a second?" She jerked her head in the direction of

Zack, whose station was towards the rear of the shop and decked out in a pseudo-Western theme with horseshoes and ornamental animal skulls. Each artist got to decorate their own area; Tinsel's favourite station belonged to a chick who went by the moniker Felony Swiff and leaned hard into a Y2K aesthetic complete with fluffy, pastel utensils and inflatable furniture.

"Ahhhh..."

Nancy pulled up Zack's schedule on the office computer, before glancing overhead at the clock.

"He should be finished up on that thigh piece in the next five minutes or so, if you want to hang around?"

"Yeah, that would be great," Tinsel murmured, catching his eye as he glanced towards the reception desk. She could see the frown of confusion on his face as he mouthed the words 'you okay?'

She nodded, pointing to the front of the store so he knew she'd be waiting outside.

"Thanks Nancy," she said. "Tell him I'm out front."

"Okie doke, will do."

There were no milk crates left, so she took a spot leaning against the wall of the building. She was about to put her headphones back in, but Madame Fazell chose that moment to slip outside for a cigarette.

"Tinsel, darling, how are you, dear?" the older lady asked, bracelets rattling as she reached out to gently touch her arm.

"I'm good, Miriam, how are you?" she smiled. "How's business?"

"Ha!" the psychic cackled, the cigarette between her lips jiggling as she attempted to light it. "This time of year is always good, you know? Any period heading towards the New Year."

She kissed the air with a blessing, laughing a little louder at herself so that a passing family turned to stare. The daughter whispered something to her mother, after taking one look at

Madame Fazell and darting around to the other side of her parents. Tinsel didn't blame her: the old woman actively dressed like a witch, so scared kids were a sign that she was doing her job right.

"How's your radio show, huh? All those night hours?"

"It's good, ratings are good... for that hour."

"When do you get that daylight gig, eh? You're a girl who's meant to be seen in the sunlight."

"Coincidentally, I saw some today."

"Ah, my dear, you should never believe in coincidences!"

Tinsel replaced her frown with a polite nod as the woman began her slow shuffle towards the park across the street, where she could watch people play with their dogs and smoke in peace. She was never much for farewells, usually preferring to end their conversations on some bizarre piece of advice before ghosting into the evening. The psychic creeped Zack and most of the other tattooists out, whereas Tinsel kind of loved her kookiness. Plus, she knew Felony was a regular customer.

The hinge of the shop's door creaked as her boyfriend stepped outside. Tinsel admired the way the light of a passing car lit his face with a warm glow. He wasn't watching her though, instead his eyes were glued to the screen of his phone. Zack was staring at the device with a mix of emotions passing over his expression so quickly Tinsel wasn't able to register them all. He looked up, meeting her gaze.

"Tinsel, what the fuck?"

She frowned, opening her mouth to reply but stopping herself the moment he held the screen of his phone towards her. She inched closer, squinting at the sudden brightness as she read the headline.

"'"SOMEONE'S IN MY ROOM!" Woman Murdered in Halloween Broadcast Bloodbath.'"

She snatched the phone from him, eyes scanning the story in a panic.

"That's in *The Herald*," he said, frustration evident in his tone. "When were you going to tell me?"

"That's what I came here for tonight," she murmured, only half-concentrating as she scanned the rest of the article. There was information in here she didn't know, including quotes from one of the neighbours who discovered the body and a timeline leading up to the crime.

Tinsel's blood ran cold as she read halfway down the piece. Feeling her own phone buzzing in her pocket, she forcefully handed Zack's back to him and glanced at her screen. She had three messages from Pandora, each popping up one after the other.

Holy shit, it's live!

Followed by: *I'm posting my story now.*

Then, finally.

Just so you know.

"Gah!" Tinsel grunted, annoyed as she swiped the messages away so she could get to her contacts.

"Seriously, I can't believe *Nancy* is the one who just showed me this," Zack continued. "I didn't even hear it from my own girlfriend."

Tinsel had saved both of the detectives' numbers in her phone, she just needed to find them–

"Hey, I'm trying to talk to you!" Zack yelled, grabbing her by the arm.

"THIS ISN'T ABOUT YOU!" she screamed, pulling herself free as she took a few steps back. He blinked, clearly shocked by her outburst as the conversations around them on the street came to a halt.

"I was trying to tell you, okay?" Tinsel started, softening her tone. "I found out at six this morning and in between speaking to the police and trying not to have an emotional breakdown, things kind of got in the way."

"Tin–"

"I came straight from Pandora's to talk to you tonight, I

didn't think the story was gonna break this bloody fast. And yeah, okay, it would have been preferable if you heard it from me instead of your fucking receptionist."

She knew most of the staff inside Wallace and Marshall were watching their fight through the front windows, but Tinsel didn't care. Her heart was racing and with shock, she realised his reaction had scared her.

"A girl died," Tinsel said, trying to keep her voice even. "And I heard it. I don't exactly have a guidebook on how to deal with that, do you? Cos I'd welcome some advice right now."

His lips parted to reply, but no sound came out as he stood there with palms raised in some kind of peace gesture.

"Hey, I'm sorry," he began, voice immediately softer from when the conversation had started out. "I was shocked, alright? I saw your name there – your show is listed – and the article interviewed someone else who was listening too. I just don't understand why you didn't come to me straight away."

"You mean this morning?" she asked. "When you were tossing eggs about and so *desperate* to get out of the house?"

"Hey, come on," Zack huffed. "I don't even eat gluten and I still went to Loafer to get your favourite bread for breakfast. You're being unfair and you know it."

She balked at him, truly and utterly bewildered by the words that had just come out of his mouth. Blinking, it was like she was seeing him for the first time. *Really* seeing him. And he looked like a stranger.

"No," she said softly, shaking her head. "Not again."

"Not what?" Zack replied, her gentle tone causing him to inch closer.

She looked up at him, staring hard at the person she realised had successfully pulled a trick like this on her a thousand times.

"You're not turning this back on me," Tinsel answered, firm. "Not anymore. And the only thing I *know* is that I'm out of here."

She spun on her heels and marched away from him before his words could undo her resolve.

"Wait, Tinsel – come on! Get back here! Where are–"

"Just fuck off and leave me alone," she snapped. "You're so good at it."

She heard his footsteps die off with that final comment, and Tinsel felt a flash of guilt at the pain she might have caused him. It lasted for all of two seconds before she got mad at herself for not prioritising her own feelings. She thought she heard someone murmur "just let her go" with a voice that sounded like Nancy, who she had long suspected had a thing for Zack.

Tinsel couldn't even find the energy to be mad, with her overwhelming emotion being exhaustion. *Let her have him*, she thought, as she hit the number for Detective James in her phone. It rang as she continued to walk, directionless and fully aware that she must look like a hot mess to anyone she passed.

"Hello?" a voice croaked.

"Detective James?" Tinsel asked, thinking that he sounded as if he'd just woken up.

"Yeah, yeah – hang on, one sec."

She sniffed, wiping away the salt from her eyes and nose at the same time.

"Who's this?" the police officer questioned, sounding slightly more alert.

"It's Tinsel Munroe."

"Tinsel, hey – are you okay?"

"I, uh…" she was surprised by the question.

"You sound upset."

"I'm okay," she lied. "I'm just calling because I saw *The Herald*'s story."

"What? Argh, son of a bitch! When did it go up?"

"Like, within the last half an hour, I think?"

"God damn it."

She thought she could hear him hastily getting dressed, a clink in the background sounding like a rattling belt buckle and that was definitely a zipper in motion.

"The reason I called was in the article they had a picture of Mera Brant taken from Instagram. They said it was the last image of her alive and she's dressed in this white outfit, covered in fake blood and posing with her friends."

"Yeah, I've seen the picture. We spoke to a few of those friends today too."

"So she attended a *Halloween* movie marathon on the night she was killed?"

"Yeah, we've corroborated that. It was a two-parter and the second half is running tonight at The Astor."

"I know, I was there."

"What?"

"I was the host. I introduced the first few movies as a cross promo for *The Graveyard Shift*."

"The one that happened last night? On Halloween?"

"Yeah, I do it every year. They pick different movies each time and people dress up. I came as a skeleton and–"

"Where are you right now?"

"Huh?" Tinsel grunted in response, coming to a halt.

"Right now, where are you?"

"I'm…"

With a jolt she realised she must have been subconsciously walking towards home, her destination only a street and a half away.

"I'm in Fitzroy," she said. "Heading home."

"Are you by yourself?"

"Yeah, I mean, kind of."

Just in her line of sight she could see two different groups of people, one walking towards her and another walking away. It was a Thursday night in the inner-city, so the place was still somewhat populated.

"I live in Brunswick, I'm going to come and get you."

"Okay," she said, trying to sound calm even though she didn't feel it. "Should I be worried?"

"Not at all," Detective James replied, Tinsel almost able to hear his fake smile through the phone. "Give me your home address and I'll pick you–"

"The Pinny."

"The pub?"

"Yeah, I live upstairs."

"Okay, go sit at the bar or something. Stay surrounded by people and I'll be there in fifteen minutes at the latest."

"I'll save you a drink."

Hanging up the phone, Tinsel stepped to the side of the footpath to allow a trio of people space to get by as they chatted and laughed about an episode of *The Bachelor*. Wrapping her jacket around her a little bit tighter, she tried not to freak herself out as she stood there on the dark street, alone. She urged her limbs to move, to push herself forward, but they were heavy like lead as she thought about the fact Mera Brant had been murdered while calling in to her radio show, only hours after they'd been at the same event.

Madame Fazell's words came swimming back to her.

"Never believe in coincidences."

Tinsel couldn't help the shiver that ran down her spine.

CHAPTER 5

Thursday night festivities were just beginning to wind down when Tinsel pushed her way through the front door of The Fitzroy Pinnacle. There was a tuckshop window that provided a view into the beer garden out the back. As she'd passed it, she'd seen that even there amongst the fairy lights and creeping vines, the crowd had dissipated.

"Baaaaaaabe!" her favourite bartender Gee yelled as they spotted her. "I was just about to turn off the frozen margarita machine but could sense in my waters you were around the corner."

The greeting did a lot to ease the discomfort that had been steadily growing until she had stepped over the threshold. A spicy, frozen marg would do even more.

Gee was in a variation of their standard uniform: bucket hat, eye catching earrings, tea towel thrown over their shoulder and cute sweater/blouse combo.

"Where's Ray?" Tinsel asked, looking around and finding only one indoor table remaining that was occupied with patrons picking over her number one dish – the pulled pork nachos.

"It was so quiet, I sent everyone else home," Gee replied, grabbing one of the cocktail glasses. "I'm doing close by myself."

Tinsel slipped behind the bar, taking the stem from Gee and

using her hip to bump them aside. "Then close away, don't let me stop you."

"Ugh, you're a gem!" They planted a kiss on the side of her cheek as they dashed off, Tinsel only half watching as Gee began swirling around the place like an organised tornado. Cutlery containers were collected, candles were rapidly blown out, tables were wiped, empty glasses were stacked and packed. While they were busy, it meant she had free reign of the music and she quickly queued a handful of Swet Shop Boys bangers to come on after the Madonna track faded away.

Until then, she grabbed a slice of lime, used its juice to rim the glass before placing it face down in the Tajin chilli seasoning until there was an even coating lining it. She poured the last of the frozen margarita mix as it churned from the slushie machine, flipped the switch off and added her original piece of lime as garnish. Tinsel took her usual spot at the end of the bar, hanging her bag on the hook underneath and let out an audible groan as she took a heroic first sip.

"Okay, I can tell your day has been drab if you're smashing half a marg on the first go," Gee commented, flying around her as they made their way to the closed kitchen.

"If only you knew," she murmured. Since the clock had ticked over from midnight until now, it felt like Tinsel had been copping kicks to the snatch one after the other. The day had started out horrific and gotten progressively terrible, with her metaphorical vadge all but dust now. Her phone rung and she flinched when she saw it was Zack.

Pandora had this motto – never sleep on an argument – yet this was more than an argument. This felt like the end, truthfully, and Tinsel cringed at the thought of all the things she'd slept on in this relationship. Years of it. When it finally stopped ringing, she blocked his number. Eventually she would have to talk to him, but that was beyond low on her priority list. Subterranean, even. She didn't want to see him and with a start, she realised that eventually when he came home, she didn't want to be there.

Wallowing was the last thing Tinsel needed to do and action made her feel foolishly positive. Downing another gulp of the frozen margarita and licking the chilli powder from her lips, she quickly texted Detective James new instructions.

Meet you at the staff door as the pub is closing up.

The dots of a message being written in response were clicked away as she stood up, sculled the last of her drink and rinsed the glass. Slipping it in the dishwasher, Tinsel hit the necessary buttons for a wash cycle and grabbed her stuff.

Gee appeared around the corner just as she was passing the kitchen, catching her by surprise and causing a scream.

"Fuck!" she yelped.

"AAAA!" Gee responded, both grabbing each other and clutching on to their arms for dear life. The panicked breaths turned into uneasy chuckles.

"Sorry," Gee started. "I didn't–"

"No, I'm sorry. Just very jumpy at the moment."

"How unlike you," they purred. "Halloween hangover?"

"Something like that. Listen, I'm going to call it a night."

"Okay hon, lubya!"

They embraced and parted ways, Tinsel taking the internal route through the backroom, past the locked staff door, and up the stairs to her apartment. Heading directly to the bedroom, she pulled an overnight bag from the wardrobe and began throwing supplies into it. Double checking she had enough of everything for a few nights, she tossed in her makeup bag and headed towards the bathroom to grab her toothbrush and a few toiletries.

Pandora had a spare room and a never-ending desire to involve herself in Tinsel's problems, so she would make the most of it for a few days. Finally throwing in her laptop, back-up hard drives, and chargers, she slung the bag over her shoulder and made her way out, flicking off the lights as she went.

Cracking open the staff door, she made herself comfortable sitting on top of one of the empty silver kegs that were positioned outside for collection. Resting her back against the wall, Tinsel watched as a loud ding heralded the arrival of a tram that sped past on the main road at the corner. It was the motion that drew her eye, and she frowned as she watched the dark figure of someone leaning against the wall of the bottle-o across the street. They were in shadow, so she couldn't see their face or make out much detail like height or clothing, but it irked her.

Now would be a good time to show up hot cop, she thought to herself, pulling out her phone to check on his status. She had just one message from him.

STAY INSIDE UNTIL I GET THERE, it read.

"Shit," Tinsel muttered. Looking up, she was the only person down this side street, which peeled off Saint Georges Road and was largely residential. There were parked cars lining the curb and she watched as a cat skittered across the road only to shimmy under a garage door. Her eyes darted back to the bottle-o, but the person standing there was gone. The neon "open" sign had also switched to "closed," casting the parking lot around it in even thicker darkness.

Her decision to wait there for Detective James suddenly felt foolish and she wished Gee was still inside. The darkened windows of the pub told her they were long gone. She had her keys clipped to the belt hoop of her jeans and she reached for them, turning her back to the street as she went to unlock the door behind her and head inside again. Her fingers were barely on the cool metal when she heard a *thump* behind her.

Tinsel spun around, pressing her back to the wood of the door. Her eyes scanned the street desperately for the source of the noise. It sounded like weight hitting the bonnet of a car, somewhat metallic and hollow at the same time. There were shadows everywhere, the branches of the banksia trees that lined the footpath blew softly in the wind and created even more. It was the fauna that caused her to look up, beyond eyelevel, and that's what made her breath catch.

A beaten-up car was parked at the top of the street, the first and last spot before you hit the main road. It had been tagged to shit, with slogans and logos spray-painted over every clear inch. The windows were long since smashed and a paper council removal notice fluttered uselessly under the window wipers. It was right next to an overgrown tree, the leaves blocking the glow from the streetlight overhead.

There was another metallic crunch, this sound sharp enough to make her flinch. She stepped away from the pub to get a better view. It sounded like someone trying to key a car door. *Or knife,* she thought before she could stop herself.

That was bullshit and Tinsel knew it. As if to prove it to herself, she grabbed her phone and hit the flashlight button, which wasn't exactly a spotlight but would do in a pinch. She shined it towards the car, the beam tracking up towards the roof. The second it shone on a pair of black sneakers, she was already running.

She barely had a moment to digest the figure dressed all in black crouching on top of the car, hunched over and leaning towards her with intent. Tinsel didn't need more time than that.

The phone slipped from her hand in panic, but that was the last mistake she'd make. She sprinted down the middle of the street, giving herself as much room as possible as she pummelled the pavement.

The *thump* repeated, telling her the figure had jumped down after her. The panting she could hear confirmed it. *They were right behind her.*

Tinsel hadn't spared much thought for where she was going, she just knew that she had to put distance between her and whoever was on her heels. She didn't even want to risk banging on a door for help – all the lights inside were turned off and the time it could take for someone to wake up and come down to her... she'd be the next Mera Brant.

The end of Taplin Street was looming in front of her, however, and she'd have to make a choice. With a start, she realised she was being herded into an even more dangerous situation. Tinsel had been almost at the top of the street and that's exactly where they'd blocked her path, meaning she was being forced away from the main road. At the opposite end was a park, with a bike path that was usually busy during the day but isolated this time of night. The whole space was, actually, with thick bushes and enough distance between there and the nearest house that it was likely someone might mistake a scream of hers for a fox taking out a neighbourhood cat.

It was the kill zone.

Tinsel took a sharp left, skidding and sliding across the bonnet of a car as she sprinted down a tight alleyway. A surprised grunt sounded behind her, and she felt a spurt of energy knowing she had caught her pursuer off guard. She risked a glance over her shoulder, seeing only a darting black mass that was closer than she would have liked.

They were faster than her. But this was Tinsel's neighbourhood. She knew every derelict alleyway thanks to years of spilling out of house parties into them with her friends.

If she could just keep running, keep ignoring the pain in her chest that burned from a shortness of breath, just keep ignoring the overwhelming fear she felt threatening to immobilise her, then she could make it.

Take this alleyway west, pop out near Saint Georges Road, sprint along the tram tracks in open space until one came along, or a car drove in sight – didn't matter which. Until that happened, she'd keep picking her way back towards The Pinny where there was a twenty-four-hour BP service station nearby that she could run into for help.

Tinsel had committed to that choice in her mind as the alleyway arched around towards her destination. She could see the clear street in sight, grateful for the Stan Smith sneakers she'd chosen that day instead of something with a heel, although she was still tripping and stumbling on every fourth step. The alleyways were largely unchanged since they were first put down, retaining some of the oldest infrastructure in the city. They were cracked, uneven, and it was just as likely you could break a neck as break an ankle if you fell.

It was on one of these near misses that she risked another glance back. The alley was empty.

There was no one there.

The long, dark and grey path stretched behind her like an insidious reptile. She slowed to a halt, slapping a hand over her mouth to quiet her panting. She strained to hear something in the dark, any rustling or footsteps from the shadows she couldn't fully penetrate visually. Not taking her eyes off the darkness, she patted herself down, looking for the lump of her keys. *Shit*, she thought. She'd left them in the lock of the fucking door.

Tinsel would have felt marginally better if she had her switchblade. Staring at the empty alleyway, she thought it might have been a trick. She couldn't be certain, but maybe they were just out of frame, waiting for her to be dumb enough to retrace her footsteps. Then they could lurch out and end this unseen, her body discarded until someone was unlucky enough to come along.

No, she wouldn't be got that way.

She should have charged at the person from the start and taken her chances at trying to make it to the main road. Slowly, quietly, she turned and started jogging towards the alley entrance. She couldn't see what was waiting for her on either side of the opening, so she put her head down and sprinted, eyes focused on Saint Georges Road up ahead.

Tinsel burst out of there in a rush and –

BAM!

She screamed as she immediately collided with a figure, knocking both of them over. The man gripped her shoulders on the way down, taking the brunt of the fall. Her palms extended outwards, the flesh ripping off as they grazed the concrete. She kicked and punched and hit him as she desperately tried to untangle herself and get away.

"TINSEL!"

She paused, recognising that voice as hands clutched at her.

"Tinsel, it's me!"

She leaned back, arching her body enough so she could see the person beneath her properly.

"Detective?"

"Hi," he replied, his bashful smile half-cloaked in the low light.

"I... uh–"

"Are you okay?"

"I don't know," she admitted, her breaths nearly turning to sobs.

"Tinsel?"

She looked behind her and down the alleyway. It was still.

"Tinsel, what is it?" he repeated, gently shaking her shoulders.

His tone was serious, believing, and he stared at her intensely.

"Someone was chasing me."

The effect was immediate. Detective James gently rolled her off him and leapt into position. He drew his gun, angling himself in front of her and towards the mouth of the alley.

"I couldn't see who it was," Tinsel continued. "It could be som–"

He held a finger to his lips. She fell silent, nodding her head to indicate that she understood. They both remained quiet, listening to the sound of the night around them. She was still sitting on the path, her hands stinging and her breath shaky as she tried to bring her heart rate back down. Detective James took one step towards the alley before changing his mind.

He spun back around, reaching a hand underneath her arms to help her up while still keeping his gun in the other.

"Come on," he said, gaze remaining fixed on the alley.

"Where are we going?" Tinsel asked.

"*You* are going to my car," Detective James replied. "Where I know you'll be safe and where *I* know your exact location."

The Pinnacle was visible over the rooftops of the houses they were passing, the pair of them not having to march far until he was opening the passenger door of a Holden Commodore parked right in front of the staff entrance.

"What?" he asked, watching as she hesitated.

"My bag, my phone…"

Detective James followed her gaze. "Get in the car, lock the doors."

Tinsel didn't question the directions, and did exactly that as she nervously watched him in the dark. Her eyes darted from his figure – gun drawn and torchlight now held under it – to the space around Detective James that could have held anything or anyone creeping towards him.

After a few minutes, he returned to the car unharmed, passing her phone towards her and tossing the overnight bag in the backseat. The vehicle doors slammed and locked behind him in quick succession as he slid into the driver's seat.

He placed his gun up on the dash, where it was still within reach, and clicked off his torch. Detective James' gaze slid to the steering wheel, where Tinsel had both her hands hovering over the worn covering there. She drew them back, feeling stupid.

"I was going to honk if someone came up behind you," she explained. "It's silly b–"

"It's not," he said, cutting her off. "You would have given me a warning."

He reached out and took her hands as she was drawing them back. Gently, he turned over her palms. His fingers examined the deep grazes, careful not to get blood on himself, which was challenging given how much she was shaking. Mercifully, he didn't comment on that. He just reached across, unclicked the glove compartment and retrieved a tiny first-aid kit that looked like it was contained in a red purse with a white cross on it.

"Are you hurt anywhere else?" he questioned.

"No," she whispered. "I don't think so. Maybe tweaked an ankle, but nothing an ice pack won't fix."

"You talk," Detective James began. "And I'll bandage these. Tell me everything that happened."

Her words came out steady despite how unsteady she felt at her very core. Tinsel only had to pause once, hissing as Detective James tweezed a chunk of gravel from under her skin. The sting of the Betadine to her wounds didn't exactly help, but by the time her hands were padded and wrapped, she was done.

"You didn't get a good look at the guy on the car?"

She closed her eyes, trying to recreate the image in her mind. All she could dredge up was the silhouette of a hunched figure.

"I couldn't even say if it was a guy," Tinsel admitted.

"Did they have the same physique as the person outside the bottle-o?"

She shook her head. "I'm sorry, I really couldn't tell in either case. I just know they were fast and…"

"And what?"

"I don't want to sound hysterical, but it felt like they were waiting for me."

He nodded as if that didn't sound hysterical at all. Neither said what they were both thinking. They didn't need to. There wasn't anyone in custody for Mera Brant's murder yet, and they both knew the killer was still out there.

She jumped as a loud screech came from within the car. A strangled choke escaped Tinsel's own mouth. It took her a few beats to realise what it was – the sound had come from a police scanner strapped to the dashboard. It was only when human voices began speaking over the transmission, with the same screech punctuating each sentence, that she was able to calm herself properly.

"Be chill," she whispered, placing a hand over her heart. "Be chill."

"This is a decidedly unchill situation," Detective James muttered, grabbing his police radio. Tinsel spaced out for a moment, his chatter combining with the scanner so that she only picked up key words like "assailant" and "assistance." The adrenaline had finally worn off and she was left exhausted. When he touched her shoulder, her lids felt heavy as she opened her eyes and refocused on him.

"Tinsel?"

"Mmmm?"

"I've got back-up on the way. Whether it was some junkie and you got unlucky or someone with other motives, we'll get to the bottom of it. Okay?"

"Okay," she nodded.

"Until they arrive, I need to go back out there and look for any evidence I can," he continued, passing her his phone which had the maps app open on their location. "Can you show me exactly where you ran?"

She traced the route with her finger, answering the brief questions he had until he seemed happy.

"Alright," he sighed. "I'm going to give you my keys."

His words triggered something in her memory, and she leaned forward, looking past him.

"My keys."

"What?" Detective James twisted around to see what she was staring at.

"I had them in the door when I heard the noise. I didn't have time to grab them when I ran. They're still there."

"Leave it with me." He handed her his own set in the meantime.

Tinsel hit the button on his keyring that locked the doors as Detective James stepped back out into the dark. Switching off the car's overhead light so she didn't look like a sitting target, she watched as he examined the area around the staff door and grabbed something metallic. Then he began retracing her steps and moving out of her line of sight.

It was excruciating waiting there, her mind unable to help but imagine Detective James moving through the labyrinth of cobblestone alleyways that snaked behind, in and around most of suburban Melbourne. The torchlight would be the only source of light as no one usually cared whether you could or couldn't see down there. She imagined he would inch past a wheelie bin, unable to see the figure crouched behind it until it was too late.

Tinsel exhaled slowly, her nerves entirely shot. There was no point imagining horrors when the ones she was dealing with in real life were just as prescient.

CHAPTER 6

Even when the flashing red and blue lights of the back-up he'd called for arrived, Tinsel didn't relax until Detective James came back into view. He was seemingly unharmed and unphased as he greeted the officers.

At first it was just a man and a woman, and she watched as Detective James gestured between her and The Pinnacle. Soon, there was half a dozen others milling about and closing off the street. She observed someone mark the car where the figure had hidden with small, yellow flags and she did her best not to freak out. It was clear they had found something.

After leading officers into the alleyway, Detective James returned and she unlocked the door. He passed Tinsel her house keys and flipped out a tiny notebook just like his partner Diraani had, details of what she had already told him jotted down there. He pulled out the audio device he seemed to carry everywhere, and recorded her as she went through it all again, making silent amendments to the notebook.

"Who has access to the property?" he asked.

"It's a pretty popular pub among locals so… lots of people I guess."

"How about when you got here? Who was left?"

"Maybe three or four regulars and the manager, Gee, who was closing up."

"How did you know they were regulars?"

"I used to work behind the bar, they come in nearly every night. They all live on the same street a few blocks over."

"And Gee was here until when?"

"Just as I went upstairs, I heard them locking up. When I came down on to the street, the whole pub was empty."

"Who has keys for the venue?"

"Gee, Jorro the owner, Ray has the spares, and me."

"I'll need numbers for each of them."

"Sure," she nodded, tapping through her phone and sending the contacts to Detective James immediately before realising she'd left someone off. "Oh, and Zack."

"Who's that?"

"My, uh, boyfriend," Tinsel muttered, not sure if that was actually true.

"Zack Tykken: Zack with a K and two Ks in the surname."

"Where's he at the moment?"

"I'm not sure."

There must have been something in the way Tinsel said it that alerted Detective James. His pen paused and he glanced up.

"Did something happen between you two?"

"Are you just intuitive by nature or–"

He smiled. "I'm not very good at my job if I can't pick up on these cues."

"Right. Um, well, we got into a fight at his work."

"Where's that?"

"Wallace And Marshall, it's a tattoo studio."

"Around the corner, I know it. And when was this fight?"

"It was tonight, maybe an hour ago? I have no concept of time anymore. It was just before I came home. I was packing stuff to stay at my sister's."

"Did he know you were coming here?"

"No, I mean, he could have guessed but I think he just went back inside the studio. He works late on Thursdays."

"Would you like us to contact him about what happened, or we can…"

He left the question open-ended, which Tinsel was grateful for as it gave her the option.

"I don't want to speak to him," she replied, somewhat surprised at how true those words were once she said them out loud.

"Okay," Detective James nodded. "Can I ask what the fight was about?"

Tinsel let out a long sigh, leaning back as she ran her fingers through her hair. "Will three and bit years of bullshit do?"

He smirked. "I might need a little more detail than that. It's pertinent."

"Fine," she huffed. "It was about the murder."

"The murder?" he repeated.

"Calm down, I can hear the excitement in your tone Benoit Blanc. It wasn't like that. He found out about what happened on *The Graveyard Shift* because of that article and was pissed I hadn't told him. I was pissed about other things."

"What other things?"

Damn, this guy followed up so quickly, she thought, annoyed that amongst everything else she had to recount this. She watched as an officer outside the car fiddled with the set-up of an industrial lamp.

"Are you familiar with The Chicks song 'Gaslighter?'" she questioned.

He snickered. "Okay, got it."

The cop finally got the lamp on; a yellow light flooded the area as he began to reposition it. The rest of Taplin Street was waking up now, with a few of her neighbours peering out of their windows with interest. One even had their phone out recording the scene.

"They're going to take a look at everything properly," Detective James said, watching her observe the set-up outside.

"What did you find?" she asked, flipping the script and asking the questions of him for once. "It must be something bad."

"I'm not sure," he replied and strangely, she believed him. There was a defeated honesty there that made her trust Detective James, despite the fact he was both a) a man and b) a cop. "But I think it's best if you do stay at your sister's until I have proper answers."

"Speaking of, I better call her," she mumbled. "She has sources everywhere and if she hears about this before I tell her, I'm toast."

"Type the address into the GPS and I can drop you there now."

"Thank you," she said, unclipping the device from the holder on the dashboard and entering the details.

"I think it's probably best if we get you to come by the station tomorrow," he said. "I'm conscious of the fact you must be exhausted right now, and talking through everything is going to take a few hours. You'll want to be rested."

"Talking about tonight? Or how Mera and I were at the same event the evening she died?"

"All of it," he replied, pulling out of his parked position and moving forward slowly as they were waved through the police barrier.

Tinsel pressed her phone to her ear, using the ringing to distract her from the implications present in his last comment. When Pandora answered, there was only one way to start the conversation.

"Alright, I need you to not freak out," Tinsel cautioned.

By the time she was done, they were passing the tattoo parlour on the opposite side of the road. Tinsel averted her gaze, not sure why she didn't want to look inside and see what Zack was up to.

"Did you feel unsafe at all?"

"What?" Detective James' question shocked her out of her melancholy.

"With your boyfriend tonight, when you had the fight. Has he ever made you feel unsafe before?"

"Stop detecting," she snapped. "No, Zack didn't make me feel unsafe and no, he hasn't made me feel unsafe before. He made me feel uncomfortable tonight, sure, but it wasn't him chasing me down an alleyway if that's what you're getting at. I would have known."

"Are you sure?" he asked as she shot him a look. "I don't mean to pry, but the line of inquiry always tends to start with friends and family before we expand out further to acquaintances and strangers."

"Because if someone's going to hurt you, it's usually someone you know, right?"

"Especially for women."

"Grrrrreat," she sighed. "So, you think whoever killed Mera, knew her? Intimately?"

"It's too early to say."

"But you don't have a clear suspect yet, sooo… I'm thinking no."

She watched a smile hitch up the side of his face. Detective James cast her a pleased sidelong look as he braked for a red light.

"I can't say anything officially."

"How about unofficially, *Vicellous*?"

His head snapped away from the road to look at her as she used his full name. It wasn't even on his business card.

"How–"

"Hey, if you leave me alone in the car with an unattended glove compartment and my eyes *happen* to scan over some of the papers shoved there addressed to a 'Vicellous James,' am I really the bad guy for snooping?"

"Please," he grinned. "My friends call me Vic."

"And my niece calls me Tintin, yet here we are."

He laughed, repeating the nickname to himself as the car was basked in green light and the vehicles around them began to move again.

"Unofficially," he started, "if you go back to *snooping* in that glove compartment, you'll notice there's a can of police issue pepper spray, which is illegal for civilian use. If you'd be so kind as to return the first-aid kit to its usual spot."

She blinked, letting the words sink in for a moment. When she didn't move, Detective James met her gaze. Tinsel took the medical supplies off the dash where they had been sitting and slipped them inside as requested. Her fingers hovered over the silver can with a black aerosol lid as it slid around amongst the collection of papers and trash.

"This better not be entrapment," she said as she took it. He let out a rough, smoker's laugh as she grabbed the contraband and clicked the compartment shut. Slipping it into the pocket of her jacket, she pressed her head against the cool glass of the window and stared out at the oncoming traffic.

The rest of the drive was quiet, but not uncomfortably. As someone who talked for a living, Tinsel found it refreshing that the detective didn't feel the need to fill the silence with meaningless chatter just for the sake of it. He left Tinsel to her own thoughts, and she appreciated it, since her head was swirling with so many of them.

As he pulled into the driveway of Pandora's place and the security lights flicked on, Tinsel felt something loosen in her chest. Detective James turned off the engine and they sat there for a moment longer, the intermittent sounds of the police scanner the only noise. The front door to the house opened, and Pandora rushed outside to greet them. A streak of blonde outpaced her sister, and Tinsel smiled as she recognised Max in his Hulk pajamas. She was barely out of the car when the air was knocked out of her as the speeding object collided with her thighs.

"Tintin!" he exclaimed.

"Mad Max," she replied.

"You're sleeping over, mum said!"

"Hell yes I am."

"Outta the way," Pandora grunted, pulling her son free.

She replaced his position immediately, yanking Tinsel into a crushing hug. "Are you okay?"

"I'm fine," she replied, smiling with amusement as her sister patted her down, looking for untold injuries. "Bag of peas on my ankle and I'll be right. Vic already bandaged me up."

"Vic?" Pandora repeated, turning around to eyeball the man himself. "So, you're the cop. Who did this? Do you reckon it was Mera's murderer? Cos you can't rule out the creeps that call into the station. You should see the kind of comments and hectic stuff Tinsel gets."

Pandora released her and wandered over to Detective James, shaking his extended hand absentmindedly as she peppered him with more questions.

"He's not a source," Tinsel interjected quickly, lifting Max into her arms. "Don't press him."

"Too late," her sister answered. "He's already shaking my hand, which is practically a deal with the Devil."

"You're a journalist?" Detective James asked, cautious.

"Trained lawyer, actually. But I run a true crime blog to keep me distracted from this monster. And the other one."

Max made horns with his fingers to emphasise the point, with Pandora creating her own above her head in response.

"What's it called? I'll take a look."

"Don't do that," Tinsel groaned, shaking her head at him. "Don't pander."

Yet Pandora already had her business card out and was handing it to him. Her sister couldn't be stopped.

Brian joined them outside, Airlie resting on his shoulder. The two men exchanged brief pleasantries as Tinsel did her best to quietly chastise her sister.

"I thought none of the cops were supposed to know my *sister* had a true crime blog," she whispered.

"Doesn't matter now though, does it? The story's up and out: I didn't break it. But I'm probably one of the few people writing about this who has had face time with a lead detective. May as well take advantage of it."

She scoffed. "Face time."

"What? If he leaves my card in his office, maybe one day he checks out the site, likes what he sees. Maybe one day they need someone to leak to who isn't affiliated with a Murdoch masthead."

"Pandora and Tinsel," Detective James said, drawing their hushed conversation to an end. "Interesting names."

"Yeah, yeah," her sister grinned. "We have kooky parents. And believe me, we've heard all the jokes."

"His real name is Vicellous," Tinsel said, elbowing her sibling. "That's what Vic stands for."

Pandora looked delighted. "Reeeeeallly."

"My parents were kooky too," he shrugged. "And Portuguese immigrants, so no name jokes here."

"That's why she had to marry me," Brian said, gripping Airlie's fat legs to make sure she didn't fall accidentally. "The only thing that could even out Pandora Munroe was a Brian Smith."

Her sister smiled affectionately at the joke Tinsel had heard her brother-in-law tell a hundred times before. Detective James laughed obligingly, and she gave him points for that.

"Come on," Brian said. "All this excitement means the kids have stayed up way past their bedtime. We should get inside."

"Thanks," Tinsel said, hanging back just slightly. "A weird understatement to be sure but still… thank you."

Detective James smiled at her, offering a small nod. "I'll see you tomorrow at the station."

She watched as he hopped back in the car and slowly reversed out of the driveway. Following her family into the house, she felt immediate relief as she shut the door and slid all three locks into place.

Even just the act of putting Max to bed and reading him his favourite picture book – *Baby's First Exorcism* – was soothing to

Tinsel as she settled into the familiar rhythms of the household. When she found her sister waiting in the kitchen with a bottle of wine and two glasses, she knew it was time for a debrief and they retreated to the guest bedroom with a farewell wave to Brian.

Cork popped, bags tossed, and bodies contorted into comfortable positions on the bed, Tinsel gave her sister the full rundown. First, of her head-to-head with Zack, and then what came after. When she was done, she took a long sip and waited for Pandora's immediate reaction which – as far as Pandora reactions go – was not disappointing.

"What a fucking asshole."

"Dora," Tinsel sighed, readjusting the bag of frozen peas she had on her ankle.

"No, seriously! You got dick-noticed and stuck with this man for three years when you should've just fucked each other's brains out then moved on."

Her words were spoken so passionately the glass of red wine she had balanced on her stomach jiggled with the movement. Tinsel looked at it with concern, worried that one more outburst would send it tumbling over the both of them as they lay next to each other.

"I am proud of you," her sister continued. "I know the things I've said about him over the years have caused friction. I was so scared of you pulling away, of *us* losing you, so I tried to hold my tongue and I shouldn't have done that. I should have been there for you to sing Britney's 'Toxic' anytime you doubted yourself. And I wasn't. I'm so, so sorry."

She couldn't squeeze Tinsel's hand, but Pandora gently touching her shoulder was nearly enough to send her over the edge.

"In the end, you didn't need me to fight for you," her sister added. "You fought for yourself."

"I still need to officially 1800-Dump-Him," Tinsel said, draining the last of her wine. She was sick to her stomach thinking about Zack and sick to her heart talking about him. "Let's change the subject."

"To someone trying to kill you?" Pandora offered.

Tisnel was quiet for a moment, thoughtful as she ran through the terrifying events in her mind.

"I don't think they were trying to kill me," she said with realisation. That didn't change the terror she'd felt in the moment or now, but with a smidge of distance she felt like she had more perspective.

"They certainly weren't trying to give you a tarot reading, babe."

She huffed a laugh. "No, I mean... I never saw a weapon. Isn't that strange?"

Pandora's hand wavered from side-to-side with consideration. "Maybe, maybe not. I will say, if they were trying to kill you it would have been easier and quieter to do it inside the pub. Once Gee left, you would have been alone. So why not there? Why come after you out on the street where there's so many opportunities to be seen and so many unpredictable variables? Mera's killer didn't risk that."

"Sure," Tinsel agreed, impressed with her sister's assessment. "I was thinking more that it felt like they were trying to scare me."

"That seems likely, but the other side of the column is timing. If I had to guess, your maybe connection to Mera is what has the police spooked. I'm dying to know what your mate Vic found in that alley."

"Me too," Tinsel replied, placing the empty glass on the bedside cabinet as she retrieved her laptop. "Also..."

"Uh oh," Pandora murmured, watching as her blog was opened on screen. The article on Mera's murder had been going through the roof, obviously, getting shared and reshared. It wasn't quite at viral levels yet, but it was by far the best and most in-depth of the pieces in circulation, which was a big coup.

"You said you'd let me read the first draft," Tinsel growled.

"And I meant it, but when *The Herald* published, I had to be quick – I only had minutes, Tintin."

"See, that's when I know you're sucking up to me: you start using the kids' nickname."

All of the information was correct, of course, and Pandora linked back to the newspaper's original post, so it was clear to anyone paying attention that *Pandora's Box* hadn't broken the story, merely followed it up. Yet the real clincher had been the exclusive details threaded throughout the piece, including a transcript of the audio itself.

"People posted TikToks of the call when they heard the whole thing live," Pandora protested. "I could have embedded a tweet with the audio, but I didn't."

"Take it out. Add a line about the audio being available if you have to, but there's no need for the transcript, Pandora. Think about her family reading this."

"Think about the clues that could be in there. It was stuff like this that helped catch Luka Magnotta! Think of the *Don't Fuck with Cats* sleuths!"

"Sleuths? You're Pandora not bloody Poirot," Tinsel snapped. "Do a separate post on that if you have to. Analyse the audio signature or whatever, but this is too much."

Her sister sighed deeply, which is how Tinsel knew she had won. Pandora had killer instincts when it came to so much of her life, but she also had a good, soft heart.

"Alright," she whispered, rolling out of bed and grabbing their wine glasses. "I'll take that part out."

"Thank you," Tinsel yawned. "You making breakfast in the morning?"

"Not for you. You're not allowed out of bed until it's well past noon."

"I've gotta be down at the police station by two."

"Bitch, I know. I'm driving you. So stay in bed until midday and then when you're up, we can head in early and get lunch somewhere. Brian's got the kids all day."

"Milf on the loose, look out."

Pandora gave her an exaggerated wink as she slipped out of the room, wishing her a good night's sleep.

As Tinsel switched out the light, she wasn't exactly sure if that was possible.

CHAPTER 7

Alona Cennoqia wasn't supposed to be here. She was meant to be in and out of the National Film and Sound Archive (NFSA) storage facility hours ago, but the idiot who'd sent her down there clearly didn't know what they were doing. This was a request that had been left by her boss Logan, who'd blurted some excuse about needing to check a Beta tape conversion at ACMI, then rushed from the office before she could ask any more questions, clearly trying to avoiding doing the actual labour himself.

Guaranteed he was having an overpriced Aperol Spritz somewhere right now, enjoying his Friday night, while she trawled the dank, dusty and dark aisles looking for a long-lost short film that no one knew the name of. Oh, there was a reference number alright – written in handwriting that gave her an anxiety attack – but no actual title, or even a decade that would have helped this hopeless quest.

"Fucking asshole," she muttered to herself, frowning as she re-examined the torn paper he'd thrust at her as he left. With frustration, she squinted until the tiny hat on the "one" could possibly make it a "two."

Part of Alona was dying to know who this request had come from. If it was something handed down from Logan, that meant it had gone through important channels – swanky channels, even. Probably some prestigious curator or documentarian chasing archive footage. Footage that mightn't exist, mind you, but for as long as she could remember, Alona had wanted to work in film preservation. If starting in the bowels of the NFSA was the ladder she needed to climb, she'd willingly scale that rung.

"No matter how creepy it is," she said, louder than one should when talking to oneself. In truth, hearing her own voice made the entire process a smidge less eerie. There was no reception down there, so it wasn't as if she could call a friend for a chat to keep her mind off what the deep shadows at the end of every aisle did or didn't potentially hide. Instead, she had rain sounds downloaded, the synthetic weather playing on low volume through her headphones, doing more than anything else to soothe her nerves.

Reshuffling reference numbers like she was in the goddamn *Da Vinci Code*, Alona marched from the aisle she had been scanning and made her way towards one that preserved student films considered notable by the archive. You'd think that would only be a few, really, but the reality was closer to a few hundred. Various schools across the country had relinquished the storage capacity as their students had become the Peter Weirs and the Gillian Armstrongs and the James Wans and the Catriona McKenzies of the world.

A particularly loud roll of thunder in her headphones meant that she didn't hear the brush of metal against metal as a sharp object was dragged along a rack. The footsteps were soundless as the shoes had been discarded at the entry. Someone watched her, socks quiet and swift over the cold concrete floors.

Alona did sense something, however, and she paused halfway down the aisle. If she'd turned around and looked over her shoulder just half a second earlier, she would have seen a figure that would have sent her running for the exit. As it was, she just shook her head and told herself not to get "freaked out" like she did every time she spent a considerable chunk of hours down here.

Not at night, though.

She was always in the archives alone, but at this time of night – even with the late shift – she should have left the building hours ago. Alona came to a stop in front of a series of numbers that resembled the ones she had in her hand more closely than anything else she'd scanned in the past few hours. She bent down as she slowly pulled the case from the shelf. Taking a beat to put on her handling gloves and placing her phone down on the ground next to her, she gently examined the negative as she pulled it from the reel.

"It's going green," she huffed, making a disapproving click with her tongue. "Who would store something so shitily..."

Alona cut herself off, frowning as she saw movement reflected on the film. She could see herself staring in the distorted view, but more importantly she could see someone purposefully creeping up behind her with –

"AH!" she shouted, pivoting on the unforgiving concrete as she tossed the reel at the looming figure. They made an *offt* sound as it collided, but Alona didn't wait to see what happened next as she scrambled back. Her brogues slipped on the smooth surface, causing her to stumble as she ran, all but losing the head start she'd managed to get. Throwing a panicked look over her shoulder, she saw the fluorescent lights overhead reflected in the blade of a knife and it made her run faster. But it was pointless.

She was in a dead-end aisle. This mysterious short film was located in one of the few rows that ended against a wall, leaving her no way out. Alona couldn't afford to stop, couldn't afford to panic, couldn't afford to ask why and who this person was, or question the odds of them waiting here for her in the exact spot where there was no escape. Instead, all she could do was leap upwards as she did her best to climb the shelves.

Her footing was desperate, kicking as she climbed, causing reels to fall off the shelf and fly backwards. She heard a grunt, knowing her attacker had to dodge them, and she screamed as the knife slashed across her thigh and through her jeans. Not deep, but painful enough.

An outstretched hand grabbed for her jumper, missing and securing around the cord of her headphones which were pulled against her throat instead, half choking Alona as she fought to continue her upwards climb. But the wire was pulled tighter and tighter and she struggled to breathe. Her fingernails brushed the top of the shelf, *so close*. Just out of reach. If she could just get up to the top there –

Alona's vision was fading with the lack of oxygen as she was yanked backwards, a hand gripping each end of the headphone cord, using it as both a ligature and leash simultaneously. Eyes wide, she watched the top of the shelf as she fell away from it, hands outstretched, before she collided brutally with the steel framing behind her.

Her neck snapped at an ungodly angle, and Alona's body slumped to the floor with a sickening sound. Her attacker kicked her legs free, so she was spread out flat. They crouched down beside her, taking their time to examine the prey they had finally caught.

She was immobile, her injuries devastating, but she was still breathing. As the knife was raised into her line of sight, Alona knew, with her last comprehensive thought, that she wouldn't be breathing for long.

CHAPTER 8

"And you had never met the victim before?"

"No," Tinsel said, conscious of the fact that Stu, the station lawyer, was sitting behind her, gently tapping his fingers. "I mean, not that I can recall. You end up meeting a lot of people hosting screenings and often you or they are dressed in costume, so it's not like you would remember a face."

Detective Senior Sergeant Diraani nodded with understanding, Tinsel watching as he made a small note on the piece of paper in front of him.

"Also," she continued. "If I had met her, I feel like she would have mentioned it when she called, you know? I remembered her name and brought that up. If we had met previously, that would have been the perfect opening."

Detective James gave her the briefest of smiles as he sat next to his colleague, the gesture fleeting but just enough to calm her down a bit.

"Are we saying there's a *definite* connection between Tinsel and the victim?" Stu asked.

"We're pursuing all lines of enquiry at the moment," the older officer said, with a sigh that indicated just how that pursuit was going. "But I don't think we can discount it. The fact they were both at the *Halloween* screening on the night of the killing, the fact Miss Brant regularly listened to *The Graveyard Shift* and had called in to the show before, the fact *someone* was at Tinsel's home within twenty-four hours after the murder... I think we'd be foolish to consider all of that coincidental."

The sushi Tinsel had scoffed just a few hours earlier with Pandora squirmed in her belly.

"There's also the issue of proximity," Detective James said. "Your Fitzroy North address isn't that far geographically from Miss Brant's. That's a concern for us."

"Why?" she asked, her eyes flicking from the face of one cop to the other in order to try and read their expressions. "Does that mean the killer has established a hunting ground or something?"

"We don't know," Diraani admitted. "It's just something we have to be mindful of at the moment. Now, I have here that you're returning to the air on Monday night."

"That's right."

"We won't be mentioning the incident or taking calls," Stu assured them. "Just playing songs, airing a pre-recorded interview with an actress from the UK, and taking requests via social media or the text line."

"Good, I think that's good," Diraani nodded. "Just out of curiosity, late night radio talk shows are a thing of the past. Why do you take calls in the first place?"

"It's a great way to engage the listener," Tinsel admitted. "Plus, it's retro: a lot of the music selection, and even the interviews, are retro too. It made sense. And for the record, I'll get back to taking calls eventually. Just probably not the first week I've returned to the air."

"Besides," Stu beamed, "you'll have caught whoever is doing this by then, right?"

There was a beat of silence that passed between the two officers before Detective James cleared his throat.

"Finally, we wanted to get a list of anyone who may fit the bill of an over-obsessed fan of the show. Any behaviour or messages, for example, that may have crossed the line."

Tinsel had come prepared, and she pulled a folded piece of paper from her bag. Laying it flat on the table, she slid it over to the detectives.

"It's a big list," Detective Diraani commented, a finger running over the dozens of names.

"Most of the audience are pretty great," Tinsel smiled. "Really respectful and just generally good people who love genre stuff as much as I do. But..."

"But what?" the older cop questioned.

"I'm still a young, brown woman in radio working in a genre space that has historically been the real estate of straight, white men. Death and rape threats online are a daily occurrence."

"What are the stars next to their names?" Detective James asked, Tinsel noticing an interesting tick in his jaw as he clenched and unclenched.

"Those are the ones I'd prioritise. They sent packages to the station, waited outside the office once until I finished my shift, tried approaching me at events, that kind of thing. The others are just regular senders of dick pics, which naturally I muted, blocked and reported across the various platforms."

Detective James frowned, his fingers tightening on the list just a little.

"We'll start working through these," Detective Senior Sergeant Diraani noted, getting to his feet. "And cross check them with anyone Miss Brant might have had issues with on her social platforms as well."

"Great," Stu smiled, extending his hand to both men as they concluded the formal interview. "And if there's any updates, you'll let us know?"

"Definitely," the older man said, holding the door open for the pair of them. "Vic, you okay to walk these two out?"

"No problem," the detective replied, already in step alongside Tinsel. She barely remembered walking through the corridors of the police station when she had entered a few hours ago, so she was glad to have some guidance on her way out.

"Don't lose my number," Detective James said to her, voice low enough so that only she heard it as Stu trailed a few steps behind, checking his phone. "Keep your eyes peeled and if you see anything out of the ordinary or something seems off – call me."

"Okay," she murmured in response, wanting to say something else but running out of time as she walked through the final door that led to the lobby area. Her sister was waiting there with Luiza, the two of them deep in conversation and seemingly unaware of the other cluster of people who sat nearby. Tinsel recognised them immediately, as her mum had sent her a link to several news articles after they had spoken on the phone that morning. It was Mera Brant's family, including her twin brother, mother, father, and two other people she guessed were cousins or partners.

Stu pushed past her, heading over to debrief with Luiza and Pandora, while Tinsel felt the smallest pressure as Detective James rested a hand on the small of her back.

"I'll see you later, alright?"

She nodded, unable to say anything else or take her eyes off the Brant family.

"Be careful."

He turned and left her then, Tinsel feeling like a zombie as she took one step after the other towards her people.

Most of the Brants had flown in from somewhere else, something she knew only by the fact they had been snapped at the airport by local media on Thursday evening. She wasn't sure where they were from initially, but as she listened to the strong twang in their accents, she guessed North Queensland.

"Hey, how did it go?" Luiza asked, suddenly realising she was there.

"Oh, uh, good? I think? I don't know what the right response is, to be honest."

"I think mine went 'uh, good' too, if that helps," her friend smiled, getting to her feet and quickly pulling her into a hug.

Tinsel resisted the temptation to squirm free immediately, conscious of the fact the people next to them would likely give anything for another bone-crushing hug with their loved one.

"I'll meet you all outside, okay?" she said, extricating herself as diplomatically as possible.

"Sure," Luiza said, "You alright?"

"Uh huh, just need some air. Tell Pandora for me, will ya?"

"I'm on it."

Her sister was pressing Stu for details as Tinsel left them, closing her eyes briefly as she stepped through the sliding doors and let herself feel the cool air on her face.

Finding a spot where she could lean against the railing, she took a moment to watch people stroll by the police station, completely unaware and happy. A mother and daughter were walking a pair of Boston Terriers, the small dogs excitedly tugging on the leads as they urged their owners to go faster. A man strolled by next with a beard so elaborate it would have made Gandalf jealous, the fumes from his coffee making her desperately want a cup. There were a number of trendy cafes dotting the length of the street and she was considering ducking inside one while she waited.

"You're that chick, aren't you?"

She stirred, following the sound of the voice. She turned around to meet the inquisitive face of Mera Brant's brother as he descended the stairs of the police station.

"Tinsel, the girl who hosts *The Graveyard Shift*. The one who heard my sister die."

"I am," she mumbled, not sure what else to say.

He watched her as he lit a cigarette, inhaling deeply before he breathed out a massive cloud of smoke.

"You want one?" he asked, rattling the packet.

Absolutely.

"No thanks," is what she replied instead.

"Smart. Mera always used to give me shit for this *dirty little habit*, saying it was gonna kill me. Ironically, I didn't think I'd outlive her."

There was no amusement in his expression as he said the line, sadness etched into every one of his features.

"I'm so, so sorry about what happened," Tinsel said. "I know that doesn't help and you're probably sick of people telling you that, but I really am sorry your sister was killed."

"It doesn't quite feel real yet," he admitted, taking a spot next to her on the railing. "You know what I mean? Like, I feel as if at any moment she's going to text me a stupid meme and I'll realise this whole thing was a nightmare."

"It is a nightmare," Tinsel agreed. "Just a different kind."

"The kind you don't wake up from."

Tinsel chuckled, surprised at her own outburst at first and clapping a hand over her mouth. Mera's brother looked at her curiously, as if she was going mad. Maybe she was.

"Sorry," she croaked, "It's just… I'm pretty sure we both recited *A Nightmare On Elm Street*'s tagline."

"Oh God, I forgot you're a horror movie nut just like her. You know, she was *obsessed* with your show. She would listen to it religiously, never missed a week, and even if she did, she'd play it back on the online stream."

"I could tell she was a die hard," Tinsel smiled. "Just from speaking to her."

There was a gentle silence as they stood there, him smoking his cigarette and her watching the pedestrians pass by.

"How long are you in town for?" Tinsel asked.

"We don't know yet. We didn't even know why we came originally. To clear up her stuff, sure, but they're not going to release the body to us until they've completed the autopsy so it's a weird state of limbo to be in."

"I know you already know my name," she started, "But it feels weird not to introduce myself properly. I'm Tinsel Munroe."

"Sebastian Brant," he answered, shaking her hand. "Seb works just as well. And hey, excuse me if this is being pushy but we're trying to do an online crowdfunder to cover the funeral costs. Is there any chance you could plug it on the show tonight?"

"They cancelled last night's show," she said. "And tonight's, out of a combination of respect and just wanting to wait until everything calms down."

"Oh, well, thanks anyway."

She saw the disappointment in his eyes and felt the spark of an idea forming.

"When's the funeral?"

"Sometime this month," he answered, stamping out the cigarette on the ground. "That's as much as we know at this point."

"I might have a way to really signal boost that crowdfunder, if you're interested?"

Seb's eyebrows shot up and he looked immediately hopeful. "Yeah?"

"You'd have to clear it with your parents first."

"Just hit me with it," he smiled, as Tinsel took a deep breath and let the word vomit pour from her mouth.

She spent most of the weekend trying furiously to set her plan in motion, with Pandora even driving by Rushelle Li's Toorak mansion so she could speak to her in person. Tinsel knew that her boss was clucky, so she had her sister bring the kids in the hope it might help. After a debrief with Stu and some of the other big wigs at the station, Rushelle agreed.

It wasn't until Tinsel was walking from the tram stop towards work on Monday evening that she realised there was probably someone else who needed to be looped in. She brought up Detective James's number on her phone, her thumb hovering over the green call button. Before she had the chance to chicken out, she pressed it and held the device to her ear as it rang and rang and rang.

"Hi, you've reached the voicemail of–"

Yes, she thought, realising his answering machine was the ideal scenario she was after. She frowned as she glanced at her screen, the red number of missed calls there as annoying to her as the unread emails in her inbox. Most had been from numbers she didn't recognise, calls she didn't answer, knowing they would be journalists looking for a comment. The ambitious ones left her a voicemail or sent a text – sometimes three – on the off chance she'd put herself on the line and call them back.

Tinsel didn't, she knew better. Yet that didn't mean she and Pandora hadn't been keeping a close eye on news stories that dropped in the weekend papers about the murder. There was little new information about the suspect or the crime itself; instead, the pieces focused on who Mera was, with fleeting comments from friends and colleagues who knew her. The family hadn't spoken publicly yet, but that was about to change.

She smiled as she reached the HitsFM office, mainly because Malu was waiting outside for her and looking bored with his hands in his pockets. A massive grin spread across his face as he spotted her, the security guard holding out his arms for a bear hug she knew there was no avoiding.

"Hey there, girl," he said. Tinsel returned the gesture and hugged him back.

"Broseph," she replied, using the nickname he'd given himself.

"How are you holding up, aye?"

"You know," Tinsel shrugged. "All things considered. Staying busy helps."

"No shit," he scoffed. "I've seen what you have planned for tonight. That why you're in early?"

"Just wanna dot my Is and cross my Ts before everyone gets here."

"I respect that, I respect that. Well, you go on through. When they get here, I'll bring them up to you."

"Thanks, Malu. It shouldn't be until a little after ten thirty I reckon."

"Sis, I got you. Don't even sweat it."

She was grateful knowing that, despite how tough he looked on the outside, Malu was a sensitive softie on the inside. That's exactly what the Brant family would need.

It was only a little after 6pm, which was way earlier than Tinsel would usually arrive before a shift, and it was strange to see the building so populated. She wasn't sure if she was imagining it, but it definitely felt as if eyes were following her wherever she walked.

Thankfully her hands had healed up enough that she'd been able to ditch the bandages, so that left one less visual cue to draw the eye. Passing one of the studios as the *Drive* show finished up, Tinsel used the reflection of the glass to scope out the scene behind her. Nope, it wasn't all in her mind: her presence in the office was not going unnoticed.

Luiza looked up from her desk as Tinsel sat her stuff down beside her and slid into her own station, fingers tapping on the keyboard as she logged in. Luiza knew what she was up to, as she'd gone to her for advice about exactly how to stage it. Her colleague was in her early forties, been in the business for a while, and always had solid wisdom to impart when Tinsel asked for it.

"Is it just me or is everyone staring?" she murmured, lips barely moving.

Luiza did a completely unsubtle swivel on her chair, spinning around so she could view the office with a three-hundred-and-sixty-degree view.

"It's not you," she replied, almost humming it. "How are you feeling? You nervous?"

Tinsel considered the question. "No, actually. I thought I would be but... I feel good. I spoke to Seb this afternoon. I'm going to do a mini-run through with the lawyers and Rushelle at six thirty, and the art just popped up."

"Awesome. Rushelle said you're not putting it out until about eight, across all the platforms?"

"They didn't want it to seem gratuitous and promotion-ey."

"That's smart. Hey, listen, can I get you after that for an audio promo?"

"Sure. Just send me a text when you're ready. I'll have my phone on silent, but I'll come right through."

Her phone buzzed on the desk and she glanced down at it, groaning when she saw it was Zack calling. It had taken him two days to realise that sending texts wasn't going to cut it. In the back of her mind, she wondered how many more days it would take before the unanswered calls led to a bouquet of flowers rocking up at the office. She let it ring out, burying herself in work for the next few hours as she cut back and forth between one of the meeting rooms and her desk.

Once everything was cleared and ready to go, all that was left to do was wait.

At ten minutes to eight, Luiza's text came through and Tinsel stepped into the studio for the first time since Wednesday night. It didn't feel strange and perhaps that's what was strange about it: it seemed perfectly natural. Luiza gestured to one of the guest stations and she took a seat, slipping the headphones on and adjusting the volume until she was comfortable listening to the song play out.

"That was Kira Puru with 'Idiot.' Before we get back into the music, we've got Tinsel Munroe here: host of *The Graveyard Shift*, which runs weeknights from 11pm until 6am. Now, after a few days off, you've got a special show coming up this evening, is that right?"

"That's right," Tinsel replied, ignoring the buzzing in her pocket. Above Luiza's head, the clock had just ticked past eight, so she knew the scheduled posts had gone live. "Obviously most people are aware of the tragic passing of Mera Brant, who was a regular listener to *The Graveyard Shift* and frequent caller. After some thinking about the best way to proceed, what myself and everyone here at the station wanted to do was celebrate Mera's life, rather than focusing on her death."

"So it's a special, memorial edition of the show?"

"Kind of, yeah. Essentially, what we're going to be doing is playing songs that were important to Mera and to help me do that, I'll be joined by her brother Seb, father Andrew and mother Lesley. She was also a massive fan of genre movies, like a lot of our listeners, particularly the work of Joe Meyer who will also be joining us live for a chat."

"Now how can people get involved, if they want to help out in some way?"

"I'm so glad you asked, Luiza," Tinsel smiled, giving her colleague a wink. "The Brant family are trying to raise funds for Mera's funeral and any donation that can help out with that would mean the world to them. I've posted links via *The Graveyard Shift*'s official Twitter, Facebook, Instagram and TikTok pages, as well as my own, and that information is also up on 102.8 HitsFM's accounts. There's a crowdfunder so any little bit you can contribute is going to make a huge difference to them. For obvious reasons, the phone lines won't be open tonight, but you can send your messages of support over text – 1800 HITS FM – or via Twitter using our regular hashtag."

"Great! That sounds like something really special y'all are doing and I know a bunch of you out there, like myself, are looking forward to tuning in."

"Thanks so much, Luiza."

"So, a reminder: that's *The Graveyard Shift* from 11pm right here on 102.8 HitsFM with Tinsel Munroe."

She waited until the broadcast light flicked from red to green before Tinsel hitched the headphones down around her neck.

"Cheers for that," she said, exhaling.

"Hey, no worries. I think the idea is pretty bad-ass to be honest."

"If it raises the money they need, then yeah."

"Besides that, I think doing an audio obituary for someone given the circumstances... you should be proud to pull this off, Tinsel."

"Talk to me at six, I'll be proud then."

"Speaking of, you mind if I hang around for the first few hours of the show? Provide some moral support?"

"Of course not," she blinked. "Luiza, that would be so sweet of you."

"Mate, I'm a motherfucking Chupa Chup."

Tinsel laughed, slipping herself free from the headphones and taking a moment to check that all of the guest stations were set up and connected before the arrival of the Brant family. She arranged the cushions on the studio couch nervously, double checked there were enough refreshments in the fridge, and fidgeted with her outfit in the reflection of the studio's window.

Inching closer towards it, she pressed her nose against the glass as she stared down at the street below. She focused on the illuminated light of a taxi as it zoomed by, indicating that it was empty and open for business as it darted between lanes of traffic.

"Hey, Tinsel?" Luiza called, her voice jerking her out of her melancholy. "Can you stop pressing your tits against the glass for a minute, cos I think Rushelle's looking for you."

She laughed as she turned around, grateful to her colleague for lightening the mood. Looking out of the studio, she saw their boss standing there and waving in her direction.

"It's the final countdown," she muttered.

With her eyes focused on the timer, Tinsel took stock of the studio as the red digital numbers ticked closer and closer to airtime. She held up her hand, indicating the seconds remaining to her guests, as she folded down her fingers one digit at a time. They weren't familiar with this environment, but she'd been careful to explain how everything worked so they were at least aware when she was on and off-air. As the music played out, she lowered her final finger.

"Hello and welcome to *The Graveyard Shift*. My name is Tinsel Munroe and tonight is a very special episode dedicated to celebrating the life of Mera Louise Brant: a twenty-seven-year-old woman who loved music, movies, and pop culture just like the rest of us. Joining me in the studio are Mera's family, with some other guests popping by later in the show. But first up, I'd like to welcome Mera's bro – her older brother by two minutes – Seb."

"Hello," he said. "Is that loud enough?"

She laughed. "Yeah, that's perfect. You just have to speak normally and everyone out there will be able to hear you."

"That's good to know," Seb smiled. "I was never very good at public speaking."

"Ah, see, that's the beauty of radio: you don't see all the listeners tuning in so there's nothing to be stage-frighty about. Now, you have a list here that you want to work your way through, is that right?"

"I do, I do. I mean, I just want to say first that Mera was such a huge fan of this show, and it would have meant the world to her having you let us all come on here."

"Please, it's… honestly, when we both started talking about the possibility of doing this, I just–"

Tinsel realised she was running out of words, something that *never* happened when she was on-air and she felt emotion pricking at the corner of her eyes. She cleared her throat slightly.

"I'm just honoured you're here and honoured we can do this," she said quietly, before regaining her confidence. "And of course, if you'd like to donate to the Brants crowdfunder, all of the links to that are up on social media and the 102.8 HitsFM website. So, this list."

"Yes," Seb said, sniffing. Tinsel understood she wasn't the only one struggling. "This is a list of Mera's ten favourite films of all time. She was very thorough with this, always keeping an updated and annotated version on Letterboxd, didn't she Ma?"

Lesley Brant nodded enthusiastically from her position on the couch, her husband Andrew gripping her hand.

"She was batty for horror movies, which is totally Dad's fault cos that's his favourite genre too."

"Okay, let's read through them, shall we? Going from ten to one."

"Okay, number ten is *Predator 2*."

"Oh my God, I think I'm in love with her."

Seb laughed. "She thought the first was too homophobic and sexist, plus the sequel had–"

"Bill Paxton," Tinsel interjected. "The only man to be killed by an alien, predator and terminator. What a legacy."

"Number nine is *Attack the Block*, which she raved about."

"Rightly so, it's a perfect movie," Tinsel nodded, feeling strange about the similarities between herself and this woman she never knew.

"And number eight was *Halloween*."

"The OG slasher, not to be confused with the 2018 reboot of the same name or the Rob Zombie version."

"Sure," Seb nodded. "I'm more of an action movie guy, so I'll take your word for it. *Halloween* was actually the first movie she ever saw."

"That's a great first movie and that leads us into our first set of songs for the night. It's only right to continue Mera's order so first up is 'Lettin' Off Steam' by Papa Dee, which appeared in *Predator 2*, followed by *Attack the Block*'s closing number 'The Ends' by Basement Jaxx, and, finally, the main title theme by John Carpenter himself from 1978's *Halloween*."

She turned up the song as she switched to off-air. Seb took a nervous breath as he slid off his headphones.

"Was that okay?" he winced. "I have no concept of how that went."

"It went great," Tinsel smiled, squeezing his hand supportively. "Look at all the love pouring in."

She drew his attention to her computer screen, turning on the television as well and linking it so his parents could see from their position. There were so many tweets being sent on social media that the feed was constantly updating every few seconds, while the crowdfunder's numbers started to tick upwards from the five hundred dollars already in there to six hundred, then six hundred and seventy-five, then eight hundred, nine hundred, and just over a thousand before the first ad break.

Mera's family were overwhelmed, with Rushelle having hung back after work and popping in to the studio to congratulate everyone. Tinsel's phone was buzzing almost non-stop in her pocket, the vibrations annoying her enough that she set it to airplane mode. Malu and Luiza were both watching from the other side of the glass, so Tinsel slipped outside for just a moment to bring them both cold drinks, before dashing back to the control deck.

Each time he was on the air, Seb got a fraction better: warming to the rhythm of the show and the messages of support people were sending through. The music was good too, thanks to Tinsel spending a solid chunk of time that evening making sure she had a few songs from each movie to pad out the first hour or so. The countdown was great, with Seb sharing anecdotes as he made his way through each of Mera's movies and why she loved them so much. He looked exhausted when he took a seat next to his mother on the studio couch, his father trading places with him.

Andrew sat in one of the guest stations and adjusted the volume dial like Tinsel had taught him. She held up her hand again to count down the final five seconds before they were live, clenching her fist just as the light above her switched over.

"What an absolute bop," Tinsel said, hoping the smile on her face was audible through the airwaves. "That was 'I Against' by Massive Attack and Mos Def, which played during that bad-ass slo-mo scene from *Blade II*, Mera's second favourite film of all time. Rounding out her list was *The Silence of The Lambs* – her numero uno – and, of course, Tom Petty's 'American Girl.'"

"She did love that movie," her father chuckled.

"That, dear listeners, is the voice of Andrew Brant, Mera's father. Now Seb told me you actually sneaked her into the cinema to see *The Silence of The Lambs*."

"Yes! It was years after the movie had come out, but they used to have the poster on display at our local video store. Mera was always fascinated by it, you know? It has that big moth over Starling's mouth."

"I know exactly what you're talking about."

"She always used to tug on my sleeve 'Daddy, Daddy, when can we get that one?' Lesley hadn't quite forgiven me for letting her watch *Halloween*, so I had to wait. On her thirteenth birthday, we got these friends of ours to play it at the local cinema they ran. It was just a small joint, only sat fifty or so people, but that movie... she loved it immediately."

"And on that note we're going to hear one more iconic song from it then: this is 'Goodbye Horses' by Q. Lazzarus."

The Brant family didn't hang around much longer after that. Seb was keen to, but understood the fatigue he saw in his parents' eyes. It was a lot for them to handle. In fact, it was a lot for everyone.

They were all emotional as they hugged her goodbye, Tinsel telling them she would call tomorrow to check in. Malu was waiting for them at the door along with Rushelle, the pair giving them an escort from the building as they stepped out into the night. Tinsel tried to watch from her viewpoint at the studio's window, but was only vaguely able to make out their ant-like figures as they climbed into a car the station had waiting for them.

It wasn't long before Malu returned with her next guest, Joe Meyer, who looked like he'd been regurgitated out of a steampunk stage play. He had what could only be described as a discreet mohawk, the hairstyle was a sharp juxtaposition to the immaculately tailored three-piece suit he was wearing. There was even the chain of a gold pocket watch dangling over the intricate design of the tweed. That was his vibe: early nineteenth century gentleman on the bottom, Smashing Pumpkins fan on the top.

"How are you holding up, Tinny?" he asked, rubbing her shoulder. "This whole thing, it's crazy."

"I know. And hey, thank you so much for doing this."

"Of course! She was trying to get tickets to my movie premiere when she died, I can't stop thinking about that. How horrible! After all, we *make* horror movies, we don't want to live them."

"Yeah," Tinsel frowned. "We want to avoid talking about the murder and the nature of her death specifically on-air. I'll lead the conversation in a safe direction, but it's a more general discussion on genre movies and why fandom is so important."

"Course, totally. Keep it classy."

She had known Joe a long time, the two having met on a visit to the set of his very first film: a low-budget horror flick that blew up in a big way. Everyone had those friendships that always felt more like a business transaction, and that's how it was with Joe. When he left Australia for Los Angeles, staying in touch with him was as much about their past as it was their present. Tinsel thought he was a good horror filmmaker, veering towards great, and she had always gotten the impression Joe was hyperaware of how beneficial it was to have a respected genre presence on his side. There was a knock on the studio door and a cheery woman was seen waving through the slit of glass.

"Ah, that's the studio publicist, Gilly. Had to bring her, I'm afraid."

"No worries," Tinsel nodded, opening the door and leading the woman to the couch as quickly as possible. "We've got thirty seconds before we're back on, so if I could make sure everyone is quiet and your phones are on silent. Joe, you know the drill: pick the guest dock of your choice."

He always took the one at the far right for whatever reason, and Tinsel got herself in order, sliding on the headphones and testing whether he could hear her okay. He held up his thumbs to indicate "yes." She pressed her fingers to her lips as his publicist got to her feet, the woman gesturing that she understood as she crept around the studio and snapped pictures "for his social media." It annoyed Tinsel, and she could see that it annoyed Joe too, but there was little she could do about it as the final seconds played out.

"We're back from the break with a friend of the show and director of several rad films you probably love, including *Band Candy* which will have its Australian premiere in Melbourne this week – Joe Meyer. Welcome back to *The Graveyard Shift*."

"Tinsel, it's wonderful to be here, even under such sad circumstances."

"We appreciate you popping by Joe and it's fitting because as we heard a few hours ago from Seb, your debut feature *Until Dark Night* was number three on Mera Brant's list of favourite films of all time."

"Clearly she had great taste!" he joked, laughing for a moment. "No, but seriously, it's such an honour that my movie – that movie in particular – connected with her. *Until Dark Night* was a film no one believed in, I had to fund it with my life savings and take a risk leaving my work as a commercial director to make it."

"You're three films deep now and I've even heard your name being circulated for a *Friday the 13th* reboot. Clearly it paid off."

"Ha, I don't know if I'll be going to Camp Crystal Lake any time soon, but it's great to be considered for those kind of gigs.

It is show business after all, and if your movies don't find an audience that's as loyal and feverish as Mera was, then your career dies out pretty fast."

Tinsel flinched at the phrasing, trying to move the conversation forward. "You began as someone who was a fan themselves, isn't that right?"

"Being obsessed with movies is how I got my foot in the door," Joe smiled. "And I think that's the same for a lot of filmmakers: fandom is the first step. It's almost inevitable you end up on a set."

Tinsel continued the talk a little longer before bridging into a cluster of four songs, one from each of his movies. She chatted to him casually as she retweeted some of the thousands of comments that were *still* coming in to the main account, long after most listeners had usually gone to bed.

She began counting them back down as the song played out, Tinsel having interviewed Joe enough times that they had a familiar rapport as they returned to air.

"Joe, this is probably the equivalent of a night shoot to you so I will let you leave soon."

"Please don't."

"If I don't, your publicist is gonna drag you out by your waistcoat—"

"Gilly, you wouldn't dare, would you?"

"Whatever it takes!" the woman chimed.

"But look," Joe began, smile fading to a more serious expression. "Before I vacate, I just wanted to extend a warm welcome to you for *Band Candy*'s premiere on Thursday night. The film was obviously something Mera Brant was very excited about and since this show is honouring her, we've got twenty-five tickets for you to give away to listeners who call in over the next few nights."

"Oh," she said, surprised, before quickly attempting to recover. "I'll definitely be there and I'm sure everyone tuning in is going to be ecstatic. Joe Meyer, thank you again for joining us and if you're not following him already, check out *the* Joe Meyer on Twitter, Instagram and Facebook. His latest film *Band Candy* is out November fifteenth or this Thursday for those of us lucky enough to see it at the big event."

"Thanks so much, Tinsel."

"Coming up now, we've got 'Zombie Conqueror' by Dirty Projectors and 'Ghosts' by The Presets."

Tinsel did her best to say goodbye to Joe and his publicist, but both were so preoccupied with their phones and the social media reach the interview was having. She was relieved when Malu appeared on the other side of the glass to take them back downstairs. She mouthed a "thank you" at him behind their backs and he tossed her a discreet shaka in response.

Once they were gone, Tinsel was by herself for the first time that shift. Luiza had left an hour or so earlier, along with Rushelle, Stu and mostly everyone else. She was used to working the shift solo, so it should have felt normal to be back there in the studio by herself again. But as she leaned against the control panel, it didn't quite feel that way.

Now that there were no other guests lined up, she dimmed the lights to a more comfortable level. Cracking her neck, she ran the past few hours over in her mind. Thanks to Joe's handout with the tickets, she realised with a groan that she was going to have to open up the phone lines again. That made her nervous, but as she took a moment to go through the messages people had written and some of the memories friends of Mera had shared, that hesitation started to ebb away.

This would be okay. This would be fine.

Probably.

CHAPTER 9

Stepping out of the studio at exactly five minutes to six, Tinsel let go of the feeling that had been weighing her down the whole night. The feeling that the show was going to bomb. The feeling that she was going to fuck it up somehow, no matter how good her intentions. The feeling that something even more horrible could happen live on-air. Yet it hadn't. She did it. She got *through* it. She was back.

She thought it was strange that producer Tim hadn't joined her behind the controls like he usually did around that time, yet she'd seen Killara across the way preparing the morning bulletin. So, she scheduled enough songs to take them to the hour and decided to liberate herself from the studio, only then understanding his absence.

Tim was standing in the hallway along with Ryan, Shea, Stu, and a handful of other people from the station she didn't know outside of saying a friendly "hello" to every now and then. She blinked, surprised by the audience clearly waiting for her. That feeling increased tenfold as they began clapping. Tinsel looked from one face to the other with shock.

"What in the–"

"Congrats, kid," Tim smiled. "You did a gutsy thing last night. It can't have been easy coming back into the shift after what happened. But the show… that's some of the best radio I've heard in the last twenty years."

"I'm trying really hard not to be offended right now," Shea muttered, but she could tell by the way he didn't slow his clapping that he, too, was genuinely happy for her.

"And the ratings!" Ryan exclaimed. "It's going–"

He didn't get to finish the sentence as Shea whacked him so hard the words were lost to the air.

"What?" he scoffed.

"Have some respect," Shea groaned. "You gross human being."

As the gaggle of people moved away and the boys let themselves into the studio. Tim hovered for a moment and placed a hand on her shoulder.

"Seriously, I meant what I said. I honestly wasn't sure how any show, let alone one called *The Graveyard Shift*, could come back from something like that. You did it though. It was tasteful, respectful, exceeded all my expectations."

"You organised this?" she asked. "The mini-cheer squad?"

He smiled, the gesture causing the edges of his rusty coloured moustache to twitch.

"In this business, people rarely tell you when you're doing something right. Besides, I know you've got to back up a show again tonight and thought you deserved a little pick me up."

"Thank you, Tim," she murmured, still struggling to believe it. "I really mean that."

"Get on out of here, try and get some sleep. You have Steve Buscemi eyes."

She laughed, gently touching the aforementioned bags that were clearly still visible despite her best attempts to cover them with concealer. He tossed her a farewell wave and ducked into the studio, already shouting commands at his two hosts to "stop dicking around." She was surprised to find Malu waiting at her desk as she scooped up her things and logged off.

"Hey, thanks for everything overnight," she started.

"Aw, no problems, sis. I just feel so bad for her folks, you know?"

"Yeah, I couldn't even imagine. Anyway, what are you still doing here? I thought you finished at three?"

"Nah, pulled a double. Can't really turn down the cash, to be honest. Thought I'd walk you out."

"Huh," was Tinsel's only response as they strolled from the office side-by-side.

It was only a little after six and the building was still mostly quiet, with the elevator ride to the ground floor filled with the lively chatter of *Breakfast with Ryan and Shea*. Swiping herself through the first of two security barriers, Tinsel frowned as she noticed a small group of people gathered outside the 102.8 HitsFM building. She could see them clearly through the glass, with at least three camera crews set up with equipment on tripods. There were a handful of others, reporters and photographers with cameras hanging from straps on their shoulders.

"What in the world?" she muttered.

"That's why I figured you might want the company," Malu said beside her as they neared the exit.

She opened her mouth to ask him what he meant, but it all became clear. As soon as the electric doors slid open, she was bombarded with noise.

"TINSEL MUNROE! How does it feel knowing someone was murdered during your radio show?"

"What was it like having the Brant family in the studio just days after their daughter was slaughtered live on-air?'

"Will you be changing the name of *The Graveyard Shift* after this horrific incident?"

"Do you think the NFSA could be connected?"

"Have the police shared any details with you about what kind of suspect they're looking for?"

Panicked, she spun around to face Malu. "Is this hell?"

"Technically it's public property, so they're allowed to be here," he shrugged. "I can't move them on, but I can make sure you get to where you need to go undisturbed."

"Undisturbed?" she practically screeched the word as someone asked if she was aware about the nature of Mera Brant's injuries.

"TINSEL! How do you respond to claims that Mera's murder is linked to a Satanic cult?" a woman asked over the shoulder of her cameraman. "Do you support the Satanic agenda?"

Tinsel froze, unable to formulate a proper response as she digested the question with shock.

"Hey, come on now," Malu snapped, stepping in front of Tinsel and essentially hiding her from view thanks to his massive frame. "Let her get by, okay? People have places to be. Scoot, moving through."

He gently guided Tinsel by the bend of her elbow, the press parting for him as he led her through the throng of people. They continued to shout questions, the light and continuous flashes from their cameras disorientating to her.

It's way too early for this, she thought. She only became aware of the bigger issue as they continued to cut through the people. Where was she supposed to go? There was nothing stopping the media throng from following her through Fed Square and to the tram stop.

That notion made her suddenly feel queasy. Yet it was clear Malu had a plan. A small sound of shock escaped her lips as she saw where he was leading her. Tinsel almost stopped dead in her tracks at the sight of Zack leaning against the bonnet of a car.

There wasn't anywhere to park on Flinders Street, and he had half-mounted the curb in a loading zone to get as close to the office as possible. His eyes scanned the faces of the people around her with a sense of agitation, but that expression softened when he saw Tinsel. She emerged from behind Malu, and Zack moved forward quickly as he told a pushy photographer to "rack off."

Propping open the car door, he got her swiftly inside and did up the seat belt after her shaking hands failed to do it

successfully. She watched, still in shock, as he darted around
the front of the car to the driver's side. Malu looked like
Polynesian Jesus as he stood with his legs slightly apart, arms
wide and extended as he used himself as a human barrier to
block the journalists from getting any closer.

Zack pulled out of there like he owned the place, tires
screeching slightly as he merged on to the main road.

"Are you okay?" he asked, taking a hand off the wheel to
touch her arm gently.

"Um…"

The sound seemed to echo through the car, but Tinsel
couldn't make herself more verbose than that. She was still
dealing with the double jolt of the media scrum waiting outside
the office *and* Zack being there to whisk her away.

"How did you know there were going to be journalists
outside?" she asked, finally.

"I didn't," he replied, slowly putting his hand back on the
wheel. "I was going to wait out the front for you when you
finished your shift anyway, and I guess I wasn't the only one.
I got lucky. Or unlucky."

"For the record," Tinsel began. "The only reason I'm not
rolling out of this car and into oncoming traffic is because of
the press outside. I don't need the lift that badly."

"I thought we could use the time to talk on the way home.
This whole thing has been really shocking for me."

Tinsel closed her eyes, needing the beat to swallow down
her deep sense of frustration. She wanted to scream. Smash
her hands on the dashboard. Actually, unclipping her seatbelt
and pulling a *Lady Bird* as she threw herself out of the vehicle
didn't sound so bad suddenly.

"Have you honestly not asked yourself how *I* might be
feeling, amid all this?" she questioned, struggling to keep her
voice level. "How *I* might be coping with it?"

He was silent for several minutes, Tinsel almost able to
audibly hear his mind ticking over the questions she'd asked

him. She and Zack had met when she accompanied a friend to get tattooed at Wallace and Marshall. He hadn't been the tattooist, but he'd seen her in the shop, and it wasn't long before she noticed the guy one station over kept stealing glances at her. Unable to take the tension after a few hours, she told him she liked his Deftones shirt and that had broken the ice.

By the time her friend – freshly inked arm sleeve covered in glad wrap – had paid up and they left the store together, Zack had followed her out on to the street and asked for her number. It was a very old school way of doing things and she'd been charmed by it. There was no swiping left or right, no sliding into her DMs – he was straight up. It was comical how wrong that initial read was. Now she felt Zack was anything but, and that she was Jack Torrance running through the icy maze, trying to navigate a path, axe in hand.

"I guess I didn't think of it from that perspective," he said, breaking the silence.

"You didn't? Not once did you think about how scared I was on Thursday night? When there was someone chasing me down our street and my nerves were still rattled from fighting you?"

To her surprise, he laughed. "Babe, come on. The cops are humouring you and pretending to take that seriously. There was no one waiting outside the house."

"Yo, jack ass, you weren't there!" she huffed. "And Vic thought it was *serious* enough to call a unit! They–"

"Who's Vic?"

"The other homicide detective."

"The uniforms?"

"No, detectives are plain clothed. The ones that came to see you were junior."

"See, you said it yourself: junior. Beat cops."

"I didn't say beat cops."

Light was beginning to crack on the horizon as he slowed

down and with surprise, Tinsel realised he'd driven her to The Pinnacle. She turned to him in disbelief as he parked the car.

"You really are obtuse, aren't you?" she questioned.

His hands froze as he turned off the ignition. "Tinsel, I didn't mean to make fun, I know you're scared–"

"No, you don't. You're a guy. You don't walk home from work with your keys wedged between your knuckles. You don't take note of a car's number plate if it slows down beside you in case you need to remember that detail later. You don't have statistically at least one out of three friends being survivors of sexual assault."

Zack threw himself back into the seat with frustration. "I can never compete with your drama."

Tinsel unclicked her seatbelt, mind and spirit light in spite of everything.

"I'm going to say this very clearly so you understand," she began. "We are broken up, Zack. I am breaking up with you. And not in the kind of way where we stay friends afterwards. I'm not going to change my mind like all the other times. I'm not staying at my sister's for a few days until I get over it. My name is on the lease. You're moving out. I'll come back next week and when I do, your stuff will be gone."

"Damn it Tinsel!" he shouted, slamming his hands on the steering wheel. She jumped, heartbeat racing as she all but leapt out of the car.

"I love you!" Zack yelled. "I can do better, give me that chance!"

What she gave him was a door slammed in his face. Spinning around, she nearly cried with relief as she heard the familiar dings of a tram arriving. Tinsel had to sprint for the number eleven, turning herself sideways so she could make it just as the doors slid shut and her bag swung through behind her.

Breathless, she watched through the glass as Zack stood in the middle of Taplin Street, waving his hands at her and shouting something she couldn't hear.

He was almost out of sight when she realised exactly where he was: mere inches from where she'd been chased. In fact, he'd parked in same spot as the beaten-up car where the mysterious figure had laid in wait.

She had to hold on to the railing for support. *No,* she thought. Her mind was making connections that weren't there, amongst the chaos of the past few minutes and the fatigue of a full night's show. *You're finding meaning where there is none,* she told herself. *You just need some sleep, some silence, some space.* Tinsel closed her eyes, listening to the stops as they were called overhead, but savouring the small sanctuary she was able to create by blocking out everything else.

"Wake your ass up, Auntie Tintin."

"Mum, you said ass!"

"I'm allowed to, cos I have one. Max, jump on her a little bit, will you? Just gently."

"*Ugh, whhhhhy?*" Tinsel whined, lifting her head from the pillow as the body of a small child jumped on the edge of her bed.

"Because I am their overlord and commander," chirped Pandora. "They do what I say."

"Is that enough jumping now? She's awake?" Max smiled at his mum.

"Two jumps more, oh – good boy!"

"Dora!"

Tinsel lurched to an upright position, hurling a pillow at her sister who pivoted away from the flying object like an NBA pro.

"Hey, you chose to stay here," Pandora smirked. "In a house full of children. Remember that."

"Yeah, but it's not the children who woke me up, is it?"

"They came home from kindy and got bored."

"More like *you* got bored," she grumbled, flopping back

down on to the mattress as Max lay beside her. Tinsel turned to face his bright, intelligent eyes as they blinked just a few inches from her face.

"Why do you sleep all day?" he asked.

"Because I work all night, Max, you know this."

"Oh yeah," he frowned, as if suddenly recalling the conversation. "Why do you work all night?"

"Because I'm a vampire who sucks the blood of little boys who ask too many questions."

He giggled and Tinsel bared her teeth for emphasis, hissing loudly. He shrieked and jumped out of the bed, his cries echoing down the hall as he sprinted from the room and into his dad's office.

Tinsel closed her eyes for a moment, feeling the weight of the bed shift as Pandora dropped down on to it.

"I swear, if you've got him into vampires now, I'm gonna be so pissed."

"What is this?" Tinsel asked, not opening her eyes. "A strictly werewolf household?"

"We just got over the pirate phase, I'm not ready for vampires."

Even with her eyes shut, she could sense Pandora looking at her.

"What?" Tinsel asked, not moving.

"You're on the news."

"I figured. Is it bad?"

"No, cos you didn't say anything, which was smart."

Sitting up, Tinsel stretched her arms above her head as she let go of the notion that she'd be going back to sleep.

"No fuel, no fire, right? But honestly, I was too shocked they were there to even mumble a coherent sentence."

"If it makes you feel better, I don't think you'll make the evening news," Pandora said, handing over her phone which had the clips up and ready to go. "They had no fresh angles on the murder, so the family speaking for the first time on your show was the only way to keep the story alive. And that's radio, there's no moving images. Most of the morning bulletins had footage of you leaving work while audio from the brother and dad played over the top."

"I can see that," Tinsel murmured, scrolling through. "The online stories have nothing either, which is…"

Tinsel didn't finish the sentence as her eyes caught on a line that made her heart drop.

"*Police investigated an incident at the radio host's residential address on Thursday evening, according to the popular true crime blog, Pandora's Box,*" Tinsel read, the volume of her voice increasing with each word. "*Victoria Police Media confirmed that an incident did take place, however, they would not state whether it was connected to Mera Brant's murder less than twenty-four hours earlier.*"

"Now give me a sec–"

Tinsel threw the phone at her sister's face; Pandora batted it away so the device landed softly on the mattress instead of the intended destination. She tossed the bed covers, lunging at her sister.

"It could have been anyone!" Pandora shrieked. "A bunch of people already posted videos online of the cops at your house, I just got it confirmed with police media so I could write about it!"

Pandora sprung out of Tinsel's clutches and to the safety of the doorway, putting distance between them.

"There's a hyperlink in the article to your blog!" she growled.

"I know, isn't it great? You should see the numbers on the site–"

"I'm going to kill you!"

"I'm a mother, *how dare you*!" Pandora replied, unable to keep the smile off her face. Tinsel didn't give a shit and took off after her as Pandora sprinted down the hall, her red ponytail streaking behind her like a fox's tail. She extended her hands to try and grab it as she had in so many fights before, but Pandora pre-emptively threw it up into a bun as she was running.

"Come on!" she puffed. "If I didn't report on it, it was going to leak to someone else! Don't you want me to have the hits?"

"No wonder the press were there!" Tinsel cried, hurdling the couch to cut her sister off as she ducked around it. "You made it seem like–"

"Hey, I didn't publish my piece until eight this morning," Pandora snapped. "You were already home and in bed, so I timed it to go live *after* I saw the morning bulletins and when interest in the story would be piqued." She scooped up Airlie from her playpen and held the dribbling baby out between them.

"Don't use Airlie as a human shield!" Tinsel said, shifting her weight from foot-to-foot.

"I know she's your favourite and you can't hurt me without hurting her so…"

They had reached a standoff. After holding her sister's stare for several beats, Tinsel sighed and relaxed her shoulders. Pandora let out a breath as well, lowering Airlie to the ground. The baby stumbled towards Tinsel on her awkward little legs and she bundled her up in her arms.

"Can I make you poached eggs and officially call this a truce?"

Looking at the clock over her sister's shoulder and seeing that it was just about to tick past four, she agreed. "Fine. But with that homemade Hollandaise while you're at it."

"Whatever princess wants," Pandora bowed.

"And gimmie my phone, so I can survey the damage."

She and Airlie settled on the couch while Pandora moved about in the kitchen. Tinsel began the arduous process of replying to every text message and phone call she had ignored while doing the show overnight. Rushelle was ecstatic with how it went down, especially how it had been received by listeners and the rest of the management team. Tinsel had to squint her eyes shut and open them again when she read the figures, certain there must have been a mistake. A twenty-two per cent audience share was almost unheard of, not only for *The Graveyard Shift*, but any night time radio show in the country. It was a dramatic spike from her usual listener numbers.

A quick check of Twitter showed her "The Graveyard Shift" was still trending, along with "Joe Meyer." She clicked into that, seeing a number of articles about Mera's final moments spent trying to win tickets to the premiere of *Band Candy*. He'd even given a comment on it, talking about how it made him feel and "what a tragedy" the whole thing had been. *At least he didn't say it on my show*, she thought, the blatant promotional angle of the whole thing making her feel icky.

There was also a text from Detective James and her throat clenched a little tighter as she read it.

Listened to your voicemail, thanks for the heads up about the show, it read. *I tuned in*.

He tuned in and then… what? He didn't say anything about what he thought of the show or how Mera's family handled themselves. He didn't mention whether he thought she did a good job or even if tying in the songs to Mera's favourite movie choices was a nice touch. It was just a straightforward, to the point text that lasted two sentences. Tinsel found her thumb hovering over the keys as she considered writing a reply before giving up.

"So, I saw a fleeting glimpse of Zack on the news too," Pandora said, dropping the plate of eggs Benedict down in front of Tinsel on the coffee table.

"Yum, thank you. And it was the second horrible surprise of the morning, believe me."

"He just showed up?"

"Mmm hmmm," Tinsel replied, her voice muffled through the first bite.

"You're here rather than there, so I take it that means you told him to kick rocks?" Pandora asked. "I mean, you don't have to tell me if you don't want to…"

"I do," she said, watching as her sister heaved Airlie into

her lap and began feeding her yogurt. "It's just so fucking embarrassing, sis. The things I put up with, the things I let slide… I feel like a fraud."

"Ha, why? Because you're Tinsel fucking Monroe, bad bitch radio presenter and producer, C List celebrity, all my independent women throw your hands up at me?"

She blinked. "I don't even know where to start with *any* of that."

"I know I'm a judgy bitch by nature," Pandora replied. "But no one knows what anyone's relationship is like from the outside. I love you. I won't judge you. You're my sister. I just want you to be okay. And happy."

"I'm trying to eat," Tinsel smiled, genuinely touched.

"And get railed on the regular," her sister pressed, causing her to nearly choke on a mouthful. "And be with someone who's not threatened by your success or trying to dampen your shine."

"Stood on my chest and kept me down," Tinsel quoted. "Hated hearing my name on the lips of a crowd."

"Oh God, we're at the reciting Lorde lyrics stage of the breakup, are we?"

She shrugged. "It's called *Melodrama* for a reason."

Tinsel was starving and she ate rapidly, unable to help her hunger, given that usually she would have been up a few hours ago. Pandora had let her sleep and after everything that had been going on, she needed it.

"On a happier note," Pandora said, wiping the corner of Airlie's mouth. "You got what you always wanted."

"What's that?" Tinsel frowned.

"A top rating radio show."

She scoffed. "Yeah, not at the expense of someone's life! I don't know if I want to hitch my burgeoning career to the death of a listener."

"Have you heard anything more from the cops?"

"No, you? I mean, you spoke to police media."

Pandora leaned forward, opening up her laptop and positioning in front of Tinsel so her sister could read the last three blog posts she had written on the murder.

Pandora had a unique ability to throw a rope around information like she was a rancher and bring it to heel. Her stories were succinct, factual, and towards the end always left a few sentences for her own introspection. It caught Tinsel up on everything she felt like she'd been missing amid the mania. When she finished the final piece, she glanced over to meet Pandora's blue eyes as they stared at her expectantly.

"Well?" she asked.

Tinsel bit her lip. "What couldn't you write?"

"That's *so* the right question!" Pandora exclaimed, spinning the laptop back around to face her and placing Airlie down. "The line from police media was the only 'on the record' one I could get, but I spoke to Stacey there who has a really great phone voice and she's low-key my favourite. Anyway, I asked her about suspects and she said 'officially, no.'"

"Officially?"

"Right? That means there's someone they're looking at and I expect we'll find out in the next few days. But what's really interesting is Reddit."

Tinsel shifted so that she was sitting next to Pandora on the couch, both able to see the screen equally as she pulled up a subreddit.

"This whole thing is dedicated to the murder," she explained. "It's where the videos of the police at your house on Thursday night were posted."

"The fuck?"

"It was definitely one of your neighbours, but it's okay because most of the print journos aren't going to find this."

"Why not?"

"You saw the people outside your work, can you imagine any of them navigating their way through a subreddit? I'm more worried about the online reporters."

"Well, someone clearly found it," Tinsel said, pointing out a topic as her sister nearly scrolled by it. "Some woman shouted at me about a Satanic connection to the murders. Click into that."

"She did not!" Pandora gasped.

"She did. I wanna see what's under that tab."

"It's nonsense," her sister explained. "I looked at it briefly, but it just seemed liked they were clutching at straws trying to make connections between the content except–"

"What?"

"That's the angle the tabloids are running with. It's juicy and it appeals to their online international readership, but it doesn't hold up under scrutiny. Like, listen to this: 'does anyone else think it's weird that at the precise moment Mera died, 'Let's Have a Satanic Orgy' was playing?'"

Tinsel couldn't stop the eruption of laughter that escaped her lips. "Oh, for fuck's sake!"

"I know," Pandora sighed.

"That song is from Twin Temple! They basically invented a subgenre called Satanic Doo-Wop. People need to get a grip. Besides, they don't know her precise time of death! 'Hungry Like the Wolf' could have been playing. Does that mean Duran Duran are behind it?"

"It would be a much better story if it was," Pandora noted, navigating her way back with a few key clicks. "Now, this is from an anonymous poster–"

"Never a good omen."

"– who claims to work at the state coroner's office where they performed the autopsy."

"They won't release that to the public," Tinsel said. "No way. There could be stuff in there that's the only tool they have to disprove someone's the killer, information only the murderer would know."

"Totally, but this person posted a blurry screen shot of notes on the report that says the stab wounds indicated there were two different types of knives used. One was a chef's knife, the other was a paring blade: both are used in cooking."

Tinsel squinted, trying to read the scrawled handwriting on the image that had unfortunately been taken in low light. Leaning back, she glanced at her sister.

"Looking for an angry chef isn't exactly going to limit the suspect pool," she remarked. "It would be more unusual to find a calm one."

"No one is saying Gordon Ramsay's the murderer, Tin, but look at Mera's address on Google Maps."

Pandora pulled up another window on the screen, tapping at a street address with her finger. Then she drew a line to a series of buildings nearby.

"That's her house and *that* is a major restaurant district. There's nearly two dozen businesses there and most of them have chefs who get off around the time that Mera was murdered."

"So this could have nothing to do with the show at all," Tinsel said, hopeful. "It could all just be a coincidence, that we were at the same screening, and that she called the show at the time she died."

"Do you remember that case I covered pretty extensively a while back? The young chef who followed a guy home in Sydney and stabbed him to death?"

"It's ringing a bell. He got thirty years, didn't he?"

"He did, but my point is the guy had never met his victim before that night. They just crossed paths at the wrong time and an innocent man lost his life because someone else was in the mood to kill."

"You think that's what could have happened to Mera? Someone wanted to do something horrible, maybe saw her walking home at that time–"

"And an opportunity presented itself."

"And the person waiting outside for me at The Pinny?"

"Could be a rando. Or it could be the original killer who had their interest tweaked after realising they murdered her while calling in to your show. The two things could be completely unrelated, but from the outside they just look eerily connected."

Casting a sideways glance at Pandora, Tinsel could see the hope in her sister's eyes. She felt it too, deep within her chest. *I really hope you're right*, she thought.

CHAPTER 10

"God damn it, Pikey!"

Indy Aposolottius swore under his breath, frustrated but not frustrated enough that he wanted his colleagues to hear him. The man was supposed to be his boss, but with less than half an hour until curtain-up, Pikey was nowhere to be found. At just nineteen, Indy knew he was lucky to have his job as the junior lighting technician at The Capitol, especially whilst studying for his communications degree with a focus in theatre. It was a gift, he reminded himself, to be able to pay his bills working in the actual field he wanted to be working in when he left university rather than making minimum wage at the Starbucks two doors down on Swanston Street.

Not that he was earning much more than that here, but he was getting experience. He was learning on the job. And he was taking on responsibilities that were *definitely* above his pay grade every time Pikey dipped as they were heading towards crunch time.

It was the premiere of *Band Candy*, some fancy new horror film that Indy honestly didn't pay much attention to outside of the specs requested from the event manager who had hired the space for the evening. This was just a film screening and with the exception of a brief introduction at the beginning, there were no key performers to spotlight or an elaborate lighting design he needed to master. All that needed to be done in theory was the bare minimum front-of-house checks before theatre doors opened in twenty, no, fifteen minutes now.

"Shit," he huffed.

"What's up?" asked Wahli, one of the two AV techs stationed at the control deck with Indy.

"Uh…" He hesitated to tell her the truth. Only a few months into this casual position, he valued the job too much to throw his boss under the bus and be branded a narc.

"Pikey's AWOL again, isn't he?" she questioned. She pushed off against the wall, rolling over on her chair until she joined Indy in front of a plethora of buttons, dials, and controls that would be enough to send even the most tech literate into an overwhelmed meltdown.

Indy, however, felt a sense of calm wash over him every time he looked at the sight before him. He took comfort in the knowledge that although you couldn't control everything, the answer to whatever his problem was could usually be found right there.

"It's okay," Wahli continued, flipping a pink strand of hair out of her face and tucking it behind her headset. "I've worked here since the reopening; I know what Pikey's like. Let me put out a call and–"

"No!" Indy blurted. "If you put out a call, then everyone will know I can't handle it."

"You're not supposed to handle it, kid. That's why he makes four times what you do. He's the lighting supervisor. Besides, I ain't dumb: I'll say AV needs to double check a timing note and he'll be none the wiser."

Indy let out a long breath. "Okay, well, if you're sure?"

"Super sure," she beamed.

Wahli did exactly what she said she'd do and provided a fudged explanation when a disgruntled Pikey returned reeking of cigarettes. The annoying thing was that even though his boss vanished occasionally, when he was there, he was incredibly good at his job. He was able to answer Wahli's question in two seconds flat, before turning to Indy with a huff.

"How's everything going here? We good to go?"

"No," he replied. "I mean, yes. The LEDs are synched and patterned."

"That I can see," Pikey replied sarcastically, glancing up at the ceiling.

"And all the other front of house checks are done, except–"

"What?"

"LX2 is not responding. I know we don't technically need it so long as LX1 is a go, but I also know how much you like to have a backup plan."

"Mmmm, I do," he murmured, taking a seat and fiddling with his lighter.

Indy could almost see the words coming out of Pikey's mouth before he said them – his superior would offer to go and check the back-up lighting bar in person, therefore providing him with another opportunity for a sneaky durry. Then the remaining window of time before Melbourne's high-profile guests started pouring through the doors would be well and truly closed.

"I can go and check," Indy offered, just as Pikey's lips parted and the scenario he'd feared played out in full. "I'll be down there and back up in ten minutes, max, and that way if anything major comes up at least the client will feel much more reassured with you here."

It was Indy who would feel reassured, but he left that part out.

"Pikey, I've got some stuff I need to check with you too," Wahli spoke up from behind him, throwing a wink over Indy's shoulder that only he could see. "Just some last-minute notes."

It took a beat before the older man nodded, his mop of grey curls bouncing in agreement. "Go, go, radio back if there's any issues. If we've got LX1 I'm not too worried."

Indy practically sprung from his seat, not wasting a moment

in case Pikey changed his mind. The control room was less of a room and more of a huge, long desk in an open-air section at the back of the theatre. Hundreds of patrons would be seated in front of them with The Capitol's stage the huge object that would command everyone's attention. That space would be clear tonight, however, with a state-of-the-art screen taking the spotlight and the film projected on to it.

Indy couldn't see any of that though, as he made his descent towards the stage, half-hopping and half-jogging as he negotiated the various levels. There was a grandiose curtain cloaking the screen from view right now, but that would be dramatically withdrawn seconds before the opening credits would roll. He loved the spectacle of it all, and took just a tiny breather to once again feel grateful for working here of all places.

Ducking through one of the doors discreetly tucked away at the front of theatre, Indy slipped around the side of stage like he'd been working at The Capitol his whole life. Pretty much everyone else on the team was cool and blasé about it, but this place was still enough of a shiny novelty to him that he couldn't quite taper down the earnest enthusiasm. Yet.

With no live performance, it was quiet back there. And dark. In fact, during his first two weeks on the gig he had hated performing in-person checks just like this because of how eerie it could be backstage without frazzled actors or disgruntled prop masters running about. When there was a film playing, it was unnerving. There was no need for a bustling backstage presence and so Indy was on his own as he weaved through the thick layers of curtains, hanging ropes and screens that would be implemented for other productions on other days.

It took a while for his eyes to adjust to the darkness and he grabbed the small yet powerful torch that was clipped to his utility belt for situations just like this. Craning his neck upwards, Indy used the rigs above him to help place his location as he began moving towards where LX2 should be. The heavy fabric of a curtain brushed against his shoulder and he jumped involuntarily, annoyed at himself as he swept it away and kept his eyes scanning above. There was another brush of material, this time at his hip, and Indy hesitated with the sensation of it. That felt more solid. Almost like a person moving past him on the other side of the curtain.

He stilled, waiting a second as he turned down the chatter on his headset and listened to what was around him. Nothing. It wasn't quiet – people were spilling into the theatre now and he could hear the excited murmurs – but there was no sound that *wasn't* supposed to be there. Still, he couldn't help the itch that crept along his spine telling him something wasn't right, even though he didn't know what that something was.

Indy halted, frowning as the beam of his torchlight hit on a twist of cables. He tracked the knotted mass downwards, understanding now why LX2 hadn't been responding as he saw the lighting bar collapsed on the floor. Besides the fact it was in the wrong place vertically, it shouldn't have been anywhere near here at all. He crouched down to inspect the damage. He wouldn't be surprised if it had fallen, partially collapsed somehow. He put his torch between his teeth and began pushing the crumpled curtain off the structure.

The black material slid away from the metal easily enough as he worked, right up until it didn't. The fabric pooled around a solid shape. Indy shoved it back as fast as he could to reveal the toe of thick, black boot.

The torch slipped from Indy's teeth and clattered to the ground as he looked up, his head jerking towards the body the feet were attached to in the hope that it was someone he knew.

Even before he met the cold stare set deep within the black hood that concealed the person's identity, he knew this was no friend of his. He knew it wasn't a colleague playing a practical joke or even an audience member who had mistakenly gotten lost back here. Much in the same way that he knew – even a second before a heavy object was raised above his head – he was in grave danger.

Indy only heard his muted grunt for a brief instant before everything went dark, *truly* dark, and there was peace for a moment.

When he stirred, he almost wished he was back in the void as pain became the primary sensation. It was sharp, but not overwhelming as he tried to move his head. There was something around his neck, so he couldn't get much leverage. When he tried to wiggle his hands, he realised they had been tied up behind him. No, this wasn't some kind of prank. This was something much, much more sinister.

"Please," he groaned, conscious of a presence as someone paced around him. "Please just let me go. I won't tell–"

Indy never got to finish his sentence as the knife cut under his clothes and into his flesh. His scream was muffled by the crowd on the other side of the curtain, the excitement palpable as the countdown to showtime crept closer. They remained unaware of his agony just metres away.

The person hurting him was certainly aware. Indy's scream died off as his windpipe was restricted and the rope strangled him with an upwards tug. He was heaved into the air, flying off the ground and upwards as he choked. The thick, sticky substance of his blood and other things, more precious things, dripped down his legs as the figure took a moment to watch from below. Then they were gone, disappearing into the blackness of the curtains like they belonged there.

Maybe they did, this demon.

Indy heard words registering in his mind as they echoed through the theatre, but couldn't do much more than that as comprehension left him. He heard the whir of the curtain being drawn, the sheen of the screen in front of him as he hung behind it, fading, dying, struggling, desperate.

There was a scream somewhere and he was jostled, someone finally having found him. The horror in that voice reflected what he felt inside as he wondered whether there was still time. Yet the weight of everything was so heavy, so pressing, that even as the screams got louder and louder and other voices were added to the chorus, Indy was fully aware that he was about to die in the theatre he loved so much.

CHAPTER 11

Tinsel's mistake had been letting herself think things could get back to normal. It took until Wednesday to realise they likely never would, at least not for a while. The press kept calling her phone and she kept avoiding their calls, but they had at least stopped waiting outside of the 102.8 HitsFM office when she finished her shift, so she considered that a win.

Although her listenership had spiked with the memorial episode, it didn't drop over the Tuesday and Wednesday shows. The number stayed staggering and even without knowing the exact percentage, she could tell it was going off by the sheer volume of tweets that were popping up with "The Graveyard Shift" hashtag each evening.

That was the other problem: the usual audience from the show was specific, niche, and loyal. For the most part, they self-policed, with any dickheads in the comments or on the hashtag reported by Tinsel's regulars so fast that she saw only about half of the nasty stuff before it was gone.

Her audience now, however, was bigger. It was like the local dive bar had been swarmed and she could barely order a pint, let alone hear herself over the racket.

She couldn't help but scan those messages. She had to, really, as part of her job was to signal boost the good stuff, but her DMs were a minefield. It was weirdly one that looked more professional and more normal than the others that raised red flags.

During a song break, she sent Detective James a text asking whether she should be screenshotting those kinds of notifications herself, or if they had someone on it. Her message barely had time to make the satisfying *whoosh* sound as it sent before her phone was vibrating with his call.

"Sorry," he said, by way of hello. "I know you're on air."

"It's okay," Tinsel smiled. "I have a full… eight minutes and thirty-two seconds to spare."

"That's oddly specific."

"Two songs and the end of this Dusty Springfield track," she replied, frowning as she strained to hear what was on in the background. She muted the speakers in the studio for a moment so she could be sure. "Wait, you're listening to the show right now?"

"I am," he chuckled. "I have to admit, I am new to the listenership–"

"*And* you have to, for work," she cut in. "To monitor any weird callers."

"Afraid so."

She had been given permission by both Stu and Rushelle to open the call lines back up if she wanted to, but she had been hesitant.

"It could be good," Pandora had said one morning. "You'll get back into the rhythm of things, you know?"

"Mmmm," was her only response as she thought about it. Unfortunately, it wasn't the only thing rattling around in her head. Mera's panicked voice played on repeat, like her brain had it scheduled there and ready for instant replay any time she thought she was doing okay. She had little choice, however, as the additional *Band Candy* tickets from Joe essentially forced her hand. By Tuesday evening, she'd gulped down her fears, and by Wednesday, things were still smooth. She was hugely grateful that only the regulars seemed to be the ones utilising the phone lines.

"Tinsel?"

"Huh?" she snapped back to the present, quickly checking how long had passed in case she'd spaced out through her cross. Just under seven minutes to go. "Sorry, I–"

"Have a lot on your mind."

"Yeah," she exhaled. "You could say."

"Tell me about these messages. We do have someone monitoring the show's social channels and yours, but everything has turned out to be harmless so far. Well, not harmless."

"I get it," Tinsel answered. "Creepy and frustrating and sexist and occasionally racist, but not the killer."

"Exactly," Detective James agreed. "What was it about these ones?"

"Okay, I've sent you screenshots. They're coming through every ten minutes like clockwork, which made me think it was a bot."

"When did they first start popping up?"

"Monday, but I missed them because that was the night of the memorial show and socials were swamped. I noticed yesterday, then when they started tweeting again tonight, I clicked into the profile and it was only created last week."

"*The Graveyard Shift* is the only account they follow," he noted. "And you're the only one they have sent messages to."

"They're all quotes from horror movies, so not original or particularly threatening in context, but it's the avi that gets me."

"Avi?"

"Avatar, their profile pic," she explained.

"A kookaburra? Are you strictly anti-bird?"

Tinsel laughed, the gesture feeling good. "I pay my swoopy taxes, thank you. It's the logo for the National Film and Sound Archive, which is weirdly professional for a spam account. When I was leaving the office in the middle of that media scrum, someone barked about the NFSA too. I barely heard it at the time, but now... I don't know, it could be nothing."

"There was a death there."

"What?" Tinsel had been rhythmically tapping against the control deck and her fingers froze. "When? Another murder? Oh my God."

"No, that's the thing," he began, the confusion audible in his voice. "I don't think it was a homicide. At least, it didn't come through to *us*, which means it was ruled accidental or a pre-existing medical condition."

"I was going to say, Pandora basically has a Google alert set up for 'murder' at the moment so this would be on her radar."

"Hmmm," he mused. "I'll need to look into it more, but hold tight. I don't know if this is something to be immediately alarmed about, yet it's always best to be safe rather than–"

"Slain?"

Neither of them laughed, the situation was a little too grim for that.

"Can I leave you with some good news?" Detective James asked.

"Please," she sighed. "I think I've actually forgotten what that is."

"Diraani picked someone up for last week, at your house."

Tinsel's grip tightened on the phone. "For real? Who?"

"He's a fifteen-year-old. Popped up on CCTV footage tagging several businesses in the area that same night in clothing fitting your description."

"An all-black outfit?" she scoffed. "That's the equivalent of a business suit for graffers."

"And he had tagged the car earlier in the evening. The paint matched."

Tinsel was quiet for a beat, knowing that she should be relieved by this news yet feeling the exact opposite.

"I don't think it was some kid," she murmured. "Do you?"

She picked up on the way he'd identified his colleague as the one who'd made the connection, leaving himself entirely out of it. His pause told her a whole lot more.

"Diraani has a lot of experience," he stated, diplomatic. "If he says he's got the guy, he's got the guy. It seems like the whole thing might have been incidental after all."

She noted the time, less than thirty seconds to go before she had to be back on air.

"My clock is nearly spent," she said, the alleged "good news" doing little to cheer her.

"Tinsel?"

"Yeah?"

"I said to text, call, whatever, if *anything* didn't feel right. And this social media situation is anything. You're not overreacting, you did the right thing."

"Thank... thank you."

She hung up, slightly dazed. Why was she so resistant to the alley rat being some kid? A random chance to scare her had been the exact scenario she'd been hoping for. Now it had manifested, why was she fighting that solution?

Tinsel had to guillotine the thought, jumping with alarm when she realised there was less than five seconds until she was live again and she needed to be fading out the song. Refocusing and clearing her throat, she tried to focus on what she knew for certain. She had a job to do, and she pushed her discomfort aside.

Several hours and a few anxiety nightmares later, Tinsel was staring at herself in the bathroom mirror trying to place what was off about her look. *Eyelashes*, she realised with a start. Dashing over to her make-up tray, she pried her favourite set of false ones from the packaging and carefully started applying the glue. It was a skill, lining them up with her liquid eyeliner perfectly, but she had just nailed the first eye when her phone buzzed on the sink next to her. She grabbed it without looking, putting it on speaker as she applied the second set of lashes to her right eye.

"Ello?" she said, her voice sounding funny as she tried to move her mouth as little as possible to keep her face still.

"I was calling to see if you wanted a ride."

She flinched, nearly sticking the lashes to her eyebrow. "Vic?"

"Huh, I like the way you say that. Sounds a lot better than–"

"Vicellous?"

"I was going to say Detective James, but sure."

She smiled, catching her own dumb expression in the mirror and attempting to correct it as she properly secured the lashes this time.

"I'm going to the premiere tonight and thought I'd see if you needed a lift."

"*You're* going to the *Band Candy* event?"

"I am."

"Dressed like a cop?"

"Dressed like a guy in a tux, but still a cop."

"Is Diraani going?"

"Just me, I'm afraid. But I look better in formal wear, so really everybody wins."

She laughed, the sound echoing around the small space of the en-suite bathroom.

"Okay then, yeah, sure. When can you pick me up?"

"In fifteen minutes?"

There was a pause on her end long enough to make him ask again. "Is that too soon? Half an hour?"

"Half an hour is good," Tinsel answered, even though she was basically ready now. "I don't want to get there too early or even on time, because then I'm a sitting duck."

"You're worried people are going to grill you about the murder?"

"Oh, they definitely are. The less time I can give them to do that, the better."

"Well, I'll be there too so I can always interrupt questions you don't want to answer with a comment on the weather."

"Mate, how's the humidity?" she mocked, immediately feeling better at the prospect of not being alone at the premiere.

"And the rains! Ergh, just wild this time of year. So should I head to your sister's?"

"Yes please."

"See you in a bit."

He hung up before she had a chance to ask him if he was driving a cop car. The thought of arriving with red and blue lights flashing made her palms sweat. Dragging her mind back to more pressing matters, she gave her ensemble a final once over. Ever since she was old enough to decide what she actually liked, she had been permanently stuck in the late fifties sartorially. Everything she owned fitted the mod aesthetic or rockabilly-lite. That evening's frock was no exception.

In a rusty shade that sat somewhere between red and orange, the velvet clung to her body like she was a femme fatale on the cover of pulp fiction. It started with a cross halter neckline that slashed across her collarbone and wrapped around her neck, before the sweetheart cut highlighted what cleavage she had. Seamed at the waist, the hem flared out into a fishtail midway down her calves, and she had teamed it with a simple pair of black heels that matched the shade of her hair. She had been tempted to try victory rolls now that her bob was just long enough, but had reconsidered. The dress was *a lot* of look, and because of it, she was able to keep her make-up relatively simple with just her signature winged eyeliner and a strong brow. Her eyeshadow was a subtle bronze that matched the highlighter on her cheekbones, and she kept her lip dark.

Popping a bobby pin in between her teeth, she teased the back of her hair slightly as it gave her some height and she clipped everything in place. She had a backup bag waiting in her room with a change of clothes. Once she dashed from the premiere to the radio station, she wouldn't have to do the whole show in red carpet attire.

Detective James was on the phone when she slid into his

car, but he paused mid-sentence as he caught sight of her. It told Tinsel everything she needed to know. She bit down on a smile that she could feel forming on her lips. He had gone all out as well, mind you, and she wasn't sure why that was so surprising to her. *Band Candy*'s big opening was at The Capitol which required a certain amount of effort from guests. She found herself looking forward to the moment when they would be out of the car and she could properly see how that tuxedo looked on him when he was standing upright.

"Sorry about that," he said, pulling the bluetooth headpiece from his ear after a few minutes of driving. "An old case goes to trial tomorrow, so I'm getting calls about it every two seconds it feels like."

"Is that a good thing or a bad thing?" she wondered.

"It's... ah, I'm sorry, but I just have to say how amazing you look before anything else gets in the way."

Tinsel felt herself blushing as she looked down at her hands clasped in her lap. "Anything else gets in the way? You mean, besides this traffic?"

"We're going *into* the city when everyone else is coming out; it shouldn't be this bad," he said, with a frustrated laugh.

"I'm not used to it. Usually when I go into work I'm walking. And thank you, by the way. You look good too."

"I didn't know people got so dressed up for horror movie premieres," he admitted.

"Depends on the venue," she shrugged, watching him from the safety of her seat as his eyes focused on the road.

He must have sensed it, however, as he thew her a sideways glance.

"What is it?" he smirked, Tinsel enjoying the dimple she watched form deep within his cheek.

"You're clean-shaven and everything."

"Boss's orders. I need to blend," he said, self-consciously running a hand over his jawline.

"So, this is work then? Something related to the case?"

Tinsel could almost sense his impulse to close up on her and she waited for it to happen. Yet strangely, he let out a long breath as he shifted the car into neutral and turned to look at her properly when they stopped at a traffic light.

"I thought coming along tonight might be smart, just in case, and especially since…" He stopped himself, clearly aware that he was saying too much.

"Since you don't have anything to go on," Tinsel finished for him. The look in his eyes was confirmation enough.

"We have plenty. We have a body, a crime scene, witnesses. I've worked cases with less. But there's still not a single good suspect or even a motive. That frustrates the hell out of me."

"Pandora thinks it could be random. A chef, even."

"Because of the knives?" Detective James shook his head. "It doesn't feel random. There was no forced entry into her home, no one saw anyone coming or going even though they heard her cries. There was no DNA left at the scene, no murder weapons disposed of nearby, no tracks we could follow or even shoe prints. All of that tells me Mera's murder was planned and her murderer was careful. He watched her, he had a course of action, and he probably had a contingency plan. Several."

Tinsel let that wash over her, watching commuters walking along the city streets outside of the car.

"Wait, how do you know about the knives? How does your sister?"

"Uh… Reddit."

"Fuck," he growled, frustrated.

"I take it you being here as my personal bodyguard means the NFSA death wasn't an accident?"

He flashed her a look that was both annoyed and pleased that she didn't miss anything. "That's tricky."

She blinked, waiting patiently for him to continue, and doing her best not to breathe a sigh of relief when he did.

"The death occurred late on Friday night. No one saw anything, no one heard anything, there was only one person recorded in the building and that was the deceased. She was a bit of an introvert, didn't have a lot of friends and lived alone, so no one knew anything was awry until a staffer entered the storage facility on Monday afternoon."

"That's so sad," she whispered.

"Her body was partially buried under collapsed shelving and the cause of death is blunt force trauma for now."

"*For now?*" she tried to keep the alarm out of her voice, but couldn't help it.

"I don't like it," Detective James said, casting her a glance. "With that much time between her death and the discovery of the body, even seemingly insignificant injuries can look worse than they are with decay and bruising and... on paper, the two victims don't have anything in common besides being women in their twenties who work tangentially in film."

"Mera worked at CinemaNova," Tinsel recalled.

"That's right, but the tweets and the timing have me uneasy. I'm getting a second examination done as we speak, so we'll have answers tomorrow probably."

He'd been pretty forthcoming with her when she was quite certain he wasn't allowed to be. So Tinsel returned the favour, starting with the subreddit and continuing right through to Pandora's theory about the proximity of Mera's house to a restaurant district and the murder weapons. She also debunked the stupid Satanic theory, not that she thought he believed it, but she'd watched *West of Memphis*. Fear and panic could contort organisations, especially if there was mounting public pressure. Detective James listened, none of this information seeming particularly surprising to him, and Tinsel noticed for the first time how tired he looked. It had been seven days since the crime, and she suspected the hours he had been working would make her radio shifts look like a vacation.

"We went door to door on every restaurant," he said, when she was finished. "Ran background checks on every apprentice chef to bloody line cook to see if anyone had a criminal record or something that leapt out to us."

"Nothing?"

"Nothing. But we've widened the net to include neighbouring suburbs as well. Diraani doesn't think it's a chef either, and that man has the best instincts out of any cop I've worked with."

She realised they were only a block away as the traffic began to slow. The illuminated yellow light of The Capitol sign was visible up ahead. A historic theatre like this was quite a weird thing to find wedged between store fronts in the CBD. Yet, it had been there since the nineteen twenties and considered by many one of the most beautiful theatres in the country, if not the world.

The usually no-nonsense foot traffic of Swanston Street was at a crawl as a growing crowd of onlookers watched the proceedings. There were intermittent flashes as photographers took pictures of people she couldn't see through the masses.

"You'll never get a park this close," she said, watching as Detective James scanned the route in front of them. "We shouldn't even be driving on this street."

"Oh really?" he asked, flashing her a smug smile as he switched a button on the dash. To her horror, red and blue lights began flashing without noise and he negotiated the car into a loading zone right in front of The Capitol. People were turning around to look, and she sunk lower in her seat with embarrassment.

"I've had nightmares about this," she choked out. "Literal nightmares."

He laughed, looking delighted at her reaction.

"Is it okay if I leave my work bag in here?" she asked, jerking her head at the bundle. "I've got to get changed and head straight to the station after this."

"Course, I can drive you if you want?"

"Are you my private security now? Because if I'd known, I would've left the can of pepper spray at home."

"Ha, no, but if you leave there's not much reason for me to stick around is there?"

"I don't know," she frowned. "Is there?"

The way he looked at her as she asked the question made Tinsel's pulse race and she was grateful for the low light. She pulled her gaze away first, feeling almost physically difficult as she did so.

Checking her make-up in a small, handheld mirror, she added a fresh coat of lipstick and adjusted her bangs, before slipping the compact back into the black purse that was designed like a mini-keyboard.

"I'm ready," Tinsel said, pretending to ignore the tension she felt between them.

"Alright, let's go."

The boning in her dress made it difficult to wiggle out of the car, but she managed it and spent a few seconds on the sidewalk adjusting everything as a tram rumbled by. She used the reflection in the car windows to examine the look top to bottom, conscious of the fact she wouldn't have another opportunity to do so before she was standing in front of a line of cameras.

As Tinsel spun, she watched Detective James watch her, his eyes pouring over every inch. She read the desire in his expression, and it made her feel formidable in the moment.

"I was wrong," he said, his voice sounding funny.

"About what?"

"I said you looked beautiful before. I hadn't seen the full impact."

She laughed. "You'd change your initial assessment?"

"I'd upgrade it. Significantly."

"Come on," Tinsel said, after a moment standing there on the street. He offered her his elbow and she smirked as she slipped her fingers through it, the mannerism very outdated to her. Detective James was creating an impact of his own, respectfully, now that he was out from behind the wheel and she could see him fully. Tinsel kept casting sneaky sideways glances, his usual hotness coming across as a rough Ronaldo, and tonight shifting firmly into that refined Ronaldo territory. To throw another R into the mix, everything from the sportiness of the tuxedo jacket to the black pleated silk cummerbund made him look like Robert Redford in *The Sting*. She gulped. It was a strong cocktail.

They negotiated their way through the throng of people, there being a natural flow towards the entrance of the red carpet. There was a duo of publicists checking names on a clipboard and Tinsel recognised one that had accompanied Joe to the studio days earlier, Gilly. Or Milly. Maybe Billie? It was something in that range. The lady recognised Tinsel too, her eyes widening with excitement as she clocked her presence.

"Tinsel! Ah great, I'm so glad you're here!"

She made a shooing motion towards other people with her hands as she dragged Tinsel and Detective James to the front of the line, not bothering to check their names off against the guest list. People moved apart to let them through, the cluster suddenly opening up as they found themselves at the start of the red carpet. There was a photo wall just up the stairs, with the film's logo and the HitsFM branding printed on to the background over and over again as various celebrities posed in front of it.

"Joe didn't want to head in until you got here so we could grab a shot of you two together," Gilly/Milly/maybe Billie said in a flurry of words. "Do you want to get in and get your solo shots while I find him? I'll be two seconds."

"Sure," Tinsel nodded, "But I'm not taking–"

The publicist had darted off through the line of media and into the crowd of guests on the other side, leaving Tinsel and Detective James standing there awkwardly.

"– questions," she finished.

She recognised one of the actresses from the film ahead of her, striking an over the shoulder pose as she looked back at the line of photographers. Tinsel saw one of them check his shot in the digital display, before glancing down the line to see who was next. His face brightened when he saw her, and she threw him a friendly wave.

"Tinsel! So good to see you out here, girl, how are you?"

"I'm good, Clyde, how are you doing? How are the girls?"

"The eldest just finished high school this week so, naturally, I'm terrified."

"I feel that," she chuckled, shuffling towards where he pointed her to stand. She cast a backwards glance at Detective James, but he had already slunk around to stand next to the photographers and out of the line of sight. He gave her a knowing smile.

"Two more steps forward," Clyde told her, drawing her attention back.

"Who are you shooting for?" she asked.

"Getty and the rest of the wires."

"Ah," she nodded with understanding. That meant these images would be in the system for any publication that had a subscription fee or was willing to buy them for a one-off sum.

She rotated through a few poses, familiar with how this whole circus worked. When she had first started at 102.8 HitsFM, someone from publicity actually gave her a "red carpet course" where she was taught how to pose and conduct herself when she inevitably attended any number of official events on behalf of the station. In the three years since, she had that act down pat and knew most of the regular photographers by name.

"Yup, that's it, gorgeous," Clyde called. "Give me one over the shoulder."

"I'll give you one over the shoulder alright," she growled, the man sticking out his tongue at her as a taunt.

"Perfect, that's it. Thanks, Tinsel."

"Tell the hubby I said hi."

"Of course."

She moved her way down the photo line, spotting one of the photographers who had been waiting out the front of her office on Monday. He looked slightly embarrassed, but not enough to stop him yelling, "This way, Tinsel, big smile!"

"Here he is," Gilly – Milly/Billie – said with a breathy gush, reappearing beside her with Joe Meyer.

"You look ethereal!" Joe purred, holding her back and giving her an exaggerated once over.

From the way the publicist darted out of the frame, Tinsel knew it was orchestrated so there would be some classic "look what great friends they are" shots in the system.

Joe brought her in for a hug, asking how she was with something she wasn't certain was real or faux concern. They posed together, Tinsel careful to position herself in a conscious manner so there was no way anyone could read into their body language and pen an "are they/aren't they?" column. *He would love that*, she thought, fully aware of the fact she wasn't high-profile enough for him to be a viable option. Generally, Joe dated actresses on the come-up and, sure enough, she could see a woman glowering at her just over his shoulder.

"How about your date, Tinsel?" someone asked. "Can we get him in here?"

She thought Detective James had gone unnoticed and as she told the photographer "Not a chance," her eyes searched the sea of people for his face. Tinsel had been there all of ten minutes and she'd already lost him, his finely tuxed frame nowhere to be found. She maintained a frozen, dead smile as she made her way off the red carpet and past the line of journalists.

"Tinsel Munroe, can we grab you for a quick–"

"I won't answer questions," she said, cutting off the reporter with a polite smile and her best Ray Shoesmith impression. She could feel Joe's hand on her shoulders trying to steer her towards the media and two television crews that had assembled. She stood her ground until he was forced to walk in front of her. He gave her a pleading glance and she mouthed the word "no" quite firmly.

"Please, Tinsel," a reporter begged. "Just two seconds about the murder–"

"I've been looking forward to seeing *Band Candy* for months, so I'm just grateful to be here and to support genre filmmaking in this country," she answered, continuing to push her way inside, thankful for the velvet rope that separated the press from guests.

Suddenly, as if sensing her distress, Detective James appeared through the mass of people at that precise moment and moved towards her. He threw an arm around Tinsel, acting as a human barrier between her and the media.

"You disappeared," she muttered.

"I was trying to avoid the cameras," he replied, their arms linked as they headed into the foyer. "Why, miss me?"

She smirked but didn't answer the question.

"Tinsel!" Joe called after her.

"I'll see you in there," she called, not turning back for a second.

She remained silent for several minutes as Detective James put as much space between them and the red carpet as possible. She nodded polite hellos to people she recognised until they found a discreet corner together. He swiped them both a glass of champagne and Tinsel downed half of the flute in one go, letting out a satisfied sigh.

"Christ, I needed this," she said, finishing the glass before grabbing another from a passing waiter.

"He's an opportunistic one, isn't he?" Detective James murmured eyeing Joe. He took tiny sips from his glass as his eyes travelled the room over the rim of his glass.

"I mean, it's got him to where he is," Tinsel replied. "Residual culture cringe means we don't support genre filmmakers the way we should. If you want to have a lasting career, you've gotta have one or two films that get noticed overseas then straddle those two markets."

"He was on your show, wasn't he? The episode you did for Mera?"

"Yup, the publicist came too. It's weird…"

"What is?" he asked as her thought trailed off. She shook her head slightly.

"I dunno, just thinking about it. If Mera hadn't died, she would have been here tonight too."

Tinsel felt something brush against her hand and she looked down to see Detective James' index finger gently touch hers, as if testing the waters. She met his gaze and felt the heat behind it as she let him take her hand. He squeezed it gently before releasing. *Oh boy*, she thought. *I am in trouble.*

"We should head in," he said.

She nodded, worried her voice might give her away if she spoke out loud. Instead, Tinsel led the way as they joined the mass of people heading up the last set of carpeted stairs and into the theatre itself.

She couldn't help the small gasp that escaped her lips once they reached the top, the sight before them doing that to her. It wasn't the hugest venue; it had been much bigger once. The bottom level had been turned into a shopping arcade in the sixties and what was left had barely been saved. Yet it was something worth fighting for – the Chicago Gothic-style architecture was breath-taking to behold, following the venue's very first historic restoration a few years back.

It looked like something out of time, with the different dimensional layers of the ceiling and walls helping to create a dramatic effect that enhanced the first silent films that played there with orchestral accompaniment. The once candy-coloured globes had been replaced with LED lighting fixtures that slowly transitioned their way through the shades of the rainbow. It was one of the few visible modern touches, the rest being things only people like Tinsel would care about, such as a state-of-the-art sound system and digital laser projection to go with the 35mm projector they already had. It was cinephile heaven.

"What are you doing?" Detective James whispered, leaning in dangerously close.

"It's my favourite part," she replied, "Walking in at the start of the night, seeing the whole place… it's so beautiful."

"It is," he replied, but Tinsel didn't have to tear her eyes away from those gathered in the box seats to know he wasn't really looking at the theatre.

She heard her name being called, and grimaced, spotting Joe's publicist again as she tried to wave her towards a set of reserved seats in the front.

Fuck no, she thought, grabbing Detective James' hand and pulling him in the opposite direction towards somewhere in the middle. She felt the breath of his laughter on her neck as he chuckled; it was obvious what she was doing.

The venue was bubbling with noise as the rest of the theatre began to fill up. Tinsel tried desperately not to notice how close she was positioned next to him as they took their seats. She definitely didn't notice the way her skin felt when he accidentally brushed up against her. Nope. Not at all.

"Do you come to premieres here a lot?" he asked, and she was grateful for any conversation that led towards safer territory.

"To be honest, most film studios can't afford the space unless it's for something big."

"And his movies are big?"

"They're… getting bigger," she admitted, the pair falling silent as the lights dimmed.

Tinsel's eyes widened as she recognised one of Australia's most prominent genre filmmakers walk on to the stage, his silver hair and thick-framed glasses part of his iconic look. He paused in front of the microphone, waiting patiently as the round of applause from the crowd eventually died down.

"It's an honour to be here tonight to introduce the latest film of someone who I have been able to mentor towards the end of my career," he began. "I've watched Joe Meyer develop from a promising film school student to a filmmaker on the world stage, all the while never giving up his love of a well-orchestrated scare and ability to thrill audiences to the point of near discomfort."

There was an appreciative chuckle from those around them and Detective James leaned back towards her as the speech continued.

"Is now a bad time to mention that I've never seen one of his movies?"

She threw him a look, genuinely surprised. "Not even one?"

"I'm not really a horror guy."

"What kind of 'guy' are you?"

He hesitated, as if reluctant to share his response. It took a beat but eventually he caved. "A rom-com kind of guy."

Tinsel held his gaze to see if he was kidding, but his face was serious despite a wariness in his eyes, like he was expecting her to make fun of him.

"What kind of rom-coms are we talking?" she quizzed. "Old school, new school, high school?"

"All of them," he chuckled. "Whatever you've got."

She felt herself smile as she replied. "I respect that."

Another round of applause drew her attention back to the stage and she abruptly started clapping, feeling guilty for not having listened to the last few minutes of whatever had been said. She hadn't even noticed when the speaker had switched to being Joe himself, asking the audience to hang around at the conclusion of the film for a question-and-answer session with several actors from the movie.

There was a final burst of clapping before everything went dim and the opening credits began to roll. The first scene was in a grimy bar as a punk band well beyond their prime played to an enthusiastic audience of scene kids dancing and thrashing to the music. The whole thing was shot in slo-mo, exaggerating the movements of the musicians and focusing in on the sweat and spit that flew from their bodies. A heavy backing track was thudding over the action, the chords hinting at the tension of whatever was to come during the next hour and a half of the film.

A scream rung out and Tinsel frowned, thinking that the sound effect seemed out of place within the context of the scene. It wasn't until Detective James stiffened beside her that she realised something was wrong. The scream increased in volume, the source of the sound being a woman who sprinted out on to the stage in front of the screen where the movie was being projected.

Tinsel felt herself rise to her feet, squinting to make out the figure properly. The lady was covered in some kind of dark substance, and she was shouting. It was near impossible for most of the people in the theatre to hear her over the sound of *Band Candy*'s dialogue. There was a break just long enough though for Tinsel to make out a few words.

"BLOOD!" she shouted. "HELP, THERE'S SO MUCH BLOOD!"

The man next to her chuckled, muttering something to his partner about a "stunt." She heard that sentiment ripple out through the crowd. Yet the woman didn't leave, instead collapsing to her knees on the stage and sobbing as someone from the front row rushed forward to help her.

A light danced down the aisle as ushers ran towards the commotion, someone asking guests to stay in their seats as their flashlight beams led the way. The movie's sound cut out completely and Tinsel could hear the chaos more clearly.

"She's saying someone is covered in blood," a voice whispered. Another scream was heard, this one deeper in tone that definitely belonged to a man. Panic began to echo through the theatre, which was still plunged in darkness despite people pulling out their phones and attempting to use the flashlight.

"SHE'S BLEEDING!" a man called. "CALL AN AMBULANCE!"

Suddenly Detective James was yanking Tinsel by the hand towards the aisle, muttering apologies to people as they bumped knees and trod on feet. She expected him to turn them towards the front of the stage and whatever was going on there. Instead, he dragged her back the way they had come and under the illuminated "EXIT" sign just as several more cries rang out in the theatre behind them. She had to jog to keep up, hands damp with sweat as she gripped the gold railing and they dashed back into the foyer.

"Vic, what are you–"

She couldn't finish her sentence as she gasped for breath, clasping one hand over her chest to try and stop her breasts painfully bouncing up and down with the motion. Her dress was not designed for physical activity. He didn't answer her, just kept them focused on the path towards the red carpet which was now empty and being packed up by event organisers.

"STOP!" she ordered, tugging him hard enough that he was forced to halt altogether. She dragged him out of the way and to the side where a discarded drinks tray had been left in the corner.

"Stop," Tinsel repeated. "What are you doing? Where are we going right now?"

"I have to go back in there," he said, breathless. "Something has happened, whatever it is, and I have to go back in there."

"Then we should go together, to help."

She could already hear the growing swell of voices as people began to spill from the theatre, shouts and screams and cries punctuating every few seconds. She doubted whether the man who had been next to her thought it was a stunt anymore.

He shook his head with frustration. "No, you don't understand. There are *hundreds* of people in that theatre, Tinsel. They're already panicking, it's going to be chaos, and if I'm going to do my job then I'm not going to be able to keep an eye on you. I can't guarantee I can keep you safe."

She opened her mouth to protest, but Detective James shut it with a kiss. It came as a shock at first, the taste of his lips on hers as he pressed himself forwards. Tinsel took an unsteady step backwards, yanking him with her as her hands wrapped around his neck like it was instinct. She kissed him back, passionately, feeling the heat of his kiss and so much more as he pressed her hard up against the wall. His hands were all over her, fingers sliding over the curve of her hips as she gripped his collar, holding him tightly.

It wasn't until one of the foyer doors clattered open that they broke apart, Tinsel's chest heaving as she stayed firmly planted against the hard stone at her back. Detective James looked as shocked as she felt, his hands idly readjusting his satin bow tie from where she had partially pulled it loose.

"I…"

Tinsel went to speak, but truthfully, she didn't know what to say. Her mind and her gaze were still focused on his lips, which were now smeared with the colour of her lipstick.

"Do you trust me?" Detective James asked, voice hoarse.

"Yes," she replied, instantly. With a stiff nod, he grabbed her hand again and they resumed their path out of the theatre and on to Swantson Street outside. People were rushing behind them now and Tinsel did her best not to throw a look over her shoulder, wondering if anyone saw. It wasn't until they were at his car that she understood it was the destination, Detective James pressing his keys into her hand.

"Where is the safest place for you right now?" he asked, gaze intense.

"The station," Tinsel murmured, pivoting on the spot as she looked down the length of the street. She could see Flinders Street Station from here, the edge of the ACMI building just peering out from behind St Paul's Cathedral. Federation Square was *that* close, barely a five-minute walk.

"Malu is there," she continued. "It's secure and locked down at night. He can stay with me if I need him to."

"Good, take my car."

"It would be quicker to wal–"

"Drive there. Now, Tinsel. You can lock the doors, it will be safer, and don't leave until you hear from me. If this is nothing, then I'll come to you and this whole thing is an overreaction."

"And if not?"

"Then I want you far away from whatever just went down in there."

His hand slid over her collarbone and up her neck, cupping her jawline in a way that made her want to lean into it. The smear of her lipstick on his lips was even clearer in this light and she couldn't help herself. Tinsel wiped the pigment away, her fingers brushing against the soft cushions of his lips and trying not to think about how they felt against hers only minutes earlier. Detective James held her gaze and didn't let go.

"Keep your phone on you. I'll call you as soon as I can."

"Okay," she whispered, not wanting him to leave but knowing he had to. He looked reluctant as well, but he stepped away from her and began jogging back towards the theatre. He spun around at the last moment, calling back to her.

"Do you know how to share your location on your iPhone?"

"Yeah, of course."

"Share it with me, so I know precisely where you are at all times."

And with that, he was gone, sprinting into the crowd as people began pouring through the doors of The Capitol in sheer panic. He was the only person going against the flow of human traffic. Tinsel watched as the dark brown of his hair bobbed in and out of her line of sight before he finally disappeared through the golden doors of the theatre.

CHAPTER 12

Tinsel's heart was pounding as she fumbled with the keys. She dropped into the driver's seat, locking the car door immediately after she did so. The silence in the vehicle pressed down on her. As she pulled out of the loading zone and into the queue of noticeably lighter traffic on a side street, she wondered how much trouble you could get in if you crashed a police car that had been loaned to you. Just the thought of it made her coast ten kilometres below the speed limit, something that wasn't such a bad idea in the CBD anyway, as she crept towards the station.

She called Malu when she was close, telling him that she was unexpectedly driving in to work, and he told her to head for the executive carpark. It was underground and access was extremely limited, with the coveted spaces only for big bosses at the radio station and the museum next door.

Tinsel relied on her memory of having parked there on only a handful of occasions as she indicated off Flinders Street. She had to swipe her pass at a digital reader to get through a rolling security gate, swiping it again as she neared the entrance of the carpark where a tiny security hut and boom gate sat ominously.

Malu had already radioed ahead when she rolled up to the window. The evening guard checked her credentials then waved her through, telling her to park on level B2 – basement two – as that wasn't occupied until advertising execs arrived in the morning.

The carpark was eerie as she drove past endless empty spots, trying to position the vehicle as close to the elevator as she could so she wouldn't have to walk far. The concrete expanse was well lit, and Tinsel knew cameras were everywhere, but that didn't help her churning stomach as she stepped out of the vehicle. She raced for the lift and frantically pressed the button over and over again.

Watching the digital reader as her ride crept closer and closer, one floor at a time, Tinsel kept glancing over her shoulder nervously. But there was no one there: not even another car was parked on her level.

The doors pinged open, and she jumped slightly, shuffling inside and hammering on the buttons again until the doors closed. Only then did she feel safe, weirdly protected in the walls of the moving metal prism. She didn't truly breathe a sigh of relief until she was on the third floor, and made a beeline for the studio as she swiped herself in and checked her phone for any messages from Detective James. Nothing.

The red light was on, indicating Luiza was live, but that didn't stop Tinsel from slipping out of her heels and into the studio. She was quiet about it, gently shutting the door behind her, but unable to put off the comfort of seeing a friendly face for any longer. Luiza was finishing her back announcement and raised her eyebrows in a question as Tinsel paced towards the couch, her shoes grasped in her hand.

The second she was done, Luiza lifted the headphones off her ears and stepped out from behind the mic.

"Hey," she started. "You look like Jessica Rabbit's classy cousin from out of town."

"Thank you?" Tinsel replied, working through the description in her head to determine if that was a compliment.

"You also look positively frazzled."

Tinsel let out a shaky laugh, nodding in agreement as she all but collapsed on to the couch. "It has been… let's start with weird night, getting weirder."

"The premiere was always going to be weird."

Tinsel unloaded, the events of the past few hours flowing from her in a stream as her friend leaned against the control deck, open-mouthed and in shock. When she got to the end of her tale, Luiza spun around and picked up the landline.

"Malu, hey, it's Luiza. When you get a sec can you come up to the studio? Sweet, see you soon."

It was only a few minutes before the security guard was tapping at the glass, Luiza waving him through as she handed both Tinsel and him beers from the fridge. He was always nervous to step foot into the actual studio itself, like there was an invisible line he never wanted to cross.

"Tell him everything you told me," Luiza said.

"Why is this necessary?" Tinsel whined.

"Because the cop told you to come here so this building and Malu can keep you safe or whatever. Bring him up to speed."

Tinsel opened her mouth to speak, before Luiza stopped her.

"Wait, let me just get this piece of audio out of the way – then go."

Tinsel did as ordered, texting Detective James in the meantime and sharing her location with him in her phone settings. There was no immediate reply, which was truthfully what she had expected, but that didn't stop her from worrying as she glanced at the clock. *The Graveyard Shift* started in under an hour and the thought of hitting the airwaves that evening seemed absurd to her.

Luiza unplugged again, dashing over once the broadcast light switched from red to green and Tinsel recited what she had just told her friend. Naturally she left out the part about the kiss. She hadn't even started to unpack that yet.

"It's his ride you parked in the underground car park?" Malu asked.

"Yeah, it's technically a police car. I followed every instruction he gave. Got out of the car, jumped in the elevator, came straight up here."

"Any word from the cop?" Luiza questioned, arms folded over her chest.

"Nothing. Mind you, I should check Twitter. There'll probably be more details on social media than anywhere else right now about whether it was legit or a stunt."

"It would be a pretty sickening stunt," Luiza scoffed. "Especially after everything that has happened."

"I know," Tinsel agreed. Nobody voiced it, but they didn't have to. It was exactly because of what had happened that none of them thought the bloodied woman was likely to be a prank.

"You don't need to worry about anything," Malu assured her. "This whole building is inaccessible to anyone without a security pass, and you have to physically get by me to access the main entrance. Plus, I'll radio Fitz just to make sure he's on the lookout for anything weird and not just watching YouTube on the desktop."

"Thanks," she said, getting to her feet as he prepared to leave. "Detective James will be coming back at some point, and he doesn't have a security pass. I've got his keys, so if you see him knocking on the glass–"

"Let him in by the hairs of his chinny chin chin."

"Please? Cos I have to go on-air soon and I mightn't see it if he tries to call my phone or message me."

Luiza scoffed. "Wait, you're still doing the show?"

"What choice do I have? I'm here, I can't leave, I may as well do something to keep me busy rather than leave a bunch of dead air for all the new listeners we've suddenly accrued."

"Ghouls, Tinsel. These people are ghouls only listening to the show because they're fascinated by the fact somebody died while on it. The killer could be one of those new listeners, did you ever think about that?"

Tinsel blinked. She definitely had pondered it, but as the seconds ticked closer to airtime, she only became more certain that she should do it.

"How old are you?" she asked Luiza.

"What?"

"How old are you?"

"I'm forty-two, you know this."

"Right, and you started your first radio gig when you were seventeen at the local station in Coffs Harbour. You have been doing this for over twenty years, Luiza. You're powerful and have experience and can flex. If you left this station tomorrow, it wouldn't matter. You could go on to have a career anywhere else."

"What's your point?"

"This is my first proper gig at a major station. Sure, it's a crappy time slot, but before this I worked in community radio *for free* and no one wanted to hire me out of uni. I got lucky sliding into this gig, but if I don't do the show – a show that's suddenly rating for them – they can fire me and replace me within twenty-four hours, and no one would care."

"That's not true," Luiza murmured. Tinsel could hear the uncertainty in her tone.

"Okay, maybe a few hundred people would care. Max. The point is, if I don't do my job or do what they want, I'm replaceable. I need this gig and the contacts and the exposure it gives me. So, until I hear from Vic, and while I'm here twiddling my thumbs trying to find out what happened, yeah, I'm going on the air."

There was a heavy silence for several moments, an indie track playing over the studio speakers while the three of them stood there, Tinsel waiting for someone to object. When they didn't, she made a move to start setting up and logging in on the nearby screens.

"Alright then..." Malu said, clearly uncomfortable. "You're

on-air. That's a good thing because it means I'll know where you are. So will the detective–"

"So will the killer," Luiza muttered. "Or killers."

Tinsel threw up her hands with frustration. What exactly did her colleague want her to do? Luiza didn't offer a suggestion, but Malu told her to text or call him with anything. She promised she would.

The final half an hour before *The Graveyard Shift* was excruciating as Luiza finished up her show, all the while not talking to Tinsel. She wanted to say something to her as Luiza stormed from the studio, but truthfully Tinsel was peeved. Couldn't she understand the restrictive position Tinsel was stuck in? It seemed drastically unfair that she was copping it from someone she had expected to be supportive in that moment.

"Good evening, ghosts and poltergeist fiends," she said. "My name is Tinsel Munroe and welcome to *The Graveyard Shift* on 102.8 HitsFM. I'm here to keep you company throughout the night and into the small hours of the morning, so let's waste no time with our first track 'Black Hole' from one of my favourite bands, Charly Bliss."

Fading out her audio and raising the volume of the song, Tinsel's eyes switched back to the Twitter feed as she continued to search for information about what had happened at the *Band Candy* premiere.

Police Media had tweeted they were attending an incident at The Capitol and that the venue had been evacuated, but outside of that there was no official line. There were plenty of tweets from people saying a protestor had rushed the stage during the screening of the movie, but it seemed none of them were as close as Tinsel and Detective James had been. She clicked on a video a film critic she knew had posted, but the footage was only twenty-five seconds of people's backs as they rushed down the main stairs while a lady next to them let out a panicked shriek and a voice off camera asked if anyone knew what happened.

Standing there in her red-carpet dress and bare feet, Tinsel shivered in the cool air of the studio and wished she wasn't so uncomfortable. With a start, she realised that in her rush to get out of the car park and into the building proper, she had accidentally left her bag and change of clothes in the police car. Her skin crawled at the thought of how Ryan was going to react when he came in for the morning shift and saw her ensemble.

There was also the matter of the other items she so desperately wanted: a can of pepper spray and a switchblade. She'd been carrying the former with her ever since it had been so gently offered, but its protective capabilities were useless to her from the pocket of the bag it was zipped in downstairs. Her keys, too. She'd left them in her rush to get inside. The purse Tinsel had with her only contained a comb, compact, lipstick and building pass. Vital as they were, she admitted none were quite as handy as defensive weapons.

Glancing at the slate of music she had scheduled and the positioning of advertisements, Tinsel wondered if she could move things around to give herself enough time to get downstairs and back up. It wasn't unheard of for the studio to be left unattended for small amounts of time, especially during a slot like hers.

There was still no word from Detective James, so she sent him a text that was just a series of three question marks in a row. There was also a missed call from Zack on her screen and as much as she wanted to ignore it, annoyingly she couldn't. When he'd sent texts about their breakup, those she ignored. When he sent texts about moving out, she'd replied. It had become enough of a pattern that he was now only contacting her about the impending move. If he'd called her, it was likely about that, and she had to be a big girl.

Please tell me you've moved out early and left your key, she thought, listening to the phone ring. *I could do with some good news tonight.* His number rang out and she peeked at the clock, knowing he'd likely still be at work. Dialling the tattoo parlour's number from memory, she felt something like relief uncoil in her chest when Fredrico, the apprentice, answered.

"Yo, Wallace and Marshall Tattoos, what's up?"

"Nancy would kill you if she heard you answer the phone like that," Tinsel smiled.

"Tinny!" he replied, recognising her voice immediately. "She ain't here right now so if you don't tell her, I won't."

"Your phone manner is safe with me," she promised. "I know he's probably with a client, but could you put Zack on for a second?"

"Nah, he ain't here either: left a few hours ago. But hey, how are you calling me right now? We've got your show playing in the shop."

"During songs no one knows what I'm up to," Tinsel told him, mildly annoyed as she opened Instagram to see if Zack had updated his stories. There was nothing.

"You'll probably see him before I do, so I don't need to take a message?"

"No, Freddy, you're good."

"Kay, but hey – while you're here. Can I make a request? Can you play 'Scary' by Meg Thee Stallion?"

"Sure," she sighed. "Mainly just because I'm impressed you know that song."

"You're the best. Bye, Tinny."

"Later."

She hung up, trying to smother the rising anxiety she felt in her stomach as she tapped a rhythm against the control deck. Sliding her fingers under the halter strap of her dress, she pulled at it with discomfort. *Fuck it*, she thought, the lure of her favourite overalls and a baggy sweater downstairs in a parked car full of weapons too much to resist.

Working quickly, she started messing around with the order of the show as she dragged tracks forward and repositioned ads. This would give her fifteen minutes to get down there and back up. Realistically she only needed five and she could get changed in the studio itself since no one was around. Fifteen minutes was being cautious.

"That was 'Which Witch' by Florence + The Machine, a bonus track off her 2015 album *How Big, How Blue, How Beautiful*," Tinsel said into the microphone. "Thanks to @ATribeCalled_ Stressed on Twitter who said 'damn, I forgot how much I loved this track – no one can do a climatic chant mid-song like Flo.' Gotta say, I definitely agree with you there. If you stay tuned, you might hear another track from our favourite red-headed songstress coming up."

Her phone buzzed and it took all of Tinsel's self-control not to glance at it immediately, telling herself she needed to finish her spiel first.

"Before that, we had a cover of Screaming Jay Hawkins' classic 'I Put A Spell On You' by the impeccable Mo'Ju. For those of you wondering what the answer was to the question I put out on *The Graveyard Shift*'s Insta stories earlier tonight – what is one of the most covered songs in music history? – welp, there's your answer."

Tinsel slipped her uncomfortable heels back on as she couldn't face the cold, dirty concrete of the carpark in bare feet, and she had to resist the urge to audibly groan as she was still on air.

"Up next, we have a special request from Fredrico and the team at Wallace and Marshall tattoos who are working hard through the night: Megan Thee Stallion and Rico Nasty's 'Scary' is for you."

She waited until the song's drums kicked in before she felt safe to take off the headphones and quickly retweet one last message on social media so *The Graveyard Shift* looked active. Snatching her pass and Detective James' keys, Tinsel looked at her phone as she set a swift pace from the studio.

It was Detective James, finally, telling her that he was on his way to the radio station. She dialled his number as she hit the elevator button, waiting for the lift to arrive.

"Hey," he said, answering on the first ring. "Aren't you on-air right now?"

"Well helloooo to you too," Tinsel huffed, although she was relieved just to hear his voice.

"I didn't mean it like that, I–"

"It's okay, I'm just teasing," she said, hopping inside once the metal doors pinged open. "Technically I am on the radio, but I've got songs scheduled so I have a window."

"A window to do what? You're not leaving the station?"

"No, no. I'm fine. Just left my stuff in your car. What happened to the woman, the blood?"

"It's not good. Diraani's down there now."

"Shit," she breathed, knowing what that meant.

"The scene is… leave… b-but it's… stagehand–"

"Hello?" Tinsel asked, holding the phone away from her ear as the lift doors dinged open and she stepped into the carpark. "You're breaking up I can't…"

"– witnesses and the – we… crime…"

"Hello? Vic? *Vic*?" She cast a look overhead, fully aware of how many levels of concrete she was under as she marched towards his car.

"Idiot," Tinsel whispered to herself as the call cut out, shaking her head. There was no way she would get reception down here. The sound of her heels echoing across the concrete was her only company. She was alone. With the phone in one hand and car keys in the other, she clicked the small button that would unlock the doors and reached for the back handle after she heard the electronic beep.

Her finger had barely connected with the cool metal when her feet were yanked out from under her. Tinsel heard her own surprised yelp as she flew through the air. She landed on the ground with a hard thud, her head connecting with the concrete. White sparks burst in front of her eyes and the shock of it covered the pain spreading through her skull at first. In the back of her mind, she heard sounds: scraping, scuffed footsteps, and something shuffling. Laying on her side, she pulled her hand back from her head and registered a reddish-brown substance that stuck to her fingers.

"Ergh," she moaned, rolling over as she attempted to sit up and failed. The harsh fluorescent lights fitted into the ceiling made her squint, but Tinsel could clearly see the dark figure that stood over her. With a jolt, her mind jumped back to a few seconds earlier and what she had felt: the sensation of gloved fingertips wrapping around her ankle. Her eyes widened and with the sharpest movement she could manage, she kicked her leg until it collided with the groin of the person in front of her. They let out a pained groan and she kicked again, this time harder as the heel of her stiletto did its job and the figure hunched over entirely.

Flipping on to her stomach, she reached for her phone which was laying nearby as she pushed herself upwards and to her feet. Her screen was smashed, but the device was still functioning as she shoved it between her boobs. Tinsel thought she had a clear route and prepared to sprint away as quickly as she could, before her legs were tugged out from underneath her again. She fell painfully to her knees, taking the brunt of another fall.

Not bothering to look back, she kicked once more but screamed as something sharp slashed across her calf. One hand released her and gripped the rim of her shoe. Tinsel shook her foot loose, the assailant left with nothing but her heel as she took off in earnest, limping in the opposite direction of the vehicle.

Unfortunately, that was deeper into the car park. She utilised the downward slope to gain speed as she tried again to sprint away. The tightness of her dress restricted her movements, and she tore at it as she moved, her fear propelling her strength as it shredded from her knee upwards.

A weird clopping noise seemed to be following her, and Tinsel realised moments later that she was the source. She only had one shoe on now. Risking precious seconds as she grabbed the remaining shoe off her foot, she glanced behind her. She was already down on to the next level of the car park and her breath froze in her throat as she made out the figure of someone dressed in black with an oversized hood calmly walking towards her. She glimpsed them for only a moment before the lights cut out, the entire multi-levelled car park suddenly submerged into darkness.

Tinsel couldn't see anything at all, the black was so suffocating. But she could hear her own breathing and the footsteps of someone moving closer and closer in her direction. She hated the panicked squeak that escaped her lips as she took off again, angry at the fact her attacker was somewhere in the darkness that blocked her exit to the higher levels and – eventually – the street. She had no choice but to run further, deeper, trying to ignore the pain in her leg that she was sure belonged to a knife wound.

Tinsel had no idea whether she was dizzy or not, because there was nothing for her eyes to focus on as she tried to put as much distance between herself and whoever had been hiding under Detective James' car, waiting for her.

A yellow light broke through the dark and she almost sprinted for it, realising at the last minute that the circular shape belonged to the electronic display of the elevators. There was one on each level, along with a glowing red logo that was supposed to look like a set of stairs. That was the fire exit, which all employees were told to use in the event of a blaze in the building.

Taking a huge gulp of air, Tinsel came to a sudden stop as she dropped down low and shuffled as quietly as she could along the width of the space. Eventually she came into contact with the cold, hard surface of the car park wall and she pressed her back against it. It was a strange thing to take comfort in, but knowing it was there gave her some certainty: the person hunting her wasn't *behind* her at least.

She tried not to let fear overwhelm her, to not revel in the thought that what was happening to her right then wasn't like the alleyway, or even the weird messages in her inbox. This wasn't open for interpretation. This was her worst fear becoming a reality.

It seemed like she was going to suffocate as she tried to quiet her breathing, her chest aching with the desire to take huge, gulping breaths but her terror being the more dominant instinct. She needed to be able to hear the footsteps as they moved past her and further into the car park, not yet registering the absence of hers as they proceeded to the lower level. Tinsel let herself inhale, her eyes growing sharper as they adjusted to the low light around her.

It didn't help much. Still, she could barely discern anything in the thick shadows. Her eyes darted to the elevator, the sound the doors made as they pinged open echoing in her mind. It would be too loud, it would draw whoever was there to her before the doors would shut again. Just the thought of being trapped inside that metal prism had the sweat on her body dripping fast as it streaked down her neck and into her cleavage. *Is it even sweat?* she thought. *Or blood?* Because she certainly knew she was bleeding from more than one source.

She was giddy and in pain, worried about whether she could make it up the incline of the car park to freedom before the person caught her. Her eyes focused in on one of the only other things she could clearly see: the tiny logo that led to the fire exit. The morsel of hope she let herself entertain was enough to distract her until Tinsel realised her attacker's footsteps had stopped too. They weren't pursuing her anymore, they were quiet, moving around silently in the dark just as she had.

She strained her ears to listen harder and barely – just *barely* – she heard a gentle shuffle. It was closer than she would like, back on her level. Just outside of the pool of light from the elevator's digital display, she could make out something solid in the shadows. They were waiting there for her, she figured, assuming that she was too hurt or too desperate to make a run for it again and would attempt to ride the elevator back to the ground level.

In her fear, Tinsel forgot she still had her phone. The glass of the cracked screen scratched against her skin as she retrieved it from her cleavage. Her first impulse was to call for help, but there was no reception. Using the flashlight was out, as that would immediately give away her location. The beginning of an idea sparked in her mind. Summoning all her courage, she turned her back to where she knew the killer was. Tinsel used her body frame to block any incidental light as she immediately lowered the brightness and pressed a series of buttons.

Wincing as she got to her feet, she switched the volume dial all the way up and she inched away from her phone, step by step. It felt like a mistake, leaving it on the ground behind her, but she was out of options. Painfully, careful to take a wide berth around the poised figure as they waited for her, Tinsel moved in increments closer and closer to the fire exit. She didn't like that she had decreased the distance between her and the attacker, but there was a sliver of relief as her fingers closed on the handle of the stairwell door.

All she had to do was wait, the minutes seeming like hours as she braced herself.

Suddenly, a sound cut through the heavy silence of the underground car park as her alarm tone went off on her phone. The noise was so shrill it made her jump, even though she knew it was coming. The attacker was quick, pivoting on the spot and sprinting towards the source of the sound immediately. It took every bit of bravery she had to stand still and wait as they moved further away, giving her every extra metre she would need to have a head start.

When she saw the light of her phone flicker, meaning a body was close enough to it, Tinsel yanked the handle and threw open the door.

She didn't know if she would be strong enough to use her

weight to block the person on the other side from coming through – she hadn't gotten that clear a look at them. Besides, her flight instinct had suddenly become much stronger than her fight one and she threw herself up the stairs, feet slapping on the rough floor. Tinsel used her upper body as well, her forearms pulling her up the railing and keeping her steady.

Lights flickered on around her, activated by her motion, and she guessed she was halfway up the second flight of stairs when the door below flung back open and the killer sprinted after her. And they did sprint, they weren't calmly pursuing her now.

There was a desperation in their pursuit that told her they couldn't let Tinsel escape.

A huge numeral two was painted on the wall in green paint, meaning she was on the same level she had parked Detective James' car and climbing higher. Panting, each breath felt like a needle as the thought of making it back brought a raspy sob to her lips. She continued to the next floor, conscious of the heavy grunts behind her.

Finally, there were only four steps left, then three, then two and then none as she reached for the door handle that would take her out into the main foyer of the 102.8 HitsFM building. It flung open and she screamed, nearly falling backwards as she dodged to avoid being hit in the face.

Malu was there, just as shocked to see her as she was to see him.

"Tin–" he started to say, before Tinsel regained her footing and streaked forwards, pushing him back and out of the doorway. Except he didn't move the way she wanted him to. He shifted to the side instead so that he slipped out of her grip and she slid on to the ground.

Malu's confused expression turned back towards the noise racketing up the stairs and she screamed at him.

"SHUT THE DOOR!"

He was caught between listening to her and staying focused

on the third person, but Tinsel saw his body move as he started to follow through on her command. He didn't react fast enough though. A silver flash registered in her line of sight just before it sunk into Malu's chest. The huge man let out a pained grunt as the gesture was repeated twice more.

Tinsel's fear was replaced with rage as she screamed, stumbling to her feet as she lurched towards the danger, tugging on Malu's wrist to pull him towards her. She tried to slow his fall as he slumped to the ground, Tinsel covering the wounds with her shaking hand while the other protected the back of his head.

"G-gg a–"

He couldn't get the words out. Tinsel shushed him as she urged Malu to save his breath. His eyes were fixed on whatever was behind her and she spun, watching with horror as the killer wiped the blood of her friend from the knife and on to the fabric of their leg. They were barely more than a metre away from Tinsel, but she had no fight left in her. She wouldn't leave Malu.

She tried to look into their eyes, but she was unable to make them out. They sat behind a layer of netting and deep within the exaggerated hood that arched out from the shoulders.

They raised the knife towards her.

BANG!

Plaster flew from a spot on the wall above. It rained down like industrial dandruff.

BANG!

A second eruption of sound sent the perpetratorperpetuator jerking backwards and through the doorway of the staircase. She watched the edge of their shoes as they fell, hearing their body make contact with the stairs during a descent.

It took Tinsel another few seconds to understand that the bangs were gunshots. Detective James ran forward – weapon extended – from behind her. With one hand still on his gun, he used his other to grip her shoulder.

"Are you okay?" he asked her. "Are you hurt?"

He wasn't looking at her, his eyes remained fixed on the now empty doorway instead. She could barely hear him through the ringing in her ears.

"I'm fine, go!" she urged. "Go!"

Detective James spared a look at her then, a question in his eyes to see if she really meant it. She did and he nodded.

"Keep pressure on the wound," he ordered, pulling out his radio as he stepped into the stairwell. She could hear him repeating commands calmly, calling for multiple ambulances and back-up as he descended the stairs.

"Shots fired," he said, repeating it several more times. Somewhere she recognised the sound of the door slamming shut and the echo as it happened again a few seconds later, but Tinsel diverted all her attention back to Malu as she tried to stem the blood flow.

She had never seen so much blood, but she urged him to stay awake, to keep his eyes fixed on her as she spoke to him about what the weather was going to be like tomorrow. She could hear the sirens close by, getting closer, lots of them, and she urged them to move faster.

The door flung back open and in an instant, Detective James was at her side, gently shoving her out of the way as he took over Malu's emergency care.

"What happened?" she asked. "Did you get him?"

"I clipped him," he replied, brow furrowed as he applied pressure. "I followed the trail of blood as far as I could, but it was too dark down there. I didn't want to risk leaving you in case he looped around before back-up got here."

There was banging on the glass and Tinsel glanced up to see the faces of several police officers and an ambulance crew.

"Go let them in," he told her. "I've got this."

It wasn't until she attempted to get to her feet, and failed, that she felt his hands on her as he carefully helped her back to the floor.

"I'm sorry," he whispered, "I'm so sorry, I didn't realise how hurt…"

His hands cupped her jaw, the blood of Malu's mixing with her own as it ran down her neck.

"I'll go, stay with him."

She nodded, unable to do much more as her hands moved back over the chest of her friend and her eyes watched Detective James as he sprinted to get help.

CHAPTER 13

Tinsel was pretending to be asleep. She knew that as soon as she was awake, people would temper the things they said to her. So it was easier to keep her eyes closed and listen. She learned more that way.

She had been brought into Royal Melbourne Hospital hours ago, refusing to leave Malu, so they both rode in the same ambulance together. They had to be separated eventually; it killed her when the nurses pried Tinsel's hand from his strong grip as they arrived at the emergency department.

He was in a critical condition but still alive, so she counted that as a small victory. Her injuries had only been superficial, yet not for lack of trying. There was a wound at the back of her head that required ten stitches and her left wrist had a minor stress fracture from when she fell, however, it wasn't bad enough that she would need a cast. A doctor had set it for her in a brace and after a few weeks of taking it easy, they could reassess and remove it.

There were a handful of other cuts and abrasions – her slashed calf requiring only butterfly stitches, which was a relief. Yet it only took one look at Malu's dried blood coating the fabric of Tinsel's dress for her to understand how lucky she was. Two nurses had gently cut her out of it, the remnants of the gown lying crumpled on the floor for less than a minute before the gloved hand of a police officer slipped under the curtain to extract it. It was needed for evidence, she heard someone say, unable to see through the white material that had been drawn for her modesty.

After being given a hospital gown and a towel, she was led to a small cubicle where she showered and used the soap from the dispenser to wash away the grime and dirt of the car park as well as some of the blood. It stung, a lot, but the pain was dull thanks to the Entonox gas she had been given in the ambulance. The emergency worker assigned to her had sensed she might be on the verge of a panic attack and handed her the mask. She had sucked down several breaths without question.

It kept her calmer than she would have been, limping through a hospital packed with police and staff members in the tissue thin frock they had given her. Even her underpants and bra had been taken. Tinsel kept crossing her arms over her chest subconsciously. She was whisked away to be examined properly, poked, prodded, stitched and finally told to rest.

An officer was sent to take her official statement and she had hoped it would be Detective James, as the last time she had seen him was leaving the radio station. Instead, it was a detective she didn't know, with the woman telling her Diraani and James were both still at the scene.

She was also told that Rushelle and senior management at 102.8 HitsFM had been contacted, which meant she would probably hear from them soon... somehow. Her phone was Lord-knows-where and a nurse had loaned Tinsel hers, with both of her calls to Pandora going straight through to voicemail. Her sister kept her phone on airplane mode overnight, so she knew Pandora would get the message as soon as whichever kid woke first. She briefly thought about calling her parents, but she knew how much they would panic. She was physically fine, after all, so she would wait until Pandora was with her and they could call together. Her older sister had always been better than Tinsel at calming them down.

She was going to be discharged the next day, there was

no reason for them to keep her more than one night. In the meantime, she was stuck at the hospital where she was safe and any potential concussion she might have could be monitored. She was going to be moved to a private room for "security reasons" eventually, but until then the curtain around her bed was drawn and an officer was stationed on the other side, keeping watch while she slept.

Or tried to. Every forty-five minutes or so a nurse came, stirred her, and asked the same set of silly questions: name, age, date, number of fingers etc. So Tinsel wasn't sleeping. Instead, she was listening.

It had been an oddly quiet night in the emergency ward until she and Malu were rolled in, so about a dozen beds around her were all empty. There was an elderly patient at the far side of the ward, but it meant her section was sparse, save for the occasional nurse and the cops. She was grateful that whoever was guarding her was popular because other officers would join him on their break, discussing what had happened that night and what was unfolding at the scenes.

Scenes, plural. From her eavesdropping she learned that The Capitol was being treated as the primary location and the 102.8 HitsFM office as the secondary one. The woman who ran out on to the stage, covered in blood, was being treated at the same hospital for shock.

"She found one of the stagehands hanging backstage," a police officer said, her voice low as she urgently shared the information with her colleagues.

"So, it could have been suicide?" a man questioned.

"People don't commit suicide like that," she answered. "Throat slit, entrails dangling from the kid's stomach on to the floor."

"*Jesus.*"

"She tried to pull him down apparently, thought he might still be alive, which is how she ended up covered in so much blood."

"Who was the vic?"

"Can't remember the name, but he was young. Like, maybe eighteen or nineteen? He was interning as a lighting tech or something."

Unfortunately, the woman had left shortly after, taking with her the information Tinsel was desperate to know. But someone had stayed with the male officer, the pair chatted casually back and forth about what they had heard. She felt like her heart stopped when one of them mentioned "the dead security guard" and she was disgusted with herself when she felt relief at learning it was Fitz, the older man who had let her into the car park that night. He can't have been killed long after Malu had contacted him on the radio, she figured.

A horrifying thought crossed her mind. What if the killer had been the one who radioed back?

The only other thing she could piece together was that Malu was in surgery and his family had been contacted. Tinsel didn't believe in God, but she prayed to whatever divine being would listen and begged for him to survive.

Eventually, she must have dozed, if only for a little while, because the next thing she knew she was waking to the sensation of hair being swept off her face.

The lights in the ward were still down low, encouraging everyone present to attempt slumber. Yet there was just enough glow from the machines beeping next to her that she could see Detective James' face illuminated by a neon blue.

He looked how she felt – deep bags under his eyes and a weariness etched into the lines of his face that illustrated his exhaustion. With a hand resting on the pillow beside her head but his body positioned further away, he looked torn between staying or going. So Tinsel made the decision for him and reached for his hand, gripping it with her own.

"Don't leave," she croaked, pulling herself upright until she was closer to a sitting position.

"I didn't want to wake you."

"You weren't, you were saving me from nightmares."

The smile that crossed his face was fleeting, the both of them knowing how true that comment was. He ducked behind the curtain for a moment, returning with the chair the officer who had been sitting guard had occupied for the past few hours.

"He finished his shift," Detective James explained. "They're sending someone else down, but in the meantime I volunteered."

Tinsel didn't want to imagine how she looked, her face stripped bare thanks to the make-up wipes a nurse had given her. She had no idea what her hair looked like, and she still felt self-conscious in the hospital gown. There was a thick blanket that prickled against her skin as she moved, but she kept it tucked under her armpits as an extra layer of protection. He was fidgeting with the dials above her head, muttering as he did so.

"The doctor said you might be sensitive to light with a mild concussion, but there's usually a lamp – ah, there it is."

"I don't know if the light is going to do me any kindness," she said.

"Me either," he replied, running his hands through his hair. It had been slicked back at the start of the evening, but whatever gel had been holding it in place was gone as it fell in front of his vision in stringy clusters. "I thought your sister would be here by now."

"What time is it?"

"Just past five."

"She'll be here soon. In fact, she has your business card on her office wall and the minute she hears my voicemail, she'll be calling you."

"I saw your phone in an evidence bag. It looks pretty smashed up, but I'm hoping we might get lucky."

"Lucky? How so?"

"Pull a print off the screen, even just a partial."

"Have you heard anything about Malu?"

"He's out of surgery. They'll keep him in an induced coma for a day or so before easing him out of it gradually, that way his body won't succumb to shock."

"But he'll be okay?"

"Yeah, he got lucky. So did you."

She let out a giggle that didn't feel quite right, but she was unable to help herself. "*Lucky.* I don't feel lucky, but given two people are dead tonight when it could have been four..."

"Here," Detective James said, handing her a bottle of water and a sandwich wrapped in a plastic.

"I don't remember the last time I ate," she murmured.

"I figured. It's tuna cucumber out of the vending machine, but it's better than hospital jello."

She took a cautious first nibble, willing herself to swallow a mouthful. "Is it though?'

They were silent for a time, the sound of her bites and the occasional beep from a machine the only noises. Eventually she looked over at Detective James, who had his eyes shut and his hands pressed to the bridge of his nose as if he was in deep concentration. His eyelids fluttered open, and he caught her staring at him, Tinsel not bothering to pretend she hadn't been.

"What is it?" he asked, his voice soft as he leaned forward. Concern was etched into the frown of his expression.

"I want to know."

"Know what?"

"Not what you're supposed to tell me, but what's really going on. I want to know all of it."

He sighed, as if he knew that request was coming, and he was powerless to fight it. Getting to his feet, he took a peek around the corner of the curtain that shielded her bed from view. Satisfied with what he saw, he was just about to sit back down when his mobile rang. Detective James frowned, clearly not recognising the number.

"Does it end in zero-thirty-three?" Tinsel asked.

"Yeah."

"That will be Pandora."

Sure enough, Detective James had barely hit the answer button before Tinsel recognised the shrill sound of her older sister's voice.

"Yes, I'm here with her right now. She's got some stitches and she's shaken up but... you know, she can speak for herself."

He offered his phone to Tinsel and she took it, Pandora already speaking down the line as if she had been there the whole time.

"– never putting my phone on airplane mode again! What if the kids had slept in? I would have never got your message."

"Pandora."

"I'm driving to the hospital while on the phone right now, that cop's not gonna fine me, is he?"

"No," Tinsel chuckled. "I'll make sure Vic gives me his word."

He raised an eyebrow at her with surprise, Tinsel smirking at the faint trace of alarm she saw there.

"Did you call Mum and Dad? Because if you haven't, then you should wait until–"

"I don't have a phone, sis. I said that in the message. It was left in the office car park and taken for evidence. And no, I'm not an idiot. I was hoping you would speak to Mum and Dad because I'm too exhausted. You can orphan whisperer them or something."

"*Horse Whisperer*. The movie was called *The Horse Whisperer*. How many times do I have to tell you?"

"Whatever. Just get here, okay? With fresh clothes. I have no underwear and only a hospital gown."

"Ugh, I hate to suggest this but..."

"What?"

"Zack is technically closer to you than I am. He could get there quicker, leave some stuff from your place in reception *and* he's desperate to get back in your good graces. Exploit it."

"I, uh, can't find him," she said, conscious of the fact

Detective James was right there and she felt super awkward speaking about her ex in front of him, no matter how D.O.A that relationship was.

"What do you m–"

"I called his cell, he didn't pick up. I called the shop, they said he finished his shift, and without my phone I don't know any other numbers by heart."

"Put the hot cop on."

"What?"

"Put him on the phone, you heard me."

Tinsel blinked as she handed the device back to Detective James. "She wants to speak to you."

He mirrored her shock, listening silently for several moments. Tinsel could hear her sister's voice, but she couldn't make out the words clearly. She found herself leaning forward, desperate to hear what was being said.

"Okay, thanks, I'll look into it," Detective James said. "See you soon."

He hung up the phone, looking at her thoughtfully for a long beat.

"What did she say?" Tinsel asked, doing her best not to squirm under his scrutiny.

"She said I should ask you about your ex-boyfriend and why you couldn't get hold of him tonight."

"Oh," she gulped. Her sister could have no idea how awkward that conversation was going to be after the events of this evening.

"And that you two had been fighting a lot lately."

"Mmmm," Tinsel replied. "We broke up."

"Your choice or his? Mutual?"

"Mine."

"And he responded to that…"

"Not great, honestly."

He frowned. "It's Zack, right?"

"Zack Tykken, yeah. And there's not much to say. I had a

missed call from him and honestly, I usually duck them. But he's moving out this week, so I thought it might be something about that. When I got no answer, I called his work, and he wasn't there."

"He works at Wallace and Marshall, correct?"

"Correct."

"And you expected him to be there when you called?"

"They're open late most nights, but especially on a Thursday. Until midnight, at least. Zack usually works that shift so I assumed I'd be able to get him on the office phone."

"And he wasn't there?"

"No, the apprentice said he'd left a few hours ago."

"What time was that?"

"Uh…" she thought back, trying to jog her memory through the haze of pain killers, trauma and lack of sleep. "It couldn't have been much after eleven, if not close to it."

She realised Detective James was making notes in that small notepad he loved, and she watched him with frustration.

"This is what Pandora told you to ask me about?"

"She said you'd get angry at her if she began asking questions, so she thought I should."

"Questions about Zack."

"That's right."

"Why wo… oh, for God's sake. She doesn't like him, okay? They have never liked each other. And she's sensitive about the subject because she didn't realise how bad the–"

Tinsel cut herself off, feeling that familiar shame creep in.

"How bad what was?" Detective James pushed, lowering the notepad.

When she didn't answer, he leaned closer so there was no escaping his gaze.

"The relationship, okay?" she snapped. "It was a bad relationship, and I should have left three months in, instead of three years."

"Bad how?"

"Fuck off, is this necessary?"

Detective James blinked before replying gently but firmly. "Yes. If he physically hurt you–"

"Never," she said, surprised by the steel she thought she'd heard in his tone. "Not once."

She could feel his dark eyes moving over her, as if scanning for a weakness or even the truth.

"But in other ways," Detective James said. No question. Just a statement of truth. He'd read it in her expression.

She watched him. Tinsel could tell there was something else going on behind the officer's eyes, but she didn't have his ability to interpret it. Slowly, she nodded.

"He was a man of big gestures, but every grand act was designed to make me feel guilty about something," she said, annoyed as she felt a sting at the corner of her eyes.

"*Gaslighter*," Detective James hummed. It was an act so surprising, she let out a laugh.

"You remembered?"

"Firstly, I love The Chicks new stuff contrary to popular opinion. Secondly, the night I drove you to your sister's, you and Zack had a falling out."

"Initiate break-up protocol," she mumbled. He handed her something and she looked down, shocked to see that he had conjured a tissue out of thin air. Even more shocking was the fact a few quick, angry tears were streaking down her cheeks.

"Ugh," Tinsel groaned, quickly dabbing. "Of all the dumb things... I'm not even upset about the stupid split, on God. I don't know why I'm crying."

"Yes, what else could possibly be going on?"

He was teasing her, but his face was soft. Kind. He went to take the tissue from her and paused, catching one last errant tear with his thumb.

Suddenly her mind was back there, on the kiss, as Detective James' fingers had gently pressed against her throat as he held her. Tinsel recalled her own desperation as she kissed him back, arching her body so that it fit better with his. She swallowed, trying to disperse the lingering sensation of arousal and replace it with guilt.

"Stop looking at me," she said, her eyes cast downwards as she picked at a spot on her blanket.

"Where would you like me to look?"

"You know what I mean," she sighed.

"Forget about that, forget about–"

"The kiss?"

"Yes," he answered quickly, looking immediately annoyed at himself. "No, but… listen, when your sister gets here, go home with her. Stay at her place again."

"I just–"

"Please, don't fight me on this."

"What am I fighting you 'on' exactly?"

"You know what Pandora said to me? Nearly half of all murdered women are killed by their romantic partners."

"Vic I am *not* a battered woman. You think I would stick around if Zack had ever laid a hand on me?"

"It's not weakness to stay, and the women who do aren't weak," he remarked. "And I'm not implying anything. I'm simply asking you to stay at Pandora's house until I can verify his alibis."

"Multiple alibis? For what?"

"The night of Mera Brant's murder," Detective James started, listing off the occasions on his fingers. "The night someone chased you–"

"He has a *key* for fuck's sake, why would he need to pursue me outside? And what happened to being so sure Diraani was infallible with the teen he picked up?"

He pressed on without pausing. "Friday evening at the NFSA. Last night when someone was killed at the premiere and later that same evening, when there was a murder and two attempted murders at your office building. You said it yourself: he was supposed to be at work, and he wasn't there.

He hasn't answered his phone. So where was he, Tinsel? Where is he?"

She opened her mouth to reply but couldn't quite formulate the words. After a long moment, she made sure her voice was steady as she spoke up.

"There's no denying Zack and I had problems, obviously. But that doesn't mean he's a serial killer."

"Actually," came a familiar voice as the curtain around her bedside was whipped back. "Technically he'd be a spree killer, not a serial."

"Pandora," Tinsel breathed, her emotions spilling over again as her sister embraced her in a hug. Her sibling knew her well enough that she paused before she pulled back, wiping away the tears from her cheek in a distinctly motherly gesture.

"You don't look as bad as I thought you would," Pandora smiled, tossing her a blue coat. "But throw this on will you, you're high-beaming."

"Oh my God," Tinsel groaned, her embarrassment making her move quickly as she wiggled into the garment. Her sister was chuckling with amusement as she perched herself on the end of the bed.

"And he's right," Pandora pressed. "This whole thing feels too personal, hun. I don't think this is some random sicko anymore, do you?"

"Honestly, I haven't spared a lot of thought on the matter."

"You should, because whoever is doing this has clearly been thinking about you." She turned to face the detective, arms on her hips. "Have you been working through that list Tinsel gave you? Of the creepy dudes who would send dick pics and jerk off to the show?"

"Slowly," he replied. "It's rapidly becoming more of a priority."

"I'll say. And if she's staying at my house, what's to say the killer won't find out where that is and strike there?"

"You're a lot more off the radar than Tinsel is."

"Barely," she snorted. "Just because I don't live on top of a landmark pub, that doesn't mean I'm cocooned."

"Agreed. That's why I have a car already assigned to your address. So, if you see a blue Mitsubishi parked out the front, that's who it is."

"One officer?"

"Two," he said, handing her a piece of paper. "And this is the license plate. They'll likely come and introduce themselves at some point, but they're happy to stay in the car if you're uncomfortable with officers inside the home."

"Fuck no," Pandora exclaimed. "I have kids and a husband who I love but would never be able to hurt another human being in a physical altercation. I'll make them cups of tea on the house if that's required."

"Wait," Tinsel said, holding up her hand to slow their mutual planning. "You said spree. Isn't this officially a serial killer now? Multiple victims?"

"No, she's right," Detective James replied, earning a smug smile from Pandora. "A serial killer has to murder three or more victims and our perp has only just gotten there. But usually there's a cooling off period of months or even years between murders. Mera Brant's death might have been meticulously planned, but last night proved the person we're looking for is reactionary."

Tinsel swivelled her head towards her sister, knowing a more detailed explanation was coming. "A spree killer doesn't have to be limited to one location, it can be many, but the cooling off period is practically non-existent. Like this guy – *or girl* – who has three notches on their belt within the space of a week."

"Four," Detective James corrected. "There was a guy in Georgia in the US, Mark Barton, who went on a rampage and over the course of three days killed his wife, children, and staff members at the offices of two former employers before taking his own life. He murdered twelve people all up, thirteen if you include him in the body count."

"The Gainesville Ripper is another one," Pandora added. "I guess you can be both a spree and serial killer, the lines are blurry."

"The person we're likely looking for is both," Detective James noted. "Serial killers usually select their victims carefully. That might fit for Mera and it might fit for you, but the kid who was killed at The Capitol seems more opportunistic than anything."

"And the security guards, Fitz and Malu," Tinsel whispered. "They were in the way, a means to an end."

"Right," he agreed. "Do you have things you need to get from your home address?"

Tinsel wasn't listening to him, she was thinking about all of the killers and all of the crimes he and her sister had just named between them. And the "accidental death" that was looking less and less like an accident after all. The idea that Zack could be responsible for any of them horrified her. They were wrong, they had to be wrong. Otherwise, what did that say about her? That she could be with someone for so long, completely unaware of what was bubbling under the surface?

"Tinsel?"

She felt Vic's hand gently touch her own and she shook her head, trying to liberate herself from the dark thoughts.

"Huh?"

"Do you have things you need at your house?"

"Oh, yeah, I need more clothes and toiletries. My backup laptop. And my bag of stuff is still in your car."

"As soon as the vehicle is processed, I'll get your bag back. It's likely you'll be discharged after morning rounds at eight, so I'll accompany you both over to the house then."

He got to his feet, his movements looking stiff after what she assumed was a full day and night of being awake, alert, and alarmed.

"What if Zack's there?" Pandora asked.

"He won't be," Detective James replied. "I've got two hours to locate him. It shouldn't take me more than forty-five minutes, at most."

With that, he left, leaving the two women sitting together under the gloomy lamp light projected from above Tinsel's hospital bed. She opened her mouth to say something, but Pandora held up a hand to stop her.

"First, we call Mum and Dad ASA-freakin-P."

She couldn't argue with that command.

"Second, we break down whatever that is."

"Whatever what is?" she asked, grateful to finally get a word in.

"I saw how he delicately touched your hand just now. Plus, the guy shot someone to save your life!"

"And Malu's, technically."

"Technically," she scoffed. "I heard he's doing okay, that he'll make it?"

"That's what I was told. Apparently a centimetre to the left and he would have bled out before anyone could get to him."

"That could have been you," Pandora breathed. "That could have been…"

Her voice broke and Tinsel watched as her sister attempted to compose herself. She may put on a brave face and quip with the best of them, but the events of the past week had taken a toll on her sibling as well. Pandora and Tinsel were close, closer even than most biological siblings despite the fact they didn't share DNA. As her sister wiped her face and tugged at the plait that hung over her shoulder, Tinsel felt a pang of warmth in her chest for the woman she loved more than any other human being on the planet.

"Alright, shit, pull it together," Pandora breathed. "I'm dialling. Let me speak first and then I'll put us both on FaceTime with them. Got it?"

"Got it," Tinsel confirmed.

"Mum, hey – yeah, I know it's early, I'm sorry to wake you. No no, everything's fine. I'm here with Tinsel and we just wanted to call you so you heard it from us before anyone else…"

Damn, Tinsel thought. Her sister really was good at this.

CHAPTER 14

She had been discharged just like they said she would be, with the doctor giving Tinsel a long list of instructions about how to care for her wounds over the coming days and what she should and shouldn't do. She would be back within a few weeks to have the stitches taken out, but Pandora was listening carefully as well and assured the medical staff she would make sure Tinsel did as they said.

"You're only four years older than me and I swear, you make me feel like a child most of the time," Tinsel said to her as a uniformed officer led them through the hospital's main foyer.

"You're my *real* baby," she teased. "Airlie who?"

Tinsel didn't mean to sound grumpy, but as her adrenaline had worn off and slowly been replaced with fear, the lack of sleep only added to her feeling of exhaustion. She had a prescription for some pretty heavy-duty pain killers that would keep her on a nice, buoyant cloud, yet they did little compared to what she'd had in the hospital. Tinsel could already feel her many aches and pains starting to flare up.

The fact that she was dressed in one of Pandora's cutesy knit dresses didn't help, but she kept telling herself it was better than the hospital gown, even if this clung to her like cellophane. She should have been grateful Pandora had anything spare floating around in her car, but that was mums for you.

Despite having pumped out two kids, Pandora was slight and had always been slight. Barely over five foot and a comfortable size six, Tinsel was not only several feet taller but at least three sizes bigger. A knit dress had been a safe bet, as the stretchy material meant it was one of the few things in Pandora's wardrobe that would come close to fitting her. Thankfully there was a thong that would suffice as underwear, but she had to go braless because even her sister's maternity range would be insufficient for her cleavage.

"Detective James said he'd be in the drop off area just out the front," the officer told them, forcing a break in their bickering.

"There's no media here, is there?" Tinsel asked, casting a look at the flip flops she was wearing on her feet. She did not want to be captured like this.

"No, everyone is focused on The Capitol thing," the cop replied. "Thankfully there was so much heat there that anyone who might have been listening to the scanner missed the call to your office a few hours later."

"Thank fuck," she sighed with relief.

"I can't imagine what it would have been like down there," Pandora murmured, her hand slipping into Tinsel's. "Running through that car park, scared and alone."

"I wasn't alone," Tinsel answered, grim. "Honestly, I was just hoping the whole thing was in my head and the footsteps chasing me actually belonged to the dog from *Bowfinger*."

"I never saw it."

"That's so upsetting," Tinsel blanched. "Please stop talking."

The officer led them over to a car where Detective James was leaning against the bonnet, phone pressed to his ear as he spoke urgently.

"No, question him without me," he said. "It's better that way. I can watch the footage later and gauge your response."

The cop cleared her throat, alerting him to their presence. He jerked around, eyebrows shooting up as he realised Tinsel and Pandora were standing right there.

"Uh huh, that sounds good. Let me know. I have the sisters with me now and we're going to the residence to collect her things... at the office, yup. See you then."

He hung up, sliding his phone into the pocket of a fresh pair of slacks. Tinsel had noticed he'd been running around in the same tuxedo he'd worn to the premiere all night, the outfit growing more and more ruffled as the evening wore on. The bowtie hanging loose around his neck was long gone, clearly he'd had enough time to grab a quick shower and change of clothes that fitted the usual uniform she assigned to him in her head.

"Thanks," he nodded, addressing the woman as she promptly turned and walked away. "Where did you park, Pandora?"

"On Tinsel's street. Figured she'd be going back there at some point, so may as well be close."

"Good, we can all ride over together then."

Tinsel and Pandora climbed into the back seat, the former wanting to be closer to the latter. There was something comforting about having her sibling brush up against her as they pulled out of the hospital driveway and into the morning traffic.

"I take it you found Zack," Tinsel said, not missing the way Detective James' eyes darted up to meet hers in the rear-view mirror.

"Yeah," he replied, the response short enough that it surprised her. "He's at the station now. Diraani is running through his alibis."

"You mean interrogating him," she corrected.

"If that's what it takes," he answered, no hint of apology in his tone.

"You're not doing it?" Pandora questioned.

"No, I'm not very sharp right now. I've been backing up night shifts with days so... Diraani is better suited."

There was a slight nudge at Tinsel's shoulder and she looked across at her sister, who was giving her *a look*. Pandora didn't need to verbalise it out loud, Tinsel knew what she was thinking: *conflict of interest?*

Tinsel had told her sister about the kiss, she had to. Talking it through helped clarify some things in her head. She knew Pandora had a strict "all cops are dogs" policy when it came to dating, so she was surprised when her immediate reaction hadn't been to recoil with disgust.

A new officer had been assigned to guard her bed, so Tinsel had to disclose the story to Pandora in hushed whispers, the two sisters' heads nearly touching as they had laid side-by-side while she recounted all of the details.

Her older sister's face had been unreadable at the time, so much so it prompted Tinsel to ask her for a response.

"I'm not saying he's *not* thinking with his dick," her sister had whispered. "But he's not *only* thinking with his dick."

"What does that mean?" Tinsel questioned, unsure whether that was supposed to serve as a dig or a compliment.

"It's his job, you realise that right? He could lose his job over this."

"I know," she lied, ashamed for being so caught up in her own feelings and the repercussions in her own life that she didn't even think about that fact until then.

"What I mean is, he likes you: enough to risk his career with an impulsive decision in the moment."

"Okay," Tinsel said, unsure of where that left her.

"The question is, how do you feel?"

She knew how she felt physically, but it was more complicated than that. Tinsel was *barely* single. Zack wasn't her first proper relationship, but he was her longest. And they'd lived together. What was the cooling off period supposed to be for that kind of thing? And what if her ex *was* a murderer? Pandora clearly thought it was possible, so did that make it okay to move on so fast? Tinsel was uncertain, but she knew one thing for sure: she was confused on many, many levels.

"I don't know," she had admitted. "I feel bad that I don't feel bad. Like, I have zero guilt. But also, am I moving on too quickly? There are just so many more important things I should be focusing on right now."

"Actually," Pandora started. "This is exactly what you should be focusing on: something sweet and seemingly trivial like this. Something positive? That's the perfect distraction from the fact a spree killer wants your head."

"Is it positive though?"

"Did it make you feel good?"

"Yeah," she laughed, surprised by the levity she heard in her own voice. "It made me feel good."

"How many things have made you feel good – genuinely good – in the past few days?"

"A bad thing making me feel good doesn't mean that it's right."

"Whatever," Pandora shrugged. "It was just a kiss. All things considered, I don't think you need to be stapling a scarlet 'A' to your chest anytime soon."

"Alright–"

"And you're not marrying the guy – have a tryst! Fool around with whoever you want, whenever you want. This is Melbourne, babe. Maybe it's time to try that polyamorous thing everyone's always talking about."

The conversation was playing through Tinsel's mind as they pulled up out the front of The Pinnacle. After being surprised by a throng of media one time, she was permanently on her guard: especially after the events of the past twenty-four hours. It's not that she had expected journalists to be waiting on the street, but she didn't *not* expect it either. She wasn't sure how she would have reacted if they had been there. Thankfully, nobody was.

Detective James instructed them to wait in the car while he did a walk-through first. It was a heavy few minutes, Pandora and Tinsel saying nothing as they watched his back disappear through the staff door, using Tinsel's keys to get inside. There wasn't a word exchanged between them until Tinsel heard her own relieved sigh as he stepped back on to the street.

Getting out of the car, a light drizzle started as they made their way over to him.

"Listen," Pandora started with Detective James. "I've left the kids with Brian and one of them could end up in the microwave. Are you okay to drop Tinsel back?"

Tinsel narrowed her eyes at her sister, fully aware of what she was doing. Pandora wouldn't meet her gaze.

"Absolutely," he nodded. "The officers should already be stationed outside your house now."

"I'll bring them biccies," she said, giving Tinsel a quick smooch on the cheek. "See you at home, no rush."

Her mouth was open, but no words came out, as she watched Pandora dart across the road and into her white Honda CR-V. Detective James gave no indication that he knew what her sister was up to, both watching as the "YETI TRUTHER" bumper sticker on Pandora's car grew smaller and smaller as it pulled away.

"Okay," he said. "Zack's at the station so it's all clear in here."

She took the hand he extended, stepping up and into the pub. The back room and bar were through a door to her left, her residence to the right and up the stairs. So, so many stairs. She stood there, looking up with resentment as she delayed what would be a slow ascent. He shut the door behind them, locking it and plunging both into gloom as he came and stood beside her. Tinsel felt the weight of the detective's gaze.

"You know," he said. "I could always carry you?"

She barked a laugh, whacking him in the chest.

"That's so insulting," Tinsel muttered as she began the upwards hobble, him following patiently behind.

"Is it?" he teased.

"I'm a feminist, let me stubbornly inch up these steps in pain one-by-one."

She'd only made it to the first landing when he stopped her, face and tone serious.

"Tinsel, are you in pain?"

He was an inch below her, the morning light from above doing frankly illegal things to his face, making him look like a film noir hunk. She touched the hand of his that was resting on her hip, as if she was about to topple back down the stairs at any moment.

"I'm okay. I'd tell you if it was too much."

"Would you?"

"Yes," Tinsel whispered, interlacing her fingers among his. "Now come on, I want to show you something while I still have the forward momentum."

Once they made it to the residence, she tugged him down a hallway and past the closed door of Jorro's office. There were more stairs, but only a dozen and it was worth it once you got to the top. It was a grey, rainy day which was *so* Melbourne, yet even if the skies weren't sparkling, it was still stunning.

"Wow," Detective James exclaimed, coming to a stop beside her.

Tinsel could hear the smile in his voice, and she risked a peek, casting a sideways glance as she watched him take in the view. *That damn smile*, she thought, trying to avert her gaze and focus instead on the three-hundred-and-sixty-degree view around them.

"There was a bell tower above us," she said, pointing at the ceiling. "And back in the day, this was the land office. People used to come up here, look at the view we're looking at now, point out a plot of land and say 'that one.'"

"Ah, colonialism," he sighed.

"Ruining the moment," she chuckled, watching as he pivoted on the spot to examine the scenery at each of the windows. The space was smaller than your standard room, but perfect size for an office as it circled around. The encased glass made you feel like you were in a bubble.

"I very much doubt that," he said, bending down to examine a small pile of pillows that were stacked next to an ash tray. "You?"

She nodded. "One of my favourite things in the world is to come up here at sunset or dawn, smoke a joint, and watch the colours."

The last time she'd done exactly that it had been with Pandora, Gee and Ray, the four of them passing a bottle of champagne between them. The memory was hazy in detail, but the feeling of it was warm. A finger brushed her jawline and she turned, not realising Detective James had inched so close to her.

"Will you bring me up here some time?" he asked, voice barely above a whisper.

"I have brought you up here."

"Now who's ruining the moment?" he scoffed, causing a smile to dance on her lips. "I'm serious, though."

"And I'm seriously not lighting up in front of a cop."

He rolled his eyes at her, taking a step back that she wished he wouldn't. "This fucking job…"

He trailed off, Tinsel watching the fatigue and frustration that seemed to wash over him.

"This fucking case, even." He shook his head, hands running over his face before he caught himself. Detective James froze as he watched her watch him. She could almost see the wall visibly snap back down.

"Sorry," he apologised.

"For what?"

"For… well, for last night to start with."

"When you saved my life?"

"You know I'm not talking about that."

Tinsel just stared at him, holding her conversational ground as she urged him to voice it.

"It was unprofessional, and I shouldn't have done it," he grimaced.

"You're sorry? That's such a dumb thing to say," she snapped, feeling that familiar flicker of anger.

"What do you want me to say?"

"That you meant it! Fuck."

She shook herself free of his grip, heading back to the stairs they had climbed up. The stiffness of her body and lingering injuries meant she couldn't stomp down dramatically like the situation warranted. Detective James patiently trailing behind her only made Tinsel madder as she huffed all the way to her bedroom.

Her eyes were stuck on the bed, the one that was perfectly made and unslept in. The blue doona was laying crisp and without a crinkle. Detective James lingered in the doorway, arms folded as he watched her grab a suitcase from inside the wardrobe and begin angrily throwing things inside it. She wasn't taking an overnight bag this time.

"Did you mean it?" he asked, breaking the silence.

"Don't answer my question with another question," she replied, speaking with her back to him as she pulled clothes off the hangers.

"Don't avoid mine. I'm older than you, and I'm a detective for fuck's sake. Know better, do better, and I didn't."

"How old are you?" she pushed. "Hmmm? Thirty-four at most? Thirty-three?"

"I'm thirty-one."

"And I'm twenty-five. Now we're both doing maths on very little sleep and I'm grumpy."

She turned to head towards the door, knowing that as soon as she was out of it, she could march down the hallway and towards the bathroom where the last of her things were. But just as she neared it, the door was shut as Detective James extended the length of his arm and closed it so she couldn't leave. Annoyed, she kicked her thongs in his general direction.

"I've been married, did you know that?" he said, voice gruff as he glowered down at her.

"Oh my god, who cares? Everyone has a past! Mine is sitting in an interrogation room as we speak."

Detective James didn't reply. Instead, he did that intense stare thing he did, the same one she'd found so intriguing in their first interaction. He was standing in front of her and the proximity thrilled Tinsel. She did her best not to admit it as she stared up at him, breathing in the faint hint of peppermint she could smell on his breath. One hand stayed on the door, but his gaze flicked to her lips. She wanted him and she wasn't afraid if he knew it. By the way he was breathing, she guessed he wanted her too.

"Vic," she whispered. "I just–"

"Say my name again."

"*Vic*," she repeated, watching him move towards her as if in slow motion. Unlike before, his kiss was slow: almost lazy, in fact. It wasn't desperate or rushed like it had been the first time. He was drawing it out, savouring her. She sighed a little, unable to help it as she slipped her hands around the curve of his neck and let her tongue push further as she kissed him deeply.

His hands slid up her thigh and moved the hem of the knit dress higher with the gesture. He was being gentle with her, fingers skirting around her injuries as if seeing how much and what she could handle. Tinsel could also feel how excited he was, his hardness pressing up against her as she rolled her body slightly.

Suddenly her dress was over her hips as he hoisted her into the air, lifting her up as she wrapped her good leg around his waist. He carried her back towards the bed and a small gasp escaped her lips. It was like fuel to him as he held her tighter. She pulled away from his mouth for a moment, kissing down his jawline until she found an earlobe, sucking on it gently before giving him a playful bite. His fist clenched the material of her garment into a knot, as if she was driving him crazy. He lowered her down slowly, watching her face, reading it to see if she grimaced or was in pain.

"Stop it," she whispered, unbuttoning his shirt slowly. "I'm fine."

His breaths were more like pants as he watched her, Tinsel's hands running over his bare chest followed by her tongue as she kissed one of his exposed nipples. He was seemingly so caught up in the sensation that he didn't realise she had the belt of his pants undone until they were sliding off, her fingers hesitating for only a moment as she realised the size of him.

That pause was all he needed. He manoeuvred her further up the bed, his fingers holding her gently under her head for protection. She reached for a condom packet in the bedside table, just in time too as he slid the dress over her head.

"*Oh*," he breathed, realising she wasn't wearing a bra. She nearly had the mind to feel self-conscious, but as he lowered his head to explore her body, she had never felt more potent in the bedroom. It was an exhilarating kind of sensation, one she hadn't experienced for so long as he admired all the shapes and curves and crooks that were completely new to him.

Everywhere he kissed felt like it left a trace on her skin, Tinsel able to feel where his lips had been long after they had left. The stings and the aches and the bruises faded into the periphery like the physical contact with him was a healing agent. The thong was long gone, and she lifted her hips, unable to take the excruciating wait much longer as she guided him inside her.

Detective James swore under his breath, repeating the curse again and again as he moved deeper. Tinsel, frankly, was speechless. Her need for him in the moment was elemental, the aftermath inconsequential. She desperately needed to feel his skin against hers, their bodies shuddering and breaths gasping.

His fingers sunk into the flesh of her waist as if he was holding on for dear life. She took charge, setting the pace as they gradually came together. He kissed her breasts as they moved, the added sensation almost too much to take as she felt her own release building. That increased tenfold as he reached down between them, circling, rubbing, pressing.

Tinsel arched her back, her own high-pitched gasp mixing with the sound of his as she thrashed her head from side-to-side with the exhalation of her climax. He fell on to her, staying inside but otherwise completely still as he rested his face in the curve of her neck. She clung to the muscles of his back, realising that she'd barely had time to appreciate his body in her rush to disrobe him. The only sound was their recovered breaths, which started fast but eventually slowed along with their heart rate.

Tinsel felt something strange bubbling up inside of herself and she laughed, the noise surprising her as much as Detective James. He turned his head to the side to examine the smile that broke out along her face.

"Usually when a woman laughs while you're still inside her, that's not a good sign," he muttered.

She twisted her neck to face him, grin going wild. "Nothing about that could be a bad thing."

A smirk twitched at the edge of his own mouth. "Then what's with the chuckle?"

"I just…" she trailed off, unsure of how to phrase it. "I didn't know it could be like that."

"Like what?"

She gently pushed him off her, rolling him onto his back. His own chest was damp with perspiration as her breasts brushed over his skin, Tinsel using her superior position to lean down and kiss him, long and hard.

"Like that," she answered, not needing further explanation.

His fingers trailed over her shoulders, stroking the baby hairs at the base of her neck and staring at her like she was a marvel. She shivered at the sensation, and Vic kicked the doona underneath them free before throwing it over their bodies like a mini tent. Carefully, he pulled her to him, and she rested her head on his chest, the hairs there tickling her face.

Closing her eyes, Tinsel dared to let herself rest for a moment. To really, truly slip away.

When she opened her eyes again, Vic was gone. She was sleeping face down on the mattress and with a groan, she raised herself up on one elbow to look out the window. It was pouring now, the rain making sharp pings against the tin of the roofing that covered parts of the beer garden below.

"Hey."

Sitting up, she turned to find Vic carrying a cup of takeaway coffee towards her and a cinnamon scroll.

"Thought you might need this," he said, sitting down on the bed next to her. She stared, wondering if she was having some kind of hallucination. He was half drenched, the downpour outside fairly recent as water had only soaked into the fabric at his shoulders while the rest of him remained dry. Droplets clung to his dark hair, and she watched as one dripped on to his cheek.

"Sorry," he said. "I didn't mean to scare you."

She leaned into his touch, and he shuffled closer, tucking her into him.

"It was just one of those deep sleeps where you wake up not knowing what continent you're on," Tinsel murmured, taking her first sip of coffee. "Dench?"

"Yeah, just tried the closest spot. And you were only out for a few hours, but that can make all the difference."

"Mmmm," she murmured, taking another hearty sip. "Split it?"

"Sure," he smiled.

They divided the pastry between them, eating in easy silence with the soundtrack of the weather outside. When they were done, Detective James reached across to retrieve something from the pile of items she'd dumped in the corner. When he handed it to her, she was relieved to see it was the painkillers she'd been given. She was only supposed to take them with food and there was something sweet about him remembering that.

"Hell yeah," Tinsel said, popping two. "Not that a quickie and coffee isn't great–"

He let out a laugh. "I can't compete with Endone."

"You really can't," she replied, getting to her feet slowly.

"Careful," Detective James cautioned, rising with her and keeping a hand under her arms to steady her. She heard him let out a sharp exhale and she cast him a glance, watching as he looked at her naked body. Desire was there, sure, but the primary emotion she could read was concern. Looking down, she understood. Her leg was bandaged and the most obvious, but her skin was also rapidly becoming a tapestry of bruises and cuts. She had fought for her life, and it certainly looked like it.

"Stop gawking and pass me a towel, will you?"

"That feels counter intuitive…"

As if annoyingly on cue, his phone started ringing. He let out an annoyed moan, grabbing it and stepping into the hall while Tinsel made for the bathroom. After a quick, awkward shower with her bad leg dangling outside so she didn't get it wet, she paused in the kitchen to scull an enormous glass of preventative cranberry juice. By the time Detective James re-joined her in the bedroom, she had her own clothes on, and her suitcase packed. She stared forlornly at the Freddy Krueger plushie by her bedside, wanting desperately to take it with her but not wanting to do so in front of him. She did snatch the framed copies of her and Pandora's adoption certificates off her desk though, the pair being part of a set that folded in on each other.

"Were you and Pandora together?" he asked, not missing a detail as his eyes ran over the item.

"Like, in the orphanage?"

"Yeah. Is that, uh, an okay thing to talk about?"

She laughed. "I don't have hang ups about being adopted.

And no, Pandora was from a home in Berlin – which is where our mother is from. I came from one in New Delhi, I mean, obviously."

She gestured to herself for emphasis, although truly not needing to. The physical differences between her and her sister were stark already.

"She was a baby when they got her and I joined the family years later, when I was two. I don't remember anything except them, though. I have no toddler memories."

His hands ran along her back in a soothing gesture, and Tinsel enjoyed the pressure there, noting how natural it seemed to her. His fingertips worked their way up to the base of her neck, delicately touching the bandaging that covered her stitches, and she arched back, smiling at him.

"What is it?" she asked.

"You are so exquisite," he muttered, leaning down to kiss her. It was gentle, but Tinsel knew what was restrained behind it now and she found it difficult to pull away.

"You're drunk," she replied, after kissing him back.

"On something, definitely." He sighed. "We should go though. I've got to get to the station."

He took her suitcase without asking, heading outside while Tinsel gave the room a once over. She had propped the windows open to dispel the scent of sex and she yanked them shut, her eyes passing over the space with a mix of sadness and regret.

Pacing towards the door, she paused. Turning back, she ripped the blankets off the bed and threw them to the floor. Grabbing the pillows, she tossed them across the room and half ripped the sheets from the mattress so that they hung loose.

Zack's clothes got hurled from the hangers and she knew it was petty, but she left the condom wrappers in the bin with the contents having already been flushed. Breathless, she felt a lazy smile on her face as she surveyed her handiwork.

The drive to her sister's was uneventful, Detective James

keeping one hand on the wheel and the other on her thigh. Tinsel absentmindedly rested her fingers on top of his, enjoying the thud at the back of her skull getting duller as the painkillers did their job. There was a ping and he checked the updates on his phone at a red light.

"You look displeased," she said, observing the deep crease that formed between his brows.

"It's nothing."

She barely had time to glare before he exhaled and provided her with an answer.

"You know when I shot him, I was hoping I did more than clip him. Forensics just found the bullet wedged into the concrete of the stairwell wall."

"And that's bad?"

"Means it went straight through and out. From the blood trail, we're guessing it didn't hit anything vital so our odds of getting lucky by picking him up trying to get treated at a hospital–"

"Not so great."

"Precisely. Looks like he had a car waiting somewhere nearby as well. The droplets disappear on Hosier Lane."

"So, another dead end?"

"Not at all," he responded, shaking his head. "There's traffic cameras to examine, which might give us a route. Eyewitnesses to canvas, security footage to trawl through, DNA I'm hoping we can get an ancestral match on from the blood splatter."

"Vic," she breathed, her heart suddenly beating faster. "Security footage… if people are going through that, what about the cameras from The Capitol?"

"What do you mean?"

"The lobby, us, caught on camera…"

She trailed off, not able to complete the thought properly. He leaned towards her but stopped himself at the last minute, as if suddenly recalling they were in public, other cars and eyes around them.

"I already checked," he admitted. "Last night, when I was having the footage pulled from various vantage points. It's a blackspot."

"Which means?"

"No cameras, Tinsel. There's nothing to worry about."

She let out a sigh of relief as they pulled into Pandora's driveway. They sat there for a minute, saying nothing. They'd passed the car and the cops stationed in it on the curb.

"I'll stop by later, when I can," he said.

"Don't," she answered. "Like, only when it wouldn't seem weird. Don't do anything to arouse suspicion."

"Tinsel–"

"You're not losing your job over this. And… I had a moment – *moments* – of weakness back there. I'll keep myself in check until this is all over. Hey, consider it something to look forward to."

She almost thought he was about to roll his eyes at her, but he ran a hand through his hair instead. "Fine. When I finish today, I'll go home, I'll sleep through the rest of my time off, and I'll touch base when I'm back on duty."

"That's all I'm asking," she teased.

His hand slid dangerously over towards her, and she batted it away. "Stop that."

"Just testing," he smirked. "And hey, since you have no phone in the meantime, that takes away the temptation."

She raised a lone eyebrow, asking the question "does it?" without needing to utter a word. He slipped out of the car, helping her with her bags. The front door opened, and Pandora jogged over to them.

"I've got it, I've got it," her sister said, waving him off. "Go do something useful, like catch a murderer."

With a nod, Detective James headed towards his car, keys jiggling in his hand. Standing there, side-by-side, the sisters watched his number plate disappear down the block, reality beginning to smash back into place with the more distance he put between them. Tinsel had big problems, as big as they could get, but it was the little ones that were niggling at her too.

"What's wrong?" Pandora asked immediately. Her sister could tell just by looking at her face that something was up. "Tell me you at least got railed?"

Tinsel elbowed her sharply.

"Ow, what? Look how far away our minders are! They can't hear us."

Pandora gestured to the two cops they could see sitting at attention in their vehicle. She threw them a big wave.

"Hello, hello," she said through gritted teeth. "Please keep us alive."

They nodded back in reply.

"How good are your sources?" Tinsel asked.

Pandora narrowed her eyes, enticed. "Good. The best, some would say. Some being me, obviously."

Tinsel grabbed the corner of her suitcase, wheeling it up the driveway as Pandora joined her with the rest of the stuff.

"We need to find out if Zack is injured," she said.

"Why?" her sister questioned.

"Vic shot the attacker. Nothing fatal, it seems like the bullet went straight through. But if your Zack theory is right–"

"Hey, not my theory! I'm just saying he was AWOL last night and AWOL most of the nights when shit has been going down."

"The bed was perfectly made," Tinsel replied. "That confirms he was elsewhere."

The house was suspiciously quiet as they entered. No kids. No Brian. It was bizarre. She turned to her sister to ask where everyone was, but Pandora already anticipated her question.

"I asked Brian to take the grublets and go to his mum's this morning when I went to see you," she said, batting away the query. "Until they assigned us police protection, I didn't want them back. And, as for Zack's maybe bullet wound, it would depend if he was arrested or picked up for questioning."

"What's the diff?"

"With an arrest they can take his DNA, search his body, all of that. But I don't think they have enough for an arrest, so if he's taken in for questioning, he has to consent to having all that stuff taken, which no one would do willingly."

"He could hide the injury under a jacket, you wouldn't know," Tinsel huffed. "How do we find out either way?"

"We need a primary source ideally," Pandora said, looking thoughtful. "And I have an idea, but you're not going to love it."

"Whatever. Tell me."

"Let's think about this logically. If they picked him up this morning, then this colleague he stayed with overnight could likely be his alibi. They'll need to verify it, so it's probable they were taken to the station too. No, actually I'd say they were definitely picked up. You couldn't risk leaving one behind in case they were his accomplice, or it gave them an opportunity to destroy evidence."

"Wallace and Marshall," Tinsel breathed, meeting the maniacal glint in her sister's eye with her own. "They'd have to be told by either one or both of them, so they'd know if it was an arrest or not."

"Right," Pandora said, as if that settled it. "This case blowing up the way it has, active police contacts are tighter than Nicole Kidman's forehead at the moment. The quickest way for us to know is his workplace."

Tinsel tilted her head, feeling a surge of energy and purpose. "Let's go."

CHAPTER 15

They had been sitting in Pandora's car for over an hour. Tinsel had downed her second coffee of the day and was absentmindedly picking at a salad sandwich that sat half eaten on her lap. Her sister was by her side, neither one of them speaking as a Haim song played on the radio.

The shop had opened late, the artists clearly knowing something was up as she watched a staff meeting called just before they officially opened their doors for the day. She saw the shocked expressions on their faces, and someone shook their head in disbelief. Whatever they had been told about why their colleague Zack Tykken wasn't coming into work that day, it must have been fairly close to the truth. And there was only one person they could have learned that information from: the other absent employee, Nancy.

Finally, she got out of the car, shaking the crumbs off her high-waisted skirt and composing herself in the reflection of the window. Her limbs were stiff after being frozen like a statue for so long.

"Why don't I go in and ask?" Pandora offered, her tone communicating clearly that she was worried Tinsel was about to cause a scene. It was a justified fear.

"They know me, I've got this," she replied, marching from where they had been parked and across the road to the entrance of the tattoo shop. She heard her sister call out after her, but Pandora would have to scramble to lock up the car and follow. It gave her a head start.

The bell above the door jingled as she pushed it open. Fredrico looked up from the reception desk where he had clearly been assigned to duties for the day. There was a light smile on his face, and it dropped almost immediately as he saw her.

"Oh shit," he breathed.

"'Oh shit' is right," Tinsel replied. "Where's Nancy, Fredrico?"

"I... uh, she's not coming in today. She called a few hours ago."

"And what did she say?"

There must have been something in the tone of Tinsel's voice, because although she was speaking quietly, she could sense the eyes of the other artists in the store focusing on her.

"She... had to go, um, to the police station," the apprentice said, warily. He was afraid of Tinsel so he wasn't going to lie, but he was still reluctant to tell her the truth. She felt the anger bubbling up within her, ignoring the bell as it rang again and her sister dashed into the store.

"She's at the police station with Zack because they're sleeping together, right Fredrico?!" Tinsel exploded. "My guess is they have been for a while, too. All these little pieces clicking together suddenly make a lot more sense."

She shook her head, furious for letting herself feel guilt for even a moment in her past relationship. Sure, she had ended it before she knew the truth, but that didn't stop Tinsel from feeling any less like a complete and utter fool.

"And you knew," she sighed. "You let me come in here and joke with you on the phone and play your damn song when you knew he was cheating on me. I bet you all knew."

"Ask him," Pandora urged. "Quick, while he feels bad."

Tinsel chuckled, but there was no humour in it. "Fredrico, was he arrested? Or was he just taken in for questioning?"

"Uh..." he faltered.

"Which one, buddy. What did she say on the phone?"

"They can't hold him, so I don't think he was arrested," he said. "Nancy gave the impression he'd be out later today."

Tinsel gave him a mock salute before her sister yanked her through the door and on to the street. Pandora set a solid pace, linking their arms together as they waited for a lull in traffic before crossing the road again and heading back to the car.

Tinsel was breathing heavily, her knees feeling like they were about to give out as she hunched over in the car park. Her eyes focused on the brace her wrist was in, the edges still damp from rushing to put it back on after being in the shower.

"Just breathe," Pandora said, rubbing her shoulders in a calming gesture. "Just breathe."

"I thought they were my friends," she wheezed. "Isn't it fucked that's what I'm most hurt by? There's no way they were having an affair in that office and everyone didn't know about it."

"I think it's most fucked that we can't rule him out as the killer, because he could be hiding that wound and Nancy could be covering for him, but anyway..."

Footsteps signalled that someone had come to join them. Tinsel looked up to see the pastel pink hair of Felony Swiff, one of the artists from the store. Her phone was clasped in a fluffy blue case and Tinsel wasn't sure why she fixated on that as the woman came to a halt.

"Tinsel," she whispered, "I'm so sorry. I didn't know about *any* of it until this morning. I swear. I tried to call you and left a voicemail saying that we needed to talk as soon as possible..."

She bit her lip as Tinsel leaned back against the vehicle.

"I just... I know you how must feel. The same thing happened to me. I only found out months after we broke up that half of my friends knew but didn't say anything. I felt so betrayed, and I know I might have overstepped my boundaries calling you and coming out here, because we're not close, but when they told us both of them were at the station and it was obvious, well... I would have wanted someone to tell me."

"The police have her phone," Pandora said. "She didn't get your messages."

"Oh," Felony replied, understanding crossing her features. "What just happened makes sense then."

"Did everyone in the shop besides you know?" Tinsel asked.

"I don't think so," she answered. "Wallace and Fredrico definitely knew for a while, cos then I started thinking back through things and I realised they had covered for him a bunch."

Tinsel frowned. "How long?"

"Honestly, I'm not sure. Maybe a few months, six at the most. I know she's had a thing for him since she started and that was a year ago so—"

"Yeah, well, didn't take him that long to reciprocate."

"I wanted to say I'm sorry," Felony continued. "I tried to tell you as soon as I could. And I know this sucks right now, but it will get better. It has for me. Anyway..."

"Don't work for those assholes," Tinsel said, watching as Felony started to walk back towards the shopfront. Her solemn expression cracked and she smiled, mischievously.

"They don't know it yet, but I just put down the deposit on my own shop: only female and non-binary artists. In three weeks, I'm handing in my notice, and I am out of here. The tattoo industry is a minefield of toxic masculinity, so why not create my own paradise?"

"Themyscira," she mumbled.

"Huh?"

"It's the island from *Wonder Woman*, no men allowed."

"Oh," Felony smiled. "Yeah, my own Themyscira. I like that."

She offered a shy wave to the sisters, before heading back over the street.

"It's weird," Pandora said, watching her leave. "I never

expected to like someone who dresses like a Furby as much as I do her."

Tinsel took a deep breath, running her hands over her face. "I fucked Vic."

There was a pause for a beat before Pandora's laughter exploded from her body like a siren.

"Ha, yes! I knew it! Oh my God, your life is so much more interesting than mine!"

Pandora practically skipped around to the driver's side of the car as Tinsel folded herself inside.

"Come on, let's go buy you a new phone and then you can text Zack telling him you banged someone else."

Tinsel chuckled. "I don't know if I'm at that level of trifling yet."

"Girl, he has been cheating on you for six months. Give it a few days and you'll be primed to trifle away."

"Can we go to the doctor's first?" she asked.

"Your stitches playing up?"

"No, but... just thinking about it, I have an IUD so Zack and I haven't used protection for the past year and a half."

"Got it." Pandora said, starting the car. "STD check first, phone vengeance second. I am on your wavelength. And on the way home, there's one more place I want to visit."

"Oh?"

"You'll see," she muttered. "It's a surprise."

"*Oh*," she answered, trying to quell the nerves about anything Pandora might have up her sleeve.

A few hours and a gynaecologist appointment later, the house they pulled up in front of was little more than a beach shack. Just outside of Brighton, sand mixed amongst the grass on the front lawn in a way that was distinctive to Australian properties a few blocks back from the beach. There was a pristine EH Holden parked under a garage and Tinsel admired the aqua paint job as they passed. Any car from the sixties was basically her pipe dream ride, and this one was in impeccable condition.

"Where are we?" Tinsel asked.

"You wanted to know how good my sources are," Pandora replied. "Now you can meet one."

A series of wind chimes dangled overhead as they stepped on to the patio, Pandora knocking with confidence as if she had been there a hundred times before. For all Tinsel knew, maybe she had.

"It's unlocked love, let yourselves in – I'm making a cuppa!" a hoarse voice called to them from inside the house. Her sister gave a nonchalant shrug as she followed the speaker's instructions.

It took a moment for Tinsel's eyes to adjust from the brightness outside to the darkened interior, but she was surprised to see the person who greeted them was a small woman. She was tiny, in fact, about the same height as Pandora. Yet she had a surety of movement that said this was someone who knew how to use their body and often. Even her wrists looked muscular as she set down three cups of tea on top of a glass dining table.

Tinsel's suspicions were confirmed when the woman shook her hand with a strong, sturdy grip.

"Tinsel, this is Veronica Watson," her sister said, making the formal introductions. "She's a former homicide detective and for the past – what, two years?"

"Almost three now, kid," the woman corrected.

"Ha, well, for the past three years she has been one of my best sources on the blog," Pandora said as the three of them took a seat. "Most of the pieces I've done with Veronica have been recounting old cases, that kind of thing."

"Had twenty-nine years on the job," Veronica said, taking a slurp from her mug. "You'd wanna hope I had *something* decent to say."

She grinned at Tinsel in a way that made her feel warm immediately, her eyes contorting into crescent moons as the gesture transformed her whole face. She had the lines and skin tone of someone who spent a lot of time in the sun, with freckles almost bleeding into each other.

"I thought it might be nice for you to talk to someone who actually has experience dealing with this kind of thing, who isn't a man."

Pandora's dig was pointed, and Tinsel didn't miss it as she warmed her hands on the ceramics of the mug she had been allocated.

"I retired five years ago," Veronica said, when she failed to speak up. "Bought the beach shack I'd always dreamed of, just a few streets away from the house I grew up in. And while you sip that tea there, I'm just going to keep talking so you can feel more comfortable and learn a bit about me in the process."

"Okay," Tinsel smirked, admiring how intuitive the older woman was.

"I started out as a regional copper before moving into the rape squad for eight years, then I worked mainly homicide cases after that. Sometimes they crossed over, sometimes they didn't, but I worked a few names you might recognise: Peter Dupas and the Frankston Serial Killer, for starters."

"Paul Denyer," Pandora added, unable to help herself.

"I don't do that kind of thing anymore, saw too many terrible things over too many years and my PTSD got to me in the end. But I follow the news. I've been following what has been happening with you, plus a little extra help from Pandora here."

"I bet," Tinsel murmured, giving her older sibling a piercing stare.

"What?" she said, innocently. "Veronica knows people and she knows her shit. That could be helpful."

"Helpful how, Pandora? I'm running solely on caffeine and maybe two hours of sleep at this point."

"They're stalling with your boyfriend."

Tinsel choked, Veronica's words causing her to spit up her tea before she regained her composure.

"You're not the only ones who come by seeking advice. Got a lot of rusty detectives who need fresh eyes from an old bird. Those detectives then owe me favours, and if I ask things, I tend to find out the answers."

"Stalling for what?" Tinsel said. "And how? By charging him with obstruction of something?"

"Everyone has a basic right to silence," Pandora responded. "You couldn't charge him with hindrance unless he was at the scene of a car accident and refusing to say what happened, for example."

Veronica nodded. "They asked him for blood and saliva. He said no. They're stalling now to give them enough time to make an application to the court for an order forcing Zack to give them a sample."

"Will they get it?" Tinsel asked.

"Yes," the older woman replied. Definitive. Sure.

Tinsel let that information sink in, the tea in her mug suddenly seeming extremely unappealing as she set it down on the glass surface with a clink.

"Please," she said. "Tell me everything you've heard."

"He's refusing to provide police with an alibi," Veronica started. "Which is stupid. You don't seem like the type who would date stupid."

"He's trying to hide an affair." The words seemed flat as she spoke them. "But we've broken up, so I don't understand the point of maintaining that charade."

"I know. They got information out of the broad who was brought in with him. But since he won't confirm whether that's true or not, there's the likelihood she could be covering for him..."

"That wouldn't be unheard of," Pandora shrugged.

"Has he got a lawyer?" Tinsel asked.

"He didn't ask for one, but somebody called someone

because a male attorney showed up at the station just as I was finishing my chat."

"But no bullet wound, no link, right? What am I missing?" Tinsel pondered.

In her bare feet, worn jeans and a crisp, white blouse, there was nothing fussy about the former detective. She was straight-up and Tinsel appreciated that. It also meant that her next question came as a surprise.

"Did you know he was in the system?"

"The system?" she squeaked. "What do you mean?"

"He served time at a juvenile correctional facility in Queensland when he was a minor," Veronica answered. "He wasn't able to leave the state for several years and he can't travel overseas."

"W-what?"

"Those records are sealed by law, but given the dates and the location I was able to piece together what he was pinged for." She already had a printed newspaper article ready and slid it across the table for both of the sisters to see.

"Cat Killers Apprehended After Six-Month Reign of Terror," Pandora whispered, her surprised expression meeting Tinsel's.

"What the fuck," she breathed, shaking her head as she read the article, digesting every line.

"It seems like the other culprit was his older brother, a Mister Declan Tykken?"

Tinsel nodded. "I only met him once. He's a few years older, works in the mines in Western Australia."

"Did you get cat killer vibes from him?" Pandora asked.

She rolled her eyes at her sister's comment. "And what vibe is that, exactly? Besides, if I didn't get them from Zack then clearly I'm not very good at picking up whatever it is you think I should be able to pick up."

"Alright, alright," Pandora replied, raising her hands in a truce gesture.

"And just because he did this when he was young and dumb, doesn't mean he's responsible for multiple murders. Think of all the stupid shit *you* did at sixteen!"

"Yes, but this does set a behavioural precedent," Veronica said. "They'd be looking for markers like this in any potential suspect. He already has a connection to several of the victims, through and including you. Not to mention an alibi he won't confirm. And even if he did, having it backed up by his girlfriend-on-the-side isn't exactly fool proof."

There was barely any tea left in Tinsel's mug, but she grasped the handle as she swilled around the remaining fluid anyway.

"We'll know in a few hours," Veronica said, watching her carefully. "Once their application is successful, Zack has to give that physical evidence. That will either prove his innocence or his guilt."

"What if there's two?" Pandora asked.

Tinsel frowned at her. "Two what?"

"Two killers. I've seen *Scream*, I know my horror movies."

"You've seen *a* horror movie," Tinsel sighed back. "Singular."

"There's plenty of precedent," Pandora pushed. "Paul Bernardo and Karla Homolka, David and Catherine Birnie, the Moors murderers, Hillside Stranglers, Toolbox Killers–"

"Now you're just making shit up."

"I'm not! If Zack killed cats with his brother, why not this?"

"The results will also show if it's family DNA," Veronica answered. "If it's not Zack's blood but there's enough shared markers, then it will also indicate which type of family member it is: parent, sibling, cousin."

Tinsel resisted the urge to stick her tongue out at Pandora, knowing how childish it would be in the moment. It would have been mighty satisfying, though.

"What you need to think about is what happens if it's not him?" Veronica continued.

Pandora opened her mouth to speak, but the retired officer stopped her with a single stare.

"I'm not saying I know anything and if I was one of the investigating officers, Zack Tykken would look like a very promising lead. Say there's no bullet wound, say those results come back negative, say the blood left at the car park scene isn't his or anyone associated with him, there's still other things you need to consider."

"Like what?" Tinsel croaked.

"Like getting out of town, for one. I'd like to think our local officers have the means to protect you, but the reality is I know better. That car on Pandora's house will be there for a week at most. Given budgetary restrictions, that's a big enough deal as it is. But it's only a matter of time before that protection gets cut and you're on your own again. Both of you."

"Is getting out of town really a solution though? Pandora questioned. "I have kids, that's gonna be tricky."

"This perpetrator is a marauder: that means a serial killer who operates within a very small geographical area. So far, Melbourne's CBD and the inner north. There's any number of reasons this could be the case. Our killer could be lazy, but it's also likely they're local. They live here and they know that area well."

"Wouldn't that mean their chances of getting caught are also greater?" Tinsel frowned. "Someone could recognise them or see them fleeing the scene. Plus, these are densely populated areas. Sure, they've only been striking at night, but they chose some of the busiest spots in Melbourne, regardless of the hour. They must know they're more likely to get caught."

"They're a very confident killer," Veronica remarked. "The places they have chosen to strike weren't exactly easy targets."

Tinsel realised for the first time that Pandora had been taking notes. Given that Veronica had already stated their chat was strictly off the record, this must have been for her own personal record. She couldn't help but zero in on one of them, which was circled several times with question marks drawn next to it.

It read: "First crimes?"

Veronica must have noticed Tinsel's gaze, because she tapped the notepad with her finger.

"I like the way you think, Pandora," she smiled. "I've been wondering about that too. No matter *who* this ends up being, I suspect there's more victims we don't know about. At least one, more likely three or four. Until we know what their modus operandi is, I'd say it's going to be difficult to find them."

"There's barely more than seventy fatal stabbings in Australia each year," her sister said. "Once you filter out bar brawls, it won't take that long to go through the past decade… maybe a few weeks."

Tinsel scoffed. "How could you possibly know how many people are murdered by knife crime per annum? Like, I know you're a true crime nut, but this is doing *the most*."

"It's public record, bitch! Every year the Australia Bureau of Statistics releases a report called Victims of Crime."

"It's true," Veronica agreed. "It breaks down homicides, kidnappings, theft, extortion, then breaks them down again to analyse the percentages."

"If you spent less time at the movies, you'd know that."

"If you spent–"

"Girls!" Veronica said, raising her voice enough that it made both of them jump. It did the job though, and they stopped bickering.

"Sorry," Tinsel mumbled.

"This is why I never had kids, Christ. Pandora, if you start going through that list year-by-year, I can help. Just text me what one you're doing, and I'll do the one prior."

"Deal," her sister beamed. If there's one thing Pandora loved, it was a project.

"And you," Veronica said, pointing her finger square at Tinsel's chest. "Be on your guard. Be double, triple, quadruple safe until this is over and don't take risks. No underground car parks, no going anywhere alone, no meeting up with people you don't know, no travelling without a weapon. Because I bet no cop has mentioned the other reason they've planted officers on your house."

Tinsel shook her head, glancing at her sister to see if she had a clue. Pandora's expression was just as blank as her own.

"If the killer isn't your fella," Veronica continued, "then they're hedging their bets by assuming they'll make a move wherever you are next. Basically, you're bait."

CHAPTER 16

Tinsel woke with a start. Her dreams had been dark and unpleasant, but the longer she tried to focus on the memory of them, the quicker the specifics slipped away. Closing her eyes, she rubbed her face as she waited to adjust properly to consciousness.

They'd left Veronica's with a plan, which made her feel good. Proactive. The three of them would work together to start picking through past cases, dividing the years evenly in the hopes of finding earlier murders that might point towards a killer, or at least similarities. Additionally, her sister had created a Google Drive that was just for the two them.

On it, Pandora collated all the information she'd used for her various stories and included links to other people's work that picked up on things she'd missed. When they got home, Tinsel watched from the bed where she was ordered to lay as Pandora worked in a flurry. There were only a few hours left until Brian and the kids returned home, so Pandora stripped the wardrobe in the spare bedroom of clutter and began turning it into what she called their "tiny, mini headquarters."

As clippings went up and columns were organised, Tinsel wanted to make a joke about her sister watching too many episodes of *Law & Order*, but in truth, she was impressed. She laughed when Pandora added some fairy lights and cushions on the floor to give it more of "cosy vibe" amongst the crime solving. Standing back from her creation, which could be hidden from the kids behind folding doors at a moment's notice, Pandora nodded with satisfaction.

"We work this," she said. "Not like cops, but like us."

"Agreed," Tinsel nodded.

"There are always taskforces for these kinds of thing, so you and I will make up a taskforce of two... well, two and a bit. Veronica and the rest of Pandora's Boxheads are invaluable."

"That is not what you call your fans, is it?"

"It is. We'll need a good name though, something cool and Final Girly. Taskforce I Will Survive, Hey Hey?"

"No."

"Taskforce Not All Men but Definitely Most?"

Tinsel barked a laugh. "I'll brainstorm something, chill."

That's what she had been trying to do before she fell asleep, her terrible suggestions scrawled and crossed out on a notepad next to the bed. It wasn't the only thing left there and she recognised the messy scrawl of Max immediately.

"For Auntie Tintin," his note read.

She smiled as her eyes inspected the peanut butter sandwiches, sliced strawberries and muesli bar positioned on a plate for her. She hadn't even heard him sneak in. Tinsel listened to the sounds of the house around her, the noise of water splashing and Brian's baritone singing a bath time song down the hall as he washed the kids.

It was calming to her as she used the time to think. She'd spoken to Rushelle just once over the phone, with her boss audibly shook up about the incident and asking Tinsel no less than five times how she was doing.

"Of course, take as long as you need," she had said. "There's no rush to come back and we won't be replacing your show with anything, we can just use one of the syndicated overnight slots until you decide..."

She had trailed off, not filling in the dead air as she waited for Tinsel to say something. There was clearly an assumption that Tinsel would need a long break after everything that had happened, even an implication that she wouldn't be coming back at all. And she didn't like that.

The very idea that she was "damaged goods" left a bitter taste in her mouth. She was also incredibly stubborn. More than anything, she hated the idea that something she had worked so hard to build had been run off the air. Her new phone was on silent and charging in the corner of the room, something Pandora had clearly done while she slept. Checking the time, she was surprised to see it was only a little past 8pm.

"More than enough time," she muttered, quickly glancing at the list of missed calls and messages. There were some from Luiza, Shea, Gee, Ray, Tim, Stu, Joe Meyer and on and on and on... She swiped past all of them, finding Vic's number and hitting the call button. He answered on the second ring. It made her smile. She knew how busy he must be but despite all that, Tinsel was still a priority.

"Are you alright?" he asked, skipping past the hello portion of any regular conversation.

"I'm fine," she purred. "Just woke up from a four-hour nap."

"Don't make me jealous."

"Have you been home yet?"

"Soon. I had a kip in the staff room for a few hours, but they're giving me the day off tomorrow. I'll still be on call, but physically I won't have to go in unless it's something major."

"Which given the track record of events lately..."

He laughed. "Ain't that the truth."

"Listen, I just wanted to give you a heads up about something because I figure there may be logistics involved."

"Shoot."

"I'm going into the station tonight for my shift."

There was silence for a moment: a heavy, pressing absence where she had expected noise to go. Not yelling necessarily, but definitely something.

"What time?" he said, finally.

"I'm supposed to be on air at eleven, so I was going to get dressed, fix myself up, and then head in."

"I'll pick you up."

"What? No, you don't have to–"

"At night you're usually by yourself in that building, aren't you? And we've already seen that it's possible for someone to get in if they're really committed. There's too many entry points, too many blind spots, and I don't know how good Malu's replacement is."

"All fair points," she conceded.

There was a heavy sigh down the line, and she could almost envision him rubbing his forehead in frustration. "You have to do this, don't you?"

"Yes," she answered. "I have to. I can't stay here, doing nothing and just thinking about everything over and over again. I'll go mad, Vic. I'm not gonna be chased away from something I love."

"That's what I thought you'd say. Alright, give me forty-five minutes and I'll be there."

"Okay."

"Oh, and before I forget, he's awake."

"Malu?"

"Yup, a few hours ago apparently. His family are with him."

"I've got his wife's number, I'll give her a call. Thanks for telling me."

"Of course."

She hung up, her body still somewhat overwhelmed from everything she had experienced emotionally in the last twenty-four hours so it took her a moment to compose herself. First, eat the food laid out for her while making calls. She did so while sitting inside the wardrobe situation room, allowing her eyes to scan documents, facts and figures as she dialled.

Rushelle was the top of the list and 102.8 HitsFM's station manager was more than a little surprised. She had to call Stu first and get him to check whether or not they were fulfilling their duty of care if they let Tinsel back on the air so soon after she had nearly been killed on their premises.

She learned that ultimately it was her decision so long as they agreed with it, but she did have to send them an email confirming as much in writing which essentially covered their asses legally. She had to check in on her parents – something she was going to need to do twice daily for the next little while – and assure them she was totally fine.

Finally, there was Malu. She spoke to his wife, Tia, on the phone for fifteen minutes. No one had been particularly forthcoming with the details of exactly what had happened, and the security guard obviously wasn't verbose coming out of a coma, so Tinsel filled her in as best she could.

"He saved my life, Tia," she said, hearing the woman's sniffles down the end of the line. "He saved it nearly at the expense of his."

"That big idiot. If he wasn't laying in a hospital bed right now, I'd kill him. Again."

Tinsel laughed, knowing there was no true threat behind those words.

"Hang on, he's gesturing to me. One sec."

She could hear a muffled exchange as Malu asked for the phone and Tia told him not to wear himself out. Eventually she relented and Tinsel heard the strained voice of her friend.

"Tinsel?"

"Hey, the hero of the hour. How are you feeling?"

"Like I got stabbed. How about you?"

"Same, only slightly less... fatal."

She heard his wheezing laugh, followed by Tia scolding him for overexertion. Tinsel – having cleared her plate – kept talking to him as she got dressed, it being important to her that Malu knew exactly who the police were holding in relation to the crime. He sounded as shocked as she had been initially, exchanging many apologetic sentiments before his tone shifted.

"I don't know," he mused. "You got a better look at him than I did, does the description fit? Physically?"

"Zack's the same height as me, five eight, and the person seemed about that. I can't really remember their size exactly. It was dark and when I saw them standing up, I was laying down, which is confusing."

"Did he seem thinner or muscly? I mean, there could be padding under that hoodie, but you didn't see or recognise anything? Even a smell can be telling."

"Nothing," she replied. "I didn't even get a good look at their eyes. There was a weird hood that was stiff and sat out from their face like…"

"What?"

"Well, I described it to the cops as similar to the Grim Reaper."

"Ya telling me," Malu scoffed.

"Right," she said, slipping into her most comfortable pair of overalls. "Anyway, I think they were wearing a balaclava under that with netting over the eyes or something. I never even glimpsed their face once: it was just darkness under there."

"I can remember it in bits and pieces. The longer I'm awake, the more it's coming back to me."

"Don't force yourself, just concentrate on getting better so that I can see you back at the station again soon and not whoever the new guy is."

"Can't imagine anyone is gonna be super keen for the night shift after Fitz ends up dead and I end up stabbed."

"Preach. I'll find out who the fresh meat is tonight and fill you in on all the goss."

"Wait, tonight? You're going *in*? You're doing *The Graveyard Shift*?"

"Is this where you petition me for more LL Cool J?"

"This is where I petition you to be careful."

"A cop is coming with me, the one who saved both our asses. I'll be fine."

"Is it weird that I actually hope it's Zack? I like that idea much more than the one where you go back into the station when the killer could still be out there, listening."

"Please stop talking. You'll make me rethink this."

"No, I won't. You're brave, sis. I'll be tuned in."

"Ha," she laughed. "You better be sleeping. Get well, Malu. I'll come see you tomorrow."

"Bring Roses."

"Only so I can eat the peppermint ones."

She looked up to see her sister watching her from the doorway as she hung up, an amused smile playing on her face.

"Witch, I knew you wouldn't be able to stay away."

"Oh yeah?" Tinsel grinned. "How so?"

"Because we're the same. If someone had tried to kill me on the job, I'd only work harder out of spite."

Tinsel chuckled. Pandora was on the damn money.

"Thanks for the meal," she said, as she began slapping on some make-up. "I didn't realise how starving I was until I saw everything sitting right there."

"You're welcome. Max helped, but I made sure he washed his dirty little hands first."

"Hey!"

The subject of their conversation stuck his head around the legs of his mother, his wet body wrapped in a towel.

"Come here and let me smell you," Tinsel ordered, grabbing him in a crushing hug and inhaling that indescribable scent of a freshly bathed child. It felt like a pain killer in more ways than one as she clung to him. Max was never able to keep still for long, and quickly wiggled free of her embrace and legged it down the hall. Pandora tapped him on the bum as he did so, earning a squeal.

"Is *Vic* picking you up?" her sister asked, Tinsel not missing the way his name dripped from her mouth.

"*Yes*," she replied, doing her best attempt to mimic the tone. "According to this text, he's ten minutes away."

"As long as we don't lose the cops on the house."

"I think your friend was right: they'll be here as long as they can afford them to be."

"What a comfort," Pandora snorted. "I need to get my own cute switchblade, I reckon."

She stepped forward with several sheets of paper as she moved into the wardrobe, sorting and pinning them up.

"What's that?" Tinsel questioned.

"Three cases that fit our perp, I think."

"Perp," she repeated. "You're even starting to sound like a cop now."

"Good, the more of them I hang around the better the blog is gonna be. Anyway, a guy is doing time for this one in Goulburn super max. But these other two are unsolved."

She laid out the documents on the interior walls, not even bothering to warn her there were autopsy photos involved.

"Jesus… this is all from the past year?"

"Past three years. While you've been sleeping, I've been busy. The thing that annoys me though is I only think this one truly fits with what we're looking for, the others seem… I dunno."

"How did Veronica go?"

"Not much better. It makes me think we're looking in the wrong spot."

"What do you mean?"

"Where are his earlier victims if not here?"

Tinsel shrugged, legitimately puzzled by the question.

"Overseas," Pandora said. "There's nothing to say Australia was his hunting ground all along, so maybe it's someone who has just moved here or just moved back. Or even a touring musician or something: any profession that keeps them mobile makes them harder to track. Like the whole truckers and serial killers thing."

Tinsel frowned. "I do not have time to ask you to explain that. Wait, this is all working off the theory Zack isn't really the person responsible, right? You're the one who put the cops on to him in the first place."

"I'm not saying he's responsible and I'm not saying he's *not* responsible. Just keeping options open until we know for sure about the bullet wound."

"Whatever you say. Also, I added everything Vic told me about the NFSA death to the Google doc, but we can't exclude that, especially now."

There was a knock on the front door and Tinsel grabbed a jumper and the rest of her stuff as fast as she could.

"That's Vic," she said, heading towards the lounge while Pandora followed her.

"It could be Astrid wanting a coffee refill."

"Astrid?"

"One of the cops: Astrid and Augustus."

"You've been giving them refreshments?"

"Why not? We want them to be alert... and loose with their tongues."

It was Vic, with Brian wrangling the kids as he opened the door. Tinsel planted a kiss on her brother-in-law's cheek before he had a chance to invite the detective in for a beer. She was able to tell just from his manner that Pandora had brought her husband up to speed on their "situation." There was no point being mad: her sister told Brian everything and the man kept secrets for the both of them.

She waved good night and told them she'd see them in the morning, quickly dragging Vic down the path and back into his car. Tinsel only breathed a sigh of relief once she was in the vehicle, doors closed and tomb of silence pressing around them. She could see Vic wanted to ask her what that was all about, his lips parting as he prepared to ask the question.

"Don't," she said, shaking her head. "Just get me to work before things get even more complicated."

He didn't need a further explanation as to what that "complication" was, but he smirked as he started the car and pulled out of the driveway. She was surprised when Gang of Youths played out of the car speakers, it being the first time the radio hadn't been playing in his car. The police scanner was still on, occasionally interrupting the gentle strumming as the closing track of *Let Me Be Clear* playing out before the album started over again. She was going to remark on it, but fifteen minutes into their journey the music choice became obvious: it was soothing. Sure, it was also a little sad in message, yet it was doing more to relax and calm her than any chemical could as they mounted the curb and pulled up in front of the 102.8 HitsFM building.

Turning off the engine, Vic answered her question before Tinsel even had a chance to ask it.

"I cleared it with security," he said, nodding in the direction of the night desk as they hopped out of the car. "This is the safest route in and out of the building. We're not taking any risks."

Neither was the station, it turned out.

Malu had not one, but two replacements. They had waited to meet Tinsel and Detective James in person, introducing themselves and sharing their personal contact details so they "could be reached at a moment's notice." There was also a police officer assigned to the building who was to constantly patrol the premises and keep an eye out for anything unusual.

Tinsel couldn't help the way her heart pounded in her chest as they talked through these details like it was the most normal thing in the world. Her palms seemed sweaty, and she wiped them on the material of her denim overalls, trying to ignore the lump in her throat as she and Vic moved towards the elevator that would take them to the third floor.

As the metallic doors pinged closed, Tinsel felt like she might hyperventilate.

"I think this was a mistake," she said, breathless. "Why did I think this was a good idea?"

"Tinsel."

"Oh God, I nearly died here last night, and my ex-boyfriend might be a murderer. *Oh God.*"

Vic lunged forward, hitting the emergency stop button so the elevator was brought to a halt. Suddenly he was in her space, clouding her vision as he pressed two hands gently to the side of her face. He was all Tinsel could see and she clung to the reassuring lines of his face, the faint acne scars she could see when he was this close, the stubble that was forming around his jawline.

"No one is going to hurt you; do you hear me?"

She tried to mumble a reply, but her breath hadn't properly returned yet.

"Inhale deeply for me, then exhale. That's it, and again, one after the other. Now slower, hold the breath for a few seconds, good girl. You've got this."

"I've got this," she repeated, Detective James never moving from the space he occupied in front of her. She realised she was gripping the fabric of his shirt tightly at his shoulders, holding him to her, and she was grateful for his presence. Tinsel closed her eyes, inhaling the scent of him and the mix of spices she now associated with *Vic*. He was watching her intently.

"You were having a panic attack," he whispered. "It's perfectly normal."

"I've never had a panic attack before. It didn't feel perfectly normal."

"It is, trust me."

"I trust you," she murmured, drawing him closer still. There was a relief that trickled through her body as his lips gently brushed hers, the action repeating as he returned her kiss just as softly. If there was heat in the gesture, it was buried deep below the surface. Tinsel recognised this as something else, something far more dangerous as the police officer held her still and kissed her in the confines of the small elevator.

When they broke apart, she knew almost immediately that something had changed. It seemed like a small worry compared to the larger ones she had. She pushed it to the back of her mind. She could tell Detective James felt it too, his touch trailing the skin on her cheek as he pulled his hand away. Sex was one thing. This was something… more. Without saying another word, he hit the emergency stop button again and they were jerked upwards towards the third floor.

Stepping out into the corridor, Tinsel looked down over the balcony that showed the entrance foyer to the station, the small figures of the security guards bringing some relief. She used her pass to swipe in, Vic going first and rounding every corner in front of her like a human shield even though he had already been informed by one of the security guards they'd just swept the floor.

Tinsel could see Luiza in the studio, but she needed to sort out some things at her desk first as she began scheduling the playlist for that night. Vic left her to it, prowling through the floor and examining every seemingly empty office, every dim corridor, every abandoned studio. He wasn't taking any chances and it eased Tinsel's nerves as she tracked his movements out of the corner of her eye.

Taking a quick trip to the bathroom and composing herself, Tinsel stepped into the studio at exactly five minutes before 11pm. It was later than she would leave it usually, but she had been inundated with emails and a considerable amount of time had gone to weeding through that.

As she pushed open the heavy studio door with her shoulder, she saw Luiza light up and her mouth pop open with surprise.

"They told me you were coming in, but I didn't believe it."

The woman's eyes flicked to the police officer who entered

behind her colleague, comprehension taking a moment longer to dawn on her face. Unhooking herself from the headphones, Luiza moved forward to embrace Tinsel in a way she never had before. It felt motherly to her in the moment, that not being a side of Luiza she often saw.

"Careful," Tinsel groaned. "I'm still tender. And stitched."

"Of course, yeah, sorry," she said, leaping back. "Sorry."

"It's okay, I'm... okay. Ish"

"That's what the calvary is for, right? At least you'll be in here with company."

"Armed company," Detective James said, patting the weapon holstered at his side with affection.

"Men and their pistols," Luiza smirked. Shaking her head, she dove back behind the mic as they began transitioning between the shows. It wasn't long before her friend had officially ducked out of there, with Tinsel falling into the familiar rhythm as she cued up the first string of ads and moved her lips closer to the microphone.

"Good evening, goblins, ghouls and all manner of night owls in between, my name is Tinsel Munroe and welcome to *The Graveyard Shift*. As we do every night Monday to Friday, I'm going to be playing you some spooky tunes and some downright bangers as we work through into Friday morning. Feel free to hit me up with your requests on the text line or via Twitter using "The Graveyard Shift" hashtag. In the meantime, Mr Cool J is going to be kicking us off thanks to the baddest mother I know, Malu."

Vic was smiling as she slid the headphones down her neck and she shrugged, offering little more by way of explanation. He mouthed something at her, clearly uncertain whether it was safe to speak or not, and she laughed.

"It's fine," she said, pointing behind her to the green light fixed into the wall. "Only time we can't talk is when that's red."

"Nobody can hear this."

"Nobody baby but you and me," she hummed, not sure if he would recognise the Penny & The Quarters tune. The blank look on his face told her he didn't. "You wanna take a look? See it from the other side?"

"Alright," he said, cautious as he pulled himself up off the couch and slipped behind the control decks with her.

"This is everything," Tinsel said, gesturing to the screens and dials in front of her.

"Whoa, how do you keep track of it all?" Detective James asked. "There's so much going on here."

"I barely need to look at the screen," she pointed, red digits counting her in and out of the various ad and announcement breaks. "It's almost like an internal backup. I just refer to it every now and again to make sure things are ticking. This screen shows me how everything looks on the website and the app, as artwork and information should be displayed with each track as it's played."

He nodded, but his eyes had that distinctly glazed over quality.

"This is a mirror of my desktop out there, so I can see what songs I have scheduled next or what ads need to be played, or if I've pre-recorded an interview," she continued. "If it's slow, I might check emails. Everything that gets sent through on the text line immediately goes into this shared inbox. Final screen is social media, so I can see feedback coming through on Twitter, Instagram, Facebook, whatever."

"A lot of questions about what happened last night," he noted, scanning the Twitter feed. "People want to know about the dead air."

"I take it that means the story hasn't broken yet."

"The police reporter from *The Age* already has it, but Diraani is buying time with exclusive comment."

"From who?"

"The commissioner."

Tinsel let out an impressive whistle.

"Even so, it will be in the paper this week some time. You won't have a mob greeting you at the end of tonight's shift, but eventually…"

"Oh goodie," she sighed. "Something to look forward to."

"Anything weird come in over social media? Any creepy emails?"

He brushed up against her as he moved closer to read, a hand naturally slipping around her waist as he did so. She cast him a smile and a sideways glance, letting him know that she knew exactly what he was up to. He smirked back, unapologetic.

"Welp, I had two job offers sitting in my inbox from rival commercial stations," she murmured. "And according to this, my ratings have never been higher. But, you know, *people are dying*. So, highs and lows."

"You could not have made that sound any more sarcastic if you tried."

"Ergh, it just seems so tacky. One even slid into my DMs."

Detective James scoffed. "Look, this line says they 'like the way you overcome adversity.'"

"Like there's any other choice. I'm about to overcome their email right into the junk folder. And hey, do you snore?"

The officer blinked, surprised by the question. "Snore?"

"Yeah, like a wailing moose sound?"

"No… although it has been a while since I had someone to tell me. Why?"

She smiled, gesturing to the couch. "It's comfy. There are blankets over there and I can dim the lights."

"Are you trying to seduce me?"

She laughed. "That horse has well and truly come before the cart. I meant for you to catch up on some sleep."

"Oh," he beamed. "It's a nice thought, but I can't do that. I'm here to guard you in case anything happens."

"There's one entry and exit to this studio. I'll lock the door, position a chair in front of it, and not leave. If I need you, I can wake you."

He looked sceptical and she rolled her eyes at him.

"Please sleep for the both of us," Tinsel moaned. "I won't begrudge you."

"*Fine*," he said, flicking the lock on the studio door as he strolled towards the couch. He lay across it, his height meaning that his feet stuck out over the other end, and he folded his arms across his chest in a very business-like fashion.

"I'll rest my eyes," he said, breath already sounding heavier just due to the fact he was horizontal.

Tinsel smiled as she dimmed the lights, returning to the controls just in time to back announce over the top of 'Hollywood Forever Cemetery's' final notes.

CHAPTER 17

By the time the breakfast show rolled in, Tinsel was more than ready to leave the station. It was fatigue, not regret. She was glad she had come in and performed her shift. There was something dominant in the act, like she was reclaiming her narrative. She could tell from the look on Shea's face that he thought it was just plain stupid. Yet the hours of *The Graveyard Shift* had also given her time to think and properly work through her thoughts while Detective James slept open-mouthed on the couch just across from her. She'd woken him an hour or so before the others arrived, and while he had been asleep, Tinsel had done some detective work of her own. The appropriate name for it was probably closer to "social media stalking," but if it got her answers, she didn't really care.

She was still friends with Zack on Facebook, the split too soon for either of them to have time to sever those digital ties. It did grant her access, however, and Tinsel opened the Google Drive Pandora had created. In it, she wrote down the dates, locations and times of every incident so far. Mera was first, obviously, then the person who had been creeping at her house the following night. Third was Alona Cennoqia who died at the NFSA on Friday evening, although wasn't discovered until Monday afternoon. The *Band Candy* premiere was fourth, then the series of events at the 102.8 HitsFM office just a few hours later. She drew herself a rough timeline, noting how everything was so tightly clustered together.

Just like Pandora said, she thought. *A spree.*

From there, she tracked through the last few weeks of activity on Zack's Facebook page: where he had been, places that were checked in to, what photos he had been tagged in, the whole lot. He didn't have a Twitter account, but he was very active on Instagram, and she jumped over there as well as she began making a dual timeline. She was looking for an alibi, she realised: something other than the fact he had been banging the receptionist. *Even Zack must have been aware of the cliche he was living out*, she thought bitterly.

Tinsel was doing her best to document his movements and see whether any or all of that synched up with what the killer had been doing. She smirked at the knowledge of how much this would please her sister, fingers swiping between screens as she looked at Nancy's account as well. They had been careful; there were no pictures of Zack on the woman's timeline and only one of them tagged together. There was a selfie of her at a concert earlier in the week, which Zack had also been checked into on Facebook by one of his friends from the gym. Tinsel frowned, knowing it was likely they were there together but didn't have definitive proof. But it did show that Zack wasn't likely the killer, as the show had been going on at exactly the same time as the *Band Candy* premiere.

She navigated over to the Facebook account of Zack's brother, it being the only form of social media the man had. Three days earlier he had been tagged in a snap of several men posing in the back of a ute, feet propped up on the tray next to the carcass of an animal. The caption read: "Successful pig hunt with da boiz." She frowned, realising that it meant he too was somewhere that was distinctly else during the nights of the murders. It was probable the police had found this information as well. She knew they had officers solely dedicated to scouring the online resources of potential suspects, Vic had told her as much. The case against Zack was growing weaker by the minute, along with any belief that they had the right man.

These thoughts consumed her as she left the station with Vic by her side. Her quietness must have concerned him, but he said nothing. Tinsel didn't miss the sideways glances he was throwing in her direction, or even the way he used reflective surfaces to watch her without her *feeling* like he was watching her. If he was worried, he didn't voice it.

He spoke with the other officers and security guards while she waited, all assuring him the evening had been "uneventful" before they stepped outside and strolled towards his car. Tinsel had never thought the word "uneventful" would be one she'd be relieved to hear, yet just listening to someone else say it out loud calmed her. She waited as Vic unlocked the car, her eyes scanning the backseat meticulously through the window.

"What are you expecting?" he asked her.

"Hey, I've seen *Urban Legend*, okay? I'm not taking any chances."

He barked a laugh. "The slasher with Tara Reid?"

"Don't omit the most important piece of information: the slasher with Tara Reid who plays a radio DJ that gets *brutally* axed to death. I will not be Tara Reid-ed."

"Who am I, in that scenario?"

Tinsel thought for a moment, climbing into the front seat and clipping in her seat belt. "Loretta Devine. She plays the cop."

"Does she live?"

"Kinda."

Vic watched her for a moment, before whipping around and doing an exaggerated inspection of the backseat. She chuckled, her response causing an amused expression to spread across his features, as if that had been his sole purpose.

"I need to ask you something," she said, seizing the lighter moment. "And I'll understand if you can't tell me."

"Shoot," Vic replied, pulling out into the non-existent traffic.

"Funny you should say that…"

He threw her a look as she pushed on.

"Zack. Did he have a bullet wound?"

Vic peered across at her, hands gripping the steering wheel. At first, she didn't think he was going to reply. Tinsel turned her head, gaze locked on the tram that tracked past the car window, only two passengers on board.

"No," he finally replied. She closed her eyes.

"What about Nancy?" she asked.

He shook his head.

"Zack's brother?"

"No," Vic responded. "He's going to be out by morning. Well, later morning."

She dropped her head into her hands, not sure if she was feeling relief or dread. The first because it wasn't him. The second because it meant the killer was still out there. The indicator sounded off and she sat up, surprised as Vic pulled off the main road.

"What are you doing?" she questioned, as the vehicle slowed to a stop behind a jeep in the drive-thru line.

"Taking your order," he replied.

She blinked.

"Food. You need to eat it. Preferably something terrible for you."

"A sausage and egg McMuffin," she replied quickly. "And two hash browns."

He smiled. "Atta girl."

"And a chocolate thick shake."

Vic reached across, fingers skimming along the arch of her cheek.

There was a sharp beep behind them and he jumped, not realising the car in front had moved on. Sliding the vehicle into gear, he crept forward and spoke their orders into the speaker. She raised her eyebrows as he ordered two serves of the pancakes and a hot chocolate for himself.

"What?" he asked, catching her look.

"I didn't realise you had such an appetite."

"Didn't you?" Vic smirked, the meaning not lost on her as she snorted at his corniness.

Five minutes later, they were digging into their fast-food feast, sitting on the bonnet of his car as dawn fought for prominence. A yellowish pink was pushing at the edges of the dark blue sky that peeked between the silhouettes of the buildings around them. It was a gradual battle, but minute by minute the light was eventually winning.

Wiping the grease from her hands on a napkin, she watched Vic thoughtfully as he sliced through his second serve of pancakes with plastic cutlery. He had the styrofoam box balanced on his knee, which Tinsel knew would have tipped and spilled maple syrup all down her leg if she attempted the same thing.

"What do you know about your birth parents?" he asked, the question surprising her so much that she was silent for a long moment. Vic looked up from his food, casting a curious glance at her.

"You look shocked."

"That was just so out of the blue, that's all."

"Are you okay talking about it? Because if not—"

"No, no, it's fine. Pandora and I have never been sensitive about the 'A' word."

"'A' word?" he quizzed, raising his eyebrows.

"Adopted," she said, in a mock whisper.

Vic smirked. "Ah, I see."

"Mum and dad are both leftie academics, you know. They believed in raising us in a very open, honest household so we always knew growing up that we had different biological parents but that they were our *real* parents, if you know what I mean."

"I think so… I come from a loud, very big family of immigrants. We don't so much talk openly about stuff as we do shout passive aggressively over seemingly unrelated things."

"How do you fare in that scenario?" she asked. Vic was passionate, definitely, but she suspected most people didn't see that side of him. On the surface, he presented a calm, level-headed exterior. He was forceful, but softly spoken. She had trouble imagining him in a boisterous feud with his relatives over the dinner table at a family gathering.

"I have five brothers and two sisters," he started.

"Eight kids?" she blanched, thinking of his poor mother.

"Yup, all older than me except Eduardo. He's the youngest, I'm the second youngest, and both of us have a similar type of personality. He's a martial artist turned mechanic and runs a workshop in Northcote now, but from an early age the two of us just stuck together and tried to keep a low profile."

"I bet," she snorted, shaking her head slightly as she brought herself back around to the original question. "And I know nothing about my birth parents, except that they were from somewhere just outside of Faridabad."

"You never looked into it? Never tried to hunt them down?"

She laughed, earning a surprised look from Vic.

"What?" he wondered.

"This isn't *The Little Princess*. You people always have this weird, Hollywood perception of orphans. Like, we're all Oliver Twisting it and desperately trying to hunt down our birth parents or we'll never be whole. For some of us, sure, that might be super important. For a lot of us though, the families we grew up with *are* our families. We don't feel like there's some crucial piece missing or some cross-country quest we need to go on to be reunited with our birth parents. We're totally fine with how things are. Or at least I am. Pandora is. I can't speak for everyone."

"I didn't mean to offend."

"You didn't. But do you know anyone who has been adopted? Anyone before me, that is?"

He shook his head.

"There you go. Meet a few more folks and your version of 'orphans' won't be so–"

"It's a hard yack life?"

"*For us,*'" she sung. "And yeah, basically. I've never had a desire to know, neither has Pandora, and our parents had us in a play group when we were younger with other adopted kids, so it was completely normal."

"These parents seem kind of awesome."

"Ha, wait till you meet them. They'll want to get into a discussion with you about the rate of Indigenous incarnation and what you're doing about it from inside the system itself. Light chit-chat they do *not* do."

He smiled, the gesture doing that thing to his face she liked where lines appeared down the side of his cheeks and into grooves that had deepened over the years with the same expression. Tinsel suddenly realised what she'd said, straightening up and feeling the cold metal of the car bonnet beneath her.

"Uh, when I said you'll meet them… I mean, like, one day. If you, er… wanted to. And they were in town. And you were free or–"

"Tinsel, it's okay," he said, placing a hand on her arm.

"I didn't mean to be presumptuous or–"

"I know what you meant," he chuckled, pulling her off the bonnet of the car and towards him. "Stop sweating."

"I'm not sweating," she retorted, letting herself be tugged into his embrace. "I'm barely schvitzing."

"Whatever you say."

She couldn't see his face from her position nuzzled against his chest, but she could hear the smile in his voice. Closing her eyes, Tinsel breathed deeply as the scents of the morning teased her nostrils. There was that distinct fast-food smell, burnt rubber from the car park, fuel cutting through it all, and beneath that, Vic. Or at least the things she associated with him: sandalwood, and just a hint of jasmine that she knew was from her own perfume. She had rubbed off on him, literally. If she had her way, she would have stayed like that, content in the rest of the city waking up and moving around them. Yet she knew she couldn't. And he couldn't either.

"I'd like to meet you parents," he said, speaking first. "I'm fascinated by anyone who could raise the women I've met in you and Pandora."

She smirked, pressing down the niggling sensation she felt deep in her gut about any implication of the future.

"I've heard relationships based on intense experiences never work," Tinsel whispered, pulling back.

Detective James opened his mouth to reply, before pausing as a frown crossed his features.

"Did... did you just quote *Speed* at me?"

"I may have."

"Wait, does that make me Jack or Annie?"

"Gender is a construct."

"Oh God! Am I Jason Patric from *Speed 2*?"

"You are thinking way too much into this."

He shook his head slightly, a lazy smile spreading on his face. "You're right. I should be thinking about how hot it is that I found someone who knows *Speed* line for line."

"Ya damn right," Tinsel laughed. She grabbed the packet of painkillers from inside her overalls pocket and quickly popped one. She looked up at the glowing, golden arches that divided the middle of a two-storey brick building with curved balconies and metal railings.

"Clifton Hill Maccas is my favourite, you know."

He twisted around to look at the sight. "Mine too. The building is heritage listed."

"Isn't that weird?" she scoffed, hopping back in the car. "You have this pristine, nearly hundred year-old example of Jazz Moderne architecture and it serves McFlurries."

When Vic pulled into Pandora's driveway a short while later, she was tempted to invite him in. She wanted to, physically anyway. But mentally she was spent. The fact two officers were still parked outside the house only complicated things further.

"I'll see you later?" she said, resisting the urge to lean across and kiss him as she kept her eyes trained on the unmarked car down the street.

He followed her gaze, not missing what had originally attracted Tinsel's attention. The muscle of his jaw twinged before he answered.

"I'll pick you up for work tonight."

"Same deal?"

"Same deal."

She went to climb from the car, her progress halted briefly as he gripped her hand, his thumb stroking the skin there gently. Tinsel gave him a smirk, before grabbing her bag and walking up the front lawn to the house. Giving the officers in the car a small wave, she kept her head down as she unlocked the front door and was immediately bombarded with a cacophony of noise.

"BUT I DON'T WANT TO!"

"Max, you eat that yogurt or I'm going to eat you, okay? Your choice," Pandora snapped, brandishing a yogurt covered spoon at her son like a weapon.

"Is threatening him with cannibalism really the best approach, honey?"

Brian had popped his head out from the hallway, where Airlie was drinking a bottle happily as she rested in his arms. He realised his mistake almost immediately as Tinsel watched her sister pivot on the spot to face him, expression furious.

"*Honey*," she said, tone deadly.

He raised one hand in surrender, quickly backing away into the hall as Pandora shot visual daggers at him. Tinsel moved slowly, careful not to make any sudden movements as she joined him en route to the office she was sleeping in.

"Rough morning?" she whispered.

Brian nodded enthusiastically. "Max is in one of his moods."

"Yikes."

"Which means Pandora is in one of her moods to combat it."

"Best to find neutral ground, I think."

"Wise," he answered. Tinsel peeled off into the spare room while Brian stepped into the nursery.

Closing the door behind her with a gentle click, she stripped out of her clothes, used a makeup wipe to clean her face, then wiggled into her favourite bed shirt. It seemed as if her head had barely hit the pillow before she was fast asleep, soft snores mixing with the sound of distant shouts as war continued to rage in the kitchen.

Vic didn't pick her up for work that evening: instead, it was a different officer, one she recognised by face only. Tinsel's mouth was already open, the question "where's Vic?" on her lips as she saw who was standing at the front door to escort her. She checked herself, however, careful not to give away too much familiarity.

Instead, she acted as if it was exactly what she expected, gathering her things and folding into the front seat for the ride to the station. The woman was clearly versed in what she was supposed to be doing, greeting the officers at 102.8 HitsFM much the same way Vic had. She even knew the station's replacement security guards by name.

After taking her up to the third floor and into the studio, Tinsel offered her refreshments as she set up for the show, which the officer politely declined. Placing a tablet on her lap, the woman looked like she was settling herself in for *The Graveyard Shift* as Luiza bid them both farewell and finished her round.

Tinsel waved goodbye with one hand, her other hitting the keys on her phone as she texted a series of question marks to Detective James. Annoyingly, the small "seen" icon and tick appeared to let her know that he had received and read the message. Her heart raced a little bit faster as the three dots loaded that meant he was writing a reply. Her eyes flicked between her phone screen and the countdown clock, with only ten seconds remaining before she was live on-air. A reply didn't come, however, and she put her phone on silent as she spoke into the mic and welcomed listeners back to the show.

"First up, I'm starting the night with a classic from Nerf Herder who are just about to hit our shores for an Australian tour. Kicking off in Melbourne next week, I'm tweeting out a link now to where you can find tickets for that show. 'Turn Off the Light' from Kim Petras featuring Elvira Mistress of the Dark isn't far behind, so stay tuned. Let's get into it!"

Raising the levels on the track as she lowered her own, Tinsel slid her headphones down and shifted to browsing the social media feed. She didn't need the daily emails from management excitedly updating her on the numbers to know that *The Graveyard Shift*'s listenership had maintained its spike following Mera Brant's death. It made her cringe, but the notoriety and press surrounding everything over the course of the past few weeks meant her audience had increased tenfold… and was only growing.

She tried to shake the idea from her head, diverting her attention back to the many screens in front of her. Scanning the tweets and sharing those she liked from *The Graveyard Shift*'s official account and her own simultaneously, Tinsel nearly scrolled past one that gave her pause. She recognised the profile picture immediately – the kookaburra logo – which meant *that* user was back. Looking up at the officer across from her as she sat there on the studio couch, Tinsel took a screenshot of the latest tweets from that night.

Hello, Sidney, the first read, following the pattern of the previous messages. It almost made her snort, the tweet itself not exactly out of context given she had just played Nick Cave's 'Red Right Hand.' It was the other tweets that worried her.

You never paid any attention. Look what you did to him.

I'm your friend till the end. Hidey-ho!

I just can't take no pleasure in killing. There's just some things you gotta do.

I know they did it, they killed her, they, killed her.

They were all lines of dialogue from horror movies, spoken by the killer to various victims. It was her job to recognise these words, her passion also. They had worked their way through various slashers from *Friday the 13th* and *Child's Play*, to *The Texas Chain Saw Massacre* and *Prom Night*. Unsure whether it was something she needed to alert her new minder to, she would have preferred to share it with Vic as he actually had the context for when the messages first started popping up.

She bit her lip, fingers hovering over the keyboard as she considered another option. *Fuck it*, she thought. Tinsel was sick of being afraid. Copying the account's URL, she opened her favourites tab and scanned the titles of websites until she found the one she was looking for.

IP Worldwide was something she had used regularly back when she first started *The Graveyard Shift* and encountered a wave of trolls disgruntled over the fact that a twenty-something brown woman had replaced the fifty-something white male stalwart who had previously had the slot for fifteen years. She would copy and paste the URL for their Twitter accounts into the website's tab, hit locate, and wait patiently while a globe icon rotated until it had a result for her. It wasn't always successful, but about seventy-five per cent of the time IP Worldwide would ping with the specific location of where the Twitter user was based if it wasn't already stated in their bio.

Usually it was a relief, with most of the trolls from the US or rural parts of Australia, so far away from her that Tinsel would exhale and close the tabs. Yet sometimes – like this one – they were close. She scratched the back of her hand with discomfort as the words "South Yarra" and the postcode "3141" appeared on screen. That was not only within the same state as her, but the same city. Hell, it was within the same five-kilometre radius as the office.

Glancing down at her phone, Vic still hadn't replied to her text. With a jolt, she realised she was nearly on-air. Quickly back announcing the last two songs and plugging an in-station promotion, she switched off her mic and considered the woman across from her. Would this cop think she was being dramatic for flagging a Twitter account with her? One that technically hadn't done anything wrong?

In the past, she would have immediately felt like she was overreacting. But after the events of the last fortnight... Tinsel tapped the desk with impatience. *I'll monitor it*, she thought, right clicking her mouse to save the page as one of her favourites just as another tweet loaded on screen.

We all go a little mad, sometimes.

CHAPTER 18

Tinsel made it to the weekend before news of the "radio station massacre" hit hard and fast. Gee sent her a text to warn her about coming back to The Pinny: apparently journalists had camped out the front since mid-Saturday afternoon. They told her there were about a dozen, with that number growing by Sunday.

"Makes sense," Pandora said, when Tinsel read their text messages aloud to her sister. "It's a stake out with double rewards: you or Zack would be super valuable. Either one is their front page or nightly news bulletin."

"Fucking gross."

"If it bleeds, it leads," her sister muttered.

Tinsel had never felt so grateful that she and Pandora had different last names, as the press weren't on to her property yet. She still had no idea how they'd found out where she and Zack had been living, but she guessed it wasn't that hard to ask around until a reporter got the answer they wanted. *Or the electoral roll*, she thought. Or one of the bloody videos her neighbours had filmed that night in the alleyway.

It didn't matter much; the important thing was that she was still under the radar staying with "the Smiths" and none of them left the house all weekend. Brian had declared a two-day long couch binge, with the three adults powering through the first few seasons of *The West Wing* even though they knew every episode practically line-for-line.

They had all agreed to a social media ban too: no checking the internet or various accounts throughout the weekend. Tinsel had overheard Brian suggesting to Pandora that it would be a good idea, that it would "help take her mind off all this horrible shit." Her sister had agreed, and Tinsel had too, yet the second her brother-in-law's snores could be heard over an attempted assassination of President Bartlett, the two sisters shared a look. They didn't even need to exchange words as they both lunged for their phones, which had been stacked on the coffee table and out of reach. Neither spoke for a solid twenty minutes as they reacquainted themselves with the digital world.

"Anything from Vic?" Pandora asked, not looking up.

"Nothing," Tinsel answered, feeling disappointment spread through her blood like oil in water. "Fuck, what is going on?"

"I asked Astrid and Augustus if he had the weekend off."

"*You did what?!*" Tinsel screeched.

"Ssssh, you'll wake the baby." Pandora pointed at her lap, where Brian's head was now resting on a pillow.

"How did you ask them? What did they say? Shit, I hope you weren't obvious."

"I was cool as ice, chill out. It was when they came by to do their morning sweep of the house and as I was giving them a muffin. I had Max ask."

"Oh no," Tinsel cringed.

"It was flawless, trust me. People are always thrown by his cuteness. We practised his lines, and I said if he got it right, he could have Cocoa Pops. So he asked them 'where the other cop cop was?' They laughed, commented that he was adorable, and said they thought he had the weekend off."

"In the middle of a high-profile murder investigation?"

"I know. I didn't buy it either."

"Which means they're covering for him." Tinsel bit her lip.

"Yo, slow down Miss Distrustful. Or he really *does* have the weekend off. Or they don't know him well enough to have heard what's really up."

"Miss Distrustful," Tinsel repeated, rolling her eyes. "Hey, remember how my boyfriend of three years turned out to be cheating on me and then the police investigated him for murder? I think I've earned the right to be a little wary when the next man I've been–"

"Bumping uglies with?"

"*Seeing*," she corrected, "drops off the face of the earth. If he does have the weekend off, why wouldn't he message me? Why wouldn't he reply?"

"Want me to ask one of the other cops? See if they've heard anything?"

Tinsel nearly said yes, before she thought better of it.

"There's more going on than my love life," she mumbled, pushing her feelings to the side.

"No shit," Pandora snorted. "Like this asshole."

She held up her phone screen so Tinsel could inspect it properly, Joe Meyer's face immediately visible under the headline *"Filmmaker Fears His Movie Inspired the Radio Murders."*

"You think they could come up with something better than 'radio murders,'" she huffed. "Or 'radio massacre.' What is that?"

"*The Guardian*," Pandora answered. "And I dunno, I think it's catchy."

Tinsel brought up the website on her phone and swallowed down a groan at the fact the story took up the top half of the homepage. Clicking into it, she scrolled down until she found the video icon embedded under the fourth par and hit play.

"It's sickening," Joe Meyer said, his face animated. "I've been told the police think there's a connection between the murder victims and my movie – *Band Candy*, out in cinemas now – and I just don't believe it. Conservatives will look for any opportunity to censor content that doesn't fit their world view and it has been proven time and time again that movies and video games with violence don't turn their audience into senseless killers. Otherwise, the whole world would be full of them! I believe that people can engage with my art without needing to recreate it in the real world. I just hope whoever is responsible is brought to justice soon."

"Ergh, did he say 'brought to justice?'" Pandora questioned, taking a large sip from her wine glass.

"Yes, he's Batman now," Tinsel, murmured as she read the rest of the article. "Is that true? Do the police think there's a connection to his movie?"

Her sister made a wanking gesture so exaggerated that Tinsel thought she might break her wrist.

"I ask because it kind of makes sense," she shrugged, attempting to explain herself. "Mera Brant was calling up to win tickets to *Band Candy*'s premiere on the same night I aired an interview with him. That nineteen-year-old lighting tech was murdered and strung up *at* the actual premiere."

"Indy Aposolottius," Pandora said, suppling the victim's name. "Respect the dead."

"Sorry."

"What about the security guard then, Michael 'Fitz' FitzWilliams? What did he have to do with *Band Candy*? And the archivist?"

Tinsel opened her mouth to supply an answer, but she paused. She didn't have one. Pandora seized the opportunity.

"And you? What does stalking you in a car park have to do with that dumb little movie? Or stabbing Malu?"

"We were… in the way?" Tinsel offered.

"Puh-lease. You know his theory doesn't make any sense; he's just trying to drum up some publicity. Fuck, he even did that interview in the foyer of a theatre with a *Band Candy* poster in the background."

"You think he protests too much?"

"Selfishly I'm glad it's taking the heat off you. But conservatives think my movie is inspiring a violent crime wah wah wah? They're not saying that, police aren't saying that, but people will sure as shit be linking the two now. He singlehandedly increased the movie's notoriety and drummed up a tonne of free publicity, all the while looking like a Social Justice Warrior."

"Clearly not everyone is buying it," Tinsel said, holding up her phone, which had just loaded her sister's blog. The latest article had only been posted that morning on *Pandora's Box* and was a surprisingly short list of violent crimes that had been inspired by movies. Next to that list was another, almost twenty times the length: it was films inspired by real-life violent crimes.

Tinsel nodded with approval. "Touché, sis."

"Sometimes there are subtle ways of pointing out someone is a dickhead."

"Sometimes. Speaking of dickheads, I got a DM from Nancy."

"Oh my God, what?! For real?"

"Uh huh. It appeared in my 'other' inbox because I'm not following her, so I don't know what it says."

"Give that here," Pandora hissed, snatching Tinsel's phone. "If you hover over the message, it shows you the contents without you having to click into the message itself. There, I took a screen shot."

Her sister handed the device back, reading Nancy's message over Tinsel's shoulder. It was lengthy – almost a novella level of lengthy. Tinsel even got bored one third of the way through, skim reading the rest just so she could get to the end. It started out as informative, letting her know that she and Zack had been cleared of all charges and had "absolutely nothing to do with all that awful stuff that has been happening." Zack had officially moved out and retrieved the last of his belongings, but had been papped doing so, and was staying at Nancy's to try and avoid the spotlight.

After that, it was mainly a grovelling apology. She said how they never intended to hurt her and that "falling in love with each other" was totally unexpected amid the craziness of their lives. The last few lines of the tome were dedicated to hoping someday they can all get past this and catch up over coffee one time, to start a new chapter... "as friends."

"I know we shouldn't be joking about murder at a time like this," Pandora started. "But I want to murder her. Heck, if you do it, I'll help you cover it up."

Tinsel smirked, closing her eyes for a moment to block out her sister's face. She wanted to look inward for a beat and examine how she felt. She tried, she really did, searching for any kind of raw emotion like anger or hurt or betrayal. She had felt those things in a back-to-back flurry just days ago, but now? She felt nothing. Her nose didn't even tingle like she wanted to cry.

When her eyelids fluttered open, Pandora was watching her closely. It was as if she was ready for Tinsel's signal and then off they would skip out the door, en route to perform a homicide. Her older sibling raised her eyebrows. Tinsel moved her thumb and deleted the message immediately.

"I don't feel a thing," she said. After a beat, she added: "Truly. It's like... it feels as if this whole thing was 'done' a year ago. I can't even muster the energy to be petty."

"Tinsel–"

"But I will *never* be friends with them."

Pandora brightened a little. "My girl. Now that retaliation is off the table, want to make an anonymous complaint to the health department about the unsanitary conditions at Wallace and Marshall?"

She laughed. "Is that your idea of 'retaliation is off the table?'"

"Yeah, there's no prison time."

Tinsel had a witty retort on the tip of her tongue when Airlie's cry interrupted her. Pandora sprung from the couch, leaving behind a startled Brian so she could hush the baby's cries before Max woke up too.

* * *

When there was a knock at the front door, Tinsel didn't give up hope that Vic would be standing there as she opened it. In a private moment when Pandora had gone to pee between episodes, she had cracked and tried to sneakily call him in a last-ditch attempt to make contact. Instead, an automated voice told her the number she had dialled was either incorrect or no longer in operation. That could have explained why her messages had gone unanswered, but then she thought of those three dots that had loaded on her screen as someone had attempted to reply on Thursday night.

Her excitement was dashed when she found Detective Gabriette Vasquez waiting patiently to take her to Hits 102.8FM. She was the same cop who had replaced Detective James last week and she had to remind herself that the disappointment she felt had nothing to do with this woman, but rather the man she had expected to be there in her place.

"Happy Monday," she said, the phrase sounding chirpy on paper, yet she delivered it with a flat tone and blank expression.

"Happy Monday to you too," Tinsel replied, closing the front door behind her as she adjusted the straps of her bag. "How was your weekend?"

"I worked."

"All weekend?"

There was a pause before she replied. "Everyone is on deck to try and catch this guy. They've set up a taskforce."

Tinsel cast her a sideways look. The woman looked serious, she always looked serious.

"What's it called?"

"Huh?"

"The taskforce, what's the name? Aren't they always given a nickname or something?"

It looked as if Detective Vasquez wasn't going to tell her at first, but she seemed to reconsider.

"Taskforce Grim Reaper."

Tinsel blanched as she reached for the passenger's side handle. "Grim Reaper?"

"Diraani has been analysing every episode of *The Graveyard Shift*, going through the archives and looking for clues. He came up with it."

"It's just so... grim."

Tinsel wasn't sure what she would have preferred. Something fluffy like Taskforce Starfish or Taskforce Jiggly Puff may have been disrespectful to the serious nature of the crimes. Grim Reaper, however, communicated that seriousness quite clearly. In fact, everything did: from the extra officers stationed at her work to Detective Vasquez taking her in through the radio station's fire exit each night for her shift so there was no chance of her being approached by journalists who were waiting at the main entrance. As she walked through the foyer, Detective Vasquez even positioned herself on Tinsel's left side so it would be difficult for the media to get a clean shot of her through the glass windows outside.

Damn, she's making it hard not to like her, Tinsel thought, a wry smile sneaking on to her face as they stepped into the elevator and pressed the button for the third floor.

"It's only a twenty-five metre vulnerability."

"Hmmm?" Tinsel blinked, the woman's voice stirring her.

"Through the foyer to the elevator. There'll always be someone with you, but just in case there's not, if you shift your shoulders towards the back wall they won't be able to get a clear picture of you."

"Oh," she mumbled. "Thanks."

The officer nodded just once, stiff and resolute, as if her job was done. It wasn't long before Detective Vasquez was settled on the studio couch and Tinsel was finishing her first on-air announcement.

"Keep those picks coming in for best haunted house movie and I'll be breaking those down throughout the rest of the show," she said, her finger hovering over the song she had lined up to play. "Mine, since you asked, is *M3GAN* director Gerard Johnstone's first feature, *Housebound*, which is a nifty lil' horror comedy out of Aotearoa. If you too are ready for the Morgana O'Renaissance then let's friggen' go."

She took a second, thinking about what she was about to do, before committing to it.

"Finally, I know a lot of you listening tonight might not be regular listeners of the show or only started tuning in recently due to certain events."

Detective Vasquez looked up sharply, it being the first real confirmation Tinsel had that the officer kept one ear listening to her show. She met the woman's stare and continued with the rest of her speech.

"Maybe you're listening because you're hoping I will say something about what happened, that I'll talk in detail about what I saw and what I went through. I'm sorry to disappoint you. That won't be happening and if that's the only reason you're listening to *The Graveyard Shift*, then I sure as shit hope you like the hip hop stylings of SWIDT, because you're about to hear them a bunch."

Luiza was still in the building and Tinsel saw her pause in the hallway outside the studio, blinking at her through the glass.

"To all the loyal listeners and even newcomers who have sent messages of support through 'The Graveyard Shift' hashtag and various forms of social media, thank you. I see you, I appreciate you, and there simply aren't enough hours in this lifetime for me to send a heartfelt reply to each of you."

Her phone lit up next to the control deck, a message from Pandora illuminated on the screen that read *GO YOU!* followed by series of about twenty emojis.

"Finally, on the off chance that the killer may be listening to this broadcast: Mera Brant, 27, Alona Cennoqia, 24, Indy Aposolottius, 19, and Michael FitzWilliams, 52. These are the people you killed. They will not be forgotten, and you will not be forgiven. They're going to find you, catch you, and frankly? I cannot wait."

Taking a deep breath, she tried to steady the shaking of her hand by making a first and then releasing it.

"Alright, back to the music. It seems only totes approp to start the week with a song from *Buffering The Vampire Slayer*. This is 'Demons To Fight.'"

As the gentle arrangement started, Tinsel's overt message became quite clear as the chorus's key mantra reverberated through her bones and said what she had been unable to.

"Any other surprises?" Vasquez asked as she resettled on the couch.

"Nope," Tinsel swallowed. "That's it."

"Good."

There was another message from Pandora on her phone, ordering Tinsel to check her email as soon as she could. Making sure the next slate of songs was prepped to play, Tinsel clicked opened a new window and typed in her email password. It was the shared Google Drive Pandora had created with an additional tab dedicated to trying to catalogue any murders that seemed similar to the crimes over the past few weeks. The second victim's autopsy report was also attached, with the document clearly a photograph that had been sneakily taken on someone's phone. Tinsel felt queasy as she began looking through everything, but her sister had written a note in the email.

If you're as serious as you sounded on the radio just now, we're gonna get this prick, Pandora wrote. *More hands make less work. The more we know, the more patterns we can identify, the safer you'll be.*

Tinsel paused, fingers hovering over the keyboard before she typed out her reply. *Taskforce Laurie Strode is a go.*

She fell into a routine over the next few days. Once she was awake, she'd help out Pandora with the kids. Her sister said it was a dream having her stay with them.

"It's like a live-in babysitter that I never have to worry about having an affair with my husband," her sister had chirped.

Detective Vasquez would pick her up right on the dot at 7.30pm. They would drive to the station, Tinsel would make her final preps for the show, then *The Graveyard Shift* would be live until 6am as the police officer sat comfortable but alert in her usual spot on the studio couch. She couldn't see Tinsel's many screens from her vantage point across the room, so she was totally unaware that she had a live chat going with Pandora and Veronica as they continued trying to dive into the identity of who their killer was.

Veronica thought she had found two other cases that fit their killer, and with the one that Pandora had discovered too, that took their tally to three murders all up. Every single one of them was unsolved. She suspected there were solved cases out there as well, with someone likely sitting behind bars for a crime they didn't commit. Their killer was prolific, sure, but that didn't mean they weren't sloppy.

Looking back at her screen, she saw Pandora had typed in the G-chat, *He's downright barely competent with these first two."*

Tinsel bit her lip, finally building up the courage to look at the crime scene photos. All of the murders had taken place in bedrooms, with the killer – whoever they were – having clearly stalked his victims long enough to know their movements, know when they would be home, and know when they would be alone. There was blood splatter everywhere, and each victim died as a result of severe organ trauma inflicted via knife blade.

Tinsel focused in on the hands of the second victim. They were clenched into tight fists, the floral pattern of the woman's blanket contorted as she had gripped it in her final moments. She wasn't sure about that "barely competent" comment. The end result was all the same.

Look at the type of victim, Veronica wrote.

Why's that important? Tinsel replied, her answer registering in the messenger box for barely a second before a response came through.

It tells us about the killer.

Tinsel's finger hovered over the 'h' on the keyboard as she was about to question it, but Veronica expanded on the initial response.

Most serial killers hunt within their own racial group. These three women are all young, white, blond. The oldest was twenty-nine and the youngest was eighteen, so I'd say we're looking for a man in his late twenties, early thirties.

White male, Tinsel added, before correcting herself. *Wait, Malu isn't white or female. And he's over thirty. Fitz was in his fifties. Both he and Indy were male. One was Irish and one was Greek. Mera Brant is the only one that fits this earlier profile.*

She paused, switching screens for a moment to check how many songs were left before she had to make another announcement on air.

Besides, she continued to write. *I was an intended victim as well. I don't fit that profile.*

And Mera was also posed, Pandora added. *Alona was battered. Indy was hung. Even if Fitz and Malu were just in the way, it doesn't fit.*

I can't help but feel like we're missing something, Tinsel wrote.

There was a lengthy pause before Veronica replied. *Me too.*

It made Tinsel uneasy, but there was little to be done about it. Working together at night during *The Graveyard Shift*, and during the day in the wardrobe situation room, at least made her feel like she was doing something. She knew Taskforce Grim Reaper was doing what they could, but she wasn't privy to any of that information. She didn't know if they were close to catching someone, if they had a list of viable suspects, or whether they were chasing their tails. She had no way of knowing. They may have had more limited resources, but Taskforce Laurie Strode made her feel a little bit less helpless.

Of course, this would have all been a lot easier if Vic was still around. He might have remained tight-lipped about official matters, yet at least he was honest with her. She'd spent so much time with him in such a short period, she could read him better than any other officer that had been assigned to her. Then there was that whole tricky *feelings* part of it. Tinsel couldn't help but let herself think about Detective James: where he was, what he was doing, whether he was thinking of her.

She was stuck in a weird position by not being able to show too much interest as she and Pandora tried to make general inquiries about where he was at. No one was forthcoming. More importantly, no one seemed to have a clue. It wasn't until she finally cracked – bored, as the weekend dragged on – that she dug through the bottom of her bag for Diraani's business card and she was finally able to get an answer.

"Diraani," he barked down the line.

"Senior Sergeant it's, uh, it's Tinsel."

"Tinsel Munroe."

She couldn't help but note the surprise in his voice.

"Is everything okay? The officers–"

"Everything is fine, I'm fine, the officers are still out the front," she said quickly, before peeking out the window to make sure that was actually true. Sure enough, she could see the two weekend shifters sitting in the police car.

"Good, that's good," he said. "What can I help you with?"

"I wanted to ask about Detective James."

"I see."

"This was his case, he was working it with you from that very first day. Now I haven't seen him in almost a week. None of the other officers have."

"He's on leave, Tinsel."

"Leave?" She sounded incredulous. "In the middle of all this?"

"It's a private matter."

In other words, none of her business. He was clear in what he wasn't saying.

"Is… is he okay?" Tinsel couldn't help herself.

"He's fine. He did some great groundwork on this. Saved a few lives. But he won't be working on the rest of the case. Is there anything else I can help you with?"

"Ah, no, I–"

"Have a good weekend, Tinsel. I'll keep you updated on any developments."

She opened her mouth to reply, yet there was a definitive click as he hung up the line. Glancing down at the phone, she stared as Diraani's number disappeared and it diverted back to her lock screen. *Personal leave my ass*, she thought.

CHAPTER 19

It was dusk as she approached the garage, the smell of oil and rubber telling Tinsel she was in the right place. That and the loud music blaring from the speakers. She wasn't sure she would believe someone was a real mechanic if they didn't have loud music blaring from the speakers, frankly. And this was a real mechanic's garage too: it wasn't glossy or new like some of the joints that popped up alongside car dealerships.

The paint on the sign above her was peeling as she walked under it, but from the sheer number of people hovering around at the end of the workday she could tell this place did a lot of business. It was one of those hidden gems, she suspected: a great mechanic that you heard about through word of mouth, looked a little dodgy on the outside, but actually provided a great service for reasonable prices. Those joints were hard to find.

Stepping into the tiny office that made up the reception area, Tinsel waited patiently behind a woman as she settled her bill. Her eyes flicked to the roadmap of Melbourne that was pinned to the wall, along with a poster on the importance of getting a regular car service.

"Can I help you?"

She jerked as the man spoke to her, her mind having trailed off. She hadn't even realised the woman in front of her had gone.

"Sorry ma'am, didn't mean to scare you."

"It's okay," she replied, internally telling herself to cool it.

"We close in five minutes, at six. But if you're wanting a check-up, I can book you in now. We don't have any spots open until the end of next week."

"Oh, no, that's alright. I was actually looking for someone. Det…"

She stopped herself, about to say the word "detective" before she course corrected.

"Vicellous James," Tinsel said, trying a second time. "I was wondering if he was around?"

"Vic?" the man questioned, thick eyebrows arching in surprise. "Who's asking?"

"Tell him it's Tinsel. He'll know who that is."

"I know who that is," the man muttered, casting her a look with newfound interest. "I'm Eduardo."

"His brother?" she replied, before she could stop herself.

"Ah, I see you've heard of me too," he answered with a smirk that was distinctly Vic's.

Eduardo wiped his hand on a towel draped around his neck before extending it to her. Tinsel felt how strong his grip was, no doubt the result of years spent under the hood of cars and twisting wrenches. He leaned over the desk, inspecting her feet.

"You wearing enclosed shoes? Great, follow me."

Tinsel glanced down at her black and white Chuck Taylors, before looking up and being greeted with Eduardo's back as he disappeared through the office door. She made to rush after him, only understanding his comment about enclosed shoes once she stepped into the interior of the garage. She negotiated her way past any number of things she could have stood or slipped on. Exposed toes were clearly a safety hazard.

The place had mostly emptied out, with only two other staff members present and cramming their stuff into a locker as she and Eduardo passed by. They came to a stop in front of a black

Mini that was raised high enough so somebody could fit below. Eduardo gently kicked the legs dangling from under the car's body, earning an unhappy bark from their owner.

"What the fuck, Ed?"

Vic's brother cast her a mischievous grin. "There's someone here to see you."

"Tell them I'm busy. Cos I am."

"I think you'll want to see her."

"Her?"

There was a metallic clank as Vic dropped whatever he had been holding, his legs bending so he could roll himself out from under the car. He was sweaty and dirty, things that didn't make him any less attractive to Tinsel as he lay there flat on his back. He was shocked to see her, she could tell, but he didn't look unhappy about it either.

"*Tinsel.*"

"Hi," she murmured, looking down at him.

Eduardo shuffled his feet as he glanced between them. "I'll, uh… leave you to it. You alright to close up?"

"Yeah," Vic responded, not taking his eyes off Tinsel as his brother tossed him a set of keys.

"You know the code."

"Yeah Ed, I got it."

"Nice to meet you in person, Tinsel."

"You too," she answered, struggling to pull her gaze away from Vic. "Thanks."

He nodded, before dipping behind the car his brother was working on and heading back towards the office. His colleagues were watching Vic and her with attentive gazes, something the police officer caught as he sat up and wiped his hands on his dirty jeans.

"Come on," he said, jerking his head in the direction he wanted them to go. "There's somewhere private back here."

Tinsel heard Eduardo chatting behind them, saying something about "drinks being on me" as she followed him to a back room. She didn't miss the way his arms looked in the black singlet he was wearing, brown muscles exposed and rippling as he opened the door for her and switched on the light. She remembered how it felt when those arms were wrapped around her, gripping her body, running down her –

"You want a drink?"

"Huh?"

"A drink," he repeated, gesturing to a fridge in the corner of the room.

"No, I'm fine."

She shut the door behind them, watching as Vic began washing his hands and his face at the sink. This was clearly a staff room of sorts, with three tattered couches positioned around a coffee table littered with empty beer bottles, playing cards, and a copy of *Playboy* magazine that was at least a decade out of date. Did they even print *Playboy* anymore? There were old fight posters on the wall, and she recognised a younger Eduardo several broken noses ago on most of them.

"How did you find me?" he asked, his back to her as he continued to clean himself up.

"I remembered what you said about your younger brother having a workshop in Northcote," Tinsel answered, setting her bag down on the floor. "It would have helped if it was called 'Eduardo's Car Repairs' or something easy. This was the third place I visited."

He sighed, turning around and leaning against the sink. To Tinsel, it looked like Vic didn't know what to do with his hands as he awkwardly shook them dry before crossing his arms and tucking them away. She hoped it was because he wanted to touch her as much as she did him. There was something reassuring about that feeling still being there, even after his absence of nearly two weeks.

"Is there a cop with you? I heard Detective Vasquez took over."

"She did, Astrid and Augustus were still on the house, but

things have been quiet now. For a bit, anyway. I guess they needed the resources back, so as of yesterday I'm a free woman again. They still have an officer stationed at Hits permanently when I'm on the night shift, but it's almost back to normal. Almost."

"So, you waited until there was no one on you to try and find me?"

He looked impressed as she nodded.

"I called Diraani and he said you were on leave. That's the only semi-straight answer I've gotten. When Pandora and I pried, no one else seemed to know much."

"Personal leave is the official line."

"And the real one?"

He ran a hand over his face, looking frustrated as she waited for a response.

"I told Diraani."

Tinsel blinked, not quite sure she understood. "About... *oh*, about us?"

"Yes and no," he shrugged. "I went to him after the last time I saw you, when I was technically supposed to be off duty. I told him that I had feelings for you."

"Vic," she breathed, taking a step towards him before stopping herself. "Did you tell him that we've–"

"No," he cut in. "I told him that I had feelings for you, but you were unaware of them. And we hadn't initiated anything."

"You told a lie within the truth."

He nodded. "I went through the ethics handbook, looking for a solution and it's the only thing I could come up with. I knew he'd remove me from the case. I thought he'd put me on administrative leave, but he made me take personal leave instead so it wouldn't be on my record."

She sunk down on to one of the grotty couches as his words washed over her, trying to understand.

"I wanted to tell you, to explain everything before I left," Vic said, eyes wide. "But I couldn't be in contact with you, I couldn't reach out to you. And almost everyone else I worked with didn't know why I took personal leave immediately. I'm sure they assumed it was a death in the family or something."

"What do you mean this was the 'only thing you could come up with?'" Tinsel whispered. "You could have just carried on, said nothing, and I wouldn't have been wondering where the fuck you disappeared to and second guessing myself."

He stepped around the coffee table, dropping on to his knees in front of her. It had been one of those middle days – not quite warm, not quite cold – and Tinsel had thrown a cropped leather jacket on over a pretty sundress that felt very nineties. Vic's fingers brushed against the floral fabric that fell to her knees as he rested his hands there, gripping firmly.

"I was thinking about what you said that morning, about meeting your parents."

"Ergh," she rolled her eyes. "It didn't mean an–"

He silenced her with two fingers placed gently on her lips, Tinsel's words coming to a halt.

"It did mean something. At least, it meant something to me. It meant that you were thinking about us, in the future, at least entertaining the idea of it. Which is fine, because if I'm honest I was too. I still am."

"You are?" she asked, eyes scanning his face as she searched for the truth.

"You were right, about the moving fast thing. So, I started to think about how we could take things slow, and how that required time, and how I could get around the job situation. Going to Diraani was what I came up with: it required honesty, to a degree, and time apart immediately. I didn't want to hurt you or confuse you, but I fucked up in the beginning, so I need to follow the rules now for us to have a shot."

Vic's fingers had slid from her lips to resting on the curve of her neck as he spoke to her. It was comforting, just having his skin make contact with hers. It felt necessary.

"You can't date someone whose case you worked on," Tinsel said, finally understanding. "You'd lose your job."

"Right."

"So, you left the case, but not your job."

"Right again."

"And you told Diraani because… if we end up together down the line, he won't be surprised. You went to him with it earlier, established a timeline."

He grinned at her as he ducked his head, a strand of hair escaping the slicked back uniformity and dropping down in front of his face.

"And here I was thinking I was the smart one."

"You're an idiot," she whispered. "A beautiful idiot."

"I'm sorry, you have *no idea* how badly I wanted to reach out to you, to tell you what was happening. I didn't want another man in your life to disappoint you when–"

Tinsel didn't let him finish, launching herself at Vic and pressing her mouth to his as he attempted to finish the sentence. Nothing shut him up like a kiss and he rocked backwards at first, thrown by her weight before steadying himself with his heels as she wrapped her arms around his neck. It took him only a second to catch up; Vic kissed her back in such a way that Tinsel could tell he missed her. *A lot.*

He pushed her backwards on to the couch, his body pressing down on her as Tinsel let herself get wrapped up in his taste, his touch, his scent, all the things she had missed. She was tugging at his singlet in a heartbeat, her fingers running over the ridges of his stomach once he was shirtless and hovering over her. He was panting, his shortness of breath telling Tinsel that she wasn't the only one who had hated their time apart.

"I missed you," Vic said, voice ragged as he stripped away her jacket.

"Me too," Tinsel replied, her own hands busy with him.

Her nerve endings were on fire as Vic slid his hands under her dress, moving towards the throbbing she felt between her legs. With the other hand, he unbuttoned up top until her breasts were exposed. As she felt droplets of sweat forming at her collarbone, he licked them off. He didn't bother to undress her fully and she was glad: there was no time.

Tinsel wanted him and she wanted him *immediately*, feeling relief as he practically ripped off her soaked panties. She heard her own gasp as he demonstrated his ability with one hand, closing her eyes as she gave in to the sensation he was building with his measured strokes. Tinsel knew Vic was observing her, enjoying the look on her face as he watched what he was doing to her.

"Don't," she managed to whisper, her back arching with pleasure.

"Don't what?"

"Don't make me wait."

He moaned, as if her words had undone him somehow, and Tinsel repositioned her hips to allow him better access as he removed his fingers and slid into her.

"*Fuck*," she breathed, Vic holding still until he was completely deep. Her fingernails dug into the skin of his back as she let out an exhale and pulled him even deeper.

Tinsel yanked his face to hers as he began to move, kissing at intervals as they both breathed heavier with the increased movements. *I needed this*, Tinsel thought, as pleasure started to spread from deep within her core to the rest of her body like ripples in a pond. *I needed him*.

It was all too easy to remember the rhythms from back at her house and they fell into them again. But they didn't have to be as gentle this time. Her injuries were mostly healed and so was her heart. Tinsel clenched around him as they neared mutual release. When he came, she wasn't far behind and within a few seconds they were both still and sweaty as their limbs tangled together on the couch.

They were silent for a long while, Tinsel listening to the *thud thud* of Vic's heartbeat through his chest.

"I really hope your brother isn't still out there," she whispered.

He laughed, the sound swift as he lifted his head up from the spot next to hers. He cupped her face in his hands, looking down at her before he kissed Tinsel long and deep.

"I honestly couldn't care," he muttered, pulling back. "I just... you being here is more than I could have hoped for."

"You spoke to your brother about me," she said, her mind catching on an earlier detail. "He knew who I was soon as I said my name."

Vic smiled, tracing a shape only he could see along the skin of her navel. "Of course he did. You and Pandora aren't the only close siblings in the world."

She chuckled. "What did you say?"

"Eduardo would take my secrets to the grave. I told him everything. He started listening to your show, actually."

"Oh God."

"No, he's a fan now. Plus, I had to give him a reason for why I was hanging around the garage, looking for something to keep my hands busy."

"I can think of a few other ways to keep your hands busy," Tinsel murmured.

"I bet you can," he answered, his smile slow as it crept on to his face.

Vic sat back, pulling Tinsel with him so that she was straddling his lap on the couch. He couldn't stop touching her, his fingers moving along her skin at every moment. She shrugged out of her dress and let it fall to the floor. Her bra wasn't doing much at that point, with Vic's fingers unclipping the back of it so it fell free. Her nipples sat at attention as they were exposed to the evening air, Vic's thumbs playing with them gently.

"You're stunning," he said, his voice heavy enough that it sounded drunk.

"That's easy for you to say, as I sit here commando and topless."

She jiggled on his lap as he chuckled, his hands moving up her neck and through her thick hair. She felt his fingers pause, tracing the space where her cut had once been, and where the hair was slowly regrowing.

"Your stitches," he breathed.

"Got them out last week."

"Wish I could have come with you."

"Were you worried about me?" she asked. "When you weren't around, with the killer still out there?"

"Yes," he nodded, stroking the back of her neck in a comforting gesture. "But I suggested Detective Vasquez as my replacement for a reason. So, no, also. Have you been okay? Has anything else been happening?"

"Yeah, I've been fine. I've been careful and…"

"What?" he asked, sensing what she was leaving out as she trailed off.

"Pandora and I have been looking into things. Murder things."

"Tinsel–"

"Nothing dangerous, just looking at unsolved cases, trying to find motive, establish a pattern."

"Between your case and the others?"

"Yeah. I guess, but nothing really makes sense. We found other victims that fit Mera and Alona's profile, but then Indy, Malu, Fitz and I don't fit. I stress that tweets being sent to me from some anonymous account are sinister, but if none of this had happened I probably wouldn't think twice about them. I worry that just because Zack's cleared, that doesn't mean he's innocent and then I worry that he is and he has been put through all this for nothing. But why should I care right? I'm still furious at him and I don't even feel bad about knowing I'm never going to forgive him. I think about that relationship and I feel nothing. Then I'm with you for two seconds and I feel *everything*."

"Hey," he said, his hand sliding over her bare breast until it rested above her heart. Tinsel knew the beat was erratic, she could feel it within her own chest. "It's okay. Everything you're feeling is okay. You're not supposed to be fine after something like this, not by a long shot."

"I know," she sighed.

"Have you thought about speaking to someone? Your work should have offered a therapist by now, for PTSD."

"They did and I went... once."

"It doesn't work if you just go once."

"I know, but the therapist had a water feature Vic. It was such a cliché."

"Was it the one with the tapping bamboo?"

"It was!"

"Okay, that is a cliché. But one therapist does not invalidate the experience. And you say you've been looking at cases, how? On the internet?"

"And old files."

He tilted his head, a question in his eyes before it was on his lips.

"Pandora knows an old cop, a woman who used to work homicide back in the day. She has been helping us too."

"Does she have a gun?"

"A... what?" Tinsel frowned. "What does that have to do with anything?"

"It would just make me feel better, knowing that when you're not with me you're out there hanging around someone who can use a firearm."

Tinsel wanted to smile, to soothe his worries with an "oh, you're being silly." Yet he wasn't. He was right to worry and so was she. She planted a kiss at the centre of his chest, shifting her head slightly so that it rested in the absence of where the kiss had been. As she lay there, Vic ran his fingers down her back and along her spine. Finally, after a long while, he spoke.

"You working tonight?"

"Mmmm, of course," she mumbled. "Why, what time is it?"

"Nearly seven."

"I still have a few hours yet." She nuzzled closer, before a thought sprung to mind. "It's the work Christmas party on Saturday night."

"This Saturday?"

"Uh huh."

"It's not even December."

"Technically it's December on Monday, so they're getting in a little early. Besides, I think management probably feels everyone deserves the morale boost."

"A serial killer will do that."

"Spree, serial, Santa fucking Claus," she sat up, leaning back so she could watch Vic's expression. With daylight savings, it was well into the evening but the sun was still only just setting. Orange light slipped through the uneven blinds in the staff room, casting a crooked glow on the detective's face.

"It's nineteen twenties themed," Tinsel continued. "So, of course, they're having it at ACMI."

He looked amused at that. "Why 'of course?'"

"Have you ever been there? The history of the moving image is the start of their permanent exhibition. It's full of zoetropes and praxinoscopes and shit that's not from the nineteen twenties at all but looked ye-olde-timey enough for the social committee to be all 'ooooh, period details!'"

"Tinsel, why are you telling me this?"

"I'm allowed to bring a plus one and I don't know if you have plans already or…"

She trailed off, Vic tracing the shape of her nose with his index finger. "Your colleagues have met me. As a cop."

"I know," she sighed. "I just thought–"

"I'll be your date to every Christmas party for the rest of our lives, just not this one. It's a little too close to everything and I think we have to play this low-key."

"The lowest of keys," she smiled. "Almost entirely underground."

"We just keep me and you between me and you. For now. Until this whole Grim Reaper thing is wrapped up."

"You're calling him the Grim Reaper too? Great."

"Yeah, how did you – ah, let me guess, a source of Pandora's?"

"I heard what the operation was called. I didn't like it, so we started our own: Taskforce Laurie Strode."

He pulled her towards him, a soft kiss exchanged for what she thought would be a lone moment but dragged out into several, long ones.

"As for between me and you, you and me," she said, taking a breath. "We have to expand that a little to Pandora and Brian as well."

"And Eduardo too," Vic answered.

Hovering just in front of him, the tip of Tinsel's nose brushed his as she looked into his eyes. She licked her lips, tasting a faint peppermint flavour there. He always tasted like peppermint, smelling faintly like it too.

"To me and you," she said, as his fingers snaked through her hair.

"To you and me," Vic replied. "And our siblings."

CHAPTER 20

The softly padded, soundproofed walls of the movie theatre made a subtle cushion for Wiley Viter as he leaned against them and watched the end credits roll on a movie he had seen the last five minutes of about fifty times by this point. What happened in the first one hundred and thirty-two minutes? He'd likely find out in a few weeks when he eventually used his staff pass and caught up on the not-so-new releases.

"Thank you," a patron mumbled, nodding their head at him as they exited the cinema and jogged down the carpeted stairs that would take them out into the upper lobby.

He nodded back, hoping they were the last audience member as he peeked around the barrier and out at the seats that lined the balcony. There was just one person left a row back from the front, slouched in their hoodie and munching on a box of popcorn the size of their head. He hesitated for a moment, knowing the managers preferred for staff not to disturb remaining customers by cleaning up around them while the credits rolled. He also knew the managers hated if a session couldn't run on time, since they only had the one theatre and couldn't play multiple titles simultaneously.

He decided the threat of not getting the balcony area clean and tidy before doors were open again in twenty minutes outweighed the risk of pissing this lone customer off. Wiley started at the back row first, as far away from the viewer as possible, then he would work his way across and down. He'd gotten lucky, because the bulk of the audience had booked seating in the stalls downstairs, with only a dozen or so people up where he was. If he hustled, he could make quick work of it.

Tucking his wireless headphones into his ears, he cranked the volume on his phone so the latest episode of his favourite podcast *Total Reboot* was playing as he got to work dumping trash into his garbage bag. His hair in a tight bun, he swept the one loose curl that always seemed to escape out of the way as he bent down to collect a discarded wine class. He knew no one had sat back here, he'd viewed the digital bookings so he could fang it straight to the messiest parts of the balcony, but he also knew that Steph had been on clean up duty the shift before him. And that chick, to put it politely, was a dropkick. So Wiley found himself cleaning up his mess plus at least half of Steph's.

That would have had him fuming under normal circumstances. But tonight, he chuckled along to the podcast. It had him in a better mood than he should have been and when he finished clearing as many aisles as he could, he was surprised to see the last audience member had left.

"Huh," he murmured, realising he hadn't seen them leave, but aware that his back had been towards them most of the time. Still, it meant he was going to be able to clear his section approximately six minutes and twenty-five seconds earlier than expected. And he could use that surplus of minutes to send Steph a shitty email.

He began descending the rows one level at a time, using the flashlight that dangled from a lanyard at his neck to sweep a light over each one in case he had missed anything. As the yellow beam danced over the back of a chair, he jumped as a dark object darted behind an aisle.

"Hey!" he yelled, pursuing what he assumed was that asshole in the hoodie trying to play some kind of trick on him. Yet when he got to the end and swivelled around triumphantly, there was no one there.

"What the…"

Taking his headphones out and slipping them back in his pocket, he strained to hear any kind of noise that would have given the trickster away over the bass of the pounding score. He couldn't pick up stifled giggles or a rustling of fabric. It sounded like it was him, just him, alone in that theatre and freaking himself out unnecessarily. He stood up on the seat of a chair, directing his flashlight beam up the aisles towards where he thought *someone* had moved while crouched down. Nothing.

The lack of a prankster didn't make him feel in any way better, however. He was on this shift until at least one in the morning and if he was cracking this early, it was not a good sign. He lifted one foot off the seat, about to step down when he felt something clasp around his ankle and yank him with force. The sound that escaped his mouth was more of a howl than a scream as he flew backwards, hitting the side of his head against a chair as he went. Wiley landed with an unceremonious thud on the ground, the pain in his head so sharp he couldn't breathe for a moment.

Blood. There was warm, sticky blood dripping around his ears, he realised as he rolled over on to his back and tried not to let the Hans Zimmer score merge with the thudding in his skull.

He squinted his eyes open and shut, his vision uneven as he tried to make sense of what he was seeing. A figure dressed all in black rolled out from under the row of seats, standing up slowly so that they loomed over him. He had a concussion, maybe a bad one, and that was the only clear thought Wiley could formulate as a long silver knife was drawn. It was the lone audience member, he realised, with their face only partially hidden beneath the black hood as they crouched down. He whimpered as they ran the cold steel of the weapon along his cheek, following the trail his tears had made.

As he stared at the face watching him, he knew it would do no good to beg for mercy. The most he could hope for was they would make it quick.

It was the last wish Wiley Viter ever got a chance to make.

His manager, Laura, was wondering where the hell Wiley was as people began lining up for the next session. But when they ducked their head inside the theatre, the balcony was spotless. It always was when Wiley was on duty. A problem for later, Laura figured, as they began scanning tickets and allowing the audience inside five minutes before the next movie was about to start. It was only when the screams began that they learned what had really happened to their missing employee.

Sprinting up the stairs, they froze with relief for a moment as they saw Wiley sitting there hunched over in the front row. What was he–

Then, Laura saw his throat, or what was left of it, as his head hunched over at an unnatural angle. The blood was so thick and dark it blended with the black material of his shirt.

When the woman in the row behind him screamed again, rushing out into the aisle to escape the scene, she bumped the body. As if it was playing in slow motion, the gathered crowd watched as Wiley's head rolled right off and over the edge of the balcony barrier.

It was less than a few seconds before the screams from the stalls below joined their own.

CHAPTER 21

"You look like Miss Munroe's Murder Mysteries," Pandora said, letting out a low whistle.

Tinsel did a slow swirl around the room for maximum effect, the beaded tassels from her flapper frock flying around her. It was sleeveless, with a V-neck in a classic nineteen-twenties silhouette that ended midway down her thighs before a fringed trim added another few inches of length. In a pale teal colour, it wasn't exactly true to the period, but it looked great on Tinsel. That was more important. Art Deco patterns in black beading and sequins ran down the form-fitting frock, with a pair of t-strap heels added for good measure. They weren't very high, and Tinsel could dance in them all night long. That was crucial.

"You can talk," Tinsel grinned, admiring her sister who was dressed in an identical frock but in a deep, red colour. "You look va-va-voom, Miss Milf's Murder Mysteries!"

"This old thing?" Pandora laughed, fluttering the false eyelashes Tinsel had aided her in sticking on not five minutes earlier.

"Here," Tinsel said, tossing something through the air to her sister.

Reflexes sharp as ever, Pandora caught it and looked down with surprise.

"What's this?"

"Your very own switchblade."

Pandora looked at it like a treasure, eyes wide and delighted as she stroked the pink heart detailing. "It matches yours!"

"Of course," Tinsel smiled. "The shipping took bloody ages, but now we have a pair."

She lifted the hem of her dress, revealing the garter at her thigh where she had her own strapped in an era-appropriate fashion. Pandora quickly manoeuvred her present to do the same, readjusting the black gemstone and feather elastic headband across her temple in the process.

Standing side-by-side in the full-length mirror of the hallway in Pandora's home, the sisters examined each other appreciatively.

"Is it a little daggy we're wearing matching outfits?" her older sibling asked.

Tinsel shrugged. "Who gives a shit? We look good."

"Yeah, we do," Pandora laughed. "Maybe I should give this rockabilly thing a go, huh? Take a page from your book?"

"There may be a slight difference between wearing fifties-inspired vintage clothing and dressing prohibition era."

"True. Plus, who the fuck has time to do finger waves every day? You're lucky you already have a mod bob."

Tinsel primped said bob with her hands, giving it one last coat of hair spray as Brian called out to see if they were ready. Pandora said that they were, grabbing their purses and heading to the car.

Max and Airlie were already inside, strapped in the backseat and fast asleep. Tinsel quietly slipped in alongside them, careful not to wake either. Brian and Pandora gently closed the doors to the front of the car, the former being their designated driver for the night and the latter hastily turning down the car radio as the ignition started. With Brian dropping them off at the Hits 102.8FM Christmas party and Pandora attending as Tinsel's plus one, it meant there was no one left at home to watch the kids so they were coming for the drive.

Bonus passengers aside, Tinsel was looking forward to a

night out with her sister. She couldn't remember the last time they had done this, let alone with an open bar and canapes covered by her employer. After all the blood, terror and fear of the last month, they both *really* deserved to let their hair down. Besides, things had been chill. Her police detail was officially dusted, work had been smooth for the remainder of the week, the ratings were holding strong and she hadn't found herself in mortal peril once. They were all big ticks in Tinsel's book, the largest one of them being the presence of Vic.

Just because they were keeping things discreet, didn't mean non-existent. It had taken her a few days to find him at his brother's garage, but soon as she had, Tinsel realised she wasn't letting him go. Even better, neither was he.

They'd reacquainted themselves on a Tuesday, with Wednesday, Thursday and Friday evenings before *The Graveyard Shift* spent entirely in his presence and at Eduardo's garage. Sure, a mechanic's workshop wasn't the most romantic place in the world, but any place where they could be together was fine with her. Plus, there was a certain charm to it. No corniness, no fakery, no frills. Vic started taking the early shift so he'd finish at four instead of the usual six, meaning they had longer to hang out. The staff room became somewhat of a sanctuary for them, with the pair even joining Eduardo and one of the other guys for Friday night beers as they shut down the garage for the weekend.

Diraani or Vasquez called her every day, touching base and letting her know the investigation was still moving. Whatever that meant. The important thing was that Tinsel felt safe and she was letting herself hope for the future.

Looking out the window, she smiled as she watched the sun set over the Yarra River. It was beautiful at twilight, the body of water like a big, brown snake as it cut through the city. The lights of the aquarium, the surrounding restaurants and shops reflected on the water as their car crept by. It was slow going, traffic always bumper-to-bumper on a Saturday evening.

"Stay in the left lane," Pandora whispered.

"That takes us around the city," Brian responded. "Going through will be quicker."

"Are you mentally regular?" she hissed back. "This is Melbourne, for fuck's sake. Stay in the left lane."

With a sigh, Brian did as his wife ordered. He even mumbled a bashful "you were right" as the path they had taken opened up and they zoomed along Flinders Street towards Federation Square. As the familiar silhouette of Flinders Station loomed ahead of them, Tinsel couldn't help but feel like she was heading to work, with the Hits office building just steps away from their party destination.

"This is good, just here – look, there's a Bonnie and Clyde," Pandora pointed. "We're definitely in the right place."

"Have fun," Brian said, pulling over and giving his wife a kiss on the cheek so as not to ruin her lipstick, like a true gentleman.

"Thanks for the lift," Tinsel added, gently squeezing his shoulder as she climbed out of the car.

The sisters took a moment to straighten themselves and once everything was in order, they linked arms and negotiated their way over the tram tracks carefully in their heels.

There was a steady throng of people heading through the glass doors of ACMI's ground floor, the 'Riverboat Shuffle' playing loudly as those in costume headed up towards the entrance of the exhibition. It was low light, the whole place dimmer than it usually was during the day which helped create a unique atmosphere.

"Hold up," Pandora said, pulling them to a stop near ACMI's shop in the foyer. "I've got a surprise for you just over… there!"

Tinsel followed the direction of her sister's gloved finger as she pointed to a man stepping out of the shadows. His hands were tucked into a brown, boxy suit straight from the nineteen twenties and a wool, trilby hat in the same shade.

"What kind of sup…"

Between the tilted hat on his head and the bandana fastened around his face, most of his features were covered. Except for the man's eyes, which is why Tinsel's words dissolved as she realised not what, but *who* the surprise was. She beamed, running forward as she threw her arms around Vic's neck and he spun her in a half circle.

"Hey there, doll," he said, words somewhat muffled under his disguise.

"It's you, you came! I didn't think... well, this is brilliant!"

She lifted up the bandana, leaning forward for a passionate kiss. She could feel the surprise in Vic's posture at first, before instinct took over and he kissed her back. Pandora cleared her throat behind them, the two reluctantly pulling apart.

"In keeping with the period, I believe all action must be kept firmly above clothes," she said. Tinsel didn't even have the sense of mind the blush as she darted forward and hugged her sister.

"You organised this?"

"I might have," Pandora winked. "I can neither confirm nor deny."

"I love you, sis. Thank you."

"I knew you were bummed he couldn't come. So, we schemed and came up with this fitting disguise. No awkward questions now."

"And minimal conversation," Vic said, lifting the flap of the bandana from over his mouth so they could hear him properly.

"You'll just have to be very handsy instead," Tinsel smirked.

Pandora made a gagging sound. "Don't make me regret this. It's still sisters' night out, just with accompaniment."

"Of course," Vic agreed, bowing in a decidedly over-the-top manner before offering his arm to each of them. "Ladies?"

Tinsel smiled at him as she took one arm, Pandora the other, and they continued in the direction of the party.

"Are we gangster moles?" Pandora asked, her head tilting

with the thought. "And more importantly, does that mean you're packing?"

"I'm always packing," Vic mumbled in reply, casting Tinsel a look so that she knew he meant it.

Pandora made a retching noise again, thinking that he meant it sexually, while Tinsel understood the real meaning. She slid her hand down his back, to where his waistband was, and felt a mix of relief and anxiety simultaneously as she touched the hard lump there. He was carrying a weapon with them into this party, and he was taking no chances that she would be left unprotected that night.

"Tinsel, ohmigooooood! You look GREAT!" Stu screeched as they neared the entrance. "Argh, but of course you would. For someone who is on the social committee I stupidly picked a theme that doesn't go with my aesthetic at all!"

"You look pretty great to me," she told the lawyer, whose outfit wasn't that dissimilar to Vic's except in black and white.

"Bless your heart, I feel so butch. Anyway, here's your wristband and the two for your guests. That will get you free drinks and food all night. Go on through, have a great time – you deserve it!"

She thanked him as the trio stepped into the exhibition, the radio station having hired the entire space for the end of year party in what was truly a bougie display of wealth. Hits 102.8FM didn't have enough staff to fill out the place, but the Christmas festivities were always attended by a mix of loyal sponsors, advertisers, local politicians and celebrities. Those invites tripled the guest list, making it as much of an end-of-year celebration as it was a promotional tool.

"Do you know what song they're playing?" Vic asked her, whispering into her ear as they passed a five-piece band.

She arched her eyebrow as she gave him a look.

"Come on," he urged. "I know you know."

"Of course I know. That's Louis Armstrong, sir. Respect a legend."

"Sir?"

"'Put 'Em Down Blues', sir."

He chuckled as they weaved their way through the curved path of the exhibition, pausing in front of a rotating zoetrope that – once it reached speed – saw models of the animated characters from *Cuphead* come to life under flickering light. Part of the space had been cleared for catering, with a food station set up and waiters milling about with themed drinks for patrons.

"Oooh look," Pandora said excitedly, tugging on her elbow. "Someone's already trying to do a drunk Charleston."

Tinsel followed her sister's gaze, chuckling when she saw the object of her observation. "Ha, it's Rushelle! Good for her."

"The big wig has had a big swig."

Vic steered them towards the makeshift bar, where they collected their drinks and made for a quiet spot in the corner near a re-creation of the Interceptor from *Mad Max* that had been mushed against one from *Bush Mechanics*. It was the perfect location, as they could survey everything safely from a distance.

Sipping her dark and stormy, Tinsel smirked as she watched Luiza drag her wife up on to the dance floor. It turned out they were the Bonnie and Clyde Pandora had spotted earlier, the pair out-manoeuvring everyone in an immediate radius with swing dancing skills even she couldn't quite believe.

She felt Vic's hand snake around her waist, gently pulling her closer to his side. They didn't need to say anything, Tinsel felt they were both probably thinking it. *It's nice having you here*, she told him with her eyes. The sentiment was reflected back at her.

"Come on," Pandora barked, grabbing Tinsel's hand. "Finish your drink, both of you, we're going up there to dance."

Tinsel laughed at her sister's bossiness, sliding the strap of her purse higher up her wrist. "Yes ma'am."

They cut through the throng of bodies, ducking under

strings of pearls that were swinging in the air and darting around outstretched jazz hands. That last one was upsetting. They finally found a small space where Tim – the breakfast show producer – was trying and failing to dance with their newsreader, Killara. The issue was that neither one of them wanted to let the other person lead. Tinsel scoffed at how on-brand it was for both of them as she threw herself into the music.

A jazz cover of Beyonce's 'Crazy in Love' had just started and it wasn't hard to get swept up, with Pandora and her moving and sashaying and swirling to the rhythm like they were teenagers going clubbing for the first time all over again. Vic wasn't much of a dancer, and he disappeared and reappeared at intervals, retrieving drinks for them as they began to build up a steady layer of sweat from all the exertion. Even the frosty museum air-conditioning couldn't prevent their gradual melting.

Tinsel felt a hand skim over her butt to rest on her hip and she was about to lean into it when she frowned. She could see Vic in front of her, doing a terrible attempt at a waltz arm-in-arm with Pandora. Spinning on the spot, she turned to face breakfast co-host Ryan who was looking at her with an intoxicated, sleazy grin. She pushed him back, gently, scanning the crowd for Shea who was smartly as far away from his colleague as he could be and holding court with a group of junior employees near the video game station.

Ryan's hands found their way back to her hips despite her having batted him away, his own body doing a gross backwards and forwards motion that Tinsel couldn't mistake for anything else *but* dry humping.

"Hey there sexy angel of Christmas past," he leered. He was slightly shorter than her, so it didn't quite have the same impact.

"Ergh, Ryan, fuck off."

"What?" he blinked, his face full of mock surprise. "This is your season, Tinsel!"

He laughed at his own joke, stepping closer towards her just as somebody pulled her backwards. She would have stumbled if it wasn't for the steadying hand as Vic inserted himself directly in-between her and Ryan.

"Hey, that was my dance partner!" he growled, spilling half of his drink down the front of his own shirt. "Shit."

"Clearly she doesn't want to dance with you," Vic said, pushing the bandana to the side of his face so his authoritative tone could be heard. "That's what 'fuck off' usually means."

"Oh yeah, you wanna go mate? You wanna go?"

Tinsel could tell just by the tension in Vic's shoulders that he was, indeed, ready to go, but it would likely be a short fight. Mercifully Tim crashed the party, bursting out of a group of people and throwing his arms over Ryan's shoulders.

"Hey hey, there's no drama here," the breakfast producer said, smile wide and tight as he tried to convince everyone around him of that. He slapped Ryan on the chest twice, hard, beginning to drag the radio host towards the food station. "Let's get a beef slider, aye? Leave these good people to dance. Come on, Shea's over there too."

Ryan's back was already to them when Tinsel heard his voice respond with excitement: "Beef slider?"

Tim kept his eyes trained ahead, flashing a thumbs up to Tinsel as the situation properly diffused. Vic turned to her, hands running gently over her shoulders.

"You okay?" he asked.

"Just fine," she said, meaning it as she leaned up and planted a kiss on his lips before pulling the bandana back in place. "Dance with me, will you?"

He flinched. "If I have to. I'm not very good."

"You have to," she said, drawing him towards her as horns started blaring and the band began a new song. It was fun, she was having *fun* as she danced with Vic and switched to jumping up and down with her sister when a jaunty piano ditty started. Tinsel was breathless, letting the music and the night and the company elevate her from the dark place she'd been in for what felt like the longest time. They were her little sparks, Vic and Pandora, and they were brightening up her world.

"I need to pee," she shouted over the music, spinning around on the dance floor to look for the bathroom sign.

"Don't break the seal," Pandora called back.

Tinsel laughed. "I have to, brb."

She let go of Vic's hand and smacked Pandora on the ass as she dipped through the dancing staff members, heading towards the illuminated sign that said "loo" that was flickering just above her. When she got there though, it was just a pot plant.

"Bathroom?" she asked the security guard standing nearby. He rolled his eyes, as if that was the one hundredth time he had been asked that same question. It probably was. A jerk of his head showed Tinsel a series of illuminated arrows that led away from the party and out of the exhibition.

"Sorry," she mumbled, returning the wave of a woman whose name she couldn't remember as she passed her en route to the toilet. She knew she was in the right place as soon as she saw the line of female colleagues spilling out of the doorway. Tinsel sighing as she settled in for a wait and tried not to think about how badly she needed to pee.

Pulling out her phone from her purse, she frowned as she saw six missed calls from Veronica.

"Crap," she murmured, her mind not immediately worried through the haze of alcohol and adrenaline. She swiped past the missed call alerts, seeing she had left two voicemails as well and several texts.

Call me when you can, the first one read. *Tried Pandora as well*.

The one after that was short: *DON'T check social media*.

Tinsel huffed, as that was obviously the *first* thing she wanted to do as soon as she was told not to. The sinking feeling in her stomach wasn't letting up as she shuffled further up the line, now only two women away from the cubicle. Hitting the Twitter icon, her screen was lit up with notifications as her timeline loaded and reloaded in a flash.

"What is going on…" she murmured, quickly nodding at the girl in front of her who said the loo was free. "Cheers."

Sitting down, she peed as quickly as she could before taking a moment to fully comprehend what she was seeing.

"Oh no," she whispered, her thumb shaking with a slight tremor as she digested a picture that was attached to a tweet from a news organisation. Parts of it had been blurred out, yet there was only so much you could censor.

The body of a movie theatre employee had been butchered and posed inside a cinema. At first glance from behind, you might mistake them for a sleeping patron… until you realised there was no head.

Then your eyes started to notice other details, like the sheer ungodly amount of red that was soaked into the surrounding surface. She didn't need to look at the text of the tweets to recognise where this horrific scene had taken place, the interior was unique. It was also somewhere she had frequented a lot, including on the night of Mera Brant's death as she had presented the *Halloween* marathon. It was one of Melbourne's most treasured cinemas, The Astor.

The symbolism wasn't lost on her. This was full circle storytelling and whoever was behind it, well, they were getting ready to wrap up their narrative by returning to where it had all started. Something that had been swimming around in her subconscious began floating to the surface, just the hint of an idea that started to solidify the longer she let it percolate. And then there it was.

Tinsel dropped her phone in a panic, her shaking hands scrambling to pick it up off the bathroom floor as she got her dress back in place and pushed her way out of the cubicle. She felt like she was going to be sick, and she had to shove a woman out of the way as she reached the basin.

"Hey!"

The girl fell quiet as Tinsel dry-retched over the ceramics, turning the tap on to splash her face with cool water.

"Are you okay?" someone asked.

"It's too early to be hitting it *that* hard," someone replied.

"Ah, excuse me. That's exactly what work Christmas parties are for, Emmy!"

The girls laughed at that, continuing to fix their make-up in the mirror as Tinsel stood at attention. Staring at her own reflection, she jumped when she saw the figure of a man standing behind her. None of the other women reacted, however, and Tinsel wondered if she was slowly going mad as she spun around to examine what she had seen.

It wasn't just the figure of a man, but several, all assembled side-by-side on a poster that hung on one of the cubicle walls. It was to promote an upcoming season of live film commentaries at ACMI, the commentary being provided by the filmmakers themselves. She focused in on a face she was sick of seeing, quite frankly. Joe Meyer's half-smirk looked back at her from his third billing and something deep, deep within her stomach dropped.

Her mouth went dry and by the time she finally went to squeak out words, she turned to see the backs of the girls as they disappeared through the doorway. There was only one cubicle occupied, the door shut and engaged. This wasn't a conversation she wanted to be overheard, but it was one that she needed to have immediately. Hands shaking, she dialled Pandora's number as she stumbled out of the bathroom.

"Oy, what are you calling me for we're on the–"

"Find somewhere quiet," Tinsel barked at her sister. "I'm coming back from the loo now, but this can't wait."

"Okay, okay, I'm near the *Priscilla* costumes. What's up?"

"Joe Meyer's alibi."

"On what night?"

"Every night, but let's start with Mera Brant's murder."

"He was on *The Graveyard Shift* with you."

"Right, but they never checked with me, Dora. That interview wasn't live."

"Wait–"

"He came on to talk about *Band Candy*. We were doing a station promo and giving away tickets for the premiere that was on that week. Mera had called in to try and win them. The interview was a pre-record from a few months ago, when he was last in town. We were careful with the language though, didn't say anything to date the chat or allude to the fact he wasn't physically in the studio."

There was a loaded pause on the line before Pandora spoke up.

"So the cops cleared him," her sister murmured. "What about the night of the tribute show?"

"He came in. That was live in the studio."

"At Hits?"

"Yes."

"Was he alone?"

"No, he had his publicist with him."

"And how does that work? Does security escort him through or–"

"Malu brought him up to the studio kind of out of courtesy. He's been there dozens of times before. We've assigned him and his publicist a visitor's pass, they pick it up from security, hand it back in at the end of the night."

"Do you know if he handed his back in? Are they set to a specific person?"

Tinsel felt her throat tighten as she marched back towards the party, squinting through the darkness of the interior hallway. The neon arrows that had illuminated her path were switched off, plunging the whole space into blackness.

"I assumed they both did. But visitor's passes are assigned to anyone: we have about fifty, I think, that are always active and in rotation. They're blank, so there's usually an identity

sticker for the specific guest and then it's peeled off at the end
and reissued for someone else. He has been there *so many times*
over the years, sis! And we always said whoever attacked Malu
and I, whoever killed Fitz, clearly knew their way around.
They knew how to get in, how to get out, and how to avoid
registering on most of the CCTV cameras."

She could hear puffing down the line, as if Pandora was
jogging and struggling for air.

"They never treated him as a suspect because they assumed
he was *live on-air* the night of the murder," Tinsel continued, in
her gut knowing that she was right.

"That was a tight alibi," Pandora replied. "But once that's
gone, the rest…"

Tinsel stretched out her hand, sighing with relief as her
fingers connected with the wall to her left in the darkness.
She used the solid structure to guide her way out towards
the exhibition, knowing that she was heading in the right
direction as the music from the party started to get louder and
she struggled to hear Pandora.

"It was his premiere, so of course he'd be there that night at
The Capitol," her sister added.

"Who had the most to gain from all this? We questioned the
motive, and it was right there, on a fucking poster."

"I don't–"

She paused, pulling the phone away from her ear for a
moment as she looked over her shoulder. She thought she heard
a noise, a large thump of some kind. As Tinsel peered through
the darkness, she realised it was no use: it was impenetrable.
The only thing she could see was the illuminated doorway of
the exhibition exit some twenty metres behind her. Everything
else was black. She picked up her pace, turning around and
marching a little bit faster as the panic began to build.

"You there? Hello? HELLO!" Pandora shouted at her through
the phone.

"Yes, yes, I'm here, sorry I–"

"Are you back at the party yet?"

"Almost, I'm heading there right now."

"Get back here Tinsel, I'm going to find Vic. We'll stay tight to him until–"

"Shit!"

Tinsel tripped in the dark, missing a divot in the floor thanks to the lack of light. Her knees hit the carpeted ground and she let out a cry as her phone slid from her hands, bouncing twice before coming to a stop. Painfully, she fumbled her way towards it on her hands and knees, Pandora's bark still audible through the speaker.

"I'm coming, I'm coming," she moaned, her hand extended for the device just as she heard another noise, this one much closer. Right behind her, in fact.

She froze, unsure what to do or whether she should make any sudden movements. It sounded like the squelch of a shoe as its wearer came to a stop. She tried to ignore the furious beating of her heart.

Finally, she looked up, craning her neck and trying to see something, anything, through the dark. She could make out the faintest outline of a person and Tinsel opened her mouth to scream. An electronic buzz cut her off before she even began, the bluish light of a taser the last thing she saw as her vision clouded.

Sprawled out on the floor, the figure bending over her, Tinsel was consumed with fear.

I've seen you before, she thought, as the person gripped her limbs and began dragging her. With a jolt of horror, she realised where. The fully covered face sitting deep inside a hood, the eyes she couldn't see but the breath she could hear.

It was the Grim Reaper.

He's going to kill me, she thought, with the last of her fading consciousness.

CHAPTER 22

There was a bitter taste in Tinsel's mouth, and it intensified the longer she was aware of it. She gagged, leaning forward as blood and spit dribbled from her lips. She groaned, her head and knees hurting as she strained against the chair. It was the rope around her wrist that fully brought her to, the unusual texture rubbing against her skin enough that it irritated her into consciousness.

"Ugh," she moaned, leaning back and feeling the rigid wooden structure behind her. She wiggled her fingers and her toes, growing used to the fact that each wrist and each ankle had been tied to the legs of a chair. And not tied well, mind you: it was a mess of knots and half bows. But they were tight. She wriggled against them, conscious of the fact someone was watching her.

Tinsel didn't want to look up just yet, she was terrified. She knew her logic wasn't sound, but hiding under the blanket was the only way the monster couldn't get her.

"If I were you, I'd quit struggling."

She closed her eyes, ignoring the sting as tears streaked down her cheeks the moment she recognised *that* voice.

"You're not going anywhere, Tinsel Munroe."

Ultimately, it was the muffled squeak beside her that caused Tinsel to glance upwards.

"Hello, Joe," she said, doing her best attempt at keeping her voice steady. She mostly succeeded, but it was his piercing blue eyes that made her want to hurl. They seemed brighter than ever, alive with excitement and intent.

"See, that's annoying," he said, clicking his tongue with frustration. "That was supposed to be my *big* surprise."

"What a shame," she replied, drily.

"You and that bitch sister stole my moment. But that's okay, I'm a director. I can craft another one."

His left eye was twitching slightly, and Tinsel couldn't stop staring at it, aware that he'd probably had a full psychotic break by this point. It was the only thing that could explain why he was standing in front of her, dressed head-to-toe in what she thought of as the killing uniform. The hood had been pushed way back, exposing his face, and the plain black mask he usually wore was scrunched up under his chin. Without all his usual trimmings and accessories, he looked almost naked to her. In a way, he was. She was getting to see the real Joe Meyer underneath, not the person he presented as.

"Don't you wanna take a look, see who our other guest is?" he asked, gesturing next to her.

Tinsel shook her head, pressing her mouth into a hard line. She didn't need to glance across to know who else was there; she knew it was Pandora with every sense, every pore in her body. Because of course it would be, she realised. He wouldn't take one without the other.

Suddenly Joe lunged forward, causing her to shriek in surprise as he pressed something to her throat. She jumped with a slight electric shock, realising it was the taser from earlier. He smooshed the skin of his cheek up against hers, using his hands to slowly turn her neck until she was looking at her sister.

"Don't close your eyes, you coward!" he shouted, as Tinsel did her best to keep her eyes shut tight. "Open them! Look at her or I'll tase you again!"

With a strangled sob, she did as he ordered. And it nearly

ruined her. She'd avoided looking at Pandora for so long because she worried she'd lose whatever resolve she had to escape this situation if her sister was badly hurt. She didn't want to fall apart, for the both of them.

As she gazed at her older sibling, she nearly did exactly that. Blood was dripping from a cut at Pandora's forehead, the gore trickling down her face and along the curve of her neck like a sick river. Yet she was conscious, her eyes wide and horrified as she stared back at Tinsel. They were restrained the same way, with the addition of a gag for her sister. Even through the ropes, Tinsel could see how violently Pandora was shaking.

"Let her go," she whispered, her voice breaking this time. "I'll do whatever you want, Joe. Just let her go."

He laughed, jerking backwards. "No, she's gonna stay. I read her blog, she's a great writer. Someone is going to need to document this all from an insider's perspective. That's Pandora's job and that's why the gag is staying on. We don't need to have a back and forth, I just need her to listen and remember."

Something unclenched in Tinsel's chest as she hoped that he was telling the truth.

"And don't even try to scream if that's what you're thinking about."

"I wasn't," she snapped.

"Just making sure. Cos no one will hear you in this soundproofed sanctuary."

His comment had her straining to look around them, her mind still foggy as she tried to process as much of the surroundings as she could see. There was only one light coming from directly above them and casting a small pool of illumination. It felt like a weight in her stomach dropped when she realised where they were: a movie theatre.

Sanctuary.

ACMI had two on site, not far from where the exhibition was, in the same building and clearly easy enough for Joe to access given his familiarity with the place. He was a storyteller, after all, and this whole thing had been about theatrics. Naturally, this was where they would end up.

"Cinema Two?" she asked, arching her neck and squinting as she tried to look through the harsh light to observe the high ceiling above.

"Please. Cinema One, Tinsel. It sits more people. Only the best."

"I couldn't give a fuck how many it sits, Joe," she spat.

He giggled, Tinsel watching with horror as he pulled an enormous knife from the sheath at his side. He brandished it through the air as he spoke.

"I heard they're calling me the Grim Reaper now," he said. "So this seemed like an appropriate setting for a final performance. Everything is state of the art of course and, importantly, it's empty. It's not The Capitol, but given I had to move up the timeline more quickly than I anticipated, this will do."

His pupils were gleaming with a maniacal energy as he told her this and while he muttered on, Tinsel narrowed her eyes at the odd phrasing. Then she spotted it: cameras, two of them, one positioned on each side of their weird little showdown.

Maximum coverage, she thought, feeling sick. She could see the red lights blinking on each of them, telling her they were already recording. He had his back to her for a moment, continuing his rant as if there was an audience before him. In Joe's mind, there probably was.

Tinsel glanced around frantically, looking for any possible way out, any avenue that she and Pandora could exploit. Where was Vic in all this? Joe couldn't have known he was with her at the party, nobody knew. If he'd managed to lure Pandora away from the dance floor, it was only a matter of time before Vic went looking for both of them and realised something was up. He was on his guard, so she suspected that would be sooner rather than later. Unless he had already been taken care of. Her lip trembled at that thought and she twisted to face Pandora, her sister's eyes glancing between her and Joe.

She cast Joe a quick look, making sure his back was still turned, as she mouthed the word "Vic." Pandora's expression lit up and she nodded enthusiastically. Tinsel let the smallest morsel of hope blossom in her chest: her sister wouldn't react like that if Vic was dead. What she needed to do was buy them time. She tossed Pandora a wink, diverting her attention back to Joe as he continued ranting. She rocked the chair backwards and forwards, doing her best to act hysterical and terrified which wasn't hard. After all, she *was* hysterical and terrified,

"ARGH, LET ME OUT OF HERE, YOU FREAK!" she screamed, increasing the movements until she eventually rocked herself right over. She landed ungracefully at Pandora's feet, white specks dancing in front of her eyes as her head made contact with the floor. Tinsel could hear her sister's panicked cries through the gag, no doubt wondering what the fuck she was doing. Joe seemed delighted, clapping enthusiastically as he dragged the chair – and her – back to a sitting position.

"Well done, veerrry dramatic Tinsel. I knew you'd be good at this! Especially after that night at the station."

She was still dizzy, but she'd achieved her aim: she was closer to Pandora. Caught up in the excitement, Joe hadn't bothered to move her back to where she'd sat before. He left her diagonal to her sibling, not at an ideal angle but close enough.

"Why are you doing this? Huh?" Tinsel shouted, trying to get him going again. "What's the point Joe? What did I ever do to you?"

"GOD!" he shouted, recoiling at her words. "This is not about *you*, Tinsel! It was never about you! This whole thing was supposed to be about me and my movie!"

"*B-Band Candy*?" she stammered, incredibly confused.

"Do you have any idea how hard it is to market a film these days?"

"Tell me," she begged. "Tell me what your grand plan was and *what the fuck* that has to do with *Band Candy*."

"Gladly," he smirked, taking a mock bow. With his arms extending on either side of him, Tinsel couldn't help but notice the knife in one hand and the taser in his other. Whipping himself up to attention, he began pacing around them as he spoke, fully aware of his best angles as he deviated between each camera's range.

"My last movie wasn't exactly a hit, Tinny. It did fine, it was a cult mover and shaker, but it didn't make enough money. I was still riding off the success of my debut and if I was gonna have any kind of enduring career, *Band Candy* needed to be big. No, not big. Huge. Colossal. Iconic."

Carefully – as quietly as she could – Tinsel lifted and shifted her body weight so the chair would move where she needed it to as Joe talked. Pandora could see what she was doing, but still not quite understanding why, until her fingers brushed against Tinsel's thigh. Pandora grabbed on to the fabric, and pulled up the hem of the dress inch by inch.

"Slowly," Tinsel whispered, worried that he'd catch them. "Slowly."

Their matching switchblades were small and dainty enough so you couldn't see the lump under their frocks where they were strapped, yet they had also given them the illusion of security at the time. They would be no match against Joe's knife, but they would be sharp enough to cut through rope.

"People are fucking stupid, you know this!" Joe pressed on. "We had our South by Southwest premiere and the reviews were fine, but the studio was cooling on it already. They downscaled the US marketing, cutting the number of festival slots we were supposed to play and only organising two junkets. Two! Can you imagine?"

Pandora's fingers had closed around the blade, but Tinsel felt her sister stiffen as Joe glared at her. Thankfully, he was the kind of man who spoke *at* you rather than *to* you. He continued venting, uninterrupted, as Pandora carefully slid the blade from Tinsel's garter and tugged her dress back down in place.

"There was talk of skipping a theatrical release altogether and selling it to a streaming service, like it was some Friday night novelty you glanced at over the top of your phone. They were giving up on the movie before it even had a chance to find its audience. Do you know how frustrating that is? I was supposed to get a tentpole job off the back of this, Tinsel. Not an A-list superhero or anything, but Booster Gold would do. A spin-off villain, even."

"So, you just started murdering people?" she scoffed, not quite sure if she believed his insanity. She moved her body slightly, using it to block his view of what she hoped was Pandora working feverishly at. She had heard the blade open and could detect the faint sound of friction.

Please, please, please, she thought, urging her sister to get free.

"Just one person, at first," he shrugged. "Mera was easy, I kind of knew her from back in the day when I was starting out. We did a Q & A screening at CinemaNova. Her uUp dating profile told me everything else I needed to know: she was a fan. It was almost too easy, I thought, slicing and dicing her right at the moment she called into your show, *desperate* to win tickets."

Tinsel risked a glance towards Pandora's hand, her heart pulsing as she saw one limb was free but still held on to the ropes so it looked as if she was restrained. Her second hand was nearly loose.

"The media are idiots though," he spat. "The story didn't even break fast enough and when it did, it was all 'Woman Murdered on Halloween' or 'Bitch Killed Live On-Air.' They didn't even mention *what* she had been calling in about, what she had spent her final moments doing!"

Pandora's chair shuffled slightly beside her until she was in a position to start working on Tinsel's own ropes. Both women kept their heads up and their eyes trained on Joe, Tinsel careful not to react as the knife nicked her skin in her sister's attempts to cut her free of the restraints.

"*Band Candy* was a footnote at best. Your tribute show helped a bit, and I kept trying to angle the story there, but it wasn't enough."

"So, Alona. In the archives. But it backfired."

"Nobody found the fuck! I kept waiting and waiting for it to hit the news and it never did. Some incompetent autopsy marked it as an accident."

"Not anymore, you've got the body count," she mumbled, conscious of the fact it was Vic who was responsible for recognising another victim of the Grim Reaper. Joe didn't seem to hear her, naturally.

"An accident! My handiwork!" he continued. "I needed something bigger, splashier."

"The Capitol," she whispered. "That poor fucking kid died for your ego."

"He died for art!"

"News flash, Joe. I've seen the movie. It's not fucking art!"

"You bitch."

"Carpenter's third film was *Halloween*. Yours was *Band Candy*. How embarrassing."

"Shut your mouth."

"Wes Craven's was *The Hills Have Eyes*. Look at yours. Big yikes energy."

He was dangerously close to her now as he swung his arm. Tinsel's head snapped back as he broke her nose with his fist. Pandora's muffled cries mixed with her own as she attempted to breathe her way past the pain. But it was far reaching, snaking up into her brain and behind her eyes with such sharp agony that even her gulping inhale hurt. Blood was running straight from her nostrils and down her lips, and Tinsel took a moment to lean forward and spit on the floor at Joe's feet.

"You watch your dirty mouth," he growled, brandishing the knife at her. "I'm killing you no matter what. But it's up to you how fast I do it."

"How long can you last?" she questioned, borderline delirious as she felt Pandora cut her other hand free. "Cos your whole plan was dumb, Joe. What did you think, these murders would make people want to see your stupid film?"

"Why not?" he laughed, bouncing on the balls of his feet. "People faint in *Psycho,* audiences rush out to see it. Someone has a seizure in *Prometheus,* suddenly the drop-off numbers stabilise. A serial killer works on *The Exorcist* and weird shit keeps happening? That film is *legendary.* Teenagers get inspired by a movie and go on a killing spree. This shit happens all the time, baby. So why can't I make it work in my favour? Why can't I make it work for Joe?"

"I can't believe you," she said, shaking her head. "All this time, I thought I knew you. I can't... I can't believe you could manage something like this."

"Eh, I'm a genre filmmaker. People think we're all sick fucks anyway. May as well lean into it. And I've been practising, refining my technique over the years, like all good auteurs."

Something moved out of the corner of Tinsel's eye, but she resisted the urge to let her gaze be drawn to it. She could sense a change in Pandora beside her, however, and the second Joe looked down to grab a phone, her eyes darted to the source of the movement. It was Vic, creeping through the dark, gun poised and ready to fire as he carefully tried to get himself into the best position. He didn't need to put a finger to his lips to keep her quiet: she wouldn't make a sound.

"I saw the texts, Tinny," Joe said, holding up the cracked screen of her phone so she could see it. "I went through this little message thread you and Pandora have going on here with Taskforce Laurie Strode. Cute. You're a bit all over the place, I admit, but you found one of my test dummies."

She tilted her head, confused. "Test–"

"Slater Hawker from five years ago in Sydney. It was around the time of SIFF, I believe."

"The Sydney International Film Festival?" Tinsel still didn't quite get it.

"When I'd go on tour, you see, promoting a film or whatever, I'd get opportunities on the road. It gave me avenues to improve myself, refine my technique. Your sister knows all about it, she wrote a whole post on *Pandora's Box*, remember? Serial killers are so much harder to track if they stay mobile. Add different countries to that and I'd say I'm damn near elusive."

"Not anymore," Vic said, a moment before he fired two shots square into Joe's chest. The man let out a startled grunt, jerking forward as he fell to the ground face first.

"Vic!" Tinsel shouted, losing all composure as he sprinted towards her. She pulled her hands free, tugging away at the final strands as he examined her bloodied face in his one, free hand.

"Are you okay? Are you alright?" he asked, breathless as worry dotted his features.

She tried to kiss him, Vic laughing somewhat as she flinched back as soon as her nose made contact with his.

"Ouch."

"You've got a broken nose, silly. Don't rush this, we've got plenty of time. Are you hurt anywhere else?"

"No, I dunno, I don't think so. My ankles are tied up though, I need to–"

"Here," Pandora said, yanking herself free from her chair and tossing the gag that had been wrapped around her mouth to the ground. "I already did mine when he wasn't looking, let me."

She dropped low as she started working on Tinsel's feet with the switchblade.

"How did you find us?" Pandora asked, looking up at Vic.

"I was already looking for you when you didn't come back from getting a drink–"

"The motherfucker tased me. Tased both of us! I don't really remember what happened, but I was getting my drink, and then someone waved me over, near where the huge Christmas tree was. I guess the second I was alone and away from people… everything went dark after that."

"Same," Tinsel nodded. "He must have been waiting for me outside of the bathroom."

"If he'd gotten to both of you in such a short space of time, I knew he must be close. Plus, I figured you were attacked while still on the phone to Pandora less than five minutes earlier."

"The fucking prick," Tinsel said, the words coming out in a sob as Pandora released her left foot followed by her right.

"Hey," Vic said, his firm grip on her neck and directing her gaze to him. His eyes were wide as he stared at her intensely, no hint of fear in his expression. "I'm here, I've got y–"

He somewhat gargled the last syllable, his eyebrows creasing into a frown as she blinked rapidly.

"Vic?" she squeaked, gripping his arms as he stayed in position on his knees and at her feet. That was when she saw the blood, followed by the wet slicing sounds as a blade sunk into flesh over and over again.

"NO!" she screamed, pushing to her feet. Joe had crawled up behind him, taking full advantage while Vic's back was turned.

"GET OFF HIM!" Pandora shouted, his arm still stabbing as both women launched themselves in Joe Meyer's direction.

Tinsel made it there first, tackling him away hard enough that he was tossed backwards and the knife flew from his grip. She heard it clatter along the floor, registering the thick padding of his body as they landed on the ground. She saw him reach for the taser and she bit his hand, not willing to release her grip on his torso but desperate not to be electrocuted again.

He cried out in pain and she bit harder, trying not to be disgusted at how the flesh of his wrist felt between her teeth. She felt a swift punch to her side and grunted as the wind was knocked out of her. Joe grabbed her hair and yanked her backwards as they wrestled.

"LET HER GO!" Pandora shrieked. "I'VE GOT THE GUN, LET HER GO!"

Time seemed to hover as Joe held Tinsel in place. With one bloody fist clenched in her hair, he seemed to consider his options. She watched her sister, both hands firm on the grip of the weapon that was pointed squarely at his heart.

"It was meant to go this way anyhow," he said, a piece of skin dangling from his lip. "The big finale. Except you were meant to go with me, Tinny."

He released her, Tinsel scrambling free as she dashed towards her sister. She knew Pandora wouldn't wait, wouldn't let him carry on if she thought Tinsel was in danger.

"This is good enough," he grinned, the smile turning into a weird chuckle as he twisted to look directly into one of the cameras.

"He's wearing a bulletproof vest!" Tinsel panted, scrambling to stand alongside Pandora just as she started to pull the trigger. She nudged her arms up just in time, throwing off her sister's aim from Joe Meyer's heart to his head. Pandora fired twice, the first bullet hitting him in his neck and the second at the base of his skull. Both women screamed as they were splattered in gore, the noise of the gun sending them momentarily deaf thanks to the simultaneous bangs. Ears ringing, Tinsel looked over Pandora's shoulder at Joe Meyer's corpse. There was no doubting that he was dead this time.

He didn't even have a face.

There was another large bang, the women shrieking as bodies began to fill the space. Tinsel couldn't make out what they were saying, but Pandora had one hand raised as she lowered the gun with the other. Men and women in uniform were filing in, among them Veronica. She rushed to Pandora, asking her questions that Tinsel ignored as she spun around, searching for Vic.

The sound that escaped her mouth didn't belong to a human. She fell towards him and lifted his head up off the ground before cradling it in her lap. He was covered in blood, so much blood. She couldn't tell if he was breathing or not as he lay there in the foetal position.

"Vic, Vic," she whispered. "Vic, it's alright."

She felt hands on her shoulders attempting to pry her away. She refused to go anywhere so long as his eyes were open and he was looking at her. But he wasn't really looking, she realised. In fact, he hadn't blinked in a long time.

"Ma'am, I'm sorry, but you have to move. There's nothing else you can do for him."

It was only when she heard Pandora's voice in her ear that she released her grip, unable to believe the words.

"Sis, I'm so sorry, but... he's dead," she said, voice ragged. "Vic's dead."

CHAPTER 23

The red light of the studio was flashing, telling Tinsel she was live and on-air. But she couldn't get her vocal chords to move, couldn't get them to function the way they usually would. *Breathe*, she told herself. *Just breathe, then start speaking.* It seemed like a simple enough mantra. Yet after everything that had happened, even just breathing was an effort.

This time, she had taken leave from work. A month of it, in fact. She was allowed more but was worried that if she stayed in the house much longer, she would drown in despair. Pandora's kids were a pretty good balm; it was so much easier dealing with children than having to deal with what she was going through. She took over the day care run for Max, and had Airlie almost permanently attached to her hip during the day. She found herself twitchy and anxious whenever the kids were asleep, always looking for something to do.

"If you're angling for a promotion, you can't have Brian," Pandora had joked. She knew her sister didn't mind. It meant that she could pour herself into her blog, which had blown up after everything that had happened at the Christmas party. It was as if the words had threatened to explode out of Pandora's chest, with Tinsel watching her older sibling with interest as she typed thoughts on her phone every few hours from their shared hospital room.

They were discharged within a day, with plenty of painkillers between them. Their parents had flown in and rented an AirBnB on Pandora's street for two weeks, until they gathered the girls were doing "well enough on their own" and returned to Sydney.

They had wanted to be there with Tinsel for Vic's funeral. And she was glad they were. With a sick thought, she reflected on the talk she had with him, about the future, of how she wanted him to meet her parents one day. She could never have guessed it would be under these circumstances. Her family and Eduardo were the only ones who knew about the true nature of her relationship with Detective Vicellous 'Vic' James.

Although, given where and how he died, she knew others would have suspected there was more to it than just a close friendship. Mercifully, nobody said anything. Not even Diraani, who gripped her shoulder firmly at the funeral before leaving without saying a word. All of Detective James' siblings were there, and Tinsel found herself fascinated as she observed his features and traits dispersed among adults who did and didn't look like him. Even his ex-wife attended, sobbing loudly as his casket was lowered into the ground.

She wanted to sob too, to scream and shout irrationally as she pounded her fists on the ground. Yet she had to keep it bottled in, squash all the emotions down, and save face. His reputation was all that was left now, and she was conscious of the media who had staked out the gates at Melbourne General Cemetery, their telescopic lens trained for a reaction. Eduardo had stood with her during the service, Pandora clasping one of her hands and him clasping the other. She thought that it was as much for him as it was for her. He had died a "hero cop." That's what the papers and news broadcasts were calling him. It was the way he should be remembered.

For Tinsel, the things she would remember was how he tasted, his mouth on hers, how it felt as his hands would run over her skin, how he sounded when he would press her head to his chest and hold her as she listened attentively to his heartbeat. The first time she caught a whiff of peppermint after he died, she broke down in tears that quickly descended into a panic attack. Pandora couldn't work out what was wrong at first, before eventually understanding that it was the scent of her gum resurrecting painful memories. That evening, Brian had carefully gone through the house throwing out anything with a vaguely peppermint scent or flavour: even three bottles of peppermint essence from Pandora's baking supplies.

The press, of course, had swamped them.

And not just local. The story had legs and it went global, with Joe Meyer's work having enough of a reach that people were fascinated with his spiral into madness.

Tinsel and Pandora's phones rang constantly with interview requests, the former turning hers off entirely. Everyone else got passed on to Pandora. She became somewhat of an official spokesperson, equipped with the specifics to provide thoughtful insight and analysis, but "no bullshit" enough that she could intimidate reporters with dumb questions through her icy stare alone. Tinsel got some satisfaction in thinking about the small measure of good that might come out of all this, with Pandora's public speaking engagements and her profile both skyrocketing.

Pandora's Box too was in a whole new place. Before her sister had written anything about what happened on the site, their parents sat both of them down in a forced mediation of sorts: having Pandora talk about what she wanted to write and why, with Tinsel voicing her opinions on how that made her feel. It was a healthy decompression of sorts, the two establishing guidelines on what exactly Pandora would be publishing and what she wouldn't. Tinsel knew her sister's true crime blog was incredibly important to her and because of that, it was important to Tinsel too.

It weirdly became like a healing instrument for both of them, Pandora working her way through a list of planned content.

She suspected her parents might have known this would be the case – they were usually smarter and more emotionally in tune than their daughters.

There was an initial first-person piece from Pandora, which was raw and heartfelt and challenging for Tinsel to read. Then there was an in-depth interview with some of her fellow researchers, including Veronica, detailing what they had been investigating as part of Taskforce Laurie Strode. That included the false leads and crimes they thought had belonged to the killer, then the ones that actually did belong to Joe Meyer which included unsolved murders in Sydney, Brisbane, Toronto, London, Austin, Los Angeles and Sundance as he had travelled for film festivals over the years. There was a third piece, on his undiagnosed psychosis, and what could be learned. Pandora also broke down the media coverage in the coming weeks, reports that were harmful and reports that were helpful. She concluded with one on the intersection between real-life horror and fictional horror, and how that could be interpreted.

Among it all was Tinsel, trying to work out where she sat and how she felt about everything. Returning to work was a no-brainer, but it wasn't until she strolled through the 102.8 HitsFM doors for the first evening back that she questioned whether it was a good idea or not. Malu was there, waiting for her with a comforting smile and an even more comforting hug. *If he can do it, there's no reason I can't,* she thought, settling in at her desk later as she prepped for the show and attempted to clear her inbox.

There was more than one email waiting there from a publishing house, offering her and Pandora a joint book deal to "tell their story, on their terms." She knew what that meant: cash in and *cash in* quick. There was likely already a true crime podcast, documentary and book all in production about what they were calling "The Grim Reaper Rampage." Yet they wouldn't be able to compete with one from the actual sisters who survived it.

She scoffed at the wording in one specific email, which had also CC'd Pandora via the address listed on her blog: "with your profile and audience, combined with Pandora's penmanship and readership, we felt like this could be a seminal true crime text."

They want your minor *celebrity and my* physical *labour*, her sister had emailed back.

That comment had made her laugh because of how true it was, with Tinsel replying simply: *Yeah nah mate.*

Luiza was waiting for her when she stepped into the studio, the two women embracing and exchanging pleasantries. They had been friends before, but it became clear to Tinsel as they talked around the subject of Joe Meyer and the murders that their relationship would never exist outside of that building.

Luiza was going to stay for the first hours of the show to "catch up on stuff I'm behind on," she said. That might have been true, but Tinsel suspected it was for a combination of moral support and Rushelle Li suggesting someone should watch over her for the first few shows. She appreciated it nonetheless, even though it felt suffocating to her as she struggled to formulate words once she was back, live on-air.

Finally, with a gulp, she was able to verbalise something.

"Hi there folks, this is Tinsel Munroe and welcome back to *The Graveyard Shift*," she said into the mic. She felt Luiza relax on the couch across from her, sensing that Tinsel was just finding her rhythm again.

"Thanks to Paarth Case for filling in for me over the break and it's... well, it's a new year. First up, we're doing a throwback with 'Jennifer's Body' from Hole. Coincidentally the title of a great, and underrated, Karyn Kusama film that I highly recommend you check out during flashback screenings that are happening this week at the Coburg Drive-In."

Her eyes darted to one of the screens that had social media open, with tweets and Facebook messages flowing in. Sweat sprung up on her skin as she observed them, the studio feeling smaller than she knew it actually was.

"After that we've got a favourite by Joseph Bishara from the *Malignant* score, then 'The Devil & Me' from The Brad Pitt Light Orchestra and…"

Her throat clenched again, and her mouth went dry as she struggled once more to find the words. Exhaling, she ran a hand over her face, not worrying if it messed up her make-up. Luiza stood from the couch, inching towards her to see if everything was okay. It wasn't. And she was done saving face.

"I'm sorry," she said into the mic, her voice cracking slightly as she slid the headphones off. "I can't do this. Ghouls, goblins, every poltergeist in between, it has been a pleasure. This is Tinsel Munroe, signing off… permanently."

She hit play on the first track she had lined up, stepping back from the control deck as the light switched from red to green indicating that she was off air.

"Tinsel, are you–"

"It's all yours," she told Luiza, cutting her off. "Tell them… tell them something cool, I don't know. I'll email Rushelle my resignation."

"What? Are you sure? You should think about this. So many people would be grateful to be in this position."

"Grateful?" Tinsel questioned, feeling a familiar spark of anger she thought was long dormant. "Grateful to work at a place that tells me I'm so great, but doesn't create a pathway for progress? Or where senior men are so busy trying to present as 'good guys' and 'allies' but never actually want to reprimand their probbo colleagues or stick their necks out?"

"Fuck 'em," Luiza gestured, as if they were all standing there in studio with them right then. "You have worked so hard on this show and built it up to be a massive success. Don't throw that away."

Tinsel let out a sharp laugh, wiping away a tear as it slipped from the corner of her eye. It all seemed so insignificant now, everything she had sweat and bled for.

Backing out of the studio, she grabbed her bag and threw Luiza a wave as she rushed from the space. Marching down the halls as fast as she could and willing the elevator to drop even faster as she entered it, there wasn't a morsel of doubt in her mind. She felt light then lighter, sure then surer of her decision. The things she had wanted, she didn't want anymore and that was okay. Her life had changed, and she needed to change with it.

Tinsel Munroe walked out of the radio station's front door, knowing that she was never coming back.

The Graveyard Shift was over.

ACKNOWLEDGEMENTS

The biggest thanks has to go to the icon and Godfather of hip hop in Australia, Hau Latukefu, for letting me come in and shadow him overnight on *The Hip Hop Show*, asking annoying questions 'n' shit. Bonus points for Sonja Hammer – champion of wahine, queers and POC – who actually ran Australia's only late-night genre radio show for several years and helped form the basis for much of what Tinsel's program could and should be.

Also, my fellow radio experts Keegan Buzza, Sosefina Fuamoli, Sophie Ly, and Rachel Junge for fielding my technical questions and super weird queries over the many evolutions of *The Graveyard Shift*. Da Boiz chat, legal eagle Stu Coote for grounding the novel in as much reality as possible, and Blake Howard for encouraging a crime romp as a great use of my energy.

The life savers, namely Kodie Bedford who kept me afloat during times full of darkness and doubt. Breaker of generational curses, Ramona Sen Gupta, MILFs Amy Remeikis and Anna Jabour, THE Opera House's lighting and Pokémon expert Mikey for letting me exploit his knowledge. Film Club! For helping navigate elaborate slayings in the venues we love so much: namely José Ortiz, Corey Te Wharau, Zak Hepburn, Laura Toister, Kubrick, KC and Tony, Chloe, and Vanessa The Stresser.

Merci to Louis B Schlesinger from the FBI Behavioral Science Unit for his time and insights into the specifics of serial killers, spree killers and marauders. Mad props to CCC TJ Hamilton, an amazing author and screenwriter in her own right and bad-ass who provided much insight into the policing aspects of this book. Hat tip to my mum, Tania, who got me into scary stories in the first place and would sneak me into slashers even though I was too young.

My agent, Ed Wilson, who specifically requested "more stabby-stabby please". Gemma Creffield for getting what I was trying to do on the first pass and the team at Angry Robot, specifically the Datura imprint homies – Desola Coker, Caroline Lambe, Amy Portsmouth – for supporting spooky tales about spooky doings and the spooky people who tell them.

Finally, thank you to Wes Craven and John Carpenter for giving me the tools to make *The Graveyard Shift*. I owe you a blood debt.